DATE DUE			
LM			

ALSO BY JENNIFER MCMAHON

Don't Breathe a Word

Dismantled

Island of Lost Girls

Promise Not to Tell

The One I Left Behind

Jennifer McMahon

HARPER LUXE
An Imprint of HarperCollins*Publishers*

This book is a work of fiction. The characters, incidents, and dialogue are drawn from the author's imagination and are not to be construed as real. Any resemblance to actual events or persons, living or dead, is entirely coincidental.

THE ONE I LEFT BEHIND. Copyright © 2013 by Jennifer McMahon. All rights reserved. Printed in the United States of America. No part of this book may be used or reproduced in any manner whatsoever without written permission except in the case of brief quotations embodied in critical articles and reviews. For information address HarperCollins Publishers, 10 East 53rd Street, New York, NY 10022.

HarperCollins books may be purchased for educational, business, or sales promotional use. For information, please e-mail the Special Markets Department at SPsales@harpercollins.com.

FIRST HARPERLUXE EDITION

HarperLuxe™ is a trademark of HarperCollins Publishers

Library of Congress Cataloging-in-Publication Data is available upon request.

ISBN: 978-0-06-222303-6

13 14 ID/RRD 10 9 8 7 6 5 4 3 2 1

In memory of my mother,
Dorothy Elizabeth McMahon—
my co-conspirator, my teller of tales,
my blue-eyed newt.

I know we'll meet again; you'll be waiting one day, with a bottle of gin and a smile. We'll climb into your old Vega, crank the radio as loud as it can go, and ride right on out into the stars.

Excerpt from *Neptune's Hands: The True Story of the Unsolved Brighton Falls Slayings* by Martha S. Paquette

It began with the hands. Right hands, severed neatly at the wrist. They arrived on the granite steps of the police station in empty red and white milk cartons stapled closed at the top, photos of missing children on the back—the whole package wrapped in brown butcher's paper, tied neatly with thin string like a box of pastry.

The medical examiner told the police to look for a surgeon or a butcher, someone who knew bone and tendon. It was almost as if he admired the killer's technique, like there was something beautiful about the cleanliness of the cuts, so perfect it was hard to imagine the hands had ever been attached to anything; objects all their own.

The killer kept the women alive for exactly four days after the removal of the hands. He took good care of them, cauterized and dressed their wounds, shot them full of morphine for pain, tended to them like precious orchids.

On the fifth morning, he strangled them, then left their bodies displayed in public places: the town green, a park, the front lawn of the library. Each woman was naked except for her bandages—brilliantly white, lovingly taped like perfect little cocoons at the ends of their arms.

Neptune's Last Victim

The first thing she does when she wakes up is check her hands. She doesn't know how long she's been out. Hours? Days? She's on her back, blindfolded, arms up above her head like a diver, bound to a metal pipe. Her hands are duct taped together at the wrist—but they're both still there.

Thank you, thank you, thank Jesus, sweet, sweet Mother Mary, both her hands are there. She wiggles her fingers and remembers a song her mother used to sing:

Where is Thumbkin? Where is Thumbkin?
Here I am, Here I am,
How are you today, sir,
Very well, I thank you,
Run away, Run away.

Her ankles are bound together tightly—more duct tape; her feet are full of pins and needles.

She hears Neptune breathing and it sounds almost mechanical, the rasping rhythm of it: in, out, in, out. Chug, chug, puff, puff. *I think I can, I think I can.*

Neptune takes off the blindfold, and the light hurts her eyes. All she sees is a dark silhouette above her and it's not Neptune's face she sees inside it, but all faces: her mother's, her father's, Luke the baker from the donut shop, her high school boyfriend who never touched her, but liked to jerk off while she watched. She sees the stained glass face of Jesus, the eyes of the woman with no legs who used to beg for money outside of Denny's during the breakfast rush. All these faces are spinning like a top on Neptune's head and she has to close her eyes because if she looks too long, she'll get dizzy and throw up.

Neptune smiles down at her, teeth bright as a crescent moon.

She tries to turn her head, but her neck aches from their struggle earlier, and she can only move a fraction of an inch before the pain brings her to a screeching halt. They seem to be in some sort of warehouse. Cold cement floor. Curved metal walls laced with electrical conduit. Boxes everywhere. Old machinery. The place smells like a country fair—rotten fruit, grease, burned sugar, hay.

"It didn't need to be this way," Neptune says, head shaking, clicking tongue against teeth, scolding.

Neptune walks around her in a circle, whistling. It's almost a dance, with a little spring in each step, a little skip. Neptune's shoes are cheap imitation leather, scratched to shit, the tread worn smooth helping them glide across the floor. All at once, Neptune freezes, eyeing her a moment longer, then quits whistling, turns, and walks away. Footsteps echo on the cement floor. The door closes with a heavy wooden thud. A bolt slides closed, a lock is snapped.

Gone. For now.

The tools are all laid out on a tray nearby: clamps, rubber tourniquet, scalpel, small saw, propane torch, metal trowel, rolls of gauze, thick surgical pads, heavy white tape. Neptune's left these things where she can see them. It's all part of the game.

Son of a bitch. Son of a bitch. Son of a bitch.

Stop, she tells herself. *Don't panic. Think.*

Tomorrow morning, another hand will show up inside a milk carton on the steps of the police station. Only this time, it will be her hand. She looks at the saw, swallows hard, and closes her eyes.

Think, damn it.

She struggles with the tape around her wrists, but it's no good.

She opens her eyes and they go back to the tools, the bandages, the saw with its row of tiny silver teeth.

She hears a moan to her left. Slowly, like an arthritic old woman, she turns her head so that her left cheek rests on the cool, damp floor.

"You!" she says, surprised but relieved.

The woman is taped to a cast iron pipe on the opposite side of the warehouse. "I can get us out of this," she promises. The woman lifts her head, opens her swollen eyes.

The woman laughs, her split lip opening up, covering her chin with blood. "We're both dead, Dufrane," she says, her voice small and crackling, a fire that can't get started.

Part One

Excerpt from *Neptune's Hands: The True Story of the Unsolved Brighton Falls Slayings* by Martha S. Paquette

The year was 1985. Madonna's "Like a Virgin" was pumping out of every boom box. Kids were lined up to see Michael J. Fox in *Back to the Future.* And in the sleepy little suburb of Brighton Falls, Connecticut, Neptune was killing women.

Brighton Falls, northwest of Hartford and just south of the airport, was a farming community that had quickly given way to suburbia. The men who worked in the insurance high-rises in Hartford moved their families to places like Brighton Falls, safe little bedroom communities with good schools, no crime, and fresh air.

Along Main Street were the most prominent shops: Luke's Donuts, Wright's Pharmacy, Ferraro's Family Market, Parson's Hardware, and The Duchess Bar and Grill. Tucked behind these shops, on the cross streets, were the gray granite police and fire station, a doll shop, Joanne's House of Nuts, a cheese shop, two bookstores (one that specialized in used romances), three churches, Talbots, the Carriage Shop Fine Furnishings, Carvel Ice Cream, Barston's Dry Cleaning, and The End of the Leash pet shop.

Most of Brighton Falls itself was idyllic, but after you crossed the river, left the waterfall and old mills turned into condos behind, as you drove north on Airport Road, past the tented tobacco fields and leaning barns, the road turned from two lanes into four. Here were the strip malls, boarded-up factories, vacant lots, fast-food restaurants, motels where you could pay by the week or the hour, X-rated movie houses, used car dealers, and bars. This was what the insurance executives considered no-man's-land, an area they carefully avoided on weekend outings in the station wagon. Here, the noise and chaos of the large airport had spilled over and was reaching dangerously toward suburbia.

Other than the occasional drunk and disorderly arrest at one of the bars on Airport Road, the biggest crime the police had to deal with in recent years had been the time the mayor's son drank too much at graduation, ran a red light, and led the police on an across-town chase that ended when he drove his Mercedes into the country club swimming pool. There hadn't been a murder since 1946, and that had been a clear-cut case of a man shooting his brother after catching him in bed with his wife.

There was nothing clear-cut about the Neptune killings.

His victims appeared to have nothing in common: an accountant with two kids; a waitress who worked the swing shift at the Silver Spoon Diner; a film student from Wesleyan University; an ex-model turned barfly. The police were dumbfounded.

In the end, everyone—the police, families of the victims, and citizens of Brighton Falls—were left with more questions than answers. Why did Neptune cut off the right hands of his victims? Why keep them alive for four days after leaving the hands in milk cartons on the steps of the police station? And what was different about his last victim, the glamorous has-been Vera Dufrane? Why is it that her body was never found?

And perhaps the biggest question of all: was he just a drifter passing through, or is he out there still, living among them? What made him stop? And—the people of Brighton Falls wonder each night as they lock their doors—will he one day kill again?

Chapter 1

October 16, 2010
Rockland, Vermont

Imagine that your house is on fire. You have exactly one minute to grab what you can. What do you choose?

Tara turned over the little hourglass full of pink sand. Her fingernails were painted cyanosis-blue, chipped in places. Her face was pale, her lips bright red as she smiled, breathed the word, *Go.*

Reggie tore down the front hall, skidding as she rounded the corner to the narrow oak stairs, galloping up, one hand on the curved snakelike rail, the other on the cool wall of damp stone.

"Your lungs are filling with smoke!" Tara called from down below. "Your eyes are watering."

Reggie gasped, jerked open the door to her room, her eyes moving over the crammed bookshelves, the desk covered in her sketches, the neatly made bed topped off with the quilt her grandmother had made. She skimmed over all of this and went right for the closet, moving toward it in slow motion, feeling her way through the invisible smoke, stinging eyes clamped shut now. She reached for the sliding door and eased it open, the little metal wheels rattling in their tracks. Reggie stepped forward, fingers finding clothes hung on hangers. She reached up, felt for the shelf.

"Hurry," Tara whispered, right behind her now, her breath warm and moist on Reggie's neck. "You're almost out of time."

Reggie opened her eyes, took a gulp of fresh, cold, October air. She was at home in Vermont. Not back at Monique's Wish. And she was thirty-nine—not thirteen.

"Damn," she said, the word a cloud of white smoke escaping her mouth. She'd left the windows open again.

Wrapping the down comforter around her like a cape, she slid out of bed and went right for the windows, pulling them closed. The trees, vivid with oranges, yellows, and reds just last week, were losing their brightness. The cold and wind of the last three days had brought many of the leaves off the trees. Out across the lake, a V of Canada geese headed south.

"You don't know what you're missing," Reggie told them. Then, in her next breath, she muttered, "Chickenshits." She squinted down at the lake, imagining it three months from now, frozen solid and snow covered; a flat moonscape of white. It wasn't all that different from Ricker's Pond, where her mother had taught her to ice-skate. Reggie could see it so clearly: her mother in her green velvet coat and gold chiffon scarf soaring in graceful circles while Reggie wobbled and fell, the ice popping beneath them. "Are you sure this is safe?" she'd asked her mother, each time the ice made a sound. And her mother had laughed. "Worry girl," she'd teased, skating right into the middle where the ice was the thinnest and holding her hands out to Reggie. "Come on out here and show me what you're made of."

Reggie shrugged off the memory, along with the heavy down comforter. She quickly threw on a pair of jeans and a sweater and headed down to the kitchen, her bare feet cool on the wood floors.

She'd laid out the house so that she'd have a view of the lake from almost any vantage point. As she descended the stairs, she faced the large bank of windows on the south side that looked out over her yard and meadow and down to Arrow Lake. It was a little over half a mile from her house to the water's edge, but when she came down the stairs, she felt as if she could just step out into the air and float across her living room, through the windows, over the yard and field, and down to the lake. Sometimes she caught herself almost trying it—leaning a little too far forward, putting her foot too far ahead so that she nearly missed the next step down. These were the moments that defined her success as an architect: not the prizes, accolades, or the esteem of her colleagues, but the way coming down her stairs made her believe, just for a second, that she could turn into a bit of dandelion fluff and float down to the lake.

For a building to be successful, it had to be connected to the landscape in a seamless way. It couldn't just look like it had been dropped there randomly, but like it had grown organically, been shaped by the wind and the rain, cut from the mountains. The rooms should flow not just from one into the other, but also into the world beyond.

4 Walls Magazine had just named Reggie one of the top green architects in the Northeast, and called the Snyder/Wellenstein house she'd designed in Stowe "a breathtaking display of integrating architecture with nature; with the stream running through the living room and the 120-year-old oak growing up through all three floors, Dufrane has created a sustainable dwelling that blurs the lines between indoors and out."

Blurring the lines. That's what Reggie was good at—indoors/outdoors; old/new; functional/ornamental—she had a gift for merging unlikely ideas and objects and creating something that was somehow both and neither; something greater than the sum of its parts.

Still foggy headed and desperately in need of caffeine, Reggie cleaned out the little stainless-steel espresso pot, then filled it with water and coffee and set it on the gas stove, turning the knob to start the flame. Her kitchen was a cook's dream (though honestly, Reggie didn't do much cooking and subsisted largely on raw vegetables, cheese and crackers, and espresso)—right down to the huge counter-hogging Italian espresso machine that Reggie only used when she was entertaining. She preferred the small stovetop pot she'd owned since college. It was simple to use and quietly elegant—the epitome of good design.

The water came to a boil. The coffee bubbled, filling the kitchen with its rich, earthy scent.

Reggie checked her watch: 7:15. She'd go out to the office, do some brainstorming for the new project, go for a run around the lake, shower, and do some more sketches. She looked back at her watch, catching it change to 7:16.

Imagine that your house is on fire. You have exactly one minute to grab what you can. What do you chose?

Reggie glanced around the house, feeling that old panic rising up inside her. Then she took in a breath and answered her old friend out loud. "Nothing, Tara. I choose nothing." Her chest loosened. Muscles relaxed. Tara didn't have that kind of power over her anymore.

Reggie wasn't thirteen. She understood that objects could be replaced. And she didn't own all that much. Losing the house would be a crushing blow, but it could be rebuilt. She owned very little furniture. Her closet was only half full. Her sometime boyfriend Len teased her: "It isn't normal for a successful adult to be able to fit everything they own in the back of a pickup truck." He'd say it with his hands shoved deep in the pockets of his worn Carhartts, a boyish smirk on his face that brought out the little dimple in his right cheek. Len lived alone in an old rambling farmhouse, every room stuffed full of books and art and furniture that didn't quite match.

"It's the gypsy in me," she'd tell him, leaning in to kiss his cheek.

"Gypsy, hell," he'd scoff. "You live like a criminal on the run."

Triple espresso in hand, Reggie went back upstairs, slid her feet into her clogs, and opened the door to the bridge that led to her tree house office. She took in a breath of cool, sharp air. She smelled woodsmoke, damp leaves, the apples rotting on the ground in the abandoned orchard on the east side of her property. It was a perfect mid-October day. The fifteen-foot suspension bridge swayed slightly under her, and she walked slowly at first, the yard and driveway below her, Arrow Lake off in the distance. *Charlie's Bridge*, she called it, though Charlie didn't even know it existed. And she'd never told anyone the bridge's secret name or the story behind it. What would she say? *I named it after a boy who once told me building a bridge like this was impossible.*

The phone in her office was ringing. She raced across the last couple of yards, the espresso dangerously close to spilling.

She opened the door, which was never locked—the only way in was to cross the bridge from the inside of her house or to scale twenty-five feet up the oak tree the office was built around. The office was twelve feet across and circular, the tree trunk at the center and windows on all sides. Len called it "the control tower."

She had a computer desk and a wooden drafting table. There was a small bulletin board with notes for her latest project, a reminder to call a client, and the astrology chart Len had done for her pinned to it. She didn't believe in clutter or in holding on to things that didn't have significant meaning, so her bookcase held only the books that she referred to again and again, the ones that had influenced her: *The Poetics of Space, A Pattern Language, The Timeless Way of Building, Design with Nature, Notes on the Synthesis of Form,* as well as a small collection of nature guides. Tucked here and there among the books were Reggie's other great source of inspiration: bird nests, shells, pine-cones, interestingly shaped stones, a round paper wasp nest, milkweed pods, acorns, and beechnuts.

Reggie went for the phone on her desk, stumbling and splashing hot espresso over her hand.

Shit! What was she in such a hurry for? Who did she expect to hear on the other end? Charlie? Not very likely. The last time they'd spoken was when they bumped into each other accidently at the grocery store just before they'd both graduated from separate high schools. Tara, maybe, teasing her, telling her she had sixty seconds to gather everything she cared about?

No. What she really thought was that it was *Him* again.

She'd been getting the calls for years, first at home, then college, then in every apartment and house she'd ever lived in. He never said a word. But she could hear him breathing, could almost feel the puffs of fetid moisture touch her good ear as he inhaled, then exhaled, each breath mocking her, saying, *I know how to find you.* And somehow, she knew, she just knew, that it was Neptune. And one of these days, he might actually open his mouth and speak. She let herself imagine it: his voice rushing through the phone like water, washing over her, *through her.* Maybe he'd tell her the one thing she'd always wanted to know: what he'd done with her mother, why she was the only victim whose body was never found. The others had been displayed so publicly, but all they ever found of Vera was her right hand.

What was it that made Vera different?

"Hello?" Reggie stammered.

Say something, damn it, she willed. *Don't just breathe this time.*

"Regina? It's Lorraine."

"Oh. Good morning," Reggie said through gritted teeth. She set down the small ceramic cup and shook her stinging hand, pissed that she'd burned herself hurrying for Lorraine. Why the hell was her aunt phoning at this hour? Usually she called each Sunday at five.

And Reggie often managed to be out. (Or at least pretended to be—lurking in a corner, glass of pinot noir in hand, hiding like a child, as if the red eye on the answering machine could see her as she listened to her aunt's disembodied voice.)

"I just got a call from a social worker down in Massachusetts." This was typical of Lorraine—getting right down to business—no useless preamble about the weather or any silly "all's well here, how are you?" There was a long pause while Reggie waited for her to continue. But she didn't.

"Let me guess," Reggie said. "She heard what a disturbed and traumatized family we were and was offering her services?"

Reggie could almost see Lorraine rolling her eyes, looking over the top of her glasses and down her nose, disapproving. Lorraine standing in the kitchen with its faded wallpaper, her hair pulled back in a bun so tight it pulled the wrinkles from her forehead. And she'd be wearing Grandpa Andre's old fishing vest, of course, stained and reeking of decades of dead trout.

Reggie picked up the cup of espresso again and took a sip.

"No, Regina. It seems they've found your mother. Alive."

Reggie spat out the coffee, dropped the cup onto the floor, watching it fall in slow motion, dark espresso splattering the sustainably harvested floorboards.

It wasn't possible. Her mother was dead. They all knew it. They'd had a memorial service twenty-five years ago. Reggie could still remember the hordes of reporters outside; the way the preacher smelled of booze; and how Lorraine's voice shook when she read the Dickinson poem "Because I Could Not Stop for Death."

At last Reggie whispered, "What?"

"They're quite sure it's her," Lorraine said, voice calm and matter-of-fact. "Apparently she's been in and out of a homeless shelter there for the past two years."

"But how can . . . How do they know?"

"She told them. She's missing her right hand. Finally the police took her fingerprints—they're a match."

Reggie's heart did a slow, cold drop into her stomach. She closed her eyes and saw it so clearly this time: her mother out on Ricker's Pond, moving across the ice, doing a perfect figure eight. Then she held out her hand to Reggie and they skated together in the middle of the pond, laughing, cheeks red, their breath making little clouds as the ice shifted and groaned beneath them like a living thing.

"There's something else," Lorraine said, her voice crisp and businesslike as ever. "Your mother's in the hospital. She's had a cough for some time and finally consented to a chest X-ray. They suspected pneumonia or TB. They found a large mass. Cancer. She may not have much time."

Now Reggie was speechless, trying to digest one insane piece of news after the next. It all felt like a cruel trick. Your mother's alive. But she's dying.

She sank down onto the floor, sitting in spilled coffee.

"I want you to drive down to Massachusetts and get her, Regina. I want you to bring her back to Monique's Wish."

"Me?"

"I don't drive much these days. Cataracts."

"But I—" Reggie stammered.

"I need you to do this," Lorraine said. Then as if sensing Reggie's hesitation, she added, "Your mother needs you."

Reggie pushed her hair back, fingers finding the scars. "Okay," she said.

Home. She was going back home.

Chapter 2

1976
Brighton Falls, Connecticut

Reggie's earliest memory of her mother began with her mother balancing an egg on its end and ended with Reggie losing her left ear.

She was five years old and her mother had taken her to a bar on Airport Road. Reggie spun herself on a red vinyl stool, pleased to be working her own trick while Vera performed hers for some newcomer who'd promised to buy her a drink if she could pull it off. Reggie pushed herself round and round, banging her legs gently against her mother's with each pass, carefully avoiding eye contact with the fellow to her left, with whom her mother had made the bet. He was a swarthy man with bulging eyes who wore oil in his hair and a thin leather jacket that didn't quite button. His nose had a bump, a slight twist to it, as if it had been broken one too many times. *The Boxer,* Reggie named him, not saying the words out loud, but in her head.

The Boxer called Reggie "Champ" and winked one of his froggy eyes at the girl behind her mother's back while Vera was busy sprinkling salt on the bar.

The key to the trick was to give the egg something to cling to, to rest in.

Reggie's mother, Vera Dufrane, who had perfected the egg trick, bore a striking resemblance to Jayne Mansfield—full busted with a head of thick platinum blond hair spilling over graceful shoulders. She had been homecoming queen and had gone off to New York City after high school in 1969 to pursue a career in acting. To help pay the bills while she got bit parts in off-Broadway plays, she took up modeling. Almost immediately, she became the Aphrodite Cold Cream girl. Her picture was in magazines and department stores across the country. *Treat Yourself Like a Goddess,* the tagline said. Her sudden fame brought more acting work, including her first leading role since her days as star of the Brighton Falls High Drama Club.

But just when her career was getting off the ground, Vera abruptly returned to Brighton Falls in the early spring of 1971, moving back into her large and strange childhood home, Monique's Wish, with her sister, Lorraine (six years her senior), and their father, Andre Dufrane. Andre had been diagnosed with ALS while Vera was in New York, and by the time she moved back into the house, he was in a state of steady decline. Her first night home, she made a surprise announcement at the dinner table.

"I'm pregnant. The baby's due at the end of July."

Her father and sister only stared, too shocked to speak.

"Could you please pass the rolls?" Vera asked.

"Who's the father?" Andre demanded, pushing his untouched plate of food away.

"He's nobody," Vera said.

Andre gave a shaky nod. "Hell of a way to bring a child into the world. Being Nobody Junior."

Andre had built Monique's Wish for his wife, who had always wanted to live in a castle. The house took him ten years to complete, as he did most of the work himself and was not a stonemason or carpenter. Andre repaired shoes. A cobbler during the day, a castle-builder at night. Monique herself died before the house was completed, from complications after giving birth to Vera.

Vera, as a teenager and adult, would often say Monique's Wish sounded more like the name of a racehorse than a home.

"A real long shot," she'd say. "Lousy odds."

Other than being made of stone, the house bore little resemblance to a castle. There was no moat, no turret or battlements. It had a sprawling, confused layout, spread over two stories, and was topped by a gable roof covered with slates. The uninsulated stone walls did a lousy job holding heat, and the house was dark and cold most of the year. Vera shivered through her pregnancy as she'd shivered through much of her childhood.

Lorraine set up a nursery in the back of Monique's Wish and did her best to prepare Vera for motherhood. She cooked her liver, forced vitamin pills upon her, and threw out countless packs of cigarettes. Lorraine did all this while caring for Andre, who was soon unable to go up and down stairs without help and began spending most of his days in the master bedroom, just across the hall from Vera, where he took to watching soap operas on a small black-and-white TV. Vera sat with him in the afternoons, lighting his cigarettes and jumping up to lock the door when she heard Lorraine coming. Vera would call out, "No admittance to the Infirmary until visiting hours! Come back at five! Don't forget the dinner trays!" and Lorraine would fume as she smelled the cigarette smoke and heard her father and sister giggling like children behind the carved wooden door.

Reggie would hear about all of this much later, from her mother.

She'd also hear about how Lorraine, in an effort to counteract Andre's insistence that "the poor bastard child" didn't stand much of a chance, said Vera's unborn child would be a lucky baby, to be raised by a mother and auntie, and that this was how elephants in the wild raised their young. Vera, amused, began referring to Reggie's father as *The Elephant.* Over the years, this nickname morphed into Tusks, which was the only name Reggie ever had for her father.

Reggie would grow up imagining her father with the body of a man and the head of an elephant, and later when, at age eight, she came upon a picture of the Hindu god Ganesh, she tore it from the book and kept it in a shoe box under her bed that held her other prized possessions: the skull of a bird, an Indian-head penny, two dozen *Star Wars* trading cards, matchbooks from various bars her mother frequented, and an ad cut from a magazine she found in the attic showing her mother holding a jar of Aphrodite Cold Cream in her perfectly manicured right hand. Vera wore a white dress that revealed bare shoulders, showing off glowing, flawless skin. She smiled slyly, like she was letting you in on a secret.

Sometimes Reggie would take the two pictures out and lay them side by side: Ganesh and the cold cream goddess. An unlikely pair.

Reggie watched her beautiful mother sprinkle salt on the bar like it was the holiest of acts. The bartender brought her an egg from the kitchen, and carefully, with her long, graceful fingers, Vera stood the egg on its end.

"Voilà," she said.

The Boxer clapped, his thick hands banging together clumsily, rattling Reggie's eardrums. The knobby-kneed girl spun on her stool, smiling, knowing her mother had performed a miracle. Understanding even then that her mother, the Aphrodite Cold Cream girl, was touched by something greater than herself, something that gave her the power to stand an egg on its end like a tiny, out-of-shape planet, send it carefully into orbit along with the Boxer and Reggie and everything else in the dingy bar down to the heavy glass ashtrays, all of them revolving gently, helplessly, around her.

"Did anyone ever tell you you're a dead ringer for Marlon Brando?" Vera asked the Boxer.

"No," he said, laughing, showing stained teeth.

"You look just like him. When he played Terry Malloy in *On the Waterfront*. Did you see that one?"

"No, honey. Can't say I did."

"Brando is a god," Vera said, lighting a cigarette, watching the smoke drift up.

Behind them, two scruffy men played pool on a table that had one leg shimmed with a phone book. The balls clacked together violently, stripes and solids battling it out. Other than calling each shot, the men were silent, chalking their cues, taking aim.

Vera had another drink, checked her makeup in the mirror of her compact. The Boxer bought Reggie a cheeseburger and said he'd give her a dollar if she could finish it. Reggie lost the bet and ended up with a horrible stomachache. Then they were all three in the Boxer's car, a big old boat of a thing with cracked leather seats that smelled of menthol and hair oil.

The Boxer's apartment was close by in a brick building, up four flights of narrow wooden stairs. He had a dog in a back room that barked so loud and hard it rattled the walls. He made drinks in a plastic blender that overheated, making the small kitchen smell like burned rubber. He called them grasshoppers, green from crème de menthe, and gave Reggie her own in a small jelly jar, thinking five was plenty old enough.

"It's like a milk shake," the Boxer told her. "Like one of them Shamrock Shakes you get on St. Paddy's Day."

He said something else as he passed Reggie the glass, but she couldn't hear him over the barking dog. The Boxer tipped her another grotesque wink. Reggie smiled even though she noticed the glass she'd been given was dirty, coated with an oily residue, thick, she imagined, with the germs her aunt Lorraine always warned her about. She took a sip and was pleased to discover it was what she'd expected a Shamrock Shake might taste like, green and cool, although she'd never had one—Aunt Lorraine didn't believe in fast food. The Boxer cuffed Reggie on the head gently, playfully, because they were drinking buddies now. Then he showed Reggie how the kitchen door opened out onto a small cement porch with two sagging lawn chairs, a transistor radio, and a large potted tree that had died long ago. The pot had become an ashtray and dumping ground for bottle caps and cigarette foil. The porch had low cinder block walls that Reggie could just about peek over.

"You play out here," her mother told her. "You'll be okay?"

Sometimes she said things that sounded like questions, but Reggie could tell they weren't meant to be answered with more than a nod.

"You like music?" the Boxer asked, already fiddling with the crackling radio, tuning into the first station he could get. It was lively music, heavy on the horns, sung in Spanish. Reggie didn't mind.

They left her out there, keeping the door to the kitchen slightly ajar. Reggie sipped her burning peppermint drink, held the crushed ice in her mouth until her milk teeth ached. The radio announcer spoke Spanish, and Reggie imagined the words were fast, brightly colored balls popping through the air. She remembered the clack of pool balls, the egg on the bar, the Boxer's crooked nose. And soon, she had finished her small green drink named for an insect that Reggie knew was not green at all, but brown.

Her head spun like she'd taken one too many trips around on the barstool, and she was thinking she'd better sit down when her eye was drawn to a shimmering sparkle coming from the corner of the porch.

She saw that there, amid the litter at the base of the dead potted tree, was a small ring with a red stone.

This wasn't some plastic gumball machine ring; it was the real thing, the cut jewel winking like an eye from a delicate band of gold.

Reggie was reaching for it—imagining her mother's delight when she slipped her surprise present onto her finger—feeling queasy and lucky all at once, when the dog came at her.

It moved too fast for Reggie to say for sure what kind of dog it was, or that it was even a dog at all. It could have been a bear, a wolverine, the Tasmanian devil. It was all mouth, teeth bared, drool spraying onto Reggie's face as it knocked her down flat and pinned her there, pressing its full weight into the two huge paws on Reggie's chest.

The cement was cool. Gritty. Tiny cracks ran through it like fault lines, like there had been a thousand small earthquakes up on this porch, all caused by this dog slamming little girls to the floor. Time stretched and slowed (a Silly Putty moment, she'd call it later) and Reggie was able to pick out the smallest details of her situation. She was resigned to the fact that the dog would kill her but she didn't know what death might be like, only that it was proceeded by this: this little window of time when things moved in slow motion and her senses were on overdrive, picking up everything, because, no doubt, it was her last chance to experience life on earth, right down to the rough, cracked cement.

Instinctively, she twisted her face away as the teeth came down. It felt as though the dog had torn a hole in the side of her head—there was searing pain and sticky heat along with a wash of hot, rotten-meat breath on her face.

She closed her eyes—surely for just an instant—and prayed to God, which is what she knew you were supposed to do when you were in such dire straits, her aunt Lorraine had taught her this. But in order for

God to come through, Lorraine explained, you had to believe, and Reggie, up to this point, hadn't given God much thought. But she tried nonetheless, picturing a white-bearded man floating off in the clouds. The God she imagined looked an awful lot like the photo of her grandfather that hung in the upstairs hall: a stern-looking man in a flannel shirt and fishing waders.

When Reggie opened her eyes, she found her savior not in the form of a skinny, golden-robed grandfather-like God, but rather of her mother, her hands dug into the thick black fur of the dog's neck, screaming, BAASSTAARD! Vera was wearing only silk panties and a pointed bra, looking to Reggie like a blond, large-breasted Wonder Woman. The dog turned from Reggie and sunk his yellow teeth into Vera's pale hand. She let out a guttural cry and punched him in the nose with her left hand. His jaw relaxed from pure surprise, and she yanked her torn right hand free with a terrible wet sound and took hold once more. This time she lifted the dog, this great bear of a thing—seventy pounds of snarling cur—and spun him like they were dancing, then let go. The dog flew out, over the low concrete wall of the porch and finished his life with one last yelp, four stories down.

Chapter 3

October 16, 2010
Rockland, Vermont

"I was just thinking about you," Len said when he answered his cell, his voice low and gravelly. He had this way of making everything he told her sound like a secret.

"Impure thoughts, I'm sure," she guessed.

"Always," he teased, his voice dropping lower, radiating warmth that hit her right in the solar plexus and worked its way down.

Behind him, she heard the dull murmur of conversations, the clanking of cups and plates. "Hey, listen, I'm just finishing up breakfast over at Hungry Mind and I thought I might swing by. Maybe entice you into a hike and picnic lunch up on Owl's Head."

She let herself imagine it for a second, she and Len in the woods, him shouldering a backpack of chilled chardonnay, Brie, and a baguette. They'd bring their sketchbooks, some watercolors maybe. Find a private place to spread out a picnic blanket.

"I thought we should talk about what happened last Friday night," Len said, shattering Reggie's romantic visions.

"Oh?" Reggie found herself saying.

"I've sensed a shift in things. Maybe it's my imagination, but it seems like you've been pulling away. We've hardly talked at all since then."

Shit. Reggie didn't want to go through this right now. Things between them had always had this playful easiness, but now Len was screwing with it.

"No," she said. "Nothing's changed. I've just been busy as hell with the new project. I'm sorry about the way I acted, Len. And we can talk about it soon. I just can't do it today. Actually, that's why I called. To let you know I'm on my way out of town."

Len was a silent a moment and Reggie heard one of the restaurant patrons laughing. "Business or pleasure?" Len asked at last, his words crisp. She pictured his furrowed brow, wished she could lay her fingers across his forehead and smooth out the wrinkles.

Reggie bit her lip. She ached to tell him the truth, but how would she even begin?

Remember my mother, who was supposed to have been the last victim of a serial killer in 1985? Well, guess what, it turns out she's alive and I'm on my way to pick her up and bring her home.

"Business. Nothing all that fun. I'm actually on my way to Worcester, Mass. I'm going to look over a site down there as a favor to someone."

"Poor you," he said, his voice a low purr again. "When will you be back?"

"I'm not sure. A couple days maybe. Depends how things go. I'll call you when I'm back home."

"We'll have that picnic then," he said. "And talk things over."

"Absolutely."

She hung up, feeling like shit for lying, but knowing she wasn't ready to tell him about her aunt's phone call yet. She promised herself she'd call Len and tell him the truth as soon as she had a better sense of the situation. Once she'd assessed things and come up with a plan, she'd tell Len everything.

It didn't take her long to pack. She was used to traveling and had perfected her packing so that she could live out of a small carry-on and messenger bag for up to two weeks. The rules for her travel wardrobe were that the items all went together and could be easily washed out in a hotel sink.

Crossing the bridge to her office, she tucked her MacBook Pro into her leather messenger bag, then added her sketchbook and pens, glasses and index cards. While she packed, her eye fell on the astrology chart tacked to her bulletin board. Len had presented her with it a couple months ago.

"Think of it as a map of the sky at the exact time and place you were born," Len had explained. "This center line represents the horizon."

Reggie had nodded and studied the chart, a computer printout Len had generated with some astrology program—three rings that reminded her of a drawing of Earth's core, mantle, and crust. The outermost ring had the symbols of the twelve signs of the zodiac; the middle ring was divided into twelve pieces of pie, which Len explained were the houses. Reggie liked that, of course. And scattered in the houses were indecipherable hieroglyphics and numbers. "The planets," Len had explained, "and their position within each sign."

"The signs that your planets are in are your inner reality, but the houses are the filters through which you broadcast that reality to the outside world," Len told her.

"Right," Reggie had said, feeling more skeptical by the second. She'd decided to go back to trying to look at it as a map.

The circle in the center of the chart was full of colored lines that made Spirograph-like designs.

"What are those?" she'd asked, pointing.

"Your aspects. They show how the planets in your chart relate to each other. See here." He'd pointed to a line at the top. "You have sun square moon. The sun represents your intellectual self and the moon is your emotional self, and the square is a dynamic, tense aspect. Basically these two parts of your self are in constant conflict with each another. It's no wonder you're so uncomfortable with feelings."

She'd rolled her eyes.

"And here." Len had pointed to a funny little glyph with an arrow, just above the horizon line. "You have Sagittarius rising. That's what makes you so frank—you don't bullshit people, you tell it the way it is, even if it isn't what they want to hear."

Though she couldn't possibly believe that the position of the planets at the time you were born could have an effect on the way your life turned out, she had to admit the design of the chart—the concentric circles, the crisscrossing lines, the inscrutable symbols—was compelling. Then her eye had caught on a little blue trident just over the horizon line, next to the Sagittarius symbol.

"What's this?" she'd asked, trying to sound casual while pointing with a shaking finger.

"Hmm? Oh, that's Neptune. You have Neptune in the twelfth house," Len had said. Suddenly, her heart was banging in her chest and her mouth was dry. "It's what makes you so intuitive. You're in touch with the forces of your unconscious. Neptune in the twelfth is a classic placement for great artists. And tormented souls."

Standing alone in her office now, Reggie reached out to touch the little blue trident, covering it with her pointer finger. Then she turned back to her open bag and threw in her cell phone and charger, looked around the office, and grabbed the rough sketches she'd done for her latest project: a small, portable home she called the Nautilus. It represented the ultimate freedom: the ability to have a home that went wherever your life took you.

"There's one thing I'm having trouble visualizing," Len had told her when he first saw the rounded, shell-shaped sketches. "How are you going to put wheels on it? I mean, does it need to be mobile? This design looks like it would work better being stationary in one place."

"Because life is about movement," she'd said.

"Movement?"

"Our ancestors," Reggie said, "were hunter-gatherers. They moved where the food was. They went away from bad weather and danger. They roamed. That ancient instinct is still alive somewhere deep inside us."

"But doesn't a house represent the ultimate stability?" he'd asked. "Isn't part of our instinct also to hunker down in one place? Put down roots?"

"We're not trees," Reggie said dismissively, covering his mouth with her own, kissing him a bit too roughly. His stubble scratched her face. His mouth tasted sour.

Damn it. She needed to focus. To get her bags packed, get on the road to Worcester, and stop letting Len creep into her thoughts again and again.

All packed up, she started to leave the office, then turned back and opened up the top drawer of her desk. Reaching back in the far right corner of the drawer, her fingers found the old silver chain and pulled it out. There, dangling on the end, was Tara's hourglass. Reggie turned it over, watching the pink sand run out.

You have one minute . . .

Then, she undid the clasp and put the necklace on, hiding it under her shirt, where it rested cool against her chest.

Punching the hospital address into her GPS, Reggie navigated the dirt roads, passing snowmobile trails and hunting camps, then hit blacktop. Turning left on Route 6, she went by the Rockland town hall, Christ the Redeemer Church, and then the Hungry Mind Cafe—the lot was full of cars there for the breakfast rush. She saw Len's old pickup and thought of stopping, but didn't want to get tied up for too long. She thought again of telling him the real reason for her trip to Worcester, pictured his intense face full of worry, and imagined he'd probably insist on going with her. But this was something she needed to do on her own.

She'd told almost no one about her mother and Neptune. Not friends, colleagues, or casual acquaintances. Len was the only one who knew. Len and everyone back in Brighton Falls. Which was a big part of the reason why she'd never gone home.

She regretted ever telling Len. He drove her crazy with his pop psychology analysis of the whole thing.

"You're Neptune's victim, too, you know," he'd said when they were in bed together last Friday night. They'd opened a couple of his bottles of homemade dandelion wine and both had had a little too much. He was drawing slow circles around her belly with his fingertips.

"How's that?" Reggie had asked. She'd known a second bottle of wine was a bad idea. Len always got very philosophical and emotional when he was drunk.

"Look at your life, Reg. You have everything, but in some ways, it's so barren." He was slurring his words a little.

"Barren?" she said. She sat up, forcing his hand away from her stomach.

"You put up all these walls around yourself. You don't talk to people."

"I talk to plenty of people," Reggie blurted out, pulling the covers up over her naked chest. "I go around the world talking to people."

"I mean *really* talk, Reg. Have you ever let yourself get truly close to anyone? Had a relationship that felt solid and long-term? I mean, look at us. As soon as it feels like we're moving to the next level, you get all freaked out and start pushing me away."

Now her hackles were definitely raised. "You're not exactly Mr. Commitment, either. As I recall, you were the one who wanted the no-strings-attached relationship. And I've gotta say, you seem pretty content to come and go as you please like a tomcat."

It was a relationship that suited them both. They'd met four years ago at a gallery that was showing several of Len's paintings. He painted abstract geometric shapes and lines that brought to mind stained-glass windows. Reggie was drawn to the cleanness and balance in his work. And she found his disheveled artist look downright sexy. She bought two of his paintings and asked him out.

He made it clear that he wasn't looking for a relationship. He'd gone through a messy divorce a couple of years before and said he just wasn't ready to get involved.

"Who said anything about getting involved?" Reggie had asked. "I'm talking about a cup of coffee, a glass of wine maybe."

"Nothing more?" Len had asked, eyebrows raised.

"If you want to know if I'm going to show up at your place with a U-Haul after the third date, the answer is no. I'm quite content on my own. But sometimes it's nice to have a little company. A coconspirator to pass the cold nights with."

He'd smiled. "No strings attached?"

"If it's no strings attached you want, I'm your gal," she promised.

They'd had an on-again, off-again relationship ever since, joining each other for movies, parties, even weekends away. They enjoyed each other's company, but after more than two days together, Reggie would begin to feel slightly panicky and claustrophobic. The closer she got to Len, the more she felt this happening, and she'd find herself doing little things to piss him off and push him away. Len was right. It just wasn't in her nature to let herself get too close to people. It was a safety mechanism she'd developed years ago, one she felt totally comfortable with. And now here was Len making her question the wisdom of her ways.

"I *am* happy," Len said. "I have a life that suits me. But the difference between you and me, Reg, the real difference, is that I'm not afraid to let people inside. I'm not afraid to love someone."

"So now I'm incapable of love?"

"I didn't say that. I said you were afraid."

"That's a big assumption. What on earth gives you that idea?"

"You think everyone's going to leave you. That we live in this world where at any second, someone you love could get snatched away."

"Bullshit," Reggie said, pissed off because she knew that on some level Len, drunk as he was, was right.

"I'm just saying I think it's sad, that's all. That because of one psychotic prick, you're going to spend your whole life being afraid to get close to anybody."

"That's not fair and you know it," Reggie hissed.

"Don't you ever wonder where all this is going?" he asked.

"All what?"

"This," he said, gesturing over the bed at the two of them with great flaps of his arms. "You and me. Christ, I'm forty-five, Reggie. Are we going to be doing this twenty years from now, slipping into and out of each other's beds, no strings, no commitments?"

Reggie squinted at him. "What is it you're saying?"

"That maybe it's time we had something more. Something beyond being fuck-buddies."

Reggie cringed a little at Len's definition of their relationship. "Like what?"

"I was thinking we could move in together."

Reggie gave a great caw of laughter. It was, quite possibly, the most absurd thing he'd ever said to her, and it had caught her completely off guard.

Len looked crushed.

"You're not serious?" Reggie said. "What, you want to have me bring you your slippers and pipe each evening, then pull a casserole out of the oven?" She thought of her house, her perfect little house, being slowly filled with pieces of Len: dirty shoes, crumpled sketches, roaches from the joints he was constantly smoking.

Len shook his head, reached for the nearly empty bottle of wine, and took a swig.

"I should have known that's how you'd react," Len said, leaning back against his pillow, closing his eyes.

"It's all there in your chart—your fear of commitment, your success, nightmares, intuition. Your need to control every situation, to be in charge." His voice trailed off. "All the things that make you who you are. The things that make you . . ." He was nearly asleep now, his voice soft and breathy. "So damned impossible."

Reggie shut her eyes tight, seeing that little blue trident, tucked down in her twelfth house. She rolled over so that she was facedown against the pillow as she listened to Len snoring softly beside her. And she was sure she could feel it then: that little piece of Neptune inside her like a fishhook, jabbing away, reminding her she wasn't fit to live with anyone.

Reggie passed Ye Olde Antiques Barn, the Maple Leaf Inn and Hotel, and the Hare on the Moon glassblowing studio. Twenty minutes later, Reggie was signaling to turn onto the entrance ramp for 89 South, the road toward Boston. As much as she traveled, the truth was, she always hated leaving Vermont. As soon as she crossed the state line, the skin on the back of her neck prickled. The billboards, four-lane highways, and skyscrapers gave her a temporary case of attention deficit disorder, left her unable to make decisions, focus or concentrate. She hated the sameness of chain restaurants and big box stores, the "planned communities" of oversize, identically ugly houses that popped up overnight like horrid clumps of mushrooms.

She cranked up the radio, listening to solemn voices talking about the global economy. All wrong for a road trip. She flipped through stations until she hit the Kingsmen doing "Louie Louie."

Fine little girl waits for me
Catch a ship across the sea

She was back in her mother's Vega, the music pumping from the crackling speakers, her mother keeping time with her fingers on the steering wheel, mouthing the words of the song, her lipstick perfect. The windows were down, the wind blew through their hair, making them feel like they were flying.

"Where are we going, Mama?"

Her mother smiled a secret, conspiratorial smile. "Wherever the wind carries us, lovie."

When they were alone together, it was the two of them against the world. Life was one big adventure and anything was possible. They could end up at the greyhound track, where Vera let Reggie put money on the dog of her choice, go to Bushnell Park in Hartford to ride the carousel, or drive to the ocean just for fried clams.

"The world is our oyster," Vera would say, wiping tartar sauce from her chin. "Or at least our clam roll!"

The Vega was gone now, turned to scrap metal and rust.

Reggie wondered if she and her mother would even recognize each other.

She tried to picture the stump where her mother's right hand had been—the hand that had once tapped out the rhythm of every song on the radio; the hand that held hers ice-skating on Ricker's Pond.

Reggie pushed her hair back, fingers finding the small crescent moon of scars behind her prosthetic ear.

Maybe, she thought, feeling her own scar tissue, they'd know each other by what was missing.

Chapter 4

May 26, 1985
Brighton Falls, Connecticut

"The ear's a keeper," Charlie said when he first saw it. "Now maybe you can do something about this mop!" Charlie tousled Reggie's long tangles, sending sparks through her scalp, down her spine, turning her into a glowing, live-wire girl.

They were up in the tree house in Reggie's yard, looking over the plans Reggie had drawn for its renovations. The sun was coming through the tarp over the unfinished roof, casting an eerie blue glow.

"You should totally get your hair cut, Reg," Tara said. She was on her back on top of a sleeping bag, and rolled over, reaching into her ratty drawstring bag for the pack of cigarettes she'd swiped from her mom. "Go see Dawn over at Hair Express. She does my hair." Tara's hair was long at the back and short and spiky in front; dyed black with blond tips. There were four earrings in her left ear and two in her right. She wore dark eyeliner, but no other makeup. With her pale, gaunt face and raccoon eyes, she looked a little like the undead, which is why everyone in the eighth grade called her a vampire.

"You got that right," she'd say to the popular girls in their acid wash jeans and cheerful blue and pink eye makeup. "Mess with me and I'll come flying into your window at night and drain you dry." Kids pretty much stayed away from Tara, just like they stayed away from Reggie—the weird one-eared kid without a dad who lived in the creepy stone house. Charlie, a nervous, spindly boy who everyone said was gay, was an outsider, too. Reggie had known him her whole life—they lived two streets away, had gone to nursery school together—and she knew Charlie liked girls. All anyone had to do was notice the way he looked Tara—his brown eyes strangely glassy and full of longing.

Tara lit a cigarette, blew the smoke out through her nose, then fiddled with her lighter. She was one of those people who always had to have something in their hands. When she wasn't smoking, shuffling cards, or scribbling out lines of poetry, she'd play with the tiny hourglass pendant around her neck, watching the pink sand fall through, then flipping it to watch again.

Tara was wearing a tight black V-neck shirt with long sleeves that had tears in them held together with safety pins. She ripped up most of her clothes, then put them back together with rough stitches, safety pins, even staples. She was pretending not to notice Charlie practically drooling as he stared at her chest. She wore a B cup already, while Reggie was so flat she was still in a training bra, when she even bothered with a bra at all. Reggie cast a self-conscious look down at her own baggy gray T-shirt Lorraine had picked up on sale somewhere.

"Can I have a drag?" Charlie asked, which was stupid, because he didn't smoke at all. He didn't believe in it. Even a month ago, he was hassling Tara, showing her pictures of blackened smokers' lungs. His mom had been a heavy smoker and had died of cancer when Charlie was ten. Reggie could remember going to his house back when his mom was alive and coming out smelling like an ashtray. His mom was real nice, though. She'd taught Reggie how to do cat's cradle and how to make a multicolored Jell-O parfait. The woman was a miracle worker with Jell-O. Once, for Presidents' Day, she brought a Jell-O mold in the shape of Mount

Rushmore for their second-grade class. It had been three years since she had died, and Reggie missed Mrs. Berr like crazy. And if she missed her like that, she couldn't imagine how Charlie must feel.

Tara pushed the pack toward him. "You can have your very own."

Tara had never met Charlie's mom. She moved to Brighton Falls last year after her parents got divorced. Her dad stayed behind in Idaho with his new girlfriend, who Tara said was half her mom's age. The girlfriend was pregnant, which meant Tara would have a little half brother or sister, but she didn't seem all that thrilled about it.

"It's not like I'll ever even see the kid," Tara had said. "I mean, why would I? My dad, he totally sees this whole thing as his second chance to get the perfect wife and kid. It's not like he's gonna want me hanging around to remind him of how crappy his life used to be." She said it like she didn't care, but afterward, Reggie watched the way she picked at the skin around her fingernails until it bled.

Tara and her mom rented a tiny two-bedroom unit at the Grist Mill Apartments, which was where people on disability and welfare lived. It was a big ugly two-story building in an L-shape with a courtyard full of broken glass and cigarette butts, where two old men were always perched on the bench like a pair of gargoyles. Tara swore one of them had once shown her his penis. Lorraine didn't like Reggie going over to the Grist Mill Apartments, so on the rare occasions she went, she lied to her aunt about it.

The first few days of school, Tara sat alone in a corner at lunch. It was Charlie's idea to invite her over to their table.

"She looks like a freak," Reggie had complained.

"Oh, and we're not?" Charlie had said, getting up to go talk to Tara without waiting for Reggie's consent.

Tara's mom had grown up in Brighton Falls and still had family around. That's what Tara said anyway, but Reggie never saw any aunts, uncles, or cousins or even heard about them. When she pressed Tara for more, Tara changed the subject. Her mom worked as a waitress over at the Denny's on Airport Road. When she wasn't working, she was in her bedroom sleeping or watching TV while she sipped coffee laced with brandy. Sometimes Reggie, Charlie, and Tara would ride their bikes out to Denny's, and Tara's mom would give them free desserts. Her eyes were always puffy with dark circles underneath and her skin smelled boozy-sweet, like she had brandy seeping from her pores.

Tara didn't talk about her dad much and it didn't sound like he ever called her or sent letters or anything.

Reggie had heard Tara's mom lashing into her when Tara had asked for new shoes. "Jesus, Tara. Why don't you call up your two-timing father and ask him to pay up all the freaking child support he owes? Maybe then we could afford your fancy new shoes. I'm sure that little baby he's having already has a hundred pairs."

Tara ended up shoplifting the shoes she wanted anyway. Her mom was always either working or sleeping, and didn't seem to notice the many mysterious additions to Tara's wardrobe. She could come back from the mall in an outfit with the price tags still attached, and her mother wouldn't bat an eye, just rush out the door, stuffing her apron in her bag and uttering some vague warnings about not staying up too late. Sometimes it seemed like a game Tara played, like she was daring her mom to notice, like she actually wanted to get caught.

Charlie pulled out a cigarette, lit it, and began to smoke without inhaling. He'd take a little puff, then let it right out. His eyes got red and his nose started to run. He was wearing the Rolling Stones T-shirt his dad hated—the one with the *Sticky Fingers* album cover showing a close-up of a guy's crotch. His dad said the shirt was obscene and made him look like a queer. He'd thrown it in the trash, but Charlie had fished it out and kept it hidden, always careful to layer another shirt on top of it when he left the house.

Charlie's dad, Stu Berr, was a burly cop who showed his disappointment in Charlie by constantly trying to remold him into his vision of the ideal son. He bought him a weight bench, dragged him to football games, stopped paying for Charlie's guitar lessons, and made him get a military-style buzz cut, which made the shape of Charlie's head look strangely crooked.

Tara sat up, eyes glistening excitedly as she looked at Charlie. "The cigarette you're smoking was poisoned with a deadly nerve agent. You have one minute to live." She pulled out the small hourglass pendant, flipped it over, and watched the pink sand running through. "Only one thing will save you."

"What?" Charlie asked nervously. Tara could go anywhere with this.

"You have to kiss Reggie. She's got the antidote on her lips."

Reggie shot Tara a panicked look—did Tara know how Reggie felt about Charlie?

Charlie looked at his cigarette, considering. He licked his lips, probably trying to imagine the taste of poison.

Reggie held her breath, wishing for the kiss, but also praying he wouldn't do it. If he kissed her, then maybe he'd be able to tell how Reggie felt. Like all her secrets would travel by osmosis through her lips and into his.

Did kisses work like that? Reggie didn't know. She'd never kissed anyone but her mother and aunt.

"Time's running out," said Tara as the sand slipped through. "Do you live or die?"

Charlie gave a soft, defeated sigh, and leaned over and kissed Reggie. His lips were warm and tasted like smoke, but only stayed on hers for a second. It was the kind of kiss a big brother might give because his mother made him, but still, it made Reggie's stomach do a flip. Her heart was pounding so hard she was sure the others could hear it. She felt her one truc ear redden as the knowledge sunk in, deeper than it ever had before: she was in love with Charlie Berr, stupid haircut and all.

Tara smiled, letting go of the hourglass. Then she squinted up at the tarp ceiling. "So are we gonna get a real roof on this place or what?" she asked. " 'Cause the blue light in here makes us all look like Smurfs. *Très sexy.*"

Reggie laughed a little too hard and loud, pleased to be moving away from the subject of the kiss. "The roof is next, definitely. Then I think we tackle the bridge."

The tree house was a relic from Reggie's childhood, built for her when she was seven by her uncle George. Turning it into a proper hangout had been Tara's idea, and Reggie immediately went to work drawing up plans for a roof, walls with windows, and a door that opened to a suspension bridge that would cross the yard and lead right to the little balcony outside Reggie's bedroom.

Reggie had scoured the library for books on design and building, taking notes on the distance between studs, the proper span of roof rafters, how to do a window header. She'd never thought about how buildings worked before, but she soon found herself hooked—here was something that took her love for drawing to a whole new level. She felt herself instinctively drawn to the neatness of plans and blueprints; the idea that you could put a design down on paper, then bring it to three-dimensional life with lumber and nails. It felt almost magical.

So far they'd framed the walls of the tree house and sheathed them with plywood. The simple shed roof was framed, and there was plywood over half of it, the other half draped with a blue tarp. They'd brought some sleeping bags up as well as a deck of cards, and an old fruit crate they used as a table. There was a stack of board games in the corner—Monopoly, Clue, Life, and an old Ouija board that had belonged to Vera. Empty Coke cans were scattered around as well as a hammer, saw, and boxes of nails.

Charlie had stashed his beat-up old acoustic guitar up there. When they hung out at night, they used votive candles stuck in glass jars and Charlie would play soft, bluesy tunes that Reggie would get lost inside; the notes carried her to a far-off place in some imaginary future where Charlie was famous and onstage, telling a crowded theater, "This song is for Reggie."

Reggie looked at the guitar now, purposely keeping her eyes off Charlie. She fiddled with her new ear.

Tara said, "Let me see," reaching out for Reggie's ear, keeping her cigarette in the corner of her mouth. "Does it come off?" Tara asked, tugging gently. When Reggie nodded, Tara pulled harder until the ear came off in her hand.

"Cool!" she exclaimed, squinting through a cloud of cigarette smoke. "Just like Mr. Potato Head!"

A few months after the dog attack (which in Reggie's family was thereafter referred to only as *The Unfortunate Incident*) her aunt Lorraine had taken her to a doctor in New Haven, who, after studying Reggie's remaining ear, fashioned her a prosthetic ear to match. Only it didn't. Not quite. The color was off a bit and the glue that held it in place itched terribly, so the ear stayed in Reggie's top drawer, hidden beneath her underwear. Her mother and aunt gave up after a while and only made her wear it on special occasions.

"Your ear!" they would cry as they were headed out the door, late for Christmas Mass or school picture day. And Reggie would run up, rummage through the drawer, and attach the ear only to remove it covertly in the car and place the lump of rubber in the pocket of her good coat, where she would feel for it from time to time, touching it the way another kid might stroke a rabbit's foot.

Her mother had also been disabled by the dog, which, ever after, Vera referred to as Cerberus. The dog's teeth had gone clean through the fleshy part of her mother's right hand between thumb and forefinger, damaging a tendon and nerve that the doctors were not able to completely repair. The result of this, in addition to the thick, semicircular scarring ruining her once perfect hand, was that Vera would never be able to bend her pointer finger. She would go through life self-consciously hiding her damaged hand, holding it on her lap or down at her side, all the fingers curled but one, which left her perpetually pointing. When she was out in public, she took to wearing long white gloves—the leather supple, soft as butter, the pointer and index fingers of the left hand stained yellow from the Winstons she chain-smoked.

In Reggie's mind, the dog truly became the three-headed beast with a serpent's tail, who, her mother explained, was the guardian of the underworld.

When she went over the attack in the months and years to come, Reggie would picture her mother in her sparkling white underclothes twirling a gigantic black three-headed dog through the air, the word *Bastard* ringing in her one good ear.

It was years before Reggie learned the true meaning of the word *bastard,* and that the dog was not the only bastard on the deck that afternoon. Reggie was a kid without a father, the very definition of bastard, which was pointed out to her rather cruelly back in the fourth grade by a gang of fifth-grade girls, led by Dusty Trono.

"Say it," Dusty said as she held Reggie pinned underneath her in the sandbox while Dusty's friends looked on, giggling. Dusty grabbed a hunk of Reggie's hair and pulled and twisted.

"I'm a bastard," Reggie had whimpered, tears streaming down her face, sand sticking to it.

"Now eat sand, bastard," Dusty said, twisting Reggie's head so that her face was pressed into the sand.

Reggie's aunt and mother had convinced her to get the new ear before starting high school in the fall, saying it would be a fresh start. Her new improved ear was made of latex and snapped into two titanium screws the surgeon had implanted in her temporal bone. The ear was purely aesthetic: the dog bite had done a great deal of damage and the subsequent scarring left her almost totally deaf in her left ear. The surgeon had suggested that Reggie have an ear reconstructed from cartilage taken from her rib cage, covered with a flap and skin graft. He showed her a photo of a patient who'd had this procedure done, and the ear looked like an actual ear.

"The benefit," the surgeon explained, "is that we create an ear using cartilage and skin from your own body. It will look and feel like the real thing. It would require two surgeries, six months apart."

Unnerved and a bit sickened even hearing about the procedure, Reggie felt content, for the time being, to stick with the removable latex ear. It was at least far superior to the older, off-color rubber ear of her early childhood. Now she'd look almost like a normal girl.

Reggie watched as Tara turned the new ear over in her hand. "It's kind of freaky how real it looks," she said. "Shit, it even feels real." She touched the ear to her cheek and closed her eyes. Reggie squirmed a little at the strangely intimate gesture.

Charlie stubbed out his half-finished cigarette. "They make sex toys out of latex, and some of them look pretty real," he said.

Tara laughed. "And you're an expert on sex toys?"

Charlie's cheeks turned pink. "I'm just saying." He reached for his guitar and strummed a few chords. His fingers were long and nimble, the nails cut short and square. He always looked more comfortable with a guitar in his hands. It was the only time he ever looked totally relaxed, his shoulders slumping a little, his body curving around the instrument, melting into it almost. Sometimes Reggie would come up to the tree house on her own and hold his guitar. She'd lay down with it on the sleeping bag, arms wrapped around the hollow body, fingers caressing the steel strings but never daring to strum them.

Tara handed the ear back to Reggie, who snapped it in place.

"So I think we've got supplies for the roof in the garage," Reggie said. "There's a couple sheets of plywood left and a box of shingles. We'll need cable for the bridge and some really heavy-duty eyebolts. Some kind of clamps to make loops with the cable ends."

Charlic leaned over his guitar, looked down at Reggie's drawing of the tree house, and scowled. "I still don't think it'll work," he said, pointing to the suspension bridge she'd drawn leading from the tree house to the little balcony outside her bedroom window.

"Sure it will," Reggie said. "We just need eye-bolts and some metal cable. We attach the wooden slats to the bottom two cables. The top two are our handrails."

"There's no way," Charlie said, shaking his head, pushing the drawing away.

"People build suspension bridges all the time," Reggie told him.

"Maybe so," said Charlie. "But for us to do it, to build a bridge all that way, it's impossible."

"It's only fifteen feet. And if we —"

"It's impossible," he said dismissively, turning back to watch his fingers dance up the fret board, bending strings, making the guitar sing.

"What do you do if you like someone and they don't like you back?" Reggie asked her mom. They were in the waiting area at Hair Express. Vera was flipping through the latest issue of *Variety* that she'd pulled from her bag. She carried a large leather purse that was more like a tote bag, and kept it crammed full. To get to her keys or lipstick, she had to pull out handfuls of receipts, notes scribbled on little memo pads, matchbooks, dried-out pens, eyelash curlers, silver bird-shaped scissors, coupons, foundation, empty packs of cigarettes, lost buttons, aspirin, and tea bags.

(Vera wasn't a tea drinker, but placed the moist bags over her eyes to help with wrinkles.)

"How do you know he doesn't like you back?" Vera asked, holding the magazine in her white-gloved hands so that Reggie could only see her eyes. Her mom's lashes were so heavy with mascara that Reggie wondered how she kept them open.

It was Sunday evening and Reggie was the last appointment of the day. The other stylists were sweeping hair into little piles, soaking combs in disinfectant, and counting out their tips. Dawn was finishing up with an old lady with peach-tinted hair.

Vera was wearing a scarlet dress and matching high heels. That was one of the things about her mom—she always dressed up like she was going to party. She put on full makeup to run down to the donut shop, because, as she always said, "You never know who you'll meet. The world is about connections, Regina. Not just who you know, but who they know. It's all one big web, everything interconnected, everyone tugging on each other's strings."

Reggie knew that after the haircut, her mom would drop her at home, then go off to rehearsal. She was doing a play down in New Haven—something dark by a local playwright who was starting to build a name for himself. The play was directed by a man named

Rabbit, her mom's on-again, off-again boyfriend, who had the temperament of an artist and was, in Vera's words, both a bastard and a genius. Reggie had never met him, but she'd heard countless stories about his temper tantrums during rehearsals and about how well connected he was. "He knows everyone," Vera always said, a proud smile on her face. "He even has a cousin in Hollywood who's worked for Martin Scorsese." Vera spoke the names of famous people in a hushed, conspiratorial tone, like they were magic incantations that you didn't dare say out loud.

Vera continued to study Reggie over the top of her magazine, waiting for an answer. Reggie bit her lip. "Because he likes someone else."

Vera nodded knowingly. "And does this someone else like him?"

Reggie thought for a minute. "I don't think so. Not like that anyway."

Vera smiled. "Then let him know how you feel. That's what I did to get Rabbit. He was seeing this little blond number until I swept him off his feet." Vera smiled in a self-satisfied way.

"But I can't do that!"

This was stupid. She didn't have her mother's looks or grace. Vera could sweep any man off her feet. Reggie was just a gangly, awkward girl with a chest as flat as a boy's. Just last week, when she'd been at Ferraro's market with her mom, the checkout boy had been unable to take his eyes off Vera. He'd said, "Can I help you out to the car with these? Or will your son get them?" Vera didn't correct him, only said, "We can manage. Thanks."

"There are other ways, Regina. But remember, you can't change what's inside a person. All you can do is help them open their eyes."

The peach-haired woman walked by. Dawn called Reggie's name and she jumped up and hurried to the chair. Vera went back to her magazine.

"And what are we having done today?" Dawn asked, moving close to put a plastic cape around her. She smelled like cigarettes and wintergreen gum.

Reggie looked at herself in the mirror, her hair long and wild, going every which way. "I'm ready for a change," Reggie told her.

Dawn nodded. "I know just the cut for you." She washed and combed Reggie's hair, then went to work, the scissors singing, hair falling in great clumps onto the floor, mixing with the wispy tendrils of peach-colored hair.

Reggie had worn her hair long since the dog attack, when it had been pale blond and curly. *Cherub hair,* Lorraine called it. It was her mother's color, the one trait they shared. As she grew, the tight curls turned to waves and the color darkened, as if the only evidence of her being Vera's daughter was slipping away, year by year. By the time she sat in the hairdresser's chair, it was chestnut brown. She looked over at her mother, who had switched to a *People* magazine and was scowling down at the movie stars and singers with a disgusted, *Who-do-they-think-they-are* look. Her platinum hair caught the light and glowed like a halo.

"Keep your head straight, hon," Dawn said.

Reggie turned back to her reflection and had the strange sensation that it was some other girl she was seeing. Her face looked longer without the unkempt bangs covering her forehead. It was thin, freckled, with dark blue eyes and pointed, elven features that made her seem younger than thirteen. She watched how carefully the hairdresser worked the scissors around the false ear, never seeming to notice that it was any different from the other.

Chapter 5

October 16, 2010
Worcester, Massachusetts

Following Lorraine's instructions, the first thing Reggie did when she got to the large, sprawling medical center was ask for the social worker—Carolyn Wheeler. The building was a confusing warren of waxed floors, elevators, beeping machines, and unimaginative art reproductions on the walls. The heels of her cowboy boots echoed in the halls. Doctors were paged. A code blue on B Wing was called. Elderly volunteers in green smocks manned information desks and wore cheerful buttons that said: HOW MAY I HELP YOU?

Reggie had won an award once for designing a community health center when she was getting her degree at Rhode Island School of Design. It was circular to represent unity and wholeness, and remind patients of their connection to the earth and nature. A curved wall was like outstretched arms ready to envelop and protect. It brought us back, on some deep level, to our original home: our mother's womb. Reggie's design included a living wall of plants and a large water feature in the center that could be heard and seen from every room. The hospital in Worcester was the antithesis of Reggie's long-ago design. With the fluorescent lights, long corridors, sharp corners, and tiny windows that looked out onto the parking lot, she couldn't imagine how anyone here could possibly get better. Reggie felt lost and off-kilter, and her forehead was damp with perspiration, even though the building was pumped full of cool air.

Carolyn led Reggie into a small office crowded with black metal file cabinets and a jungle of overgrown spider plants. Papers and file folders tottered in unorganized, precarious stacks across Carolyn's massive gunmetal gray desk. There was a framed cross-stitch that said BLESS THIS MESS—only upon further inspection, Reggie saw that it was just a picture cut from a magazine, not fabric and embroidery floss at all.

Carolyn wore a black turtleneck and a corduroy blazer with elbow patches. She had terrible glasses with aviator frames and something green stuck between her teeth. She smelled faintly of garlic. Reggie had been hungry when she came into the hospital, and now her stomach churned in an unfriendly way. Carolyn gestured to an upholstered chair with suspicious dark stains that Reggie had no desire to sit in. Looking around and seeing the only other choice was standing, Reggie sat perched on the edge of the chair, her leather messenger bag by her feet.

"As you can imagine," Carolyn said, scooching forward in her own chair so that her belly was pressed against the overflowing desk, "we're doing our best to handle this as quietly and sensitively as possible. As far as I know, the press haven't got wind of it yet, but I can't guarantee how long that will last. We've tried to limit the visits with detectives and special agents and so on, as they seem to exhaust her. And the truth is, I don't think there's much she could tell them."

"Has she said where she's been all these years? Or anything at all about Neptune?" Reggie asked, her throat closing around his name. She thought of the phone calls, the sound of his breath in her one good ear.

"Not a word. Nothing that makes coherent sense anyway. And we haven't been able to piece together much. We know she's been in and out of the homeless shelter for the past two years. She didn't disclose anything about her past to any of the staff or residents. She used a false name—Ivana Canard. The staff at the shelter requested that a mental health evaluation be done, but she refused. She's had a bad cough for some time. When she collapsed at the shelter last week, she was taken here by ambulance. She seems to like her doctor—he's the one she told her true identity to."

Reggie laughed out loud. "Let me guess—he's tall, dark, and handsome?"

Carolyn seemed flustered. "Dr. Rashana? Yes, I suppose, he is," she said, sallow cheeks turning pink. "She told him she'd been the Aphrodite Cold Cream girl."

"I'm sure she did," Reggie said. It was her mother's standard pickup line. *Did you know I was the Aphrodite Cold Cream girl?* She could just picture this poor doctor's face; a homeless woman probably twice his age telling him she was once a beauty queen. Shit, he probably didn't even know what Aphrodite Cold Cream was. The company went out of business in the early 1980s. "It was always her claim to fame," Reggie explained.

"Now I suppose she's got a new one," Carolyn said.

Reggie nodded. Felt her guts coiling like a nest of snakes.

Neptune's last victim. The only one to survive.

She could only begin to fathom the shit storm that would descend when the media learned Vera was alive. She remembered how ruthless they'd been when her mother's hand showed up on the steps of the police station: camping out in front of Monique's Wish, following Lorraine and Reggie wherever they went, asking horribly invasive questions. Some slimebag writer named Martha Paquette wrote a true crime book on the Neptune killings that pretty much portrayed Vera as a prostitute, and you didn't need to read between the lines to understand that Martha believed she got what she deserved. Martha spent months stalking their family, waiting for Reggie outside of school, saying things like "This must be so hard on you, Regina. If you ever need someone to talk to, just to get things off your chest, you know I'm here." Right. The very last person Reggie wanted to talk to was Martha Paquette and her goddamn tape recorder.

Carolyn cleared her throat. "According to my notes, your mother disappeared back in 1985?"

Reggie nodded. Her head was starting to hurt.

"She's been through a great deal since then, Regina." Carolyn blinked behind her ugly glasses, gave Reggie one of those empathetic therapist looks that must have taken six years of school to master.

Suddenly remembering all the reasons she hated therapists, Reggie found herself struggling not to roll her eyes. Did this woman think she was some kind of idiot?

"It's Reggie, and I can well imagine. Can we go see her now?" The office was feeling small and airless to her. The gangly green and white spider plants seemed to be growing before her eyes.

"I just want you to be prepared. She's not going to be the woman you remember."

No shit. When Reggie last saw her, she was twenty-five years younger and had both her hands. "I'm aware of that."

"She might not recognize you."

"The last time she saw me, I was thirteen years old. I don't expect her to recognize me." She shifted in her chair, brought her hand up to touch the scar tissue around the prosthetic ear on the left side of her head, but stopped herself. She didn't want to run the risk of this woman seeing it and giving her another doe-eyed empathetic look.

"I don't know how much your aunt told you, but your mother has been very agitated, very confused during her stay with us. She's been paranoid and delusional. There are a number of possible causes for this—underlying psychiatric issues, long-term alcohol abuse, her current illness."

What about the fact that she's been held captive by a goddamn serial killer? Wouldn't that make anyone a little crazy around the edges? Reggie bit her lip to keep from blurting the questions out. She could picture Carolyn Wheeler jotting down a note that agitation seemed to run in the family. Instead of speaking, Reggie gave her an understanding nod. She wanted to get the head-shrinking crap over with and go see her mother, whatever shape she was in.

"We've got her on some meds that have helped her to be more . . . calm, and I'm sure Dr. Rashana will go over all of that with you. I know he's been on the phone with your aunt and that arrangements are being made for palliative care at home. Your mother will, as we've explained to your aunt, need round-the-clock care."

Underlying psychiatric issues. Palliative care.

The words banged around like pinballs in Reggie's brain, ringing bells and buzzers, making her head and jaw ache.

"There's nothing they can do?" Reggie asked, hating how little-girlish her voice sounded. She cleared her throat and spoke in her best professional tone, each word carefully enunciated, "I mean as far as treatment for the cancer?"

"That's really a question for Dr. Rashana. But my understanding is the disease is far too advanced, and at this point, it's really a matter of keeping her comfortable. And safe."

It's a little late for that, Reggie thought, but bit her lip instead, this time so hard she tasted blood.

Chapter 6

May 27, 1985
Brighton Falls, Connecticut

"Wake up, Worry Girl."

"Mom?"

"Maybe. Or maybe I'm someone else. Old Scratch coming to get you."

Reggie smelled gin, cigarettes, and Tabu perfume. Her mother had crawled under the covers, curling herself around Reggie's sleeping body like a snake seeking warmth. Vera squeezed Reggie tight, pressing the breath out of her.

Reggie opened her eyes. "Very funny."

"Don't turn around, you might catch a glimpse of my horns. Feel them poking you?" She jabbed a pointed fingernail into Reggie's back.

"Ow! Quit it."

Vera let out a breathy cackle. "Did you know that you frown in your sleep?" she cooed, pressing her lips against Reggie's cheek. Vera's hair hung down, tickling Reggie's neck. "Now come on, wake up or I'll have to get out my cloven hooves."

"Whattime'sit?" Reggie moaned, squinting at the red numbers on her digital clock. 2:15. Sometimes rehearsals would go late, then Vera would go for drinks with the cast and crew. Often she'd spend the night on someone's couch or at Rabbit's loft.

Reggie touched the scars and metal nubs on the side of her head. She'd taken the ear off and put it in the drawer of the bedside table, unable to sleep with it on. The two titanium posts reminded her of the end of a battery. Like she was a robot who had to be plugged in and recharged.

"I have a secret," Vera said, stroking Reggie's forehead gently. "Do you want to hear?"

Vera's voice was bright and bouncy, like a kid's Super Ball.

"Mmm," said Reggie, struggling to keep her eyes open. The charge had run out. "Tired robot," Reggie mumbled.

"I've met someone. Someone special. I think he could be *the one*." She said this the way she pronounced the names of famous people, in an excited whisper.

"Nice, Mom," Reggie said, letting her eyes close.

Reggie started to drift. She heard only a few words of what her mother said: *important, two houses, the cleanest car you ever saw.*

"But what about Rabbit?" Reggie asked, struggling to stay awake, to understand what her mother was saying. Vera sounded so excited, so happy, Reggie wanted to be a part of it.

"He's not in the picture anymore," Vera said.

Reggie doubted that. Rabbit was always in the picture, even if he was way in the back for the moment. Vera dated lots of other men, but Reggie didn't know many details about them. There was Sal, who was a professional photographer and might just be the ticket to getting her modeling comeback off the ground; a man named Jimmy, who worked in a restaurant; and once in a while a handsome young man in a VW bus would pull up in their driveway and beep twice for her. Reggie didn't know his real name, but called him Mr. Hollywood because Vera said he'd been an extra in a couple of blockbuster movies—she'd promised Reggie she'd rent the videos one of these days and they'd sit down and watch them together.

"It's someone new," Vera said.

"Mmm," Reggie said, drifting.

"This is the man who's going to change everything," Vera said. "I can feel it."

Reggie dreamed of machines. Of cogs and wheels and batteries. Things that clicked and popped and smelled of grease and electrical charges.

When she woke up, it was after ten. "Shit," she mumbled, realizing she was already late to meet Charlie and Tara downtown.

Her mother was gone. The only trace of her was a smudge of lipstick on the pillow.

Reggie sat up, snapped the ear in place, and opened her closet. The clothes her mother had bought for her were all tucked to one side—skirts and dresses, designer jeans, tight nylon parachute pants, shirts with necklines cut too low. She never had the heart to say no to her mom when they were out shopping, and Vera held up one outfit after another, saying, "This would be cute."

Would be. If you were a different girl.

Reggie passed over those clothes and went for the old standby: Levi's and a faded T-shirt that Lorraine had bought for her.

She dressed quickly, checked out her new haircut and ear in the mirror, and headed into the kitchen. Lorraine was there, lightly buttering a piece of wheat toast. It's what she ate for breakfast every morning—weak tea and nearly dry toast.

"Mom up?" Reggie asked.

Lorraine shook her head, pursed her lips. "I heard her come in last night," she said.

Reggie opened the fridge, grabbed the orange juice, and poured herself a glass.

"You should really start locking your door," Lorraine said.

"Huh?" Reggie closed the fridge and turned to face her aunt. Lorraine's hair had been gray since Reggie could remember, and she wore it pulled back in a tight bun. She had pointed, birdlike features, murky blue eyes, and thin lips that seemed to always be chapped and peeling. She worked in the office at Brighton Falls Elementary School. She typed up memos, filed, and kept track of who was absent. During the summer, she worked only two afternoons a week. Today she was dressed in her usual at-home attire: baggy pants and shirt, and the stained and worn fishing vest and hat that had belonged to her father and were much too large for her, making her seem strangely little-girlish for a woman of forty-one.

"It's not right," Lorraine said, making her best sour-pickle face. "Waking you up when she's in that state."

"She was out late at rehearsal," Reggie said. "They must have gone out for drinks after. You know what Mom says—it's all part of life in the theater."

Lorraine scowled. "Lock your door at night, Regina."

Reggie chugged her juice, nodded, and hurried out of the kitchen.

She grabbed her ten-speed from the garage and started off down the driveway. The Memorial Day parade would have already started by now—it was the biggest event of the year in Brighton Falls and marked the beginning of summer. Poor Charlie was stuck scooping ice cream in the park with the Lions Club. His uncle Bo, who owned the local Ford dealership, had roped him, along with Bo's son Sid, into it. Charlie's dad would be driving one of the police department's new Crown Victorias in the parade.

As Reggie rode she imagined Charlie's reaction to her new haircut—he'd do a double take, unsure it was even her at first; then he wouldn't be able to take his eyes off her. The haircut was chic, her mother had told her. "For once in your life, you're not hiding behind your hair."

Reggie turned left at the bottom of the driveway onto Stony Field Drive, then right onto Country Club.

The thin tires of her bike bumped as she crossed the railroad tracks. The breeze ruffled her short hair, the sun warmed her new latex ear.

She passed the town garage, Millers' Farm, and went under the railroad trestle that was painted each year by the graduating class: CLASS OF 1985, ROCK AND ROLL FOREVER, said the letters in dripping red paint.

Main Street was lined with people in lawn chairs. Reggie could hear the high school marching band as she approached, sweat gathering between her shoulder blades. They were playing "The Stars and Stripes Forever." Little kids were waving tiny American flags. A guy on the corner was selling balloons, plastic swords, and popguns, which went off like champagne corks as boys fired at each other across the street.

Reggie zigzagged her way through the crowd, heading south on Main, along with the parade, toward the park. She felt the rush of excitement from the crowd and had this sense that she was a part of something so much larger than herself. This was her town. These were people she knew. People her grandfather had made shoes for. People her mother and aunt had gone to school with. She held her head high as she rode, wishing for someone in the crowd to recognize her, to say what a lovely, chic haircut she'd gotten, how grown up she looked now.

She reached the park and hopped off her bike. At the edge of the grass a one-legged old man in a wheelchair was at a table collecting donations for disabled veterans and giving away bright red artificial poppies. Reggie smiled at him, reached into her pocket for a quarter, and wrapped the wire stem of the poppy he gave her around the handlebars of her bike.

The Lions Club had set up tents in the park with long tables underneath. They were grilling hot dogs and slicing watermelon. Reggie spotted Charlie down at the end, scooping ice cream. He was wearing a Lions Club apron and looked totally miserable. His cousin Sid was next to him, and Reggie thought the two couldn't have been more different. Charlie was small and wiry with his too-short hair and huge brown eyes that reminded Reggie of a lemur. And there was Sid—a tall, muscular boy with pale, shaggy blond hair and a slack-jawed expression that gave him a look of content bewilderment.

Sid was a senior at Brighton Falls High, drove a Mustang, and sold pot, though word was he smoked most of his profits. He worked after school and weekends as a groundskeeper at the country club. Sid was wearing army fatigue shorts and a white polo shirt with the Brighton Falls Country Club crest. Covering his perpetually bloodshot eyes was a dark pair of Ray-Bans.

Tara was standing nearby, eating an ice cream cone with long, slow licks.

"Oh my God!" Charlie yelped when he saw Reggie. He took a step back, looking shocked and vaguely frightened. "What happened to your hair?"

Reggie felt as if she'd been hit in the stomach with a two-by-four. "You said I should get it cut," she said lamely.

"I said *cut*, not totally hacked off."

Sid just smiled this goofy, vaguely amused smile.

"I think it's perfect," Tara said, licking around the edge of her ice cream cone. "She looks like a pixie!"

"She looks like a dude," Charlie muttered, turning away.

"Come on, man," Sid said. "The androgynous look is totally hot. Look at Annie Lennox."

Reggie's stomach was still clenched in a hard knot. Her face and ear burned and tears prickled the corners of her eyes.

Tara studied her a minute, then took her arm, gave it a squeeze, and said, "Don't listen to these boneheads. You're gorgeous."

Reggie looked down at the ground.

"Nice to see you, Regina." Charlie's uncle Bo had come up behind Charlie and Sid. He was just putting on a Lions Club apron and looked flustered.

"Where've you been, Pops?" Sid asked him. "Everyone was looking for you. Freaking out big-time. There was some kind of, like, drama with lost hot dog rolls?"

"We were running low on ice for the soda coolers. Ferraro's was closed, so I had to go clear out to Cumberland Farms to get some."

Bo was a big man with a face like a ham—all meaty, shiny and pink. He heaved up a bag of ice and sliced the top open neatly with his pocketknife, dumping the contents into a cooler. "How's your mom, Reg?"

"Fine, I guess," Reggie said, squirming. She thought of her mother crawling into bed with her in the wee hours of the morning, reeking of gin, pretending to be the devil. Bo gave her a funny little smile that made her stomach hurt. Her mom and Bo had gone to high school together, had even dated once upon a time. Now Bo was married with a teenage stoner son, and they lived in a big old house out at the base of the mountain that was paid for by people buying Escorts and F-150s.

"You tell her I said hi, will you?" Bo said with a wink. His eyes moved up and down Reggie like he was searching for some sign of Vera there. Finding none, he gave a little snort.

"Sure," Reggie said, thinking, *Like hell, slimebag.*

Tara leaned in to whisper to Reggie again, "Who is this pervert? He's totally checking out my tits. Gross. And he's so lying about getting ice, I can tell. He was probably banging some Girl Scout or something."

Bo looked over at them, and Reggie thought for a second he must have heard. Tara looked right back at him and took a big brain-freeze-inducing bite of her ice cream cone, then licked her lips in a slow, satisfied way, never breaking eye contact. She was sick. Definitely sick.

"Guess I better go solve the mystery of the missing buns," Bo said abruptly, jerking his gaze from Tara. He looked sweaty and distracted as he headed down toward the grill.

"Charlie's an asshole," Tara said at Reggie's house later. They were in the living room, watching MTV and sharing a bag of Doritos. "You shouldn't listen to a word he says. That haircut's very you."

"Mmm," Reggie said.

"News is on in ten minutes and we're changing the channel," Lorraine called from the kitchen.

"*Bor-ring,*" Tara moaned. Tara's mom was working a double shift, and Reggie knew Tara wouldn't go home. She hated to be alone. Tara pretty much lived at Monique's Wish when her mom was working lots of hours.

"Can I ask you something?" Reggie said to Tara.

"Go for it," Tara said, stuffing another orange chip into her mouth.

"Do you like him?"

"Charlie?"

"Yeah."

Tara chewed, thinking it over. "He's fine and all, but he's not my type."

Reggie wondered what Tara's type was. Maybe someone like the guys in drama club who listened to The Cure and had spiked hair. But Reggie had never seen Tara talking to anyone like that. The only kids at school Tara ever seemed to hang out with were Reggie and Charlie.

"Someone like Charlie," Tara went on, "he could never get me. There's stuff about me, secret stuff, that I'd never tell Charlie in a million years."

Reggie nodded.

Tara looked right at her. "Maybe I'll tell you, though. One of these days."

Lorraine bustled into the living room. "Time's up. Channel Three. Let's see what Andrew Haddon has to say tonight." Reggie was sure Lorraine was secretly in love with the Eyewitness News weatherman, Andrew Haddon. He was a gangly scarecrow of a man whose shirts never seemed to fit him right. During the weather, he always pulled this stupid slot machine that was supposed to sum up the forecast. Instead of apples and cherries, it had pictures of suns, clouds, snow, and raindrops. He'd spin the wheel with a smile, like he was using his machine to make the weather, then peer down and announce: *It's a four-sunshine day! Get out there and enjoy it!* Or *Nothing but raindrops today, folks. Be sure to pack your umbrella.*

Reggie reached for the remote and changed the channel. There was a commercial with a guy in a chicken suit doing an ad for Bo Berr's Ford Dealership. *No credit, no problem. Don't be chicken. Come on down.*

"Do you think that's actually dear old Uncle Bo in the suit?" Tara asked, eyes wide as she leaned forward a little, studying the television. Reggie remembered the suggestive way Tara had bit into her ice cream cone, then licked her lips while she stared Bo down. It made Reggie queasy to think about.

"Nah," Reggie said. "He probably got one of the poor sales guys to do it. Or maybe it's Sid!"

"No way," Tara said.

"Who's Sid?" asked Lorraine.

"Bo Berr's son," Reggie explained. "He's kind of a pothead."

Lorraine made a sour face.

"Mom and Bo were an item once, right?"

"I don't recall," Lorraine said in a dismissive tone.

"No way!" Tara squealed. "Really?"

Reggie nodded. "My mom told me. It was back when they were in high school. Bo was like this big football star then."

Lorraine fiddled with a loose string on the arm of the couch and said nothing.

"Where is Mom, anyway?" Reggie asked.

"I don't know," Lorraine said. "She got up just before noon and left without a word."

After the news, Reggie knew Lorraine would go to the garage for her fly rod and waders, then make her way down the slope of the backyard to the creek, where she'd stay until it got too dark to cast flies. The left side of the couch where she sat night after night was infused with the tangy, fish smell that seemed to follow her everywhere she went. Reggie half expected to look at her neck one day and see gills.

"Two more weeks till summer vacation," Lorraine said, still focused on the loose thread.

"Mmmm," Tara said, reaching for another Dorito. "Then it's good-bye, Brighton Falls Junior High. Thank *God*."

"Maybe you two should get jobs," Lorraine said.

Tara laughed. "We're too young."

"I was working in my father's shop when I was twelve," Lorraine said.

"That was back before the days of child labor laws," Tara shot back. "The Dark Ages," she added, wiping orange cheese powder on her black jeans as she gave Reggie a conspiratorial wink.

"I don't think it's good for young people to be idle," Lorraine said.

"We're not going to be idle. We're going to finish the tree house," Reggie said. "And I'll probably help Charlie do lawns," Reggie added. Charlie had been cutting grass around their neighborhood since just after his mom died. He made good money and was always looking for help.

"Speak for yourself, Dufrane," Tara said. "I plan to be as idle as possible. Lay around. Eat bonbons. Work on my tan."

Reggie laughed. The idea of Tara sunbathing was bizarre. Reggie had never even seen her in short sleeves. "Don't you die if sunlight hits you? Spontaneously combust or something?"

Tara smiled. "Can't see my reflection in a mirror either. And keep your damn crosses away from me!"

"Tara!" Lorraine snapped. "That's quite enough."

"Sorry, Miss Dufrane," Tara said in a singsong voice.

The six o'clock news came on and the lead story made them all hold their breath, leaning toward the television and the newscaster with perfect hair and a square jaw who sat behind the Eyewitness News desk.

"A woman's right hand was discovered on the front steps of the Brighton Falls police station earlier today. An unidentified source in the police department reports that the hand was left in a milk carton wrapped in brown paper."

Reggie had this sense of slipping into a movie, leaving real life behind.

"What the hell?" Tara said, and Lorraine was too shocked to reprimand her for swearing.

Reggie jerked her leg involuntarily, like when the doctor tapped her knee with a rubber hammer. Her body felt twitchy and strange, like it was pulled on by invisible strings.

There was now a detective being interviewed and he had little else to say. He was a red-faced man with a bushy mustache and green polyester sport coat.

"Oh my God," Tara yelped. "That's Charlie's dad!"

"Is not," Reggie said, moving closer to the TV.

"Regina, don't hog the television," Lorraine scolded. "You're blocking our view."

Reggie went back to the couch.

"It totally is," Tara said. "He's like . . . famous now."

"Do you have any idea whose hand this might be?" the newscaster asked. "Or whether it was taken from someone dead or alive?"

"I'm afraid I can't comment on that at this time," the bushy-mustached detective said. He asked anyone who might have been downtown and seen a person with a brown paper package to call the station. Reggie looked at his face. Tara was right. It was Charlie's father. He looked fatter, more washed out and potato-like than in real life. But then again, she hadn't seem him a lot lately. Charlie didn't invite her over all that much these days, and when he did, his dad was always working.

"Je-sus!" Tara said, her mouth staying open, her eyes huge and hungry, all lit up like they got when she was playing one of her end-of-the-world games.

Lorraine smoothed the front of her stained fishing vest and shook her head, then closed her eyes for a moment, like she was making a wish.

Reggie reached up and touched her new ear, pulling it loose, then attaching it again with a satisfying metallic click.

Excerpt from *Neptune's Hands: The True Story of the Unsolved Brighton Falls Slayings* by Martha S. Paquette

Officer Thomas Sparrow was the first one to notice the package when he returned from the parade at approximately 11:45. It sat at the top of the granite steps leading to the main entrance of the Brighton Falls police station. It was a plain brown package, tied with string. Officer Sparrow, the newest member of the force, untied the string without notifying his superiors or screening it as a possible explosive device.

"I don't know what I was thinking," he told me in an interview later. He was a fresh-faced twenty-two-year-old who'd gotten an associate degree in criminal justice from the local community college and joined the force right away. He'd grown up in Brighton Falls and had always wanted to be a police officer. "I guess I figured it was a mistake, you know? Someone set it down and left it by accident. It looked like something from a bakery, all wrapped up like that."

Under the brown paper, Sparrow found a red and white milk carton, stapled closed. His curiosity piqued, he pulled open the top and discovered a woman's right hand, the well-manicured nails done in a fresh coat of coral polish. Officer Sparrow set the carton back down, hurried inside to alert the desk sergeant of his discovery, then ran down the hall to the men's room and vomited.

Chapter 7

October 16, 2010
Worcester, Massachusetts

"Regina?" the woman under the covers crooned. "Is that you?"

Her face was skeletal, her skin so thin and white you could see the blue veins pulsing behind it. Her hair, once a radiant platinum blond, was now limp and colorless as rice noodles. But it was Vera, no doubt.

Reggie froze in the doorway, a tight squeezing sensation in her chest pushing all the breath out of her, nearly stopping her heart.

Go on in there, you fucking coward, she told herself.

"It's me, Mom," Reggie said. How strange, to find herself wondering who it was her mother saw. Was there some part of the kid she used to be peering out from under the dark bangs of curly hair, the five-foot-eight frame—still all elbows and knees like some absurd marionette? Maybe not much had changed after all. In her leather jacket, jeans, and boots, she was still dressed like the tomboy she'd always been.

The walk from the doorway to the bed seemed to take forever. Reggie's boots slid on the freshly waxed floor like it was ice. Like she was ten again, back at Ricker's Pond, skating toward her mother.

She got to the edge of the bed and put a shaky hand on Vera's shoulder. There was very little flesh there—Reggie could feel the knobby bones making the loose framework that held her mother together. Reggie was reminded of the Lincoln Logs she'd played with as a kid, putting several sets together to build a tower right up to the ceiling; a tower that leaned and swayed and eventually came crashing down to the ground. Vera's arms were tucked under the covers, and Reggie found herself staring down at the shapes they made, trying to imagine the right one ending at the wrist. The blanket covering her was thin and white, the words PROPERTY OF UMASS MEDICAL CENTER stenciled in blue letters. Vera's knees were bent, making a tent of the covers. The pillow beneath her head was damp and stained.

Their eyes locked. Reggie turned her head slightly, pushed the hair away to reveal the scars around her prosthetic ear. Proof. Vera smiled, then whispered something Reggie didn't catch.

She leaned down. "What was that?"

"You have to be careful here. People aren't who they say they are. Like her." She stared past Reggie at Carolyn Wheeler, who hovered in the doorway. "She knows Old Scratch." Vera's breath was warm and yeasty smelling. She was missing several teeth.

"Would you like me to send her away?"

Vera's eyes widened. "You can do that?"

Reggie smiled. "Just watch me." She stood up, went over to the social worker, and asked if she and her mother could have some privacy. Carolyn looked flustered. Her eyes went from Vera to Reggie, then back to Vera. Was Reggie supposed to be untrustworthy? Dangerous even? Maybe she was in on it with Neptune?

"Of course," the social worker said at last. "I'll be right down at the nurses' station if you need me."

Reggie smiled sweetly but couldn't think of a single situation in which she'd need Carolyn Wheeler. Reggie shut the door. She would have locked it if that had been possible.

"Better?" she asked, returning to her mother's side.

Her mother. God, even though she was here, touching her, breathing her in, she couldn't believe it. Vera, alive. Reggie did a quick calculation and realized her mother was fifty-nine years old. With her gaunt features and sagging skin, she looked closer to eighty. Was this the result of the cancer or years of hard living? What did it take, to break a person down like this? To turn them into a shrunken doll that only faintly resembled who they'd once been?

Carolyn Wheeler seemed to think her mother's mind was too far gone to be able to reveal anything helpful about the killer. But she must remember something, right? And whatever details she did remember weren't likely to get spilled to strange-faced detectives or a social worker with broccoli in her teeth.

"I'm going to take you home, Mom."

"Home?"

"To Monique's Wish. Would you like that?"

Her mother looked up at her with watery gray eyes. "Is that where you live?"

Reggie stiffened. *Hell, no. Not for over twenty years.*

"No," she said. "But I'll stay with you there for as long as you like." Reggie could see it so clearly: how she would bring her mother cups of tea and custard, and Vera would tell her all about what had really happened to her after she was taken. Reggie would get the answers the police hadn't been able to. She'd crack the case wide open like a regular private detective, make sure that bastard got what was coming to him. If Reggie were in charge of the justice system, she'd have Neptune strapped to a table and give a big old carving knife to the relatives of the women he killed. An eye for an eye, a hand for a hand.

"Mmm," Vera said, closing her eyes. Then, she opened them wide. "They do things to people here," Vera said, lowering her voice and looking worriedly at the door. "They take them into the basement and slice them open. Then they put stuffing inside."

Reggie stared down at her mother, unsure of what to say. She decided an understanding nod was best. *Yes, I'm sure they do, Mom.*

Vera began coughing. It was a wet, racking cough. Her eyes watered and her tongue stuck out. Her whole body thrashed. She brought her arms out from under the covers and Reggie saw the stump: the cut had been made just below the knob of her wrist. The skin there was glossy and pale—ghost flesh. If Reggie squinted, she could almost see the shape of the missing hand still attached, pointing up at her. Her mother heaved forward, coughing and retching with such force it seemed like she'd crack a rib. Reggie's hand hovered by the red button on the bedrail—should she call a nurse? And then it was over. Vera readjusted herself in bed, reached into her mouth with her left hand, going so far back she gagged. Then pulled her hand out and held it open.

"See?" she asked.

Reggie looked down. The knuckles of her mother's fingers were swollen and her pointer and middle finger were stained yellow with nicotine. And there, in her heavily creased palm, was what looked like a tiny piece of mucus-slathered white thread.

Reggie shivered, felt bile rising up into throat. "Let's get you out of here," she said.

She found a plastic PATIENT BELONGINGS bag and hurriedly loaded what little she could find into it: hospital-issue toothbrush and toothpaste, shampoo and deodorant, yellow plastic comb and body lotion. There were no clothes hanging in the closet or in the dresser. Only a coat—a large black, man's wool dress coat. The lining was coming loose and it was threadbare in places. There was a hole in the left elbow.

"Is this yours, Mom?" Reggie asked, taking the coat off the hanger.

Vera nodded.

The coat was heavier than Reggie expected and soon she understood why: the lining had been cut here and there and little makeshift pockets had been formed by resewing squares around the cuts. Reggie smiled at the magician's coat her mother had created. That was Vera—ever resourceful, even homeless, even crazy.

Reggie reached into one of the pockets and pulled out an empty plastic grocery bag balled up inside a dozen rubber bands.

Rummaging through the other secret pockets, Reggie found matchbooks, a crushed cigarette, a broken cell phone, two cellophane packets of crumbling saltine crackers, bobby pins, and a wallet that was empty except for an expired coupon for Herbal Essences shampoo. Patting down the sleeves, she found one last hidden pocket at the end of the right sleeve, held closed with a safety pin. She undid the pin, reached in, and pulled out a worn red velvet jewelry box. Flipping it open, she discovered an engagement ring and wedding band inside. Reggie was no expert, but these didn't look like cheap costume rings. A homeless woman carrying around valuable jewelry? It didn't make sense. Unless . . .

"Are these yours, Mom?" she asked, lifting the wedding ring from the box. It was heavy and solid, no doubt real gold. "Did you get *married*?" The word caught on her tongue and she had to force it out.

Reggie knew her mother had never married her father. Vera had never even told her the guy's name, claiming it wasn't important.

Tusks, Reggie remembered, visualizing the picture she'd once cut out of Ganesh—the peaceful look on the elephant-headed god's face, the four arms outstretched, hands poised and waiting.

Vera whispered into her covers and the only word Reggie caught was the last one: *Soon*.

Turning the gold band in her hand, Reggie saw there was an engraving inside—words in neat script:

Until death do us part
June 20, 1985

Reggie nearly dropped the ring, as though the engraving had reached out and stung her.

June 20, 1985.

The day Vera's hand showed up on the front steps of the police station.

Excerpt from *Neptune's Hands: The True Story of the Unsolved Brighton Falls Slayings* by Martha S. Paquette

Thirty-six-year-old Andrea McFerlin was a stylish woman with frosted hair and impeccable makeup. A certified public accountant, she worked for LaRouche & Jaimeson, where her coworkers described her as dedicated and conscientious. She was the one who remembered birthdays in the office and organized the secret Santa gifts at Christmastime. She had left for a weeklong business trip on Saturday, May 25, but never made her flight. Her family and coworkers thought she'd been too busy with the conference to check in by phone, and none of them worried when they didn't hear from her. Her car was later found in the long-term parking lot at the airport, suitcase still inside.

On May 27, a hand with coral nail polish was discovered on the steps of the police station—a hand that would be identified as Andrea McFerlin's only after her body was found later in the week.

"I didn't realize she was dead at first," said Rebecca Hartley, twenty-nine, who jogged through King Philip Park every morning and discovered McFerlin's body just after dawn on May 31. "I thought it was someone playing a prank. A drunk high school kid in a game of truth or dare or something. Then when I got close and saw her, I knew."

McFerlin was naked, her wrist bandaged, and she had been placed in a sitting position, her back leaning against the center of the fountain.

"Her eyes were open," Hartley described. "You'd think a dead person would look all peaceful, like they were sleeping. Not her. I'll never forget it. She was there, in the center of that fountain, water running down over her, and when I looked into her eyes, what I saw was pure terror."

State of Connecticut Chief Medical Examiner Dr. Aldous Ramsey determined that McFerlin had been killed by strangulation just hours before her body was found. Other than the missing hand and the ligature marks around her neck, there was no sign of any other trauma or sexual assault. There were traces of adhesive around her arms and legs, likely from being bound by duct tape. Dr. Ramsey found her stomach full of boiled lobster with drawn butter, eaten only an hour or two before she was strangled.

Chapter 8

June 1, 1985
Brighton Falls, Connecticut

"I know the lady who found her."

The man behind the counter was named Dix and was an old friend of Vera's. He owned Airport Lanes and was a thin, gray-skinned guy with a bulbous pockmarked nose that resembled the bowling balls he was surrounded by.

"She's in the Friday night ladies' league," he was saying, "—was here last night, all shook up still. Sweet little gal. Becky, her name is. Real tiny, just like a doll. She runs through King Philip Park every morning around six. Don't think she'll be going back anytime soon."

Dix passed them their shoes, the leather worn and scuffed, the sizes marked in stitched-on numbers at the back. Reggie was a six. Her mother an eight. Uncle George brought his own freshly polished ball and shoes.

"That McFerlin gal was totally naked," Dix continued, "except for the bandages over her right wrist. Strangled. Had to be. Becky said she could see bruises all around her neck."

Vera made a little tsk-tsk sound with her tongue, then reached up and touched her throat.

George, evidently thinking that this was too much information for a thirteen-year-old's ears, grabbed Reggie's shoulders and guided her away from the counter toward lane three. "Going to bowl some strikes today, right, Reg?" he said. He was a small man with receding hair and a pointy rodentlike face. He wore little round glasses but probably needed the prescription changed because he squinted all the time anyway. Reggie's secret name for him was Uncle Mouse, but she meant it in a sweet way.

"How about it?" George asked again, a little too enthusiastically. "I bet you're a natural with a bowling ball."

Reggie shrugged. She really hadn't wanted to come. She wanted to be back at home, nailing shingles to the roof of the tree house, stealing glances at Charlie and remembering the way he'd kissed her, even if he hadn't really meant it. But her mom had insisted. "Georgie's taking us bowling," Vera had told her.

"I don't bowl," Reggie had said. "And besides, I thought you said George was a dud."

Reggie loved George, but her mom was always teasing him, mocking him, making fun of him behind his back.

"Well, it's time you learned to bowl," Vera replied. "And Georgie may be a dud in certain ways, but he's a gentleman through and through. After Airport Lanes, he's taking us out to that new steak house for dinner. I hear you can get your baked potato five different ways! Get your shoes, Regina."

George had been friends with Vera since high school. "He's always been a little sweet on me," Vera would say, smiling. "But he's just not my type. I'm sorry to say it, but any man who spends that much time with a bunch of wooden ducks is kind of a dud." George collected duck decoys. And he also made his own in the woodworking workshop he'd set up in his basement—he made other things too: wooden bowls and bookshelves. He'd even made a desk for Reggie and a big mirror for Vera.

The bowling alley was dark and smelled of polish and disinfectant. The rust-colored rug was full of stains and cigarette burns. Beer signs lit up the small lounge area in the back, which seemed almost cozy compared to the wide-open cavernous space where the ten lanes were laid out. Her mom headed straight back to the bar and ordered drinks.

There was a man in dress pants and a collared shirt sitting at the bar, nursing a glass of beer. He said something to Vera and she put her head back and laughed. She returned with a gin and tonic for herself and root beers for Reggie and George. Reggie felt awkward in the stiff shoes and walked like a penguin, which made Vera laugh.

"Will they catch him, Mom?" Reggie asked.

"Who?"

"The man who killed Andrea McFerlin."

Vera nodded. "Of course they will. A crime that terrible. The police won't rest until he's behind bars."

Vera picked a red ball out for Reggie and a sparkly silver one for herself.

"You know what to do, Regina?" she asked.

Reggie shrugged. She hadn't bowled since coming here to a birthday party when she was nine.

Vera put down her drink and showed Reggie how to approach the foul line in four steps, back swing, and release.

"Let the ball do the work," she instructed.

Reggie's first tries were gutter balls, but her mother and George applauded anyway. George stepped up and bowled a strike with his custom-made ball. He bowled in a league and had won all kinds of trophies.

"Not bad, Georgie," Vera said. "Not bad at all. I guess duck-making isn't your only talent."

He smiled at her, pushed his glasses up. "Everyone's got more than one talent, Vera. You know that."

"You know," Vera said, taking a long sip from her glass, "honestly, I'm a little hurt. All these years you've been making your mallards and ringtails—"

"Pintails," George interrupted.

"What's that?"

"The ducks are pintails," he said, looking sheepish as he stood, holding his ball. "A ringtail is a lemur. Or a mammal like a raccoon."

Reggie looked down at the floor, wishing George hadn't corrected her mother. And lemurs made her think of Charlie and his big lemur-eyes, which made her remember how badly she didn't want to be here in the first place.

"Is that so?" Vera murmured, draining her drink, rattling the ice around, smiling ever so slightly. "The point is, you've never given me one."

George looked genuinely puzzled. "I had no idea you'd like one."

"Of course I would. Honestly, George, sometimes I wonder if you know me at all."

George turned back and took his shot. The ball went right down the middle, then veered off to the side, catching only two pins.

"Damn," he muttered.

Vera ordered another drink from the bar, talking to the guy in the white shirt while she waited. When she returned, she removed her leather gloves and bowled with her left hand, telling Reggie she'd really been much better when she could use her right. George whistled and said, "You should have seen your mother, then. Back in high school, she could out-bowl anyone. She was a star here."

Vera bowled strike after strike with her left hand anyway, and Reggie wondered how much better she could be. She wore a pale blue dress and matching scarf to tie back her hair. Reggie thought she looked like the sky, like heaven.

She caught herself staring at her mother's scarred hand, and when Vera noticed, she held it out to Reggie, offering it as some form of proof.

"All great heroes have a flaw," she told Reggie, her voice loosening from the gin as she reached to touch Reggie's new ear, her fingers searching knowingly for the scars behind it. "It's one of the things that makes them heroes."

Vera strolled back toward the bar. "I'm gonna grab a refill and a quick smoke," she said. She stood beside the man with the white shirt and ordered a third drink, pulling out her pack of Winstons.

Reggie was up again and George stood behind her, giving her pointers.

"Don't hold it so tight. That's it. Relax your arm. Now step into the swing," George said. "Imagine a line between the ball and that front pin. Bowl straight down that line like it's an arrow."

She released the ball, watching it travel right down the middle, knocking down all but the two pins in the back right corner.

"Nicely done!" George said. Reggie looked back to see if her mother had seen, but the bar was empty. She got a funny, nervous feeling in her stomach, swirling around with her too-sweet root beer. Reggie listened to the chunking and grinding of the ball return, waiting. When her ball came back, she put her fingers in the holes and moved into position.

"See if you can get a spare, Reggie," George said. "Visualize that line leading right up to those pins."

Reggie aimed for the two remaining pins, but the ball veered too far to the right and ended up in the gutter. Turning, she saw her mother wasn't back yet. Had she gone to the bathroom, maybe? Or outside for some air?

George bowled his frame, then said, "Your mother's up." He glanced over at the empty bar grimly. "I guess I'll take the opportunity to go to the men's room. If your mom's not back in a minute, go ahead and take her turn."

"But I'll wreck her score!" Reggie squeaked, and then immediately felt like an idiot. No need to be a baby, no need to freak out.

George made a strange sound—half grunt, half sigh—and walked away.

Reggie headed for the bar, her chest feeling tight. There was an old guy polishing glasses behind the counter.

"Help you?" he said.

"Um—I'm looking for my mother."

The bartender shrugged.

Reggie went to the back door and opened it, squinting into the early evening sunlight. Her mother was nowhere around. A tan car was taking a left out of the parking lot onto Airport Road. Reggie made out two people in the front seat, sitting close together. Then she looked down and saw the size eight bowling shoes to the left of the door.

She felt a hand on her shoulder and spun. "How 'bout you and I go for that steak dinner?" George said, forcing a smile through his clenched jaw.

"Thanks, but I'm not all that hungry."

"I'll bring you home, then." His voice was so low she could barely hear him and she was suddenly sorry she'd said no to dinner. "To tell the truth, I've kind of lost my appetite, too."

They returned the shoes, watching Dix spray them with disinfectant and shelve them. George paid and they went out to his van. George had his own produce business, supplying restaurants all over the valley with vegetables and fruit. He was the only person Reggie had ever met who could get excited over beets and rutabagas.

"Buckle up," he said to Reggie with a smile. Then he pushed a cassette in and Johnny Cash started to sing "Ring of Fire." George eased the van out of the parking lot. He was a careful driver who never went over the speed limit and always seemed to have an eye on the rearview mirrors. His van was always freshly vacuumed; the dashboard sparkled. A tree-shaped air freshener hung from the rearview mirror. The back of the van was covered in AA bumper stickers that said EASY DOES IT; FIRST THINGS FIRST; ANOTHER FRIEND OF BILL W'S.

"I'm sorry," Reggie said.

"You've got nothing to apologize for, young lady."

"She shouldn't have left like that."

His jaw clenched again. "No, she shouldn't have," he said with an edge to his voice that Reggie hadn't expected. "It was our night. The three of us." He gripped the wheel tight, then turned to Reggie. He smiled. "Listen, kiddo, your mother's gonna do what she's gonna do. I learned a long time ago that there's no point trying to change her. Live and let live."

They drove in silence a minute, coming into the center of town now. Reggie looked at the neat row of shops—The End of the Leash pet store had once been her grandfather's cobbler shop.

"How've things been at home, Reg?" George asked.

Reggie bit her lip, thought of her mother crawling into bed with her, telling her about a new man; Lorraine warning her to start locking her door. "Fine, I guess," Reggie said, staring down at her sneakers.

"Good," he said, smoothly switching lanes. He sounded like he was smiling again. "That's real good."

That evening in the tree house, Reggie, Tara, and Charlie were crowded around the *Hartford Examiner.* POLICE FOLLOWING LEADS IN MCFERLIN MURDER said the headline.

"What leads?" Reggie asked, leaning in for a look, but Charlie was hogging the paper. The dim light coming through the open windows was hardly enough to see by. The blue tarp over their heads flapped and rustled in the wind.

"They don't say," Charlie said. "Only that this is the official statement from the police department."

Tara's cigarettes were out on the floor and Charlie reached for one, his long fingers circling the pack. Reggie hadn't told them about her mom ditching her and George at the bowling alley. She'd only said they'd decided not to go out for dinner, which was great, because that meant they could put a few shingles up before it got too dark. But so far all they'd done was fight over the paper.

Reggie lit the candles and set them up on the floor so they could see better. She looked out the tree house window. The sky was dark and full of clouds, a storm on its way.

Tara pushed Charlie aside and scanned the article on page two: FAMILY AND COLLEAGUES STUNNED BY LOSS. It was written by a reporter named Martha S. Paquette. There was a photo of Andrea McFerlin. She was a chunky woman with frosted hair and lots of makeup. She was wearing a white blouse with a ruffled collar and a mauve blazer. "Christ," Tara said, looking up from the *Examiner*. "She had two kids. Little girls. Three and six."

"What about a husband?" Charlie asked, trying not to choke as he puffed on his cigarette. "It's almost always the husband. Or a boyfriend."

Tara scanned the article, shaking her head. "She's a widow. Her husband died in a car crash two years ago."

"Guess that rules him out," Charlie said. "Maybe she had a boyfriend, though."

"Oh my God," Tara squawked. "Listen to this: 'An unidentified source at the Brighton Falls Police Department has confirmed that Andrea McFerlin's stomach contents showed her last meal, eaten only hours before she died, was lobster with drawn butter. There was also a large amount of morphine in her bloodstream.' "

"Lobster?" Charlie said. "Weird."

Raindrops hit the roof and tarp, slowly at first, then harder.

"Has your dad talked about it at all?" Reggie asked. "I mean it's his case, right?"

Charlie shook his head. "He never talks about work. Not even now, when the story's all over the news like this. Shit, I know more from reading the paper than I do from talking to him."

"I don't get it," Reggie said. "This lady leaves for a business trip, makes it to the airport, but never gets on her plane. Was the killer just there, waiting in the parking lot? And it's an airport parking lot, right? If he grabbed her, how is it that no one saw anything?"

"Maybe it was someone she knew. Maybe she never intended to take that business trip and was planning a romantic weekend getaway with her secret lover," Tara said. Her eyes were wide and her normally pale face was flushed. "I mean, the guy gave her lobster! He took care of her."

"He cut her freaking hand off!" Charlie shot back.

"But he did it carefully," Tara said, closing her eyes. She reached out and circled her own right wrist with her left hand, running her fingers over the knobby bone of her wrist, then up the tendons on the back of her hand. "Lovingly." She popped open her eyes, stood up, and paced in a slow circle; then she stopped right in front of Charlie and Reggie. Her whole body seemed to be vibrating, and she couldn't seem to hold still. Reggie had never seen her this worked up about anything.

"This wasn't some drooling psycho with a chain saw in a dirty garage," Tara said, her voice crackling and dramatic. "This guy must have used a tourniquet, proper surgical tools. He gave her morphine. I'm guessing he knew this lady. He cared about her." Tara gave a rueful smile. "Maybe even loved her in his own sick puppy way."

Her eyes moved to the pile of board games in the corner of the tree house. "I've got an idea," she sang, practically running to the games, pushing aside Clue and Monopoly.

"What are you doing, Tara?" Charlie asked.

She turned back to them, holding the Ouija board. "We've gotta try to talk to her. Maybe she can tell us who the killer is!"

"You're kidding, right?" Charlie said, brown eyes practically popping out of his head.

"Comc on, Reggie," Tara said, taking the board out. "Do it with me."

Reggie and Charlie had tried the Ouija board once when they were ten—Charlie made nervous wisecracks while Reggie asked again and again, "Is anybody there?" and got no answer. Eventually their hands got tired, and their legs full of pins and needles from sitting too long, so they packed the game away.

"Please?" Tara begged. "You need two people to make it work."

Reggie sat across from Tara, legs crossed, her knees touching Tara's, the board held on both their laps. They rested their fingers lightly on the plastic, heart-shaped planchette. Reggie studied the board with the sun in the upper left corner, the moon in the right; the two curved rows of letters; the word *Goodbye* at the bottom.

"We call to the spirit of Andrea McFerlin. Can you hear us?" Tara asked, her voice loud and teacherlike. The candlelight flickered, making Tara's face glow.

"You shouldn't mess with stuff like Ouija boards," Charlie said. "Look what happened to that kid in *The Exorcist.*"

"Shh!" Tara hissed.

"Captain freakin' Howdy, that's all I'm saying."

"Would you please shut up?" Tara said. "You're interfering with our connection to the spirit world."

Charlie made a disgusted chuffing sound and picked up the newspaper, turning to the comics. Reggie looked down at the letters on the board, staring without blinking until everything looked blurry.

"We wish to speak to Andrea McFerlin," Tara repeated, trying to sound proper, speaking in what sounded like her unique attempt at an English accent. Reggie wondered if Tara was playing out a scene from some movie she'd watched.

"It's not like making a long-distance call," Charlie snorted, not looking up from the paper.

Reggie thought about *The Exorcist,* wondered if you could really get possessed by using a Ouija board. What if it really was like opening the door to the spirit world and inviting any old ghost or demon in?

But that kind of stuff was made up. Only in movies. Then again, killers who cut women's hands off, then fed them lobster before strangling them, sounded like something from a Hollywood blockbuster, too.

Suddenly the planchette moved, nearly jumping out from under Reggie's fingers. She made a little yelping sound without meaning to.

She knew Tara must be moving it, but at the same time, she wanted to believe it was real. Reggie's breath came fast and shallow; the candle between them gave them each giant shadows that hung on the walls like ghosts themselves.

"Andrea? Are you here?" Tara asked, nearly breathless.

The plastic marker moved up to the top of the board, the little window hovered over the word *Yes.*

"Tara's totally moving it," Charlie said to Reggie, but he was leaning in to watch over the top of the newspaper, his brown eyes wide.

"Shut up, Chuckles," Tara hissed under her breath. And then, clearly: "Andrea? Do you have a message for us?"

Nothing. Reggie willed it to move again, wanted it so badly she felt herself start to drag the planchette, but then, realizing what she was doing, stopped.

"Can you tell us who the killer is?" Tara asked. She was leaning down over the board, studying the letters. Her face looked orange-red, like a devil. Like Captain Howdy, maybe.

Reggie held her breath, waiting.

Tara's eyes rolled back into her head and she started to tremble, gently at first, like her body was made of leaves and the wind was passing through her.

"Tara?" Reggie whispered. "You okay?"

She responded with a low groaning sound and her chin dropped down to her chest, eyes closed tight. Her shivering became more exaggerated.

Was she having some kind of epileptic fit? Or was all this possession stuff real? She knew it was neither, that Tara was just putting on a show, but still, as she watched Tara twitch, panic rose.

"Charlie?" Reggie said, "Something's wrong with —"

"It's cold here," Tara said, her voice a snake-like hiss.

"Huh?" Charlie said, scrambling backward a little.

"It was cold where he kept me. There was a concrete floor, metal pipes."

"What are you talking about, Tara?" Charlie asked, his voice sounding high and squeaky.

"My name is not Tara," she said. Now that she'd raised her voice, Reggie detected the hint of a new and different accent, but couldn't tell where it was from.

"Who are you?" Reggie asked, her mouth going dry. This wasn't real. This was just Tara playing one of her games, taking things too far. But just like with all of Tara's games, what choice did Reggie have but to play along? And wasn't it kind of thrilling? Pretending that it just might be real. Tricking herself into believing so that her heart hammered while she waited for Tara to answer, even though she knew just what Tara would say.

Outside, the rain pounded on the roof. It was coming in through the windows, some drops making it all the way to Reggie's arm, which turned to gooseflesh.

"Andrea," Tara said, smiling. "My name is Andrea McFerlin."

Reggie felt like she'd been hit in the stomach with a ball of lightning. The electricity moved through her, into arms and out her fingers, making them tingle as it discharged. She jerked her hands away from the Ouija board.

"Oh for God's sake!" Charlie shouted, standing up and throwing the paper down. "That is so totally fucked up on so many levels, Tara. You are *sick*." He slammed open the trapdoor and disappeared down into the rainy night. There was no denying that he was mad, but Reggie knew him well enough to see there was fear there as well. Charlie didn't do well with the unexplained.

Tara remained in her trance state—if it was a trance—her chin resting on her chest. Reggie held her breath, not sure what might happen next. Tara didn't move. Her breathing sounded raspy and strange.

"Do you know who he is?" Reggie asked, at last. "The killer?" More rain was coming in through the tarp, icy and cold. Reggie wrapped her arms around her chest, shivering.

"He's no man and every man," Tara said, her voice little more than a flutter. Reggie listened to Tara breathe in and out. Then she said, "There's something else I know."

Reggie leaned down, put her face right against Tara's. She smelled like ashes and smoke. "What is it?" Reggie asked.

Tara sank lower down on the floor, her body going limp as a rag doll. When she spoke, it was a barely audible sigh:

"He's already picked his next girl."

Chapter 9

October 16, 2010
Brighton Falls, Connecticut

"Cocksucking Walmart," Reggie hissed. She gripped the steering wheel tight, clawing into it with her thumbnails. "Didn't we just pass a Walmart?"

She would never have believed it possible that she'd get lost in her own hometown. Sure, it had been twenty-five years since she'd been back, but it was like the geography itself had changed.

In the beginning, Lorraine had invited Reggie back for Thanksgiving and Christmas (never going so far as to say anything like "It would be so nice to see you" but instead with a comment like, "George and I will have more than enough food—it's a waste to have to throw things away"), but Reggie always made excuses: homework, projects, trips abroad. Eventually Lorraine stopped asking.

Reggie had turned off the GPS shortly after getting her mother into the truck back in Worcester. Vera was very suspicious of the device. "Who's that talking? How does it know where we are? Who, exactly, is monitoring our whereabouts?"

Finally, Reggie pulled the plug, sure she could get back to Monique's Wish from memory. She'd done fine until she hit the Airport Road exit; then it was as if she'd been dropped into a hall of mirrors.

"It's the same Walmart," her mother said in a sage voice.

"It can't be the same," Reggie said. "Because that would mean we've just gone in one big circle." She wanted to cry.

Reggie took a deep breath, reminded herself that just months ago, she'd gone to build houses in Haiti during a cholera outbreak, for God's sake—surely she could handle Brighton Falls, Connecticut.

Vera chuckled, wheezing. She whispered a word Reggie couldn't quite hear. It might have been *cocksucking*.

Neck tense and head beginning to pound, Reggie scanned the four lanes of traffic along what she was sure had once been Main Street. If it hadn't been for the WELCOME TO BRIGHTON FALLS sign they'd passed a mile back, she would have doubted they were even in the right town, never mind on the right street. Thickets of glossy signs sprouted from shopping plaza after shopping plaza: STARBUCKS, KFC, DICK'S SPORTING GOODS, CHILI'S, OLIVE GARDEN, HOME DEPOT.

"I mean really, it doesn't even seem like the same town, does it? I feel like we could be anywhere."

Vera nodded. "Anywhere," she said. "Say, did you remember to pack my clock?"

"Clock? What clock? I didn't see any clock."

"The grandfather clock in the front hall."

Reggie knew just the one she meant; it was at Monique's Wish. "You'll see it soon, Mom."

"Runs slow," Vera said.

"You're right, Mom," Reggie said, remembering how once a day, they'd need to push it forward about fifteen minutes.

"We just have to find West Street, right?" Reggie said, more to herself than her mother. She'd ended up in a left-turn-only lane again somehow, and had to cut in front of a silver minivan to avoid being forced to turn into the parking lot dominated by an enormous liquor store. The driver threw up her hands, blasted the horn. Reggie waved in what she hoped was an apologetic manner.

Then Reggie's eye caught on one of the signs up ahead: BERR FORD. The dealership run by Charlie's uncle Bo. It was still there and had, in fact, grown to nearly three times its original size. There was a letterboard out front that said: *No tricks, just treats. Let us put you in a new truck by Halloween.*

"Look, Mom! Bo Berr's Ford dealership. Do you remember Bo?"

Vera's eyes glazed over. "Little Bo Peep has lost her sheep and doesn't know where to find them."

"Um, you went to high school with him? Bo Berr?"

Vera didn't respond.

Down the street from Berr Ford was First Avenue—the little turnoff that led to the police station. Reggie could see it there, set back from Main Street—an imposing gray granite building that had a new addition tacked onto the left side. The new part of building was covered in windows and had a roofline that was all wrong. Instead of blending with the original roof, it sort of *collided* with it. Reggie's eye went from the offending addition to the original front steps, where the milk cartons had been left. The milk cartons and their gruesome contents.

"Okay, there's West Street," Reggie said, taking the sharp right turn a little too hard and fast. The railroad tracks that had once run alongside West Street had been paved over as a rails-to-trails bike path—the only development Reggie had seen yet that didn't make her want to scream.

There were many more houses than Reggie remembered, and the once open field across from Millers' Farm was now condos, each building holding identical rows of black front doors, vinyl-clad windows, and balconies with Weber grills. Reggie wondered how its occupants found their way into the right home each night.

At last they turned onto Stony Field Drive. The house on the corner had a fake graveyard on the front lawn. A green hand reached up, clawing its way out of its grave.

Reggie's chest felt tight.

"Almost there, Mom," she said, white-knuckling the steering wheel as she eased the Escape down the street, passing the ranch and Colonial houses that were just as she remembered. Neighbors whose lawns she and Charlie had mowed, who'd bought lemonade from her when she'd set up a stand, given her popcorns balls and Hershey bars on Halloween. Plastic bats and bedsheet ghosts hung from the trees, put up by a new generation of parents—perhaps the kids Reggie had gone to school with, now with little goblins of their own.

"Where?" Vera asked.

"Home," Reggie said, the word catching in her throat as she signaled to turn up the gravel driveway, passing the old black metal mailbox. It still leaned to the left, never righted after Reggie sideswiped it when she was first learning to drive.

DUFRANE.

Monique's Wish was smaller than Reggie remembered, more like the woodsman's cottage in a fairy tale than the castle a princess might live in.

When she was growing up, it had felt large and sprawling—too big and dark to ever get warm. The stone walls sucked in light and sound and were always ever so slightly damp.

Glancing through the dusty windshield now, she guessed it to be about thirty-five feet long and maybe twenty wide—a big rectangle of dull gray cement and stone. The corners weren't square or true, making the house list this way, then that. The cement was crumbling in places. Some of the stones had fallen out, leaving gaps like missing teeth. The white paint on the sills and eaves was peeling, hanging off in places like dead skin. The roof was in sad shape, bowing in the middle, the slate shingles cracked and loose.

The house was laid out west to east, all wrong for a hilltop that got such great southern exposure. If Andre had studied the landscape, worked with it a little, faced the building to the south, put in more windows, considered the placement of trees more carefully—it could have been a warmer, brighter place. The density of the stone might even have worked in their favor, acting as thermal storage. As it was, the house was in shade most of the year, and the walls and roof were spotted with moss. The building looked as gray and damp as a poisonous toadstool.

"Do you remember what you used to say?" Reggie asked her mother as she squinted out at the crooked walls. "How Monique's Wish sounded more like the name of a racehorse than a house?"

Vera grinned and bobbed her head, but seemed to be studying something in the sky. Reggie had no idea if she had heard or understood the question.

"Lousy odds," Reggie mumbled, thinking that if the building were a horse, it was old and lame, ready for the glue factory.

Just then the heavy wooden front door slammed open and a cloud of smoke came pouring out. From behind the screen of black smoke came a woman in a faded housedress and fishing vest. Reggie blinked, thinking she was an apparition at first, a body born of smoke and dust and ruin. But then she came into focus. It was Lorraine, walking down the steps, her right hand held up in a strange, forced-looking wave that could have also been a warning to stop, don't come any closer.

Reggie opened the door of the truck as Lorraine came closer. Her body was stiff and gangly, puppetlike as she jerk-walked to them.

"I'm afraid we're on fire," Lorraine said, stinking of fish, eyes streaming, hair wild and singed.

Excerpt from *Neptune's Hands: The True Story of the Unsolved Brighton Falls Slayings* by Martha S. Paquette

The Silver Spoon is a classic American diner about a mile south of the airport. The exterior is gleaming stainless steel, the booths are red and white vinyl. A miniature jukebox adorns each table. The specials are listed on a chalkboard above the counter: *open-faced turkey sandwich, blueberry crumb cake, cream of tomato soup.* Open twenty-four hours, it's a hot spot with local teens—a place to catch up after the double feature at the drive-in or share a banana split with your date. It's also popular with truckers and is usually packed come 2:00 A.M., after the bars close, when folks come in to sober up with coffee and a western omelet.

Forty-two-year-old Candace Jacques had been a waitress at the Silver Spoon for seven years. At 11:15 P.M. on Thursday, June 6, she punched out and her coworkers saw her get into a tan sedan driven by a man no one got a good look at.

Candace was an outgoing woman who'd lived in town all her life. She had a lot of friends who popped in and out of the diner.

"She seemed to know most everyone in town," said the diner's manager, Lou Nordan.

Candace's late-model Skylark had blown its transmission a week earlier and she was saving up for a new car, picking up extra shifts whenever she could. Friends and coworkers gave her rides to and from work.

"She'd had some hard knocks," Lou Nordan said. "But she always got back up and had a real positive attitude about things. People were happy to help her because they knew she'd do the same for them."

Candace's elderly mother, with whom she shared an apartment, was waiting up because Candy always brought her a slice of pie. At 3:00 A.M., when there was still no sign of Candace or the peach pie she had left the diner with, her mother called the police.

"Something's happened to her," the frail-looking woman said when interviewed by the Eyewitness News Team. "This isn't like Candy. I just know something's happened. A mother knows."

Chapter 10

June 7, 1985
Brighton Falls, Connecticut

"My mom totally knows her," Reggie said when she met up with Charlie and Tara at the Silver Spoon that evening. "She brought me here one time and introduced us."

"No way!" Tara said. "What was she like? How's your mom know her?"

Going to the diner had been Tara's idea. As soon as she heard about the missing waitress, she said they had to go—just *had* to.

"Imagine it," Tara said dreamily, "touching saltshakers she's filled, sitting in her section, in the very seat the killer might have sat in when he was stalking her."

"We don't even know he's got her," Charlie said.

"Of course he does," Tara said. "I can feel it."

"How convenient that you all of a sudden have these newfound psychic abilities," Charlie snapped. "I mean, dead people are talking through you, giving you messages . . ."

"There's more to this world than meets the eye, Chuckles."

Charlie teased her, rolled his eyes, and said going to the diner was a little twisted, but he went. It turned out they weren't the only ones with the idea: the place was packed, and they had to wait for a table. And as soon as they walked in, they heard the buzz of customers anxiously talking about the missing waitress and saying maybe she'd been taken by the same man who'd killed Andrea McFerlin. There was this strange electricity in the air. Maybe it was danger, and they all wanted to be close to it.

Reggie explained that she had met Candy Jacques only once, when her mother took her to the Silver Spoon for ice cream when she was seven or eight. The waitress was a woman with fried blond hair and a tired face who wore thick blue eye shadow and had candy cane earrings and a candy cane sticker on her name tag even though it was only October. She was finishing a cheeseburger when they arrived.

"Hey, Vera," she said when they first sat down, side by side at the counter, on spinning stools once again. "Long time no see. How are you, hon?"

"Good," Vera said.

"See much of Rabbit lately?" Candy asked.

"Now and then," Vera said, looking away.

"You tell him I said hello, huh?" Candy said. Then, her eyes moved to Reggie. "Who's the little lady?"

"My daughter," Vera said. "Regina."

"No kidding?" Candy dabbed at her lips with a paper napkin.

She looked at Reggie and said, "Yeah, I can see the resemblance. Around the eyes. You've got your mamma's beautiful eyes. And just look at those lashes! You're gonna be a heartbreaker, little Regina, just like your mama." She reached out and brushed the unkempt hair away from Reggie's face.

"How about a little sugar for Candy?"

Reggie looked up at her mother, who said, "Go ahead, Regina, give her a little peck on the cheek."

Reggie stood up and the waitress leaned down, offering her cheek. Reggie gave her the tiniest kiss, her lips barely touching the waitress's warm, sticky skin. She could smell cooked meat and onions on Candy's breath.

"Just like a butterfly," Candy said. "Hardly a kiss at all. I hope you do a little better than that when you get around to kissing the boys." She chuckled.

Reggie spun on her stool and buried her face in her mother's coat, smelled the cold air, perfume, and Winstons. Vera laughed, too.

"I bet I know what you'd like, little lady," the candy cane waitress said. "How about one of my magical mystery sundaes? I only make them for my most special customers."

Reggie pulled her face from her mother's coat and nodded, and when the waitress returned, she carried a sundae with three different ice creams and every topping imaginable.

"This is a real treat I'm giving you," she promised. "It's not even on the menu."

Later, when they were on their way home, Reggie asked her mom how she knew Candy. "Is she an actress, too?"

"Once," Vera said, lighting a cigarette, then fiddling with the radio, searching for a song she liked. "She was once."

"Just think of it," Tara said now, sipping a cup of black coffee once they were seated in a booth. Reggie and Charlie had milk shakes and were sitting across from Tara. Reggie had moved her knee so that it was touching Charlie's. They were all splitting an order of fries and onion rings. "We might have our very own serial killer. Hell, he could be here, in this restaurant, right this minute."

"If he was here, wouldn't you be able to tell?" Charlie asked. "Aren't you supposed to be psychic now? Wouldn't you go all rigid and start speaking in tongues if he was nearby?"

Reggie knew his teasing was just his own stupid way of trying to flirt with Tara. But she also knew it wasn't working—it was just pissing Tara off.

"It doesn't work like that," Tara hissed. She shot Reggie a look like *Can you believe how ignorant some people are?* Reggie smiled back and shook her head empathetically.

Reggie scanned the crowd: truckers, tables of high school students in letter jackets, families with kids who were kicking each other under the table and fighting over packets of sugar.

Charlie frowned and stirred his milk shake. "For all we know, this waitress has just shacked up with her boyfriend."

"But she hasn't called her mother. And on the news, they said she was scheduled to work today. If she wasn't missing, she'd probably be waiting on us *right now,*" Tara said.

Reggie, making up her mind to ignore the bickering, had pulled a pen from her pocket and was doodling on the backside of her menu. She drew the ketchup bottle, capturing the faint and distorted reflection of Tara on its left side.

Charlie shook his head. "But if she wasn't gone, we wouldn't even be here, Sherlock."

Tara turned away in disgust, not bothering to reply.

As she drew, Reggie thought of how, just an hour ago, riding her bike to the diner, she'd seen pictures of Candy plastered all over town, like the lost kids on the back of milk cartons: HAVE YOU SEEN ME?

The photo showed her heavy eye shadow and candy cane earrings, though they looked more like fishhooks in the blurred image. She smiled out from telephone poles and bulletin boards in her greasy Silver Spoon uniform, and Reggie could still smell the charred meat and onions on her breath.

A little sugar for Candy.

She thought of her mom's theory, about how everyone was connected by these invisible threads, making this big web. Reggie had a string that went right to Candy. She'd met her once, kissed her cheek. Somehow this made her feel all the more frightened and jittery at Candace's disappearance.

Tara looked down at Reggie's drawing, seeing herself in the ketchup bottle. "That's totally awesome, Reggie," she squealed. "No one's ever drawn my picture before. Can I have it?"

Reggie shrugged, looked down at the drawing, and realized she'd given Tara's reflection the candy cane earrings.

"It's not really that good," Reggie said, but Tara folded up the place mat and put it in her bag.

"Please, Reggie," Tara said, rolling her eyes. "You've got more talent in your left pinkie toe than most people have in their whole bodies."

"Hey, cuz!" came a shout from across the restaurant. Charlie's cousin Sid was meandering up to their table. His curly hair had a shaggy, just-out-of-bed look. He wore low-slung Levi's, a tie-dyed T-shirt, and black Converse high-tops. He had two blond girls with him, wearing hippie clothes and reeking of patchouli. One was quite overweight, her belly spilling over the top of her Indian-print wraparound skirt. The other had horrible acne. "How goes it?" Sid asked. His pale blue eyes were bloodshot and glassy, and he had a lopsided smile.

"Good," Charlie said, running a hand over his own close-cropped hair. "How 'bout with you?"

"Can't complain," Sid said, still grinning stupidly.

"Can I ask you something?" Tara said, looking at Sid.

"Shoot."

"I hear you're the go-to guy if someone happened to be interested in a certain something."

One of the girls giggled. She wore a string of red glass beads and little round glasses with pink lenses. Her hair was long and crazy as a nest of snakes. There was a purple feather roach clip dangling from the left side.

"I could be your man. We should talk. My cuz here knows how to reach me. Y'all enjoy your snack." He loped off, the twin hippies like bookends beside him.

Charlie glared at Tara and shook his head.

"What?" Tara asked. "I thought a little weed might be fun sometime. Don't you think?"

"Yeah, right," Charlie said. "Just imagine what would happen if my dad got one whiff or found one seed on me—I feel like I'm half a step away from reform school as it is, I don't need to give him an actual, legitimate reason. "

"Too bad," Tara said, keeping her eyes on Sid as he stood in line at the register.

"Sid's a total waste-oid," Charlie said, noticing that Tara was still staring at his cousin. "No brain cells left. My dad told me that Uncle Bo's real pissed because Sid didn't get into a single college he applied to. He's gotta go to community college in the fall and take remedial English and shit."

Tara watched Sid and the girls leave, then turned back to Reggie.

"Your mom must be tripping, Reg," Tara said, stirring Sweet'N Low into her coffee. She stirred too fast and hard, making the spoon chink against the white ceramic mug and spilling coffee over the edge. "Are she and Candy still friends? How do they even know each other? When's the last time she saw her?" Sometimes Tara's sentences reminded Reggie of a bumper car ride—one slamming into the next, pushing it out of the way until the next one came along, faster and more furious.

Reggie shrugged. "I'm not sure. And my mom hasn't been around the last few days, so I haven't been able to ask her."

"Where is she?" Tara asked.

"Don't know," Reggie admitted, then, reluctantly, told Charlie and Tara the story of what had happened at the bowling alley—how Vera had taken off with the man in the white shirt and hadn't come home since. "She's been doing this play down in New Haven. She's probably down there, staying with friends."

"So wait . . . ," Tara said, setting down her coffee so hard it sloshed over the side. "This guy in the white shirt your mom took off with, he drove a tan car?" Her voice turned high and squeaky like a dog toy.

"Yeah," Reggie said. "So?"

"Hello! Tan car, Reg. Like the guy that picked up Candace Jacques! The guy who might have killed

Andrea McFerlin! What if your mom was picked up by a serial killer?"

"Jeez-us!" Charlie yelped, slamming the bottle of ketchup down. "I don't get it, Tara. How is it that your mind goes to the most messed-up places so quickly?"

"I'm just connecting the dots. It's not my fault that you don't like the picture that shows up."

"But they don't connect!" Charlie snapped, rubbing his temples as if he was getting a headache. "You're assuming all kinds of shit, jumping to conclusions based on nothing! I hope you're not paying any attention to this, Reg."

Reggie shook her head, to say, of course not. She picked at the fries that Charlie had dumped too much ketchup on, suddenly not feeling very hungry at all. She wiped her hands on a paper napkin, leaving red smeary fingerprints.

"Reggie?" George said when he opened the door. He squinted at her through his glasses like he was trying to decide if it was really her. At last he smiled warmly. "What a nice surprise. You rode your bike all this way?" He looked past Reggie at her Peugeot, resting on the grass. "Do you have a headlight or something?"

"Reflectors," Reggie said.

"Well, if you're going to be riding around in the dark, we'll have to get you some decent lights for the bike. Come on in."

Reggie followed George through the doorway of his little ranch house and into the kitchen. It was small and dark with fake wood paneling. The countertops were white Formica, scrubbed until they gleamed. George had a small table with four chairs with a fake Tiffany lamp hanging above it. The shelf behind them was lined with wooden duck decoys and bowling trophies.

Reggie liked the way the rows of ducks watched her, as they did each time she came to George for advice or help with homework. Her mother wasn't exactly the help-with-homework type, and whenever she asked Lorraine, her aunt told her to go to the library and look things up herself. So she came to George's kitchen table whenever she had a particularly tricky assignment or a test she was sure she'd fail. He had a way of breaking things down into tiny pieces that made even the hardest tasks seem manageable.

"Want a Coke?"

Reggie nodded.

"I was just finishing up a project downstairs," he said, handing her a can of soda from the fridge. "Want to see?" His eyes were all lit up, the way they got when he was hard at work on one of his decoys.

"Sure." She followed George down the painted steps into the basement. Fluorescent light fixtures hung from chains on the ceiling, illuminating George's workshop. He had a table saw, a jigsaw, a drill press, and a huge workbench with various clamps and vises attached to it. The Peg-Board wall behind the workbench was neatly hung with tools, each tool's place carefully outlined with yellow paint.

Reggie loved George's workshop. She loved the neatness, the rows of tools, the idea that you could just follow a pattern and plans and end up with a duck or a dresser. "There's a right tool for every job," George would say when he asked her to hand him things: a $^{3}/_{16}$-inch wrench, a no. 2 Phillips head screwdriver, a $^{1}/_{32}$-inch nail set.

"This is the latest," George said, holding up a nearly finished duck carving. His gouges and chisels were lined up beside it. "A female mallard. Everyone always does the males because they're so flashy with their green heads, but I thought a female might be nice. She can keep the males I've got upstairs company." He gave Reggie a wink.

"It's great," Reggie said, meaning it. She thought it was amazing that George could take a simple block of wood and find a duck inside it.

"What's this?" Reggie said, looking at a set of plans on the bench.

"A surprise for Lorraine. I thought I'd make her a cabinet to hold all her fishing rods. Don't say anything, huh?"

"Or course not," Reggie said, her eyes still on the plans, trying to understand what part she was looking at.

"Your mother know where you are?" George asked.

Reggie shook her head.

"Maybe we ought to call her."

"She's not home. That's kind of why I'm here."

George set the duck back down on the workbench and gave Reggie a questioning look.

"She hasn't been back since she took off with that guy at the bowling alley."

George ran his hand through his hair. "That's not exactly unusual, is it? I mean, you know your mother and men—"

"No," Reggie admitted, cutting him off. "It's not unusual. But something's been bugging me. The guy in the white shirt, the one she left with, he drove a tan car. I saw them pulling out of the parking lot in it."

"And?"

"And that waitress that disappeared, Candace Jacques, she was picked up by a guy in a tan car, too."

George smiled gently. "So you rode out here on your bike at ten o'clock at night to say you think your mother may have been kidnapped?"

"Kind of." She looked down at her can of soda in her hand. This was exactly the kind of situation she depended on George for. The kind where she needed a normal grown-up to do and say the normal grown-up thing.

"Reg," George said, lowering himself so that she made eye contact with him. "Now, it's true that I didn't see your mother leave with the man from the bowling alley, but I'm more than sure that she went willingly. He probably reminded her of some movie star or something. Trust me, your mother's fine. She can take care of herself. She'll come back home when she's ready. You know how she is."

Reggie twirled the Coke can in her hand.

"Right?" George said.

"Right," Reggie agreed, feeling better.

"Hey, how about you help me get started on that fishing cabinet? I can call Lorraine so she doesn't worry, tell her we're working on something, and that I'll bring you home in an hour or so. How does that sound?"

Reggie nodded enthusiastically and George reached for the plans.

"We can rough-cut the lumber tonight. I got some nice oak. See, look at this," he said, pointing at one of the drawings. "Dovetail joinery. Beautiful, isn't it? It'll be a little tricky to get all the cuts right, but it'll be worth it, don't you think?"

Reggie nodded, feeling her body relax—all the craziness of the tan car, missing waitress, and hand in a milk carton faded away as she studied the neat drawing showing a close-up of the little trapezoidal shapes that would fit like puzzle pieces, binding the walls of the cabinet together tightly, perfectly almost, no need for nails or screws.

Chapter 11

October 16, 2010
Brighton Falls, Connecticut

The smoke billowed out of the open door behind Lorraine.

"Call the fire department," Reggie instructed, holding her cell phone out to her aunt. Lorraine looked at the phone like it was a laser gun. Her face was carved by wrinkles and her hair was completely white—except in the places where it was singed at the ends. She had a slight stoop, shoulders hunched and neck stretched out, reminding Reggie of an elderly turtle.

The last time Reggie had seen Lorraine was when Lorraine and George had come to Reggie's graduation from RISD. Since then, Lorraine had called every week but never pushed Reggie to come home for a visit. Reggie was always careful to talk about how busy she was, plans she had to travel out of the country. She never dreamed of inviting her aunt up to visit her, and Lorraine never hinted that she wanted an invitation. Reggie knew from her weekly calls that Lorraine had retired from the elementary school a few years ago, and now spent a lot of her free time volunteering at the Brighton Falls Historical Society.

"Just dial 9-1-1 and push the CALL button," Reggie said, placing the phone carefully in her aunt's bony hands. Lorraine began tentatively pressing buttons. Reggie ran around to the back of the truck and grabbed the fire extinguisher clamped in beside her toolbox.

Wielding the heavy red extinguisher, she stopped at the passenger window. "Stay in the car, Mom. Don't get out. Do not come inside. Okay?"

Vera gave her a nervous smile. "Did he beat us here?" she asked.

"Who?" Reggie asked.

"Old Scratch."

Reggie stiffened, eyes focused on the doorway where the smoke reached out, beckoning her, daring her to come inside. "I don't think so, Mom. But I'm gonna go check it out."

Lorraine was giving the address to the 911 dispatcher. She held the phone in front of her face and away from her mouth like she was using a walkie-talkie.

Reggie took a deep breath of clean air and headed up the stone steps, looked through the open door and into the smoke. She couldn't see flames or even tell where the fire was.

You have one minute to grab what you can. What do you chose?

Had her early morning dream been trying to warn her, to prepare her for this very moment?

And if she got inside and discovered the house was burning and that there was no way to stop it, what would she choose to save? She wasn't at all sure there was anything of hers left inside.

One way to find out.

She reached up and touched the hourglass necklace hidden under her shirt for luck, then pulled the pin on the extinguisher. She put the nozzle in her left hand and held the lever with her right, then stepped through the door. Behind her, sirens had started in the distance.

Hurry, she heard Tara say in her ear. *You're running out of time.*

Even through the thick haze of smoke, Reggie could see the entryway and hall were exactly the same as they had been the day she'd left for college. There was a worn Oriental rug, coat hooks, a simple Shaker-style bench with a mirror above, and the grandfather clock, which seemed to have stopped altogether. To her left, against the wall, was the stairway leading up to the bedrooms. Straight ahead was the hallway that led to the living room, dining room, and kitchen. The source of the smoke was somewhere back there.

She blinked and coughed as she moved forward, but the smoke played tricks on her. She walked into a wall, sure the hall was right in front of her. She turned and looked at her image in the mirror above the bench—it wavered, seeming to grow large, then small; then she disappeared altogether. It was as if she'd stepped into a nightmare fun house.

Maybe, she thought, for half an irrational second, it was just Monique's Wish getting back at her, punishing her for abandoning it so easily. If buildings held memories, had souls, didn't it stand to reason that they could get angry, too?

She felt her way along the wall in front of her until she got to the hallway and caught a hint of movement up ahead.

Was there someone in the house with her? A wispy body moving through the smoke, beckoning, *This way.*

"Hello?" she called out, feeling silly when she heard her own voice. Of course there was no one there.

She heard her mother's voice in her head: *Did he beat us here? Old Scratch.*

Holding the fire extinguisher in front of her, Reggie headed down the hallway. The smoke stung her eyes and burned her throat, but she continued on, promising herself she'd turn back if things got too bad.

She turned left into the kitchen, where the teasing lick of flames caught her eye.

Compared to the smoke, the actual fire wasn't all that impressive. A pan on the back burner of the stove was lit up, the flames shooting up the wall. Reggie aimed the fire extinguisher and squeezed the lever, sweeping over the flames. The fire sputtered and sighed; in less than a minute the flames were gone.

The big cast-iron pan was full of white foam and oil. Reggie could just make out three blackened trout peeking through the mess. Their heads and tails were still attached, the way Lorraine always liked to cook them, no part wasted. Reggie pulled the chain to start the vent fan on the wall near the stove and threw open the window above the sink. The sirens were louder now—a ladder truck and police car were coming up the driveway.

She stumbled through the kitchen, bumping against the old round table and chairs, and into the dining room to open those windows. They were the original wooden sash windows her grandfather had installed, and they had always stuck terribly. She had to pound one with her fist to get it to budge at all. The glazing didn't hold—an entire pane of glass fell out, breaking against her arm, giving her a good gash just above her wrist, before shattering on the pine-board floor.

"Shit," she hissed, inspecting the damage.

"Hello?" a voice called from the open front door.

Reggie got to the front hall just as a group of firemen were coming in.

"Fire's out," she said.

"Mind if we take a look?" said a young man who looked like a little kid playing dress-up in his oversize coat, hat, and boots.

Reggie led them into the kitchen, where they inspected the charred remains of fish and the blackened wall. Satisfied, the little parade made their way back out of the house where an older fireman was talking with the police officer in the yard.

"Fire's out, Chief," reported one of the men. "Flare-up from a pan of oil on the stove. The lady got it with an extinguisher."

"Oil gets hot like that, it's gonna ignite," the chief said to Reggie sagely. She nodded and caught him looking at her arm. Blood had seeped through her shirtsleeve.

"I'm fine," she told him before he could say anything. "Just a little scratch. We'll be more careful while we're cooking. Thanks for coming out."

"Was it Old Scratch?" Vera had let herself out of the truck and now stood just behind Reggie. The fire chief glanced over at her, and then his gaze seemed to catch on her, going from her face to the spot where her hand should have been, and back again.

"Dear God," he said, "Vera Dufrane?"

Reggie's skin prickled. She looked at the circle of volunteer firefighters—seven men altogether, along with a cop.

"No," Reggie said, stepping in front of her mother. "I'm afraid you're mistaken."

Vera immediately maneuvered out from behind Reggie.

"Did you know," asked Vera dramatically "that I was the Aphrodite Cold Cream girl?" The men all stared. Vera smiled flirtatiously at them, showing brown teeth.

"Yes, I know," the chief said. He took off his hat. "It's Paul, Vera. Paul LaRouche. We went to school together?" Vera continued to look at him blankly, smile glued on. "My God," Chief LaRouche said. "I'm seeing it with my own eyes, but I can't believe it."

"Wait a minute," said the young police officer, stepping forward to give Vera a closer look. "Vera Dufrane? Neptune's last victim?"

Reggie got between her mother and the group again. “The police have already interviewed my mother. Now please, I need to get her inside. She’s not well.”

She guided her mother gently toward the house, but Vera resisted. She kept turning, pulling back toward the circle of men. They were talking quietly, excitedly among themselves. Reggie only caught bits and pieces: *hand; the only body never found; where in God’s name’s she been all this time?*

“It happened so fast,” Lorraine was saying at the edge of the circle, wringing her hands, talking to everyone and no one. “I fry fish all the time. I’ve never had a problem. But today . . . today everything went to hell.”

“Come on, Mom,” Reggie cooed softly in her mother’s ear. “Let’s go in and see the clock.”

“Ticky tocky, ticky tocky,” her mother said.

The young cop was on his radio now. One of the volunteer firefighters got out a cell phone and made a call. Shit. So much for slipping back into town without being noticed.

Reggie led her mother into the smoke-scented hallway.

“Welcome home,” Reggie said, inhaling the acrid, smoke-tinged air. It smelled like ruin.

Chapter 12

June 8 and June 12, 1985
Brighton Falls, Connecticut

Two days after the waitress's disappearance, on the first official day of summer vacation, a package arrived on the granite steps of the police station. The officer who was assigned to keep an eye out for any suspicious activity near the front steps had somehow missed the drop-off. There were a lot of people coming and going—press, citizens coming in to argue about parking tickets, and it was the start of the day shift, so even the cops were flowing in and out of the building. The officer went to hold the door for an elderly gentleman, and then stepped inside to direct him to the window where he could report a lost cat.

When the officer returned to his post, he noticed the package.

Like the first, this one was a red and white milk carton stapled closed at the top, wrapped in brown butcher's paper, tied neatly with thin string.

Inside was Candace Jacques's right hand.

It was identified by the bubblegum-pink nail polish and the little gold and amethyst pinkie ring she'd been wearing.

Candy's mother appeared on Eyewitness News at noon sobbing, begging for the killer to let Candace go. "She's all I've got," the old woman said into the camera. "Please, please, have mercy."

"Kind of pathetic," Tara said, rolling her eyes. She was sitting with Charlie and Reggie in Reggie's living room. Lorraine had gone out back to the brook dressed in her huge rubber waders, carrying a fly rod and net. Tara had taken a bottle of blue polish out of her ratty drawstring purse and was painting her short, ragged nails.

"It's her daughter," Charlie snapped. He was fingering a plastic tortoiseshell guitar pick he'd pulled from his pocket. "What's she supposed to do?" He was wearing his most beat-up jeans with a hole in the knee. Reggie could see the tiny hairs on his leg poking through and wondered what it would feel like to touch them.

"I just don't think they should have let her go on like that. It makes things seem . . . I don't know, more out of control than they should. Like everyone knows the cops haven't got a clue, so they're hoping to appeal to whatever sad little scrap of humanity is left in this guy or something by having her beg for her daughter's life. It just seems so . . . desperate." Tara began flapping her left hand in the air, trying to dry her nails. She turned to Charlie. "And *anyways,* the dude's obviously a psycho. Like he's going to be turned from his evil ways by a crying old lady."

"What do you mean, everybody knows the cops haven't got a clue?" Charlie asked. "My dad's practically living at the station! They're gonna solve this. I know they will."

Tara snorted. "The killer is taunting them. Leaving the hands on the steps of the police station like that . . . he's pissing on their territory. No way the cops are going to solve this. They don't even know where to get started."

"Oh, and you do?" Charlie said, stuffing the pick back in the pocket of his jeans. "Why don't you get your bad-ass psychic Nancy Drew self out there and catch the killer then, Tara?"

Tara scowled at him. "You're just all pissed off at me because I said no to going to the stupid junior high dance with you tonight. I won't hold your hand in the dark or pin an ugly-ass flower to my dress or dance to some cheesy Journey song with my head on your shoulder, so now you're gonna be a total asshole? Way to win a girl's heart, Romeo."

Reggie sank back into the couch. She suddenly felt breathless.

Charlie's face turned red, and he opened his mouth to say something, but then thought better of it and snapped it closed. He stomped out of the living room, slamming the front door.

Reggie wasn't surprised that Charlie had asked Tara to the dance, and she was glad that Tara had refused. But still, she couldn't help feeling this sort of sickly green resentment for Tara bubble up from the pit of her stomach.

"Jerkwad," Tara mumbled, staring at the door Charlie had just slammed. She finished her nails, screwed the top on the bottle of polish, and dropped it into her purse. Then she blew on her fingertips, inspected her handiwork, and turned to Reggie and asked, "Any word from your mom yet?"

Reggie shook her head.

"I don't like it. Your mom disappearing right now like this. Maybe we should go, like, look for her or something."

"She's down in New Haven," Reggie said. "She's probably hanging out with her theater friends."

"Probably," Tara said, fiddling with her hourglass necklace.

"Is it true?" Reggie asked. "Did Charlie really ask you to the dance?" She knew she should let it go, that hearing more about it would just add to the torture, but since she couldn't stop herself from thinking about it, she figured asking wouldn't make it much worse.

Tara gave a quick nod. "Can you believe it?" she asked.

Yes, Reggie thought. *Yes, I can.* The dance was that night, and practically the whole school was going. They'd had their stupid graduation ceremony in the auditorium the day before, all of them lined up while parents clapped and fanned themselves with programs because there was no air-conditioning and it was airless and hot as hell. Reggie's mom hadn't shown, but Lorraine and George had been there, sitting in the front row, fidgeting like their clothes didn't fit them right. George had brought Reggie a bouquet of really ugly carnations that had been dyed orange. Tara's mom hadn't shown up either. Charlie's dad came at the last minute, once the ceremony was over, and gave Charlie a congratulatory thump on the back that nearly knocked Charlie off his feet.

"Are you gonna go?" Reggie asked. "Not with him, I mean, but at all?"

Tara shook her head. "No way. It's for losers."

"Yeah," Reggie agreed. "I'm not going either."

So that was it. She would never set foot in Brighton Falls Junior High again. Somehow she'd expected a more dramatic ending to that part of her life. She'd expected to feel different in some way, like the eighth-grade diploma that sat rolled on top of her desk actually symbolized something.

Stupid.

"Hey, can I tell you something?" Tara asked.

Reggie nodded.

Tara's eyes looked big and owlish. "I went to her house."

"Whose house?" Reggie asked.

"Andrea McFerlin's," she whispered excitedly. "His first victim."

"Wait, what?" Reggie stammered. "Why would you go to her house?"

Tara's eyes glistened. She licked her lips. "I don't know, Reg. After that day with the Ouija board, in the tree house? I just couldn't stop thinking about her, you know? So I looked her up in the phone book. She lived over on Kemp, way out at the end. A little yellow house with a kiddie pool in the yard. I rode my bike.

I knocked on the door, but no one answered. So I went around back. And I peeked in the windows."

"Jesus, Tara! If anyone had seen you, they would have called the cops."

She shook her head dismissively. "But they didn't. Anyway, I looked in, and you know what I saw? This big old dollhouse. One of those Barbie Dream Townhouse things with the elevator and shit? Right in the middle of the living room. And I was thinking about those poor little kids losing their mama, and how cool the Dream Townhouse was, but how it didn't really matter anymore because they'd lost the most important thing and their little lives were pretty much changed forever. Then the next thing I knew—" She stopped, looked at Reggie, said, "You gotta swear not to tell anyone this. Not even Charlie."

Reggie nodded.

"The next thing I knew, I was in Andrea's house. The freaking back door was unlocked. So I walked right in." Tara eyed Reggie cautiously, like she was wondering if she should be telling her all this.

"You broke in?" Reggie gasped.

"I *said,* the door was open," she snapped. Then she seemed to relax, brushing a strand of hair out of her eyes. "And it didn't feel like trespassing," she said almost dreamily. "It felt like . . . like the place was familiar. It was like I wasn't me. Like I was her and I was coming home." She gave a shy smile.

"Tara," Reggie said, "I don't think —"

"Just let me finish, Reg," Tara said, holding up her hand with its freshly painted nails. "I got inside and I sat down at the dollhouse. All the furniture was in the wrong place—there was a bed in the kitchen and the bathtub was up on the roof. It was like Cyclone Barbie had hit—clothes everywhere, naked dolls on the floor." She reached into the pocket of her torn jeans and pulled something out, holding it clasped tightly in her fist.

"I found this there," she said. Then, like a magician producing a rabbit from the air, she opened her hand in a dramatic, tah-dah way. And there in her palm was a tiny pink doll's shoe with a high heel.

"You took that? A Barbie shoe?" Reggie said, squinting in disbelief at the shoe. "Why?"

Tara shrugged, clearly disappointed by Reggie's reaction, and tucked the tiny shoe back into her pocket. "I just wanted something from her. From Andrea. A little piece of them. Something solid and real. Something they'd never miss. Do you understand?"

Reggie just stared. She did not understand.

"Swear you won't tell anyone, Reg. Please."

Charlie spent the next few days avoiding Tara and keeping himself busy with his lawn-mowing business. Reggie hated not seeing him, so she offered to help him do lawns. Charlie put her in charge of the Weed-wacker and gave her a third of whatever he earned. On Wednesday morning, when they were in front of Charlie's house, gassing up for the first lawn of the day, Reggie finally brought up Tara.

"You really like her, huh?"

Charlie didn't respond. He poured gas into the Lawn-Boy, then screwed the cap on.

"I just miss us all hanging out together," Reggie said. "Summer vacation is gonna suck if you two don't start talking again." She didn't say what she really wanted to—that she was actually kind of worried about Tara. The thing with the Barbie shoe seemed . . . well, it seemed more than a little eccentric; it seemed possibly certifiably crazy.

"You don't get it," Charlie said.

"What? What don't I get?"

"How impossible it is for me to be around her."

Reggie bit her lip. "I do get it," she said.

Charlie shook his head dismissively, like she was a kid who didn't understand anything. He stood up and started pushing the mower down the street. Their first lawn was the widow Mrs. Larraby, who lived five houses down from Charlie. Reggie finished putting gas in the string trimmer and joined him. They worked together, both engines screaming, the smell of cut grass and gasoline following them. Reggie did around the house and along the rock wall at the back edge of Mrs. Larraby's yard. Charlie walked back and forth in neat rows.

When Reggie was done, she sat and watched him finish up. The morning was hot and Charlie's back was soaked with sweat. She could see it running down the back of his neck, which was already tan. She imagined herself touching him there, how warm and moist it would be, how if her fingers circled around, they'd be at the front of his neck, touching his Adam's apple, moving down to the hollow beneath it. She longed to put her fingers there, in this soft indentation above his collarbone.

Mrs. Larraby came outside with two glasses of cold lemonade and Charlie stopped the mower.

"Have you heard?" she asked as she handed Reggie a heavy glass wet with condensation. "That waitress from the Silver Spoon was found this morning. Strangled, poor thing, just like that other girl. She was on the front lawn of the town library, naked except for the bandages. Her body was laid out right next to the statue there." Mrs. Larraby shuddered.

Reggie could picture it clearly—the granite statue of a stack of books, the word *Knowledge* engraved beneath. And there, in its early morning shadow, was Candy's body.

How about a little sugar for Candy?

When Reggie got home to Monique's Wish, she headed down the hallway to the kitchen. Lorraine was talking in the living room, and she sounded pissed off. Was she on the phone? And then, Reggie heard her mother's voice. The relief flooded through her, a physical sensation. She stayed in the kitchen, out of sight, and listened.

"I won't have it," Lorraine hissed. "Not in this house. If Father were here—"

"Don't you dare start in about what Daddy would say," Vera warned. "And if you want to go down that road, may I remind you that you of all people are in no position to judge me."

"I don't know what—"

"Oh you know exactly what I mean. Call me whatever names you want. You're no saint, Lorraine. Don't think I don't know what goes on in that garage of yours."

Then Reggie heard the unmistakable sound of a hand slapping a face and little grunting noise.

Footsteps came toward her. Reggie looked around the kitchen frantically—could she hide somewhere? But then Lorraine was in the kitchen.

"Regina," she said, voice shaking. Lorraine's face was pale. She had on the old fishing vest and hat. Reggie froze, waiting to see what might happen next. Lorraine looked at Reggie a moment, then continued through the kitchen, down the hall, and out the front door. Reggie looked out the window and watched Lorraine cross the driveway and enter the garage.

What did Lorraine do in the garage other than tie flies for trout fishing?

Reggie went into the living room and found her mother sitting on the couch, hand on her cheek. She was wearing a shiny blue dress Reggie had never seen before.

"Hey," Reggie said. "You okay?"

"Fine," Vera told her. "Just fine." She pulled her hand away from her cheek and Reggie saw that it was bright red.

Reggie looked away, down at her sneakers covered in grass clippings, and fiddled self-consciously with the new ear.

Reggie had always been a quiet kid, even with her own family, and part of the reason for this was that she never knew the right thing to say. Words didn't come easily to her, they were stumbling blocks rather than lines of connection. And only later, after the fact, when she was replaying conversations in her head late at night, did the right words come—a cruel joke, too little, too late.

Now, as she watched her mother move her ruined hand up to her reddened cheek again, Reggie had to say something that would break the spell. But even as she opened her mouth and felt the words tumbling out, she realized once again she was saying the wrong thing.

"Candace Jacques is dead," Reggie told her.

"What?" her mother asked, moving her scarred hand away from her face, putting it carefully in her lap, under her left hand.

"They found her body in front of the library this morning. Strangled. Just like Andrea McFerlin."

As soon as she saw her mother's face, it hit harder than ever: this was real life, and Candace Jacques had been a real person—a woman who ate burgers with onions and took the time to wrap up a slice of pie for her mother at the end of a long shift. She wasn't just a news story but an actual, physical person. Reggie suddenly understood why Tara had ridden out to Andrea McFerlin's house; why she carried that little pink

Barbie shoe everywhere. It was proof. Proof that this woman existed beyond the full-color photo on the front page of the *Hartford Examiner.*

"My *God,*" was all Vera said, the tears starting. Then she turned and left the room, climbing the dark wooden steps of their failed castle.

Chapter 13

October 16, 2010
Brighton Falls, Connecticut

"I don't really care for pizza," Lorraine said for the third time as she frowned at what remained of the slice on her plate.

"Well, we had to eat, didn't we?" Reggie snapped, honestly a little relieved that Lorraine had set fire to the fish that would have peered up from their plates with gruesome little eyeballs. "And Mom seems to be enjoying it."

Vera was sitting up in bed, having her second slice. The medical supply store had delivered an electric hospital bed, a walker, and a bedside commode and set everything up in Vera's old bedroom. Reggie and

Lorraine had dragged two dining room chairs up and were eating greasy Domino's Pizza off of good china plates balanced on their laps. It was only seven o'clock and Reggie was exhausted. The pizza was the first solid food she'd put into her stomach all day, and she was starting to wonder if it had been the greatest choice.

Reggie had offered to cook, only to discover the fridge was empty except for skim milk, margarine, some limp carrots, and a freezer full of Stouffer's macaroni and cheese. "I'll go shopping first thing tomorrow," Reggie had said.

The live-in nurse Lorraine had hired was due to arrive any minute.

Reggie had been very skeptical of her aunt's ability to hire someone qualified. "Did you find her through a service?"

Lorraine smiled tightly. "She's someone I know."

"But she's experienced, right?" Reggie pushed. "You asked for her résumé and references?"

"She's a registered nurse with hospice experience. More importantly than that, she's someone we can trust."

Reggie imagined one of the dowdy old women Lorraine knew through her work at the Historical Society, probably hadn't worked for fifteen years. It couldn't hurt to explore other options.

But she had spent nearly an hour on the phone with Medicaid, the county home health and hospice service, and a private duty nursing agency. In the end, she hadn't been able to find anyone who could start right away. There was all kinds of bullshit about Vera not being a Connecticut resident, and Reggie had to agree to give her aunt's candidate a try. She'd meet her, ask for references, and make different arrangements as soon as possible if necessary.

The doorbell rang and Lorraine shot up excitedly. "She's here. I'll show her in."

Reggie stayed in the bedroom, pulling her phone out to check for messages. There was one from Len. Reggie smiled, listening: "Hey. Just checking in to see how Worcester's going. I miss you. Call me when you get back to town."

The truth was, she missed him, too. She wished she could call him, tell him everything that had happened to her today. Soon, she promised herself. When she had a better handle on things. Once things with the nurse were squared away, maybe Reggie would drive back home for a couple of days to catch up on some work and see Len.

Reggie stuck the phone back in her bag and grabbed another slice.

"Good pizza, huh, Mom?"

Vera said nothing but took another bite.

"Who am I kidding? It's crap. But anything's better than hospital food. And whatever they fed you in the shelter. Did you have meals there at the shelter? Or did you have to go someplace else? A soup kitchen or something?"

Her mother smiled. "Sister Dolores made sure I got enough to eat. Ham on Tuesdays. Fish on Fridays. Learn and clean and serve."

Reggie set down her plate. "Sister Dolores, huh? Did she work at the shelter?"

What the hell was *Learn and clean and serve*? It occurred to Reggie that she should have asked the broccoli-in-her-teeth social worker for a few more details about where her mother had come from. Reggie had Carolyn Wheeler's card in her bag—she'd give her a call in the morning.

"Regina?" Lorraine said from the doorway. "Everything okay?"

"Peachy," Reggie said, plastering a nice fake smile on her face as she prepared to meet the stodgy old nurse whom she could hear shuffling down the hall toward them. Reggie visualized a woman in an old-fashioned nurse's uniform, complete with a little white cap. White chunky shoes, maybe, with orthotics and support hose.

Behind Lorraine, a figure appeared in the doorway who was neither old nor dressed in anything resembling a nurse's uniform. She wore jeans, knee-high biker boots, and a Jackson Browne T-shirt with a hooded zip-up sweatshirt over it. She had long coppery hair in a braid and a pierced nose, and was shouldering a black backpack.

Reggie did a double take.

"Tara?"

"Mrs. Dufrane," Tara said, going straight for Vera's bed and touching her lightly on the arm. "It's so good to see you again."

Reggie would know her anywhere, even without the thick black eyeliner, spiked hair, and hourglass necklace (which Reggie herself now wore, hidden under her shirt). Tara ignored Reggie, her gaze focused on Vera. Reggie flashed her aunt a what-the-hell-is-this? look and Lorraine responded with a big, proud smile.

"I'm not Mrs. Dufrane," Vera complained, dry lips pursed in a tight little bow. "I'm not Mrs. Anyone."

Tara smiled. "How about Vera, then? Would that be okay? And you can call me Tara. I'm not Mrs. Anyone either." She gave Vera a wink. "I'm an old friend of Reggie's. Do you remember?"

Vera nodded, but there was no recognition in her eyes.

"I had crazy hair back then, black with blond tips."

Vera smiled. "Did you know I was the Aphrodite Cold Cream girl?"

"I did. And you know what—I remember seeing the old ad. I'm going to see if I can find a copy and we can frame it and put it right on your wall. Would you like that, Vera?"

Vera smiled.

"Now I'm going to go put all my stuff away and get settled while you finish up your dinner. Then I'll come in and make sure you have all your medicine and maybe help you get ready for bed. That sound like a plan?"

Reggie's mother gave a little nod and went back to picking at her pizza.

Tara turned toward Lorraine, adjusting the backpack on her shoulder. "Which room am I in?"

"Father's old room," Lorraine said, smiling. "I've fixed it up for you, put on clean bedding."

Reggie stepped between them. "I'll show you," she said. Tara looked at her for the first time, a familiar mischievous sparkle in her eyes.

"Good idea," said Lorraine, gathering the china plates they'd eaten on. "You go help her get settled."

Reggie's head was spinning. "You're a nurse? For real?" She sounded like an awkward thirteen-year-old. So much for the third degree she was planning to give Lorraine's candidate.

"Yep. For the past fifteen years. I worked on the oncology floor at Hartford Hospital for a few years, then for a home health and hospice agency. I still do that some, but mostly it's private duty these days. I like it. I'm on my own, no one breathing down my neck. You want to see my license?" Tara said. She'd laid her backpack out on the neatly made single bed and was unzipping it. "I'll show you mine if you show me yours," she said with a teasing grin. "If architects even have licenses."

"How'd you know what I do?"

Tara gave a barking laugh. "Shit, Reggie! You think that just because you move away and never come back that you're off the radar completely? That you don't exist anymore?" Tara took out a stack of neatly folded T-shirts and carried them to an open drawer. Reggie noticed an ornate tattoo on Tara's right wrist—a black bird with a wing that was all wrong—bent and broken. It circled Tara's wrist like a strangely macabre bracelet. Reggie imagined the sleeve of Tara's hoodie pulling up, wondered if she'd still be able to see traces of the scars. Tara caught her looking and Reggie's face flushed.

"No," Reggie said, looking away. Then she faced Tara again, telling herself it was ridiculous to feel the same childish awe, the familiar sense of being undone and entirely at Tara's mercy. "It's just that—"

"You're not just any architect, though, are you?" Tara cocked one eyebrow. "You're one of the top green architects in the Northeast according to *Four Walls*." There was a slight mocking tone to her voice.

"How did you—"

"Have you heard of the Internet? Google? Amazing the shit you can find on there."

"Mmmm, very funny, Tara."

Tara gave a little nod and a smirk—an acknowledgment—*yes, that was funny, thank you for noticing.*

"But believe it or not, I actually subscribe to *Four Walls.* I like to read, and I have this thing for magazines, especially all those glossy house mags. They help take my mind off the fact that I live in a hovel. They're full of such promise, aren't they? I mean, they're selling you the actual magazine, but it's more than that—it's the fantasy of the ideal life you'll have once you get a perfect kitchen with classic triangle work area and stainless steel appliances. It's kind of sickening, but fascinating and addictive, too."

Reggie smiled. "You haven't changed at all."

Tara took another pile of clothing from her bag and gave Reggie a sly grin from over the top of it. "Do any of us really?"

Reggie liked to think she'd changed, morphed into a new self-confident woman who was in charge of her own life. But standing there, she felt like she was thirteen again, and Tara was in control of whatever happened next.

"I still can't believe you're a nurse," Reggie admitted.

"What, you don't think I'm the *nurturing* type?" Tara laughed. "Yeah, it's weird. But I love it. I can't imagine doing anything else. I don't know . . . probably a shrink would tell me I got into nursing because of what happened with Sid. Because part of me is still trying to save him, to fix what happened." She looked at Reggie, who turned away. Reggie had locked so many memories away in boxes in the back of her mind; she couldn't open them all at once.

"I still don't understand. How did Lorraine come to hire you?"

"We ran into each other a few months back. I was taking care of a friend of hers from the Historical Society. She stopped by for a visit and I was there working. We talked a little then, mostly about you. Then, when she got the phone call about your mom this morning, she looked me up and asked if I was available. How could I refuse?"

Reggie shook her head. "I'm sorry. I guess I'm still in shock. I didn't expect that you'd still be in town, much less that you'd be the nurse Lorraine hired to look after my mother."

Tara grinned. "Funny how things work out, isn't it?" There was that mischievous little sparkle in her eyes, giving Reggie the absurd idea that Tara had been expecting this all along, planning for it, maybe. Reggie pushed the thought away—there was no way Tara could have predicted Vera's return. But wasn't it a little odd that Tara didn't seem at all surprised by this new turn of events? Here she was unpacking, settling into Monique's Wish like it was the most normal thing in the world.

Reggie, for the first time in years, thought about her mother's theory about everyone on earth being connected by threads, making this great big spiderweb. Maybe some connections were stronger than others and pulled people back into one another's lives when they least expected.

"So, do you have a family?" Reggie asked. "Husband? Kids?"

Tara shook her head. "Are you kidding? Who would I find to put up with me?"

Reggie laughed a little too loud.

"How about Charlie?" Reggie asked. "Have you heard anything about him?"

Tara nodded. "He's still in town. Sells real estate. He has an office downtown, near the green. You should stop in and say hi." Tara looked directly into Reggie's eyes, gauging her reaction to this news.

Reggie gave a careful poker-faced nod, thinking how bizarre it would be to pop into Charlie's office. She tried to imagine what he might look like now: Charlie the Realtor. Had he gotten married? Did he have a house full of little Charlie Juniors with a tree house in the back? Did he ever sit with them there in the afternoon, feeling the tree sway, and tell them, *I used to have a friend with a tree house. . .*

Tara continued unpacking. Reggie felt like she was spinning through time: here one minute, then back to her thirteen-year-old self the next. And there was Tara: the sun Reggie orbited around.

"What's that?" Reggie said, her eye catching on the paperback that was clearly visible now that Tara had unpacked the last of her clothing. She felt the hairs on the back of her neck rise.

"What?" Tara said, looking down into the bag. Her face reddened. "Oh, this," she said, pulling out a dog-eared copy of *Neptune's Hands: The True Story of the Unsolved Brighton Falls Slayings.*

"What are you doing with it?" Reggie snapped. It felt like another one of Tara's tests, one of her games. The book was there in plain sight—she was just waiting for Reggie to notice, waiting to see what Reggie would do next.

"Like I said, I read." Tara held the book out and Reggie leaned away from it, as if it were a venomous snake.

This was bullshit. Bringing that book into Monique's Wish was a completely fucked-up thing to do.

"But that woman . . . the things she said about my mother . . ."

"I know," Tara said. "She crossed the line."

"Why do you even have it? And what were you thinking, bringing it here?"

Tara looked down at the old paperback, running her fingers over the cover—a raised shiny silver trident dripping blood.

"When your aunt called, told me about your mom, and offered me the job, I didn't hesitate. You remember how things were with my own mom—working all the time, drinking, hardly even noticing if I was living or dead. Your family was like my second family, my real family, the one that mattered. The one that cared if I ate dinner or how much I swore. Remember that? The way Lorraine would always get so flustered and offended when I even said the word *damn*?"

Reggie nodded, feeling like she was being manipulated, like Tara was doing what Tara did best. There was a familiar comfort in being pulled along, told just what she wanted to hear.

"Anyway, when I got off the phone with Lorraine, I remembered the book. I bought it when it came out, haven't read it since. But I thought I might reread it now. I know it's shitty, the way she wrote about your mom, but this Martha Paquette lady did her research. She got a lot of the facts of the case right. There are police reports and interviews in here. Dates, times, facts about the victims. It's full of clues, Reg." Tara's eyes were all lit up and she was rocking on the balls of her feet. Then suddenly, as if realizing that Reggie noticed her building excitement, she toned it down a notch. "Anyway," she said, clearing her throat, "I was thinking that I should brush up. You know, in case your mom says anything. Or remembers anything."

"So what, you're hoping to crack the case by rereading the book and listening to my mom's morphine-addled paranoid fantasies?"

Tara shrugged.

"Just don't let Lorraine catch you with that," Reggie said, nodding at the book. "She'll fire you on the spot."

Tara nodded, looking around the room. She walked over to the bookcase full of heavy bound classics and tucked *Neptune's Hands* behind *Gulliver's Travels* and *War and Peace*.

"Our secret," Tara said, and just then, she pulled up the sleeve of her sweatshirt, exposing just the faintest edge of the pale skin of her forearm, and Reggie made herself look away, not wanting to see.

"I'm going to go do some unpacking myself," Reggie said, turning to go.

"Reg," Tara called. Reggie stopped and turned back to face her. "It looks like you're bleeding."

Reggie looked down at her arm and saw her cut had reopened and blood was seeping through her sloppy Band-Aid work.

"Let me see," Tara said, reaching for Reggie's arm. Tara's touch gave Reggie a little electric jolt. "Do you remember?" Tara asked quietly, peeling back the Band-Aid to inspect the cut.

"I had a little accident with window glass," Reggie said, cutting Tara off before she could go any further. Tara let it go, turned away, grabbed a kit from her backpack, and pulled out gauze and tape. She cleaned the area with an antiseptic towelette, then put a fresh pad of gauze over it.

"Reg, I'm sorry," she said as she ripped off medical tape. "About everything."

And Reggie nodded, though she wasn't sure if Tara was talking about Vera, or about all that had transpired years ago between the two of them.

Tara's next words answered her question. "It wasn't your fault, you know. I'm the one who made him do it. And it was my idea to run away after." She kept her eyes on the work she was doing, carefully applying tape around the edges of the gauze.

Reggie breathed out a long, slow breath. "There's this thing. It's called free will."

Reggie had never told a soul what had happened that night. Lorraine had asked her after, why it was that Tara and Charlie didn't come around anymore. Reggie would look away, make up some story about new friends, people changing, moving on. Lorraine imagined that it had something to do with what had happened to Vera: that it was all just too much for Tara and Charlie somehow.

There were times, over the years, when Reggie ached to tell someone the truth. To confess.

Me and my friends, we did this terrible thing.

Tara finished with the tape. She smiled, shook her head, and looked at Reggie, then away. "Sometimes we're at the mercy of other people. We don't even understand the power they have over us until it's too late."

"But Charlie—"

"I'm not just talking about me and Charlie. I'm talking about me and you."

Chapter 14

June 15, 1985
Brighton Falls, Connecticut

"Ho-ly shit!" Tara said, smacking the latest edition of the *Hartford Examiner* with her open palm. They were in the garage, and Tara was sprawled across the old, patched leather couch in the corner while Reggie searched her aunt's workbench. The garage was dark and airless; the only light came from a small, dusty window and a metal lamp clamped onto the wall over Lorraine's workbench. So far, all Reggie had found was fly-fishing junk—vises, clamps, scissors, wire cutters along with endless quantities of hooks, feathers, beads, and fake fur.

"Candace Jacques had eaten lobster, too!" Tara squealed. "He cut off her hand, kept her alive for four freaking days, fed her boiled lobster, and strangled her—just like Andrea McFerlin! And listen to this—the son of a bitch has a name now!

" 'An anonymous source at the Brighton Falls Police Department reports that after Candace Jacques's stomach contents were discovered, the detectives working the case nicknamed the killer Neptune.' " Tara looked up from the paper, eyes glittering. "That must have been Charlie's dad. How cool is that? His dad gets to name a serial killer! God, this reporter is awesome. What's her name . . . Martha! Whose name is really Martha? Anyways, sounds like she's got some secret inside source. She's getting stuff the TV news people don't have a clue about." Reggie could practically feel the electric hum of excitement pulsing off Tara's body.

Tara went back to the paper and read aloud, " 'The official statement from chief of police Vern Samson is that they are following leads and actively looking for a connection between these two women.' " Tara scowled. "No shit!" she yelped. "I wonder how much they really know. Maybe Charlie's heard something. His dad can't be totally secretive about every little detail."

Charlie and Tara hadn't spoken in a week, since the day of the eighth-grade dance, and work on the tree house was at a standstill.

"Maybe you should call Charlie and ask?" Reggie said quietly.

Tara shrugged. "So tell me again what we're doing in Lorraine's lair?" she asked, tossing the paper aside and getting up off the beat-up couch.

"Looking."

"For what?" Tara asked.

"I'm not sure. Anything that doesn't have to do with fishing, I guess. All my mom said was 'I know what goes on in that garage.' "

"Ooh, I love the idea that Lorraine's got some kind of dark secret," Tara said, looking around. She pulled a pair of green rubber waders off a hook on the wall. "Maybe Lorraine puts these on, rubs fish guts all over herself, and struts around naked."

"Eew!"

"Hey, I almost forgot to tell you," Tara said, hanging the waders back up. "I'm a sister."

"Huh?"

Tara kept her back to Reggie, rubbing her thumb over the rusty nail that the green waders hung from. "Remember how I told you about how my dad has this young girlfriend and she was pregnant? Well, we got a card in the mail yesterday. She had the baby a couple weeks ago. A girl."

"Oh," Reggie said. "That's cool, I guess."

Tara turned back to face Reggie. "My mom's freaking. She actually kind of slapped me last night."

"Really?"

"Yeah." Tara snorted. "Can you believe it? She was all like, 'Maybe if you hadn't been such a freak then he wouldn't have wanted another kid.' Like it's my fault he knocked up this chick?"

Reggie let out a shaky breath. "That really sucks," she said lamely.

"Yeah, whatever. She'll get over it. Drink enough brandy and she'll forget damn near anything. Which reminds me, okay if I crash at your place tonight?"

"Of course, yeah."

"Cool," Tara said, coming over. She dropped down to her knees to examine the boxes stacked beside Lorraine's workbench.

Reggie turned back to the bench. She'd been through it and found nothing out of the ordinary—no secret stash of booze, horse-racing forms, or pornography. Lorraine's fishing rods, some nets, and a metal chain stringer hung on a wall. Pushed to the back of the garage were tires, boxes of old Christmas decorations, some scrap lumber, and a trash can full of sand they used on the driveway in the winter.

"Oh my God, are those eyeballs?" Tara shrieked, pulling out a cardboard box from the pile and peering in, disgusted, but clearly captivated.

Reggie looked in and saw tiny glass eyes with wires on the back, a filleting knife, scalpel, box of Borax, spool of black thread, and needles. There was also a plastic bottle of formaldehyde solution and a paper bag full of sawdust.

"Lorraine's taxidermy stuff."

"No shit? She actually stuffs dead things?"

"She's just done a couple of fish. One was a total wreck and had to be thrown away, but she kept the second." Reggie went over to the mounted fish nailed to the back wall of the garage. Its color was all wrong, the scales were falling off, and it had weird bulges in the middle, like a snake that had eaten a sledgehammer. The whole thing was strangely shiny, like it had been dipped in lacquer. The worst part was the visible stitching, done in thick black thread, along the fish's belly.

"Oh my God," Tara said. "It's Franken-fish!"

"She actually had it hanging in the living room for a while, but my mom kept throwing it away. Lorraine finally got the hint and put it up out here."

"Your aunt is one strange lady."

"No shit," Reggie said, turning from the grotesque trout.

"But then again, we've all got our weird stuff. Our little secrets we don't tell anyone." Tara reached for her bag, pulling out cigarettes. She held the pack out to Reggie, who shook her head.

Tara sat back down on the couch and smoked in silence for a minute, watching Reggie, maybe even waiting for her to confess secrets of her own.

Reggie's head was starting to ache. The garage felt dark and airless and she was sure she could smell a trace of formaldehyde in the air mixed with the fishy scent that seemed to follow Lorraine wherever she went.

"I have something show to you," Tara said. "A secret thing just between me and you," she promised. "Come closer."

Reggie crossed the garage and perched on the edge of the couch next to Tara.

Tara put out her cigarette on the stained cement floor, then reached into her black tattered bag. She pulled out a small silver box the size of a Zippo lighter and opened it, revealing a rectangular piece of black fabric. Tara unfolded it slowly as Reggie watched. Inside was a razor blade. Tara picked it up carefully, studied it a moment, a grin on her face.

Reggie's heart started to pound. "Is it for cocaine?" she asked, wondering if maybe Tara was a secret drug addict. She'd heard of kids in high school doing it at parties, but she'd never seen any in real life, only on TV.

"No, dummy. It's something way better than that. Watch," she said. Tara pulled up the leggings on her left calf and brought the blade to her skin. Slowly, carefully, she drew the blade across, her eyes wide. A little sigh escaped her mouth. Reggie could see that the calf was covered in thin scars, like delicate etchings on glass. She was making her own spiderweb across her leg.

"Now you try," Tara said, holding out the blade, still wet with her own blood.

"What?" Reggie gasped. Her eye went back to the trout with its row of sloppy black stitches.

"It's easy. Just one little cut."

"I can't," Reggie said, panic rising.

"Sure you can."

Reggie shook her head. "I'm not like you."

Tara smiled, leaned closer to Reggie, so close that when she spoke, Reggie felt the vibrations of Tara's words sinking into the skin of her face, down through the bones of her skull, reverberating in her addled brain.

"Yes, you are," Tara said. "You're just like me. I've known it all along."

Reggie took the blade, pulled up the leg of her jeans. Her hand trembled as she let it hover above her skin. What was she doing even considering this? Trying to impress Tara? To do this sick little bonding ritual just so that Tara would consider her an equal?

No, Reggie decided. This wasn't about Tara. This was about Reggie being scared of something and wanting to prove to herself that she could do it anyway. And shit, if she could survive a dog ripping her ear off, this would be a piece of cake.

"You know you want to," Tara said. "One cut. That's all. It'll make everything else go away. I promise." Tara kept her eyes focused on the blade in Reggie's hand. "Trust me."

Reggie made the cut quickly, pushing the blade down just a little, feeling the bright flash of pain as it bit into her skin, the amazing rush that came with it.

"That's it," said Tara, eyes huge. "Not too deep."

Reggie pulled the blade away, watched the blood seep from the cut, hers and Tara's mixed. At first it was like she was watching a film of some other girl with a razor blade in her hand. But the pain brought her back inside herself and she felt connected to her body in this whole new way. She was Reggie Dufrane, a thirteen-year-old girl. And for the first time she could remember, she was in control of something big, something dangerous.

"Didn't that feel good?" Tara asked.

"Mmm," Reggie said, closing her eyes, concentrating on the pain, melting into it.

Tara was right: for those few precious seconds, everything else faded away.

Charlie was on his knees on the front lawn, tinkering with the string trimmer.

"Hey, stranger," Tara said, practically skipping right up to him. After putting the razor blade away, Tara and Reggie had left the garage with this weird high—the world was suddenly brighter, and anything seemed possible. As they walked to Charlie's, they'd kept catching each other's eye and smiling these huge we've-got-a-secret smiles.

Charlie grunted a quick hello, barely giving Tara a glance before focusing back on the trimmer, which he was loading with new bright red nylon string.

"Hot day, huh?" Tara said.

Charlie kept winding string. His white T-shirt was soaked with sweat and grass stained. He smelled like gasoline.

"You got any Coke or anything inside?"

Charlie finished his job, reattached the spool, and stood up, wiping his hands on his grimy work shorts. "Come on in," he said. They followed him toward his house.

"Crap," he said, trying the door and finding it locked. "My dad must have locked it on his way out. He does things on autopilot these days." Charlie grabbed the carved wooden house number, 17, that hung to the right of the door and rotated it counterclockwise. Charlie retrieved a key from the little niche hidden there and unlocked the door.

The little ranch house was cramped and dark, the dusty shades drawn. Reggie was sure she could still smell Mrs. Berr's cigarette smoke. She half expected her to come around the corner from the kitchen, her latest Jell-O creation in hand.

Tara picked up and examined knickknacks and pictures arranged on dusty shelves while Charlie went to get them all Cokes.

"So is your dad at work?" Tara called out, wiping her hands on her jeans.

"It was supposed to be his day off, but he got called in." Charlie passed them each a cold can of Coke and sat heavily on the Naugahyde couch. "Did you guys hear? Another hand was left."

"What?" Tara said, so excited that she spilled soda all over her shirt. "When?"

"Just a couple hours ago." Charlie watched as Tara lifted the dry lower edge of her shirt and used it to pat down the wet area, right over her chest. They could see her bare belly and the tiny bit of her black bra. Charlie looked like he was holding his breath.

"He's picking up the pace," Tara said excitedly. "Last time there was, what . . . a week or more between killing Andrea McFerlin and leaving Candace Jacques's hand? It's only been three days this time."

Charlie nodded. "You know what my dad told me . . . he said he thinks this guy's just getting started. He's got a real taste for it now. It's like an addiction. He won't be able to stop."

Reggie gave a little involuntary shiver. "Do they have any idea whose hand it is?"

"Don't know," Charlie said, taking a long sip of soda.

Tara reached into the pocket of her jeans and fiddled with something—the doll shoe probably.

"Has your dad said anything else about the case? Any suspects? A connection between the ladies he killed? I mean, do they even know the killer's a man?" Tara asked, firing off the questions rapidly, letting them slam into each other. "Maybe it's a woman, or a couple, or a crazy Satanic cult or something." Her eyes were huge as she leaned toward toward Charlie, waiting for his response.

Charlie shook his head. "He hasn't told me anything. Just the addiction thing he said as he was leaving today. To tell you the truth, I'm kind of worried about him." Charlie set down his soda and began picking at loose thread on his shorts. "He's barely eating. Not sleeping much. When he's home, he's shut up in his office.

I guess I should be grateful that he's off my back, but it's weird the way he's become kind of like the Invisible Dad. Sometimes I wake up in the middle of the night and he's not here—he's gone into work at like two in the morning. He looks like a freaking zombie."

Reggie looked over at the shelves and studied the school photos of Charlie, snapshots of family vacations. Charlie had his mother's eyes and nose. She'd been a slight woman with huge brown eyes, blond hair, and a toothy smile. There were also pictures of Stu Berr in his police uniform, and before that, in the army. He'd served as a medic in Vietnam. He was, Reggie guessed, about fifty pounds lighter back then. There was a snapshot of Stu and a bunch of other uniformed men standing in front of an ambulance, all holding tin cups, raising them into the air in a toast. They all had tired, haunted looks beneath their helmets, and wore heavy flak jackets, with what looked like a hundred pounds of gear strapped to them. And what were they toasting? Reggie wondered. Getting the hell out of Vietnam? The life that would come after, she imagined, glancing at the other photos—the wife, the son, the little green house, the promotion to detective?

"So he's got an office here? Can we take a peek?" Tara asked, doing her best to sound nonchalant.

Charlie shook his head. "No freaking way. My dad would shoot me. Besides, he keeps it locked."

"Seriously?" Tara asked.

"He's got guns and shit in there. And confidential police papers. He's gotta keep it locked."

Tara made a sour face. "We could try picking it. If it's an easy lock, I might be able to do it with a bobby pin." She started looking through her bag. "I'm sure I've got one in here somewhere."

Reggie thought about Tara going into Andrea McFerlin's house. Had the back door really been open or had Tara picked the lock? The cut on her leg stung and she rubbed at it through her jeans, looked over at Tara, remembering the crisscrossed lines of scars on Tara's leg.

"Is that why you came over?" Charlie snarled. "To look through my dad's crap?"

Tara closed her bag and shook her head. "Nah. We came because we missed you. Now quit being a paranoid spaz."

"Well, forget about the office," Charlie said. "He's got a huge padlock on the door."

"Maybe—" Tara started to say.

Charlie interrupted her, eyes flashing with anger. "No way. I'm not even gonna let you try."

"That's fine," Tara said. "Whatever."

They were all silent for a minute. Tara tapped her chipped blue nails on her Coke can. She was bouncing her legs up and down, unable to hold still.

"I know," Tara said, her body still for the moment. "Let's play a game. Close your eyes, Charlie."

He stared at her for a few seconds, then closed his eyes.

"Good boy," she said. "Keep 'em closed nice and tight." Tara slid off the couch and made her way over to the chair where Reggie was sitting. She put a finger over her lips, *Shh,* then straddled Reggie's legs and leaned forward, and for half a second, Reggie thought Tara was going to kiss her. Instead, she gave her a crooked smile—a we're-sharers-of-deep-secrets-smile—and put her hands gently around Reggie's neck. Reggie looked up, a what-the-hell look, and Tara mouthed, *It's okay. Trust me.*

"Open your eyes, Charlie," she said.

"Tara, what are you —"

"I'm Neptune," Tara said, tightening her grip around Reggie's neck. The smile was gone now and her eyes looked dark and cruel. Her hands were cold and smelled like cigarettes. "And I'm giving you one minute to save my latest victim. Tell me why I do what I do."

"This is stupid, Tara," Charlie said.

"Answer the question," she instructed, tightening her grip. Reggie tried to swallow and couldn't. She held perfectly still, tried not to even breathe.

"Because it's an addiction," Charlie said impatiently.

"And?" Tara squeezed just a little tighter. Reggie made a gagging sound and reached up to pull Tara's hands off her. She gripped Tara's wrists, pulled and twisted, but Tara held tight.

"Quit it, Tara! You're hurting her!" Charlie said, jumping up off the couch.

"Stay back and play by the rules, or she's dead. I'm not Tara, I'm Neptune," she hissed, voice deep and gravelly. When she spoke again it was a shout, "*Now why do I do what I do?*"

Reggie felt light-headed. She dug her nails into Tara's wrists, tried to speak, but no words would come. She was inside a tunnel and there at the end of it, looking down at her, was Tara. Only she wasn't Tara. She was a Neptune. A man with a shadowy face and lobster claws for hands—it wasn't skin she was pinching and pulling on, not human wrists but a hideous exoskeleton.

"Tara!" Charlie grabbed her around the waist, yanking her off Reggie and throwing her to the floor. Reggie gasped, sucked in air. Her hands flew protectively to her aching neck, her crushed windpipe.

"You fucking idiot," Charlie said, pinning Tara's wrists to the ground, sitting on her hips so that she couldn't move.

Tara smiled up at him. "You feel it now, don't you?" Tara asked. "It's power, pure and simple. The girl's under you, her life is in your hands. It gives you a big old hard-on and there's only one release. You've gotta kill her. And when you do, the whole universe is there in your hands. You're like God."

Chapter 15

October 17, 2010
Brighton Falls, Connecticut

Reggie woke up in a cold sweat, heart pounding. She'd dreamed she was tied up in a dark cave and that someone was slipping a ring onto her finger. Then chopping her hand off.

Until death do us part.

"Shit," she said, sitting up in her childhood bed, under the same quilt she'd slept under growing up—a Drunkard's Path pattern her grandmother had made. The grandmother she'd never met, who'd died giving birth to Vera. When Reggie was a little girl, she'd heard the story and pictured her mother exploding out of her grandmother's belly, like it was the force of Vera's very being that killed Monique somehow.

Reggie looked down at the pattern, remembered her mother staggering through the front door, straight for Reggie, curling up beside her, breathing gin-soaked secrets under the quilt. Drunkard's Path.

The quilt, once a vibrant red and white, had faded to blotchy pink and dingy yellow. Reggie could see the tiny stitches done by hand connecting the blocks together, making the shapes into a path that seemed to stagger and sway.

Reggie stared up at the ceiling, the plaster crumbling and water stained. The roof must have been leaking for some time. Some of the stains were built of many rings, reminding Reggie of a topographical map. She studied the imaginary landscape on the ceiling, picturing mountains and valleys, wondering what it would be like to live there.

The door to her room creaked—she looked over and saw it closing slowly. Someone was behind it, out in the hall.

"Hello? Lorraine? Mom?" There was a shuffling sound, footsteps going back down the hall.

Her cell phone began to buzz. She rolled over, reaching it off the bedside table, and saw the glowing numbers on the digital clock: 7:32. Shit. She rarely slept past six. The phone vibrated in her hand and she checked the display: Len.

"Hey, you," she said sleepily into the phone, one eye still on the door.

"Didn't get you up, did I?"

"Nah. You know me, the queen of the early birds."

"How're things in Worcester?" he asked in almost a mocking tone, like he somehow suspected she wasn't there at all.

"Not what I expected," Reggie answered, telling herself she was being paranoid. Len was just being goofy. There was no way he could know she was lying to him. Still, guilt gnawed at her belly, and as good as it was to talk to him, she was eager to get off the phone before he picked up on it.

"And is that a good thing or a bad thing?" he asked.

"Hard to say."

"Mmm," Len said. He was silent a minute, waiting. She heard one of his cats meow, listened as he picked up his coffee and took a sip.

Reggie squirmed, switched the phone to her other ear.

"I'll call you when I get back to town," she said. "We can have that picnic."

"Sounds like a plan," he agreed.

"Talk soon, then."

"Reg?"

"Yeah?"

"Nothing." He sighed. "I'll see you when you get back."

She got out of bed and stretched. The room was the same way she'd left it, which was damn creepy. There was a framed M. C. Escher print above her bed—*Drawing Hands*: a lithograph of three-dimensional hands drawing themselves into existence. Some of her sketches were still on the bulletin board, including a self-portrait she'd done in charcoal—the lines blurred, her eyes two dark hollows: a ghostly raccoon girl looking up from the paper, asking her future self why she'd come back.

Reggie turned from the drawing, opened the closet door, and found the few pieces of clothing she'd left behind when she went off to college. There, on the top shelf, right where she'd left it, was the memory box.

A month after her mother's hand was found, Reggie was sent to a counselor who specialized in grieving. He was a doughy-faced young man with sad eyes who was fond of argyle sweaters. One of the exercises he had her do was to make a memory box: a special treasure box full of Vera memorabilia. Reggie had used one of her grandfather's old wooden cigar boxes, and, following the dough-boy's instructions, had stuffed it full of things that would always remind her of her mother. Then she'd buried it on a shelf at the top of her closet and left it behind when she ran off to start a new life. Not exactly what the grief counselor had had in mind, but it worked for Reggie.

Reggie reached up and lifted the box down, blowing a layer of dust off the top. There was a full-busted, scantily clad woman on the label, leaning against a large globe. With trembling fingers, Reggie opened the hinged lid, peered in, and saw a jumble of notes, matchbooks, a folded page torn from an old magazine—her mother, the Aphrodite Cold Cream girl. *Treat Yourself Like a Goddess.*

Reggie snapped the lid closed and tucked the box back up on the shelf.

The room felt stuffy and airless. Reggie went to the window and tried to lift it, but it was stuck shut. She was about to pound on the bottom of the frame, then glanced down at the bandages from yesterday's window glass mishap and thought better of it.

She pulled on a pair of jeans, grabbed her messenger bag, and went into the hallway, stopping to peer in at her mother, who was fast asleep. Vera's mouth hung open, lips and chin crusted with sticky, white drool. The door to Tara's room was closed, and she walked up to it, listening, but no sound came from the other side.

Reggie slipped down the stairs, carefully avoiding the ones that creaked—her body on autopilot, remembering little details she hadn't thought of in years.

The kitchen was tidy but still smelled like smoke. She set her bag down by the table and inspected the damaged drywall—it would be an easy repair. She'd also need to take measurements and buy glass to fix the dining room window. She'd pick up materials when she went into town.

After searching through Lorraine's carefully arranged cupboards, she finally came upon an old Mr. Coffee machine, a box of filters, and half a can of Chock full o'Nuts. God only knew how long it had been sitting in the cupboard, but it was better than nothing. While the coffee sputtered and perked, Reggie pulled out her sketch pad and made some notes. She made a grocery list, a reminder to go to a building supply place for window glass, drywall, tape, and Spackle, and to call the social worker to get the name and number of the shelter where Vera had been staying. She wrote down the name *Sister Dolores* and circled it. Then added, *Learn and clean and serve.*

There was a low knocking sound and Reggie froze, looking up at the ceiling, wondering who'd gotten up. Then she heard it again, louder this time. It was coming from the front door. Smoothing her hair, she went to the door, glanced through the window, and saw a young man in a cheap suit with overly large ears. A salesman? Or Jehovah's Witness, maybe? Curiosity got the better of her and she cracked the door.

"Can I help you?"

He showed her a badge, and she had to work to hide her surprise. "Detective Edward Levi, Brighton Falls Police. I was hoping I could speak with Ms. Dufrane." His large ears were redder than his face.

"Which one?" Reggie asked.

He looked taken aback.

"There are three Ms. Dufranes here at the moment, Detective." She smiled when she said it, wanting to show him she wasn't being a smart-ass.

"Yes, of course," he said, rocking forward slightly to make himself look taller. "Vera. I'd like to speak with Vera Dufrane."

"I'm afraid she's asleep."

"And you are?" He took out a notebook.

"Her daughter. Reggie Dufrane." She watched him write down her name, misspelling it—*Redgie.* He held the pen so tight his fingers went pale. He fumbled in his blazer pocket and took out a business card, passing it to Reggie.

"Maybe you could call me later? When she wakes up?"

"Detective Levi," Reggie said, looking down at the card with the embossed Brighton Falls Police Department seal. "I'm not sure you're aware of my mother's condition? She's very sick, both physically and . . . otherwise. And the Worcester police and FBI already questioned her in the hospital."

He nodded. "I understand. But no one from our department has met with her, and the crimes took place here in Brighton Falls. It's procedure."

Reggie smiled again, wondering why on earth they'd sent this young, bumbling detective. Then a sinking thought occurred to her—maybe this was the best Brighton Falls had to offer.

"Of course. You can see for yourself. I'll call you later to set up a time to meet with her."

"I appreciate it," he said, backing up and nearly losing his balance on the steps.

"Did I hear someone at the door?" Lorraine asked, coming into the kitchen once Reggie had settled back down at the table.

"Brighton Falls' finest, looking to talk to Mom," Reggie said, holding the business card out to Lorraine, who glanced down at it, scowling.

Lorraine made a little clucking noise. "He was here yesterday, before you arrived. It seems he's been assigned the Neptune case."

Reggie laughed. “Well, it’s comforting to know they’ve put their very best cop on the case. The kid looks like he’s in high school, for God’s sake.”

Lorraine shook her head. “I know his parents. He graduated at the top of his class from Yale. He could have gone anywhere to work, but he chose to come back home and join the Brighton Falls Police Department. He’s their brightest star these days, rising right through the ranks. His mother’s very proud.”

“I’m sure she is,” Reggie said, unable to keep the sarcasm out of her voice.

Lorraine shuffled to the stove and put on the kettle.

Reggie looked back down at her list. “I don’t suppose you have wireless here?”

“Wireless what?”

“Um, Internet access? Wait—do you even have a computer?”

Lorraine shook her head. Reggie wasn’t sure if she imagined a certain smugness in Lorraine’s expression.

“I’ve been looking around—the place could stand some repairs, Lorraine,” Reggie said as she stood up, went to the counter, and poured herself a cup of coffee. It tasted like sludge, but she forced it down. “You need someone to come out and do some work on the roof. The slate shingles are in rough shape. It’s leaking in places. The boards underneath are probably rotted out, maybe even the rafters, too. Get one heavy load of snow and you're in trouble."

Monique's Wish wasn't in great shape, but at this point, it was still fixable. God knew Reggie had seen worse. Last year, she had done a passive solar retrofit she'd designed for a Quonset hut an old hippie couple had turned into their full-time home outside of Bennington—the *Boston Globe* did an article on it. It was an original hut that had been on the property since it was purchased as a surplus military building in 1948. When Reggie first saw it, she didn't have much hope. But then she'd drawn up plans, gutted the building, reangled it, added insulation, put in masonry walls and floor for thermal mass, and covered the south side with windows. It ended up a light, cheerful place that the couple heated with only one cord of wood all winter. The *Globe* had quoted the owners as saying, "Dufrane is a magician. She makes the impossible possible."

Lorraine pursed her lips as she fished a tea bag out of the box.

"Look," Reggie said, "if it's a question of money—"

Lorraine scowled. "It's a good strong house. Father built it to last."

"All houses need upkeep, Lorraine."

The phone rang and Lorraine practically leapt for the old black rotary dial on the kitchen wall. Reggie couldn't believe the phone still worked—it was probably old enough to be considered an antique.

"Hello? Yes, this is she." Lorraine listened for a minute, then scrunched her face up as though she had smelled something hideous. "No! No comment. No. Absolutely not." Lorraine slammed the phone down.

"Everything okay?" Reggie asked.

"It was a reporter from the *Hartford Examiner.*" Lorraine's voice was shaky. "It seems they know your mother is alive."

"Shit." Reggie breathed. She'd expected it, but not this fast. But then again, she hadn't expected the welcoming committee of firemen.

"No need for profanity," Lorraine said.

"Okay," Reggie said after taking another gulp of horrid coffee. "I'm going to run out and get some food and supplies. Stay here and lock the door. Don't open it for anyone. Not even Detective Boy Wonder."

The phone rang again.

"And don't answer the phone," Reggie advised, grabbing her bag and keys, hurrying from the kitchen.

Reggie returned to Monique's Wish nearly three hours later, after a high-stress trip to the Super Stop & Shop (why, Reggie wondered, did everything have to be Super?), Starbucks, and Home Depot. She opened the back of the truck, and as she was grabbing several bags of groceries she heard tires crunching on the gravel behind her. She turned and saw a blond woman behind the wheel of white sedan. Reggie froze, bags in hands, as the woman jumped out of the car, a friendly grin on her face.

"Regina Dufrane? My God, is that really you?"

Reggie squinted at the woman with frosted blond hair. She was wearing a smart little business suit and pumps. Her face was heavily lined with wrinkles covered in pale foundation. There was something very familiar about her. A friend of Lorraine's, maybe? Or a distant relative?

Reggie set the bags back down in her truck and walked around the car to study the woman face-to-face. "I'm sorry. You are—"

"Martha Paquette," the frosted-haired woman answered with a smile that locked her face in a frightening grimace. She held out her hand to Reggie. "It's so good to see you again, Regina."

Reggie stepped back.

"How is she? Your mother? Has she said anything about her captivity?"

"I don't know what you're talking about," Reggie said, hating how her voice shook. "This is private property. I'd like you to leave."

Neptune's Hands was Martha Paquette's only big success. She'd written other books, but none of them worked. Reggie had seen the horrible reviews and couldn't help but feel strangely satisfied.

Continuing to smile, Martha reached into her leather handbag and pulled out a photo. "I know she's alive. And she's here." It was a picture of Reggie pulling her mother away from the group of firemen in the yard yesterday. Shit. The young firefighter with the cell phone must have snapped it. It was probably all over the Internet by now.

"You can't just keep her hidden away," Martha said. "There are questions that need answering. Now I know your mother turned up in a homeless shelter up in Worcester two years ago. And I also know that with her diagnosis, we don't have much time. So what I think we need to focus on is—"

"Where did you hear that?" Reggie hissed, taking a menacing step toward Martha.

"If I could just talk to Vera, ask her a couple of questions, then I'm sure—"

"You're not going anywhere near my mother! Now get the hell off our property before I call the police."

Martha nodded, turned to open the door of her car. Then she looked back at Reggie. "He's still out there, you know. I think we owe it to his victims, to Vera, to do all we can to bring him to justice."

"And selling a few more books in the process wouldn't hurt, would it?"

Martha ducked down and sat herself in the driver's seat, shutting the door. She rolled down the window. "I'd invest in a security system. Some decent dead bolts at least."

Reggie sighed deeply. "Why are you still here?" She pulled out her cell phone.

"You think that Neptune just let her go, Regina? You think that whoever he is, he's going to just sit back and let her tell the world everything she knows?"

Chapter 16

June 18 and 19, 1985
Brighton Falls, Connecticut

"I've got something for you, Reg," George announced when she came into the kitchen. "It's there on the table."

George was sprinkling cheese on the top of the lasagna he'd just made. Lorraine was in front of the sink, washing lettuce for a salad. Vera sat at the table, legs crossed, sipping a gin and tonic. George came over and ate with them once a week or so, and sometimes he'd cook. Lorraine's meals were a consistent rotation of fish, cube steak, and scalloped potatoes from a box. Vera didn't make anything at all beyond coffee and cocktails. Reggie wasn't even sure Vera knew how to turn on the oven. When George cooked, it was usually something Italian: meatballs, manicotti, stuffed shells—he made sauce from scratch and claimed it was his Sicilian grandmother's secret recipe.

The kitchen smelled amazing—garlic and tomatoes and fresh basil all mingling together and making Reggie's mouth water. She went to the table and saw a paper bag with her name on it. She opened it up and found a headlight and taillight for her bike, along with a pack of batteries.

"Thanks, Uncle George," she said, and he gave her a you're-welcome nod. She held the lights out for Vera to inspect. Vera gave an approving smile and lit a cigarette.

"We're all a lot safer with George in the world, aren't we?" Vera asked, hissing out a curl of smoke in his direction. He had his back to them, but Reggie could see his body stiffen.

"I brought some tools over, Reg. You and I can put the lights on after dinner," George said, opening the oven and easing the heavy Pyrex dish of lasagna in. "I've got something for you too, Vera," he said, wiping his hands on a kitchen towel.

"I've heard of Christmas in July, Georgie, but isn't this still June?" she asked, smiling slyly. She held up her glass, rattled her ice cubes in his direction. "Be a love and fix me another drink, will you? Or is that against the AA code of conduct or something?"

George gave her a look Reggie couldn't read—worry? Maybe even pity?

Lorraine was slicing tomatoes now but stopped and gave Vera an icy glare. "Don't you think you've had enough?"

"Never mind, I'll get it myself," she said, pushing herself up, doing a swaying stagger-walk to the counter, where she mixed herself another drink that was heavy on the gin, light on the tonic.

"The lights really are great, Uncle George," Reggie said again, voice as chipper and bright as she could make it. She loaded the batteries in and turned on the red flashing taillight. It blinked like an ambulance.

"Ready for your gift?" George asked once Vera was settled back at the table, fresh drink in her hand. He crossed the kitchen and grabbed his jacket from the back of the chair. From the right pocket, he pulled out a small present wrapped in tissue paper.

"For you," he said, handing it over to Vera.

She put down her cigarette and accepted the gift. George watched, expectant and nervous, while Vera unwrapped the tissue paper, revealing a tiny, beautiful carved wooden bird.

"This isn't like any duck I've ever seen," she told him, turning it in her hand. Reggie leaned in to see that it had a long, gracefully curved neck, the feathers of the wings carved in perfect detail.

"Yes it is," he said, smiling and adjusting his glasses. "It's the ugly duckling," he told her. "All her life she compares herself to others, thinks she doesn't fit in; then she grows up and realizes she's really a beautiful swan." He stared at Vera, who kept her eyes on the carved bird in her hand.

Reggie held her breath, expecting her mother to come out with some mocking comeback line—*Who are you calling an ugly duckling, Georgie*?—but Vera was silent as she studied the swan, her head dropped down. Only when she raised it, Reggie saw that Vera's eyes didn't look mischievous or even angry—only sad.

Lorraine made a disapproving clucking sound and went back to cutting the tomato. "Damn!" she yelped, dropping the knife and clutching at her finger. Blood dripped onto the cutting board, mingling with the tomato juice.

George jumped up and went to her. "Let me see," he said.

"It's nothing," Lorraine snapped.

George gently unwrapped her fingers from the cut hand. "You got yourself good," he said, grabbing a paper towel from the roll and folding it up. He held the towel against her hand, said, "Let's go clean it up and get a bandage and ointment on. The last thing you want is an infection." Together they moved down the hall toward the bathroom, George's hand on Lorraine's.

Reggie and her mother sat in silence, listening to the ticking of the oven, the water coming on in the bathroom sink. George said something and Lorraine laughed.

Vera turned the swan over, running her fingers over the feathers of its belly.

After a minute, she stood up, swaying, steadying herself on the table.

"You okay, Mom?"

Vera offered Reggie a forced smile and said, "I'll be right back." Her voice sounded shaky and strange.

Vera went across the kitchen and down the hall. Reggie heard the front door open, then close. In a minute, her mother's car started.

Reggie leaned forward and put out her mother's cigarette, which had burned down to the filter, giving off a poisonous chemical smell. The swan was perched at the edge of the table, like it was thinking about taking flight.

"Where's your mother?" Lorraine asked when she reappeared in the kitchen, Band-Aid on her finger.

"She said she'd be back," Reggie said, biting her lip.

"The last thing she should be doing in her state is getting behind the wheel of a car," Lorraine announced, tugging at the bottom of her fishing vest. She went to the kitchen window and looked out at the driveway, eyes sweeping over the place where Vera's Vega had been. "I have half a mind to call the police."

George went and stood behind her, put a hand on her back. She leaned back into him, then, as if thinking better of it, swayed forward, resting her hands on the counter.

"Who's up for a game of rummy?" George asked, turning away from her, opening the drawer the cards were kept in.

Reggie, Lorraine, and George sat around the kitchen table, playing cards while they waited for the lasagna to cook. Vera did not return. They ate in uncomfortable silence, all of them listening for the tires on the gravel driveway, the wooden swan in the center of the table abandoned.

When Reggie got to her room, she went to the desk, found her X-Acto knife, and drew the blade slowly, tentatively, across her forearm. The pain was bright and beautiful, driving all the darkness away.

Neptune's hands were around her throat, tightening. She was someplace deep and cold—the underground chamber of a cave, the bottom of a well. She was tied up, held down, unable to move.

She heard Tara's voice: *The whole universe is there in your hands.*

Reggie opened her eyes, focusing on the clock radio beside her twin bed.

Red fingers, reaching for her.

No, she told herself, blinking, only red numbers: 2:20 A.M.

Her heart was pounding, her skin damp. The fresh cut on her arm stung.

She felt her mother's hot gin breath on the back of her neck. Vera was curled around Reggie under the twin-size Space Invaders sheets, pressing her ruined hand against Reggie's chest and holding her tight, so tight Reggie could barely breathe. Vera put her lips against Reggie's good ear and whispered, "Wake up."

"What is it?" she asked.

"I have news."

"Jesus, Mom! Can't it wait until morning?" She was getting tired of these middle-of-the-night, after-the-bars-closed confessions. And she was pissed off that her mother had just walked out on them at dinner, leaving behind George's gift like it meant nothing.

Maybe Lorraine had been right—maybe it was time to start locking her door.

"It's important," Vera hissed, squeezing Reggie tighter.

And Reggie felt a little dark stab of fear, starting as a flutter in her rib cage.

Her mother moved her lips to Reggie's one remaining ear again and sighed into it, her breath sharp with the piney gin smell that reminded Reggie of Christmas trees. "I'm getting *married.*"

Reggie felt a fist close inside her chest.

"Did you hear me, Regina? Isn't it wonderful?"

"Great. Great." *Liar.* "Is it the new guy? The one you met at the bowling alley?"

Vera laughed. "No, silly. It's not him."

"Well, who is it, then?"

"It's a surprise. But you'll see soon. I want you to come and meet him."

"Now?" Reggie asked. She tried to shift around to face her mother, but Vera held Reggie in place. Her mother's strength often surprised her. But then again, this was the woman who had twirled a gigantic dog through the air to save her. Reggie reached up from under the covers and touched her mother's scarred hand, remembering.

"No, silly. Tomorrow. Meet me at the bowling alley. Seven o'clock. Will you come, Regina? Please say you will." Her voice sounded hopeful, pleading. The words buzzed the back of Reggie's neck like worried bees.

"Okay. I'll be there."

"Good girl," she said, kissing Reggie's cheek. "Oh, and do me a favor, huh? Don't say anything about my news to Lorraine. I want to tell her myself. But I want you to meet him first."

"Whatever you say," Reggie told her.

"Good girl," she said, kissing Reggie's ear. "We're going to live in a real house. Maybe get some cats. Have a flower garden. A nice, normal life. You'd like that, wouldn't you, love?" She sounded so strangely wistful it was as if she were reciting lines from one of her plays.

"I want you out of this house!" Lorraine stood in the doorway of Reggie's room, the light from the hallway coming in all around her. Her face was in shadow, but the outline of her silhouette seemed to glow. Reggie looked at the clock. It was a little after three. They had fallen asleep.

Vera slid out from under the covers and stood without a word.

"Mom, wait!" Reggie started to get out of bed. "Aunt Lorraine, what're you talking about?" Reggie stammered. "It's the middle of the night—"

"Shhh, don't worry, baby," Vera said. "Everything's going to be okay. You just go back to bed."

"But— " Reggie began.

"Everything's under control," Vera promised. "You get some sleep now."

Vera left the room and closed the door gently behind her. Reggie could hear them arguing in the hall. She crept out of bed, padded across the floor, and pressed her good ear to the door.

"How dare you belittle me in front of my daughter?" her mom said.

"I've made it clear that I will not tolerate this," Lorraine said. "This is not some flophouse where you come and go as you please. What do you think it does to Regina, seeing you like this? Having a drunk for a mother?"

"You have no right," Vera hissed.

The floor creaked with the sound of footsteps.

Then a third voice, low and gentle, chimed in. "Let's all calm down." It sounded like George, but what would he be doing there in the middle of the night?

Lorraine said something Reggie didn't catch. Then "My decision is firm. I want you to leave. Now."

This was followed by more whispers, then footsteps.

Soon it was quiet, but Reggie stayed, her real ear pressed against the door until she drifted off to sleep.

Chapter 17

October 17, 2010
Brighton Falls, Connecticut

Reggie stormed back into the house after her confrontation with Martha in the yard.

"Who did you tell about Mom?" Reggie snapped at her aunt as she dropped the plastic grocery bags on the kitchen counter. One of them fell over and a plastic tub of lemon-scented disinfecting wipes rolled out.

"No one." Lorraine turned from the sink where she'd been rinsing out the coffeepot.

"You called me. And Tara. Who else?"

"No one." Lorraine straightened up, bracing herself against the counter.

"No one else?"

"I don't appreciate your tone, Regina." She reached for a dish towel and dabbed at her soapy hands.

"Martha Paquette was just here. She had a picture of Mom taken by one of those goddamn volunteer firefighters."

"I'll call the chief," Lorraine said. "That's got to be against the code of conduct. Surely he'll be reprimanded."

"The picture is really the least of our problems. Martha knows that Mom had been in a homeless shelter in Worcester. And she knows about the cancer."

Lorraine's mouth fell open, giving her the appearance of one of her much-loved trout. "How?"

"*Someone* told her, I'd imagine." She stared at her aunt, waiting.

Lorraine's eyes opened wide. "You don't think it was *me*?" She touched a hand to her chest and kept it there, fumbling with one of the pockets on her ancient, stained fishing vest.

"Not directly, no. But I need to know who else knew about the shelter."

"I told you," Lorraine said, clenching her jaw. "You and Tara. I'm not an idiot, Regina. Don't you think I have some concept of what's at stake here? I haven't breathed a word to anyone else and I resent the implication that I'm a dotty old lady who can't keep her mouth shut. You should know I have only the best intentions as far as your mother is concerned."

"Oh, really?" Reggie said. "That's a switch, isn't it? Do you think I've forgotten what you did? You threw her out of her own house, Lorraine!" Reggie bit her tongue before she finished the thought out loud: *right into the arms of a killer.*

Lorraine's whole body went rigid. She turned away from Reggie and ran hot water into the sink. The steam came up, and Lorraine leaned into it, holding on to the counter like her legs alone could not support her; she looked like a woman being enveloped by fog.

"There are angels walking among us," Vera said. "They're disguised like humans. Sometimes they're wearing rags. Sometimes business suits. You never know when you might meet one. That's what Sister Dolores says."

"Sister Dolores sounds like a smart woman," Tara said. She had a plastic tub of warm water and was giving Vera a sponge bath. Vera was half naked, her hips and legs covered with a blanket, a towel draped over her shoulders. Her breasts sagged like empty sacks onto her protruding rib cage. Every bone seemed visible through paper-thin skin.

Reggie had hurriedly pushed open her mother's door and now stood frozen in the doorway. She looked away from her mother and down at the floor, feeling like an intruder.

Tara glanced up, apparently unsurprised by the interruption. "I'm just getting your mother cleaned up. We'll be through in a minute." She'd dropped the washcloth into the tub and had started to gently blot Vera's skin with a towel.

"We need to talk," Reggie stammered, reminding herself what she'd come for as she backed up into the hallway.

"Let me finish this up and I'm all yours." She carefully dried Vera off, lifting her legs and arms gently, artfully using the blankets and towels to cover up whatever part of Vera she wasn't working on, toweling off the stump where her right hand had been as if it were no different from her other arm. There was no look of repulsion or horror. She hummed a little tune while she worked, uttered reassurances—"Almost done, Vera." "Am I freezing you to death? Sorry, my dear, nearly there."

Vera smiled up at Tara. "I think you're one," she said, her voice barely above a whisper.

"I'm one what?" Tara asked, sprinkling baby powder on Vera's torso.

"An angel."

"Perfect, because I think you're one, too," Tara said, smiling down at her, carefully easing Vera into her pajama top.

Vera closed her eyes and sank back into the pillow with a look of complete tranquility on her face. Tara grabbed the bath supplies and carried them past Reggie, down the hall to the bathroom. She washed her hands, carefully soaping up each finger, while Reggie stood hovering in the bathroom doorway. Tara's sleeves were pushed up and Reggie stared at her arms, remembering the scars, thinking she could see the faint outlines of them. Tara caught her looking and Reggie glanced away, embarrassed. Then her eyes met Tara's in the medicine cabinet mirror.

"You didn't talk to Martha Paquette by any chance, did you?"

"Who?"

"The woman who wrote *Neptune's Hands.*"

Tara gave her a quizzical look. "No. I don't know why she would have come to me. I didn't know any more than you did about the killings. She was busy talking to cops and stuff. Why would she have bothered with a thirteen-year-old kid?"

"I'm not talking about back then. I mean *now.* Did you talk to her yesterday or today?"

Tara turned off the faucet, shook off her hands. "What the hell is this, Reggie?"

"She was just here. She knows my mom is alive and in this house. And that she showed up in a homeless shelter in Worcester. She even knows about the cancer."

Tara began drying her hands. "And you think *I* told her?"

"Someone did. And the only people who knew were me, Lorraine, and you."

Tara gripped the towel as if she was trying to throttle it. Reggie remembered the way Tara had once choked her, pretending to be Neptune. For days after, Reggie had walked around with the faint yellow bruises from Tara's fingers.

When Tara spoke, her voice crackled and popped as it worked its way up to a roar. "Yeah, you, me, Lorraine—*and* all the people she met in the hospital in Worcester: nurses, doctors, aides, transport people, Christ, even the people who came in to mop the floor! Then there are all the cops who went in to interview her. You think someone like Martha Paquette doesn't still have some police connections? What about the shelter workers or other homeless people? Any fucking *one* of them could have tipped her off."

Reggie took a step back. "Of course. You're right. I hadn't thought of all that, I'm sorr—"

"No. You didn't bother to think, you just went right for the one person you trust the least, didn't you?" Tara's eyes blazed.

"That's not true," Reggie said, moving toward Tara, wanting to reach out and touch her, to find a way to show her she was wrong. She felt like a kid again, at the mercy of Tara and her moods, wanting desperately to make things right.

Tara shook her head and stepped back. "You know, as much as I want to be here for your mom, I'm not sure I'm the right person."

"No. You *are* the right person. My mother trusts you. She just called you an angel!"

Tara twisted the towel in her hands.

Reggie gave Tara a pleading look. "Please say you'll stay."

There was total silence for a beat, as if they were both holding their breath.

"It's funny, isn't it?" Tara asked. "The way life works. You don't even try to look me up in twenty-five years and now here you are, begging me to stay. Did you even think of me, Reggie? Even once in all those years?"

"Tara—"

"Did you?" Tara interrupted, the same burning look in her eyes she'd had all those years ago when she'd talk about Neptune.

Reggie reached inside her shirt and pulled out the hourglass necklace, holding it out so Tara could see it.

Tara's eyes widened. "Oh my God! You kept it? All this time?"

"Of course." The pink sand was running out. "Do you want it back?" Reggie started to take the necklace off, but Tara shook her head.

"No. You should keep it. It takes me back, though. Seeing it again. Total time warp, you know?"

Reggie nodded. "There's a lot of that going around."

Tara bit her lip. "Do you really want me to stay?"

"Yes."

"Okay. But no more weird shit, okay? We've got to stick together here. Things with your mom, they're going to get really intense in about a million different ways. If you can't trust me, I need to know now."

"I do trust you," Reggie said, remembering years ago, when she'd sat next to Tara in Lorraine's dank, fishy-smelling garage and Tara had handed her a razor blade and said, *Trust me.*

Tara nodded.

"Thank you," Reggie said. "For agreeing to stay. I'm sorry for accusing you like that—it was fucked up."

Reggie started to tuck the necklace back under her shirt, then pulled it back out, turned it over, thought, for just a second, of saying the words that would start one of their old games:

You have one minute . . .

Instead, she did the grown-up thing and turned and walked away.

Excerpt from *Neptune's Hands: The True Story of the Unsolved Brighton Falls Slayings* by Martha S. Paquette

The body of the third victim, Ann Stickney, was found at dawn on June 19. She was on the green in the center of town, underneath the descendant of the Charter Oak. She was curled on her side, looking like someone who had just fallen asleep. Like Neptune's previous victims, Stickney was naked and freshly bathed, clean bandages applied over the stump where her right hand had been. This time, the killer left a mark—a trident carved into her abdomen, apparently acknowledging his fondness for the name the police had given him.

The girl was twenty-one years old, a film student at Wesleyan University in Middletown, forty-five minutes south of Brighton Falls. Her roommate assumed she'd gone home to New Jersey for the week and hadn't reported her missing.

After the discovery of Stickney's body, a frenzied pandemonium hit Brighton Falls.

Women were warned to be on guard and not walk to their cars alone. Stores began selling mace, and a women's group passed out bright orange whistles. Citizens formed posses to patrol neighborhoods. Parson's Hardware did a booming business in dead bolts and new lock sets. Bud's Gun Shop out on Airport Road sold twice as many handguns in one week as they usually sold in a year.

The chief of police, Vern Samson, announced that as it was clear that they were now dealing with a serial killer, the FBI had been called in to assist. "We are hopeful that their expertise will help bring a swift resolution to the situation and aid in our capture of the killer known as Neptune." Samson also appointed a special task force to look into how so much confidential information was being leaked to the press.

The *Hartford Examiner* began printing letters to the editor from citizens who felt the police were bungling the investigation. People were calling for Vern Samson to resign. One popular theory in town was that Neptune might even be a member of the police force. That would explain how he got the packages onto the steps of the police station without notice, how information about the case was leaked, and even, perhaps, how he entrapped his victims.

Because, after all, who didn't trust a police officer?

Chapter 18

June 19, 1985
Brighton Falls, Connecticut

Reggie woke up at ten, stiff and cold, curled up on her bedroom floor. She remembered Lorraine's shadow filling her doorway as she bellowed, "I want you out of this house!" Trying to shake the memory from her head, Reggie went downstairs to the kitchen and found Lorraine with a bowl of soggy cornflakes.

She wanted to start screaming at her aunt, to say, *How could you kick her out? What gives you the right?* But she just stood there, speechless, half afraid Lorraine might decide to throw her out, too. And unlike Vera, she really didn't have anywhere else to go.

Yesterday's paper was laid out in front of Lorraine, and she was studying the crossword puzzle, pencil in hand. The radio was playing low in the background, a murmur of voices. Reggie heard the words: *Body. Charter Oak. Neptune.*

"Did they find her?" Reggie asked as she poured herself a glass of orange juice.

"Who?" Lorraine bit down lightly on the pencil's eraser as she contemplated the puzzle.

"Neptune's next victim. It's the fifth morning."

"Yes," Lorraine said, not looking up from the paper.

"Well, who is she? Where did they find her?"

"I don't really know," Lorraine said. "I haven't been paying attention." She filled in one of the words in the puzzle: *gratitude.*

Reggie slammed her juice glass down. "How could you not pay attention? The guy is killing women in our town! One of them was a friend of Mom's. Did you even know that?"

"No," Lorraine said, finally looking up from her puzzle. "I didn't."

"It was the waitress. Mom introduced us once. She was a really nice person."

Lorraine pursed her lips and nodded. "I'm sure she was."

Reggie stared at her, anger bubbling inside her.

"It wasn't right, what you did," Reggie said. "Kicking Mom out in the middle of the night like that."

Lorraine stood and dumped her ruined cereal down the sink, turning on the garbage disposal. She kept her back to Reggie, making it clear that she had nothing to say on the subject.

Reggie saw the little wooden swan in the center of the table, where it had been all night.

"Was there someone else here last night?" Reggie said. "When you and Mom were fighting, I thought I heard another voice."

Lorraine narrowed her eyes, shook her head. "No. Of course not."

Reggie grabbed the carved swan, stuffed it into the pocket of her shorts, then marched out of the kitchen.

"Regina," Lorraine called after her, "if you go into town today, just make sure you're not alone. Have Charlie go with you."

Reggie didn't acknowledge her, she just kept right on walking.

The flat happened before Airport Road turned from two lanes to four. Out in the tobacco fields. The workers had gone home for the day and there was no one around but passing cars. Reggie didn't have any tools with her. No repair kit with patches and glue. George had taught her how to repair a bicycle tire and had bought her all the tools she needed. But she always forgot to bring them with her when she rode.

The headlight they'd put on last night after dinner was there, front and center on the handlebars. George had chastised Reggie for using the wrong size Allen wrench—it was a little too small.

"You'll strip the inside of the bolt," he'd told her. "Take the time to find the right tool." She looked through the little set of wrenches until she found one that was the perfect fit, then tightened the clamp that held the headlight on.

Reggie wished George and his toolbox were here now.

"Shit," she mumbled, inspecting the ruined tire. She hid her bike with the torn rear tire in the bushes beside a drainage ditch and set out walking.

One car after another passed her by.

And what if a guy in a tan car slows down and offers me a ride? she wondered. She'd find some excuse not to hop in. But it was a moot point anyway, because no one was slowing down, much less stopping.

She checked her watch. She had fifteen minutes to get there. She started running.

Then, as she was just getting into her rhythm, imagining she was half running, half flying, the second disaster of the night happened.

She was running at top speed, going along on autopilot, when she saw, glued to the side of a faded red tobacco-drying barn, a huge billboard-size blowup of Candy Jacques's face, earrings like whale hooks, pouting red lips.

HAVE YOU SEEN ME? printed in letters two feet high.

Reggie lost track of her own feet somehow, and suddenly she was off balance, landing hard on her right arch. Her ankle folded and she went down in a comic-book-style roll, limbs flailing. KA-PLUNK!

She landed in such a way that when she opened her eyes, the first thing she saw was Candy's immense face staring down at her.

"Shii-t!" Reggie moaned, rolling away from her.

Her ankle was screaming in pain. It began to swell immediately, and by the time she'd dragged herself up from the ground and hobbled the half mile to where the road changed from two lanes to four, she was beginning to wonder if perhaps she'd broken it. She found she could move forward only by doing a hopping sort of shuffle, her face a grimace of pain and the words *shit, double-shit, god-DAMN* spitting out each time she put any weight at all on her right ankle. Then it started to rain. Not little happy "I'm Singing in the Rain" kinds of drops, but water by the bucketful fell from the sky.

At long last—soaked to the marrow, her stomach sick and head swimming with pain—the red, white, and blue sign of Airport Lanes came into view. It was half past seven. Reggie hop-shuffled toward the giant glowing pin, mouthing *shit, shit, shit* in steady rhythm each time her right foot hit the ground. Cars roared past her, slowing, but none stopped, no one even rolled down the window to ask if she needed any help.

As she got to the edge of the parking lot, she saw her mother.

Vera stood smoking under the red-and-white-striped awning, well protected from the rain. Her blond hair was perfectly sculpted, her green dress undulating in the breeze. Reggie raised her arms to flag her down, but her mother was looking away from her, out past the giant bowling pin, down toward the airport, where a plane had just taken off.

"Mom!" Reggie yelled, imagining her mother would turn, see the shape she was in and come running. She was, after all, Reggie's rescuer in times of great need. She didn't need the heroics of Vera twirling a dog in her underclothes this time, only a shoulder to lean on and a promise to take her home, picking up the bike with its flat tire on the way.

Vera's head was still turned, and now Reggie saw what it was she was looking at: a car had just pulled into the parking lot and was making its way to the front of the building, headlights on, windshield wipers slapping. The driver slowed. Vera waved, put out her cigarette.

"Mom!" Reggie screamed, hobbling as fast as she could across the parking lot.

Maybe it was the pouring rain, the jet overhead, the engine of the car in the lot, or the combination—but her mother didn't hear her.

The car pulled up right next to the awning and Reggie noticed the left taillight was broken. The driver leaned across the seat and the passenger door popped open. The only detail Reggie could pick out was that he was wearing a baseball cap. Vera slid in. She never glanced in Reggie's direction.

"Mom!" Reggie cried out once more, cupping her hands around her mouth. "Don't!"

Too late.

The tan sedan pulled away.

Chapter 19

October 17, 2010
Brighton Falls, Connecticut

After her truce with Tara, Reggie headed back down to the smoke-scented kitchen. Lorraine was sitting at the table, sniffling. George was beside her, holding her hand and rubbing her back. He glanced up when Reggie walked in. He looked nearly the same as Reggie remembered, with his pointy, Uncle Mouse features, but there were tiny creases around his eyes, his hair was flecked with gray, and his hairline had receded farther. He wore round glasses with silver metal rims. He was dressed in khaki pants and a neatly ironed blue button-down shirt.

"Reggie," George said, rising for what Reggie assumed would be a hug. He was shorter than Reggie remembered, or maybe he'd developed a stooped posture, shoulders hunched forward like a man who'd suffered countless defeats.

Instead of embracing Reggie, George stepped past her and said, "Let's go out for some air," and headed down the hall. Lorraine stayed in place at the table, head down, dabbing at her eyes with a crumpled tissue.

"What did you say to Lorraine?" George asked once they were in the yard, the shadow of the house surrounding them, darkening everything. They stood facing Reggie's old tree house. The roof was still in good shape, but the windows had never been finished. The rope ladder swayed, wooden steps rotted through in places, but still, she half expected to see Charlie's face appear in the doorway, beckoning her up, asking where she'd been.

"Do you think she deserved it, is that it?" George asked. His voice was quiet, controlled, but he was obviously furious. "Do you think there's a day that goes by that she doesn't think about what might have happened if she had done things differently that night?"

"Look," Reggie began, "George, I—"

"It isn't right to blame her for what happened to your mother."

"I don't!"

"Yes, you do. You always have. Isn't that why you left home and never so much as called? You couldn't stand even looking at her. I remember how it was those last four years of high school. You just stopped speaking to her. You broke her heart, Reggie."

Reggie shook her head. This was insane. Lorraine had shut Reggie out of her heart the day she was born, just because she was Vera's daughter.

George ambled across the driveway and into the old wooden garage, Reggie following. Lorraine's fly-tying bench was still there, covered with an assortment of pliers, hooks, thread, and feathers. Tucked underneath was the dusty box of taxidermy supplies: little eyes on wire, sawdust, knives, and chemicals. Beside the bench stood the oak fishing cabinet George had made Lorraine. George caressed the front door, then opened it, revealing four fishing rods, a net, and Lorraine's worn fishing vest on a hanger. It reminded Reggie of a box a magician might put a woman in, then saw her in half. Or maybe he'd wave his wand, close the door, and make her disappear completely.

"Losing Vera, that was hard enough," George said, closing the cabinet. "That tore us all to pieces. But then we lost you, too."

This was too goddamn much.

"I'm sorry," Reggie said, standing up straight. "But I refuse to be made to feel guilty. I was only a kid, and I did the best I could. Lorraine treated me like crap my whole life, because I was my mother's daughter. She hated Vera, George! Don't you remember?"

George nodded. "They had their differences, yes, but—"

"Differences? Lorraine was always awful to her," Reggie interrupted. "She used to warn me to stay away from Mom, to lock my door at night."

"She was only trying to protect you!" George snapped.

"I didn't need protecting," Reggie hissed, the anger coming through. "Not from my own mother."

She turned away from him and saw Lorraine's mounted trout watching from the wall, dust covered and deformed, the rough black stitches on its belly showing. Franken-fish.

George was silent a minute, biting the inside of his cheek. "Sometimes," he said, "I wonder if you remember things the way they really were."

Reggie's head was pounding.

"Then maybe you'd be more appreciative for the sacrifices your aunt has made," George said.

"Oh give me a break," Reggie snarled, turning from the trout to stare at George. "What sacrifices?"

"Do you have any idea what it took to send you to the Brooker School for four years? And then there was college. You got to the place you are today because of Lorraine. She gave up a great deal for you."

"Is that what she told you?" Reggie said. "Yes, she paid for Brooker, but that was her choice, and I honestly think she sent me there because she was so ashamed of the way my mother had soiled the Dufrane name. And she never paid a dime for college, George. I worked my ass off for grants and scholarships, did shitty work-study jobs all through school, and still graduated with a shit-ton of debt, all of which I paid off *on my own*." She felt her anger spiraling up and out of control, and it felt good. She took a step toward George and pointed at him fiercely. "I did whatever it took to get as far away from this place as I could, this place where I was a stranger in my own home, where pain and loss were everywhere. So don't you dare stand there and try to make me feel guilty. I am where I am because of *me*. No one else."

Reggie turned away, breathing hard. She looked through the small window toward Monique's Wish. It seemed crooked from this angle, the afternoon sun hitting the worn and broken shingles on the roof, the stone walls seeming to list left, then right.

George muttered something, but her false ear was toward him and she didn't catch it. All she heard was one word: *ungrateful*.

"I'm done," she said, and stalked out of the garage.

Reggie moved across the driveway toward the house, slowly at first, then with determination. Before she knew it, she was jogging, only one thing sure in her mind: she was wrong to have come back. George and Lorraine obviously had their own version of history, in which Reggie was the nasty, ungrateful villain, responsible for all the pain in their fucked-up little family unit. To hell with all of them.

"Regina?" George called after her, but she didn't turn back.

She went inside, passing the kitchen, where she could hear her aunt making tea. She went hurriedly upstairs and into her room, where she shut the door tight and rested for a second with her back against it. She heard George come in downstairs. There was the scraping of chairs on the kitchen floor, the low murmur of voices. She turned, pressed her good ear against the door, trying to make out what they were saying.

"Did our best," George said. And then Lorraine began to cry again.

"Oh, give me a break," Reggie hissed.

In the room next door, she heard Vera say, "Have you ever been to Argentina, dear?"

"No," Tara told her. "No, I haven't."

Reggie looked up at the water stains on the ceiling, the circles like crooked yellow bull's-eyes. The stone wall on the north side of her room was like the wall of a prison—dark, thick, and impenetrable. And like the wall of a prison, she imagined that over the years it had picked up pieces of the lives it surrounded. The stones in the wall, like hundreds of dull eyes, had watched Reggie grow, knew all her secrets.

Heart hammering furiously, stones in the wall watching, she packed her things quickly—pulling the neat stacks of clothing from the bureau and tucking them into her rolling case. Reggie zipped her suitcase, shouldered her messenger bag, and went back down the hall, down the stairs, through the living room, and out the front door. Just like that, she was seventeen again, sneaking out at dawn to the taxi that waited in the driveway to take her to the Greyhound station, where she'd board a bus for Providence without even saying good-bye. It was that easy.

Reggie jumped in her truck, cranked the ignition. Tara's face appeared in the upstairs window of Vera's room, pulling back the curtain. Tara pressed her hand flat against the pane of glass, her palm pale and ghostly.

Reggie slammed the truck into reverse, turning around, tires spitting gravel. She turned on the GPS and pushed the button that said GO HOME.

Chapter 20

June 20, 1985
Brighton Falls, Connecticut

Reggie's clock radio said 8:58 A.M. The phone was ringing. Reggie put a pillow over her head, waited for Lorraine to answer it. The pain in her ankle was down to a dull throb. The bag of frozen peas Lorraine had sent her to bed with lay clammily on her toes.

After Reggie had called home from the pay phone outside the bowling alley, Lorraine had come to pick her up, retrieved the bicycle, and taken Reggie to the emergency room. It was only a sprain, but she was supposed to stay off it as much as possible until it healed. Reggie had told Lorraine about her mother getting into a tan car driven by a man whose face she didn't see. Lorraine said the color of the car didn't mean a thing, that Reggie had an overly active imagination, and that there was far too much nonsense and hysteria in Brighton Falls for her liking. Reggie was quiet after that.

In Reggie's dreams her mother got into the car with the broken taillight over and over again. Sometimes the driver was the devil. Sometimes it was Lorraine. The last time it was Reggie herself behind the wheel, and there was a big knife with a jagged blade on the seat between her and Vera.

The ringing stopped, then started again.

Reggie sat up, damp with cold sweat, shaking off the dreams, and grabbed the phone on her nightstand.

"Hullo?" she said in a groggy voice.

"Reg!" Tara shrieked. "Are you okay? Have you heard?"

"Heard what?"

"Oh shit! Listen, turn on the news, okay. I'm coming right over." Tara hung up before Reggie could respond.

Reggie lay back in bed, flipped on her clock radio. She dozed through the national news—something about President Reagan—but bolted upright when she heard the top local story.

A fourth hand in a milk carton had appeared at the police station. This one, the police spokesman said, bore a distinguishing mark: it was badly scarred from an old injury.

Severely disfigured, was how the policeman described it.

Reggie knew instantly that the hand was not only thick with scars, but was also stuck pointing, as it had done for eight years now, toward some unnameable place off in the distance.

Part Two

Day One

Excerpt from *Neptune's Hands: The True Story of the Unsolved Brighton Falls Slayings* by Martha S. Paquette

Neptune's final victim, Vera Dufrane, was a washed-up beauty queen with platinum blond hair who wore kid gloves, chain-smoked Winstons, and would convince men to buy her a drink by telling them she was once the Aphrodite Cold Cream girl. If you look back through old magazines, you might spot a copy of the one ad Vera was in: *Treat Yourself Like a Goddess,* the tagline said. And there was nineteen-year-old Vera, in a form-fitting white gown, pouty lips painted glossy red. In her hands, a jar of Aphrodite Cold Cream.

Aphrodite, the goddess of love and lust, a fitting deity for Vera. Her face was always perfectly made up, her clothing a bit too nice for the bars the now thirty-four-year-old Vera would frequent on Airport Road. She stood out like a movie star, and when a newcomer wandered into Silver Wings, Reuben's, or Runway 36, he'd inevitably be drawn to Vera, like a moth to a flame.

Neptune, no doubt, spotted her right off. What we don't know, what we can only speculate about, is whether he watched her for some time, waiting, hunting her down. Was he one of the regulars, a face Vera knew and trusted? Or was he someone new—a handsome man who stepped into the bar, saw her, and knew she had to be his?

Chapter 21

Wednesday, October 20, 2010
Rockland, Vermont

Logarithmic spiral. The swirling of tropical cyclones, a hawk circling its prey, spiral galaxies, the nautilus shell. Reggie drew spirals on paper, in her head, starting at the center, radiating out, growing. Reggie drew a spiral with a Sharpie, cut it out and glued it to the end of a pencil, twirling it, the pattern moving, hypnotic as she stared into the center. She studied the pattern, trying to put the perfect tiny mobile house inside it.

What did a person really need to live? Protection from the environment. Warmth. Food.

Add to this the ability to move—to pick up and go at a moment's notice.

Follow your dreams.

Follow your heart.

Run.

Run as fast and as far as you can.

Sometimes I wonder if you remember things the way they really were.

Fuck.

She'd thrown herself into her work since returning to Vermont, doing her best to forget all about her mother and Monique's Wish. Her home and office had always been her safe haven—the one place where she was in absolute control and nothing could touch her. And now she'd come back there like a dog with its tail between its legs.

Fucking coward.

She'd picked up the phone a hundred times to call since she ran off Sunday, to try to explain herself, but she never had the guts to actually dial. Reggie hated feeling powerless. She was used to being in control, knowing what to do in every situation. But she'd run away like a child and now she couldn't shake that little-girl feeling of uncertainty. It permeated everything, made her unable to focus.

What kind of daughter leaves her dying mother like that?

"They're better off without me," she told herself out loud, thinking of her mother lying naked on the bed, calling Tara an angel while she sprinkled powder over Vera's shriveled skin.

And if they wanted her, if they needed her in any way, they knew where to find her. She'd half expected George to call and apologize for being so hard on her, to beg her to come back. Or Tara to say, *I thought we had a deal—no more weird shit.*

But the phone didn't ring.

Reggie looked into the center of the spiral, trying to calm her mind. *Focus, damn it. Your work has always been the one thing you can get lost inside, the thing that saves you time and time again.*

But it was no good.

She glanced up, looked at the astrology chart Len had made, which was pinned to the bulletin board above her desk. She saw the little blue trident, Neptune in the twelfth house.

"It's what makes you so intuitive," Len had told her. "It's also why you're so tormented."

Reggie's skin prickled. She looked across her desk, her eye going to the coffee cup she used to hold her tools. She touched the handle of the X-Acto knife, then pulled her fingers away.

Restless, she left the office, changed, and went for a run—her usual five-mile loop around the lake. But even this wasn't right. She couldn't get into her running groove. She struggled, pushed herself too hard on the hills, muscles screaming, shaking, until finally she had to slow to a jog. "Goddamn it," she hissed. Feeling pissed off and defeated, she headed for home, relieved to see Len's truck in the driveway.

"You're home," he said, eyes gray and steely.

He was wearing paint-splattered Carhartts and a denim work shirt. His hair, black with streaks of silver, had that just-got-out-of-bed look Reggie loved. She stepped closer to him. He smelled like turpentine and marijuana.

"I'm sorry I didn't call. I've just been working too hard. Trying to get a handle on this new project. Come on in," she said, unlocking the door.

Len followed her into the kitchen. Reggie got herself a drink of water and gulped it down.

"How was Worcester?" Len asked.

"Draining," Reggie said, wiping the sweat from her forehead with her sleeve. "It turned out there wasn't much I could do there, so I came back." She set down her water glass and walked toward him, thinking that sex with Len might be just what she needed to break this rotten spell she'd been under.

"That's too bad," Len said, a strange stiffness in his voice. "When did you get back?"

"Sunday night," she admitted. "I really am sorry I didn't call. My head wasn't on straight after my trip and I just wanted to make some headway with the Nautilus house. You know how I hate being stuck with a project." She leaned forward and touched his chest, running her fingers up to his throat, along the side of his face where they scratched against the stubble.

"Reggie," he said quietly, "I know where you were. I know what happened."

"What?" She jerked her hand away.

"We get the news up here, too, remember? Did you really think I wouldn't find out? Christ, I saw the picture of you and your mom. It's a huge headline, Reg, Neptune's final victim showing up after all these years. Why didn't you tell me?" His voice sounded slightly strangled, the way it did when he was trying to keep his temper under control.

"Oh shit." She sighed. "I . . . I really don't know."

"Right," he said disgustedly.

"Maybe you were right," Reggie said. "Maybe it's because my sun and moon are at war with each other, and having Neptune in the twelfth house makes me prone to self-inflicted isolation?" She gave him a hopeful look.

"You don't believe in any of that," Len said, "and even if you did, having some hard shit in your chart is no excuse for treating the people who love you like crap."

It was like being slapped in the face. "When have I ever treated you like crap?"

"You lied to me, Reggie. If I really mattered to you, you would have told me about your mother."

"Of course you matter to me! Jesus, Len, how could you say that?" Her heart hammered its way up into her throat, the words *I'm sorry* getting stuck there until she swallowed them back down.

"I can't do this anymore," he said in a dull voice, backing away slowly, like his legs were extra heavy. He walked out of the house, closing the door behind him gently.

Reggie felt frozen, numb, the sweat on her body giving her cold chills. What the hell had just happened? "Len?" she called after him. "Len, wait!"

His truck started in the driveway, the sound of the engine jolting her to action. She ran across the room, threw open the door, and got outside just in time to see his taillights pulling away.

"Len!" she yelled after him, but he did not slow. "Shit!" she yelped again, hitting her open palm against the door frame. "Shit! Shit! Shit!" She hit the wood again and again until her hand was red and aching.

What you need, she heard a little voice tell her, *is something sharp.*

Inside the house, her phone was ringing.

She hurried back into the kitchen to answer, suddenly worried that it might be Lorraine with news about Vera: *Your mother took a sudden turn for the worse and you weren't here.* Or maybe, just maybe, it would be Neptune: *I gave her back to you and you ran away like a spineless, heartless little girl.*

"Hello?" Reggie said, nearly breathless, her throbbing hand wrapped tight around the phone.

"Regina?"

Reggie felt a lump in her throat. It was Lorraine. Reggie held her breath, waiting, trying to brace herself for the worst.

Lorraine was silent.

"Is Mom okay? Has something happened?" Reggie asked.

Reggie could hear her aunt breathing, panting almost, her breath ragged and desperate-sounding.

"He's back," Lorraine said at last. "Neptune. He left another hand on the steps of the police station this morning."

"What?" It didn't make sense. It had been twenty-five years.

"It's Tara," Lorraine whispered. "He's got Tara this time."

Chapter 22

June 20, 1985
Brighton Falls, Connecticut

Reggie had only been inside the police station twice before. Once, shortly after losing her ear to the dog, Lorraine had deposited her on a bench just inside the entryway with a *Josie and the Pussycats* coloring book and a Baggie of broken and wrapper-less crayons. When Lorraine returned, Vera was with her, staggering a little, her makeup smeared.

"Idiot cops," Vera spat. "I'm going to sue them for police brutality. They had no right to even pull me over. If they think for one goddamn minute—"

Lorraine silenced her with one deadly look.

They all went back to Monique's Wish, no one saying another word, and Vera was gone the next morning before breakfast.

The last time was on a class trip in second grade, which Reggie had done her best to forget about. But now, smelling the floor wax and hearing the hum of police radios and voices, it came back like a kick in the stomach.

She remembered the officer giving the tour had a sweet face that reminded her of John-Boy Walton. When he'd asked who was brave enough to get locked inside the holding cell while their teacher took the rest of the class to the dispatch room, Reggie's hand shot up, eager to prove herself. He had locked her and four other classmates behind bars. There was a wooden bench bolted to the wall, a sink, and a metal toilet with no seat. The walls were painted white cinder block. The place smelled so strongly of ammonia that the back of Reggie's throat burned. Then John-Boy had disappeared, jiggling the keys happily. Several minutes went by. The children called out to the officer, who didn't return. Reggie had to pee terribly but was unwilling to sit on the seatless toilet in front of the other kids.

At first, it was fun. They rattled the bars, talked about how they'd break out, teased each other about what kind of crimes had been committed by the bad guys who'd been held there. But the mood began to change, and a scared silence had descended upon the five of them. Finally, one of the boys said in a hollow voice, "He's not coming back. Is he?"

Panic swept through Reggie's body, clenching every muscle, and her bladder let go, the warmth spreading down the front of her jeans.

The squeals of laughter and disgust from her classmates—"You shoulda worn your diaper!" Becky Shelley cawed—finally brought the officer back. He was smiling cockily as he unlocked the cage.

"Didn't think I forgot you, did ya?" he asked.

When he saw Reggie's wet jeans and the puddle on the floor, he'd frowned and shook his head.

"Jesus," he muttered and called for the teacher.

As Reggie stood at the front desk between Tara and Charlie, her face reddened with that old sense of shame. She had wrapped up her ankle in an Ace bandage, dressed in a clean white button-down and tan chinos, thinking that might help the police take her seriously. She made herself stand tall. She was no accident-prone little kid anymore.

Going to the police station had been Tara's idea. She'd called Charlie, then told Tara's mother they were going to hang out and do some shopping, and could she give them a ride downtown? Lorraine was nowhere to be found. As soon as Tara's mom pulled away, they crossed the street and helped Reggie hobble up the steps of the police station. Two uniformed cops were standing guard outside, watching over the stairs. The left side of the granite steps had been closed off by yellow crime scene tape, and Reggie stared, picturing the milk carton with her mother's hand inside.

They'd had to weave around the knot of reporters and television crews who stood in the front hall, anxiously waiting for an update. Reggie heard one of them say, "It won't take them long to find who it belongs to. Not many ladies have hands all scarred up like that."

"We need to see my dad," Charlie told the desk sergeant once they pushed their way through to the sliding window below a sign: ALL VISITORS STOP HERE.

"He's busy, son," the desk sergeant said. He was a uniformed cop with a ruddy face, small eyes, and a strange patch of pale skin on his cheek. A burn, Reggie decided. Reggie considered herself a connoisseur of scars.

"It's important, Sergeant Stokes," Charlie said, lowering his voice. "We've got information about the hand."

Stokes squinted at Charlie. "What kind of information?"

Charlie gave Reggie a gentle tap on the shoulder. "Go ahead. Tell him."

Reggie glanced back over her shoulder to make sure there were no reporters listening. They were all still standing in a tight mass by the front doors, being held back by an officer who was promising another press conference soon.

Reggie cleared her throat. "I know who she is. The scars are mostly between the thumb and index finger, right? They're from a dog bite."

The desk sergeant studied the three kids a minute, then turned, picked up the phone, and mumbled into it. A minute later, a side door opened and Stu Berr appeared. He'd always been a heavyset man, but Reggie could see he'd put on weight since she'd last seen him. His navy blue suit jacket was buttoned but straining around the middle. His face was ruddy and bloated, his eyes small and bloodshot with dark circles under them. He had a mustache and hair that was starting to go gray.

"Detective Berr!" one of the reporters shouted, pushing past the uniformed cop in the hall and coming their way. "Do you know who the hand belongs to?"

Stu gave him a disgusted look. "If you can't stay back in the area reserved for the press, I'll have you escorted from the building."

"But the hand—the scars—"

"Officer MacMillan," Stu called to the uniformed cop, "please see that this gentleman is removed from the station." He watched the reporter leave through the double doors, then turned to face them.

"Hello, Charlie," he said. He studied Reggie a minute, blinking. "Regina? Good to see you again." Then his eyes moved to Tara and seemed to narrow. "Hello, Tara," he said.

Tara stuck out her hand. "Nice to see you again," she said, voice chipper and bright. He shook her hand with a puzzled and wary look. Tara pumped his hand up and down, her whole body bouncing like she had a giant spring inside her.

"Stokes says you have information?" he said, backing away from Tara.

"The latest victim," Tara said. "We know who she is. The hand was scarred from an old dog bite." Her voice was coiled with excitement.

Stu Berr didn't show any sign of a reaction, just studied Tara for a few seconds before speaking again.

"So who is she? This gal you know with the dog bite."

Tara nudged Reggie, in a way that was more of a body check than a nudge. "Tell him, Reg. Tell him everything."

Stu Berr turned his big, jowly face from Tara to Reggie.

Reggie took in a breath and spoke the words. "I think it's my mother, Vera Dufrane." Stu Berr looked at Reggie, then scanned the hallway. The reporters were keeping their distance, but Stu wasn't taking chances. He pulled the kids farther back down the hall toward a bench and had Reggie sit down next to him. It was the same bench Reggie had been left on when she was five and Lorraine came to the station to pick up Vera.

"What makes you think that?" the detective asked in a low voice.

"The scars are between the thumb and index finger, right? A dog attacked me when I was five, she pulled it off, and her hand got all torn up. She could never bend her pointer finger after the accident. The dog . . ." Reggie reached up and touched her new ear, felt the scars behind it.

A light seemed to go on behind Stu Berr's eyes, making them glitter in the dim hallway.

She wondered if Stu remembered, if he'd ever seen her mother's hand. She tried to remember a time when Charlie's dad and her mom were ever together, and couldn't. She could picture her mom talking with Charlie's mom a few times at birthday parties and school events, but Charlie's dad was never around. And

Vera usually wore gloves in public to hide her ruined hand. People thought she was being chic in an old-fashioned way.

Stu Berr pulled a small pad from the front pocket of his jacket and scribbled something down.

"When was the last time you saw her?" he asked, still holding pen to paper.

"Yesterday. At the bowling alley. I was supposed to meet her there but my bike got a flat tire. Then I twisted my ankle running, so I didn't show up in time. She said . . . she said she wanted me to meet some guy. A guy she was gonna marry."

Tara gasped. "You didn't tell us that!"

Reggie looked back at Stu Berr. "But I was late. By the time I got to the edge of the parking lot, she was getting into a tan car. I called, but she didn't hear me."

"Did you get a look at the driver?"

"No, I was too far away. He was wearing a hat. A baseball cap. And the left taillight was out."

Stu Berr scribbled furiously in his little notebook. "So it wasn't a car you recognized? "

Reggie shook her head. "No. But a couple weeks ago, she met a man at the bowling alley and ended up leaving with him. He drove a tan car."

"The same car?"

"I can't say for sure, but it could have been."

"Of course it's the same car!" Tara squealed. "How could it not be?"

Reggie told Stu everything she could remember about the man in the bowling alley.

Stu Berr closed his notebook. "Is there someone at your house now?" he asked Reggie. "Someone to look after you since your mom's not around?"

Reggie nodded. "My aunt Lorraine. She lives with us."

Stu Berr nodded. "Thanks for coming in," he said. He stood up and started to walk away.

"Umm, Detective Berr?" Tara called. "Do you think we could get a ride home? Reggie's ankle is all messed up. My mom dropped us off here, but she had to get to work."

"Sure," he said. "Go wait outside and I'll send a cruiser around."

They crossed the cool marble floored entry hall, passing the throng of reporters, and made their way out the thick glass doors into the sticky morning. Reggie's ankle throbbed and she was limping.

The cop at the top of the steps held the door for them. "You all have a good day, now," he said, eyes hidden behind mirrored sunglasses.

"Can you believe it?" Tara practically squealed. "We get to ride in a cop car! Do you think we can ask them to turn on the lights and siren?"

Charlie rolled his eyes. "Jesus, Tara! What are you, seven?"

Reggie hobbled down the side of the steps that wasn't taped off, Charlie holding her arm.

They plunked themselves down on a bench at the bottom, and Reggie bit her lip hard, willing herself not to cry.

"It hurts bad, huh?" Charlie asked, nodding toward her ankle.

Reggie nodded, wiped at her eyes, and turned to look at the steps behind them where, just hours ago, her mother's hand had been left in a milk carton.

At the top of the steps was the arched entryway they'd just come out of. The two cops stood on opposite sides, like gargoyles in uniform.

The words PROTECT AND SERVE engraved above the doors seemed, to Reggie, an impossible promise.

Chapter 23

October 20, 2010
Brighton Falls, Connecticut

"When was the last time you saw her?" Reggie asked her aunt. They were seated at the kitchen table of Monique's Wish. It was nearly seven o'clock. Reggie had thrown a bag together quickly, stopping in the kitchen long enough to grab her espresso pot and a bag of ground coffee. She'd driven back to Brighton Falls as fast as she could, hesitating only when she got to the front door of Monique's Wish. She had stood, hand on the knob, feeling as if the house was alive, breathing and hungry. That it just might gobble her up and spit out the bones. Then she'd touched the hourglass necklace, thought of Tara, and stepped inside.

Now, the coffee bubbled on the stove, filling the kitchen with its familiar rich aroma, comforting Reggie on some deep level.

Len had called and left a message on her phone an hour ago, just as she'd crossed the state line into Connecticut. She nearly answered.

"Shit, Reggie, I just heard Neptune's left another hand! I'm at your house and it's all locked up. Where are you?" His voice was crackling with panic. She should call him. She knew she should. But part of her was still good and pissed about the way he'd walked out of her house and got a little twinge of satisfaction from letting him stew in worry. It was twisted, and she knew it. She told herself she had bigger things to worry about than whether she and Len might have a future together.

The *Hartford Examiner* was on the table between Reggie and Lorraine. The headline read HAS NEPTUNE RETURNED TO BRIGHTON FALLS? And there was a brief article describing how a new hand had been found in a milk carton on the front steps of the police station. The article said the police knew who the hand belonged to but refused to comment at this time. Reggie knew it wouldn't take the papers long to find out who Tara was and that she'd been working as Vera Dufrane's private nurse. The media were going to have a field day with this one. Martha Paquette was going to be over the goddamn moon.

"Monday morning. She left to go pick up a prescription refill for your mother and to do a few other errands. She never got to the pharmacy. I've told the police all of this over and over," Lorraine said. She looked exhausted and wrung her hands together as she spoke. "That young Detective Levi was here. He asked so many questions my head was spinning. Then he went up and searched through Tara's room. It was just like before. Just like when your mother—"

Reggie cut her off.

"Did Tara say what other errands she had to do?"

"No," Lorraine said. "But she was in a hurry. She seemed very tense, but Vera had had a bad night, and Tara was up with her. I don't think she got much sleep."

"A bad night?"

"A horrible night, actually—she woke us up screaming, insisting that Neptune was here, in the house, that he'd come through a door in the wall above her bed. I went in and tried to help, but that just made her more frantic. Tara finally had to sedate her. They were up for a while after that, whispering. I even heard poor Tara singing to her—I think that's how she finally got to sleep."

Reggie's shoulders slumped. She shouldn't have left. She should have been here for her mother, for Tara.

Maybe if she'd stayed, Tara wouldn't have been taken. But why Tara? Maybe the answer wasn't so complicated. Reggie remembered the copy of *Neptune's Hands* Tara had pulled out of her bag, the way she'd confessed to hoping Vera might give her some clues to help her figure out who Neptune was.

What if she finally got her wish?

Be careful what you wish for. That was something Lorraine used to say all the time when Reggie wished out loud for things like not having to take the SATs or eat fish again for supper.

"Do you think Mom could have said something to her? Given her a clue that might have led Tara to Neptune?"

Lorraine frowned. "Regina, don't be ridiculous. Tara's a smart girl. I can't believe she'd go chasing after a killer on her own."

Reggie nodded, thinking, *But you don't know Tara like I do.* Going after Neptune was *exactly* something Tara would do. But that was the Tara of twenty-five years ago. Did the grown-up Tara have just enough of a reckless streak to try something so dangerous?

Reggie stood up, took the espresso pot off the burner, and poured a cup for herself. She made Lorraine a cup of peppermint tea.

"Okay," Reggie said. "First thing is, we talk only to the police. No press. Second, I think we need to get some decent locks put on the doors here."

"What about another nurse for your mother?" Lorraine said.

"No," Reggie said. "We'll take care of her ourselves as long as we can. I don't think it's safe bringing in a stranger."

Lorraine nodded, then stared down at the tea Reggie had placed in front of her. She continued to clutch at her own hands, which were dry and chapped. "Poor Tara," she said.

Reggie took a sip of espresso. "It's day one," she said.

"What?" Lorraine said, picking up her cup and taking a tentative sip.

"If it really is Neptune and he sticks to his regular schedule, I've got to find her before day five." If Tara could be brave and reckless, then so could Reggie. She thought of Levi, the bumbling boy detective, and knew that the police couldn't save Tara. It was up to Reggie. And this time around, she wasn't a scared thirteen-year-old kid. She was no detective, but she was good at problem solving, at putting a string of unlikely things together and having them make sense. If she could design an award-winning house, couldn't she put those same skills to use to figure out a way to capture this son of a bitch before he killed Tara?

Lorraine choked on her tea. "And how are you going to do that?" she asked once she was done coughing.

"However I can," Reggie said, reaching absent-mindedly for the hourglass, turning it over.

Upstairs, a bell jingled.

"That's your mother," Lorraine said, standing. "Tara got her a bell so she can call for us whenever she needs anything."

"I'll go," Reggie said, sucking down the rest of her coffee and heading for the stairs.

"It's you," Vera said, peering up at Reggie.

"Yes," Reggie said, squinting at her mother in the dim light. There was a radio playing an old Bob Seger song. The room smelled of medicine and talcum powder.

"But they said you went away."

Reggie smiled down. "I came back."

"Where's my angel? The one who sings?"

"Tara's not here, Mom."

"Where is she?"

"I think he's got her," Reggie said.

"He?"

"The man who took you. The man who cut off your hand. Neptune."

Vera closed her eyes tight, the muscles of her face contracting, accentuating the bones, making her look like a skin-covered skull.

"Do you know who he is, Mom? Do you know where he's taken Tara?"

When Vera opened her eyes, she smiled, and Reggie felt a glimmer of hope. "Do you know the weather in Argentina?" she asked.

Reggie sighed. "No, Mom, I don't."

"The seasons are reversed. Fall here, spring there. You just have to look around you and know that down there, it's the exact opposite."

Reggie nodded. "Can I get you anything, Mom?"

"Some ice cream would be nice," Vera said.

"Coming right up."

Reggie went down to the kitchen, put a scoop of chocolate ice cream in a little dish, and brought it back up. Her mother was fast asleep. Reggie set the ice cream on the bedside table, next to a clipboard that had a chart to help them keep track of medications. Her mother got long-acting morphine every twelve hours, short-acting morphine every four, clonazepam for anxiety every six. And if she was especially agitated, she could have lorazepam. It looked from the chart like she'd been getting the maximum dose of everything since Sunday night. No wonder she wasn't making any sense.

Reggie left her mother's room and went across the hall, into the room Tara had been staying in. The bed was made. Tara's empty backpack sat on a chair, and Reggie went through the pockets but found nothing. Reggie opened dresser drawers, finding underwear, socks, T-shirts, jeans, and sweaters. It felt invasive, pawing through another woman's clothing like this, but she was desperate to find any sort of clue. The neat piles of clothing Tara had made were all disheveled—Detective Levi had already searched through them and found nothing. It seemed foolish, looking anyway. But she told herself that maybe there was something he'd missed; something only a kindred spirit, a blood sister, might be able to find.

The bedside table held only a flashlight, a purple pen, and a half-full glass of water.

What did you expect? she asked herself. *A treasure map leading right to Neptune?*

If only.

Her heart sank into her stomach. She was failing Tara already. She looked down at her watch, seeing the seconds click by while Tara sat tied up in a dungeon somewhere, her right arm ending in a club of bandages.

Reggie felt like she'd been thrust into the middle of one of Tara's old games. *I've been taken captive by a serial killer. You have four days to follow the clues and find me.* It felt like a test and a cruel joke and a nightmare all tangled up together.

"I'll find you," Reggie said to the empty bed. She picked up the half-full glass of water, took a sip, imagining Tara's lips on this same glass the night before last.

Reggie went over to the bookshelves, hesitating a moment before she finally gave in and pulled out *War and Peace.* There, behind it, she found Tara's hidden dog-eared copy of *Neptune's Hands.*

"Ha!" she said out loud. Evidently the boy detective had neglected to search the shelves.

She moved her fingers over the raised silver trident on the cover, felt the gaudy crimson drops of blood that dripped from it.

Reggie tucked the book under her shirt in case she met up with Lorraine in the hall, and headed back to her own room, checking in on Vera—still sleeping.

Back in her old bedroom, she closed and locked the door, and set *Neptune's Hands* down on the bed, neatly made with the Drunkard's Path quilt. She grabbed her messenger bag and pulled out her sketchbook and pens. Then, with sure steps, shoulders squared, Reggie went right for the closet, flung open the door, and reached for the old cigar box on the shelf, carrying that over to the bed as well.

She opened the lid with trembling fingers and with a horrible sense that she'd just let the genie out of the bottle.

Chapter 24

June 20, 1985
Brighton Falls, Connecticut

"You've gotta say something," Tara said.

Reggie, Charlie, and Tara were in Reggie's living room, listening to Lorraine in the kitchen. She was cleaning fish for dinner, humming as she worked. They could hear water running, the sound of a knife on a cutting board and sticky scraping sounds. Reggie pictured Lorraine deftly slitting open the belly, pulling out skeins of entrails, her fingers covered in sparkling scales.

Lorraine had been gone all day, and Reggie was starting to get worried. Then, half an hour ago, she, Charlie, and Tara had spotted Lorraine stepping out of the woods in her huge rubber waders and fishing vest, carrying her fly-fishing pole and a string of trout. From a distance, she looked like a strange monster—half frog, half woman—squishing her way up the bank.

Now she cleaned fish in the kitchen, oblivious to the news that a new hand—a hand thick with scars—had been found.

Tara was pacing, unable to hold still. "Vera's her sister! She should know."

"I already tried," Reggie said, sitting because she felt queasy. "Last night I told her about my mom getting into a tan car. She said she didn't want to hear another word about it."

"The scarred hand, Reg," Tara said, stopping to gesture at Reggie with her own intact right hand with its chipped blue nail polish. "The tan car. Did you see Charlie's dad's face when you told him that part? And that thing about what your mom said about getting married—what if that's how Neptune lures the women away? You need to tell Lorraine all of it. Tell her you went to the cops and that they're checking into it."

"I can't tell her I did that!" Reggie yelped. "She'd shoot me!"

"Why?" Charlie asked.

"Because. She's kind of a freak about my mom. And besides, I promised her I wouldn't even leave the house. If she finds out I went to the police station this morning—"

"But this is her sister!" Tara shrieked. Maybe she was hoping Lorraine would hear them, come in to see what all the fuss was about, and learn the truth. "And Neptune might have her right now at this very minute. Don't you think she might want to know?"

Reggie shook her head. "I think she'd be glad."

Charlie gasped. "What? How can you say that?"

"You should have heard Lorraine the night before last. She threw my mom out of the house! She hates her."

"I don't believe it," Charlie said. "Lorraine may be a little weird, but she's not like that."

"That's what you think," Reggie said.

"I don't get it," Tara said, scowling. "Your mom is so cool. How could her own sister hate her?"

"I don't know. But she always has. Maybe she's jealous. My mom's got the looks, the talent, and what has Lorraine got? A bunch of dead trout, her weird little bench in the garage where she sits for hours tying flies being watched over by Franken-fish."

"Holy shit," Tara said, eyes huge as she smacked herself in the forehead. "What if Neptune's not a guy at all? Maybe it's Lorraine!"

Sometimes Reggie really couldn't believe the things that came out of Tara's mouth. Her dowdy aunt in her fishing vest a serial killer? Reggie had to swallow down a laugh.

"You're nuts!" Charlie yelped. "There is no way Reggie's aunt is a serial killer."

"Think about it, Charlie," Tara said, voice raised with excitement. "She's jealous, antisocial, and great with a filleting knife. And you should see all the crazy stuff she's got in that garage—I mean, what kind of person is into taxidermy?"

Charlie rolled his eyes and let himself sink farther back into the couch.

"And didn't you say you couldn't find her this morning?" Tara asked Reggie. "That you called out over the bank and she didn't answer? If she was really fishing at the brook all day, then wouldn't she have heard you?"

"Maybe she walked down to the pond," Reggie said, a lump forming in her throat. There was no way Lorraine was a murderer. But isn't that what all the people close to actual serial killers always said?

The doorbell rang and they heard Lorraine running water, then walking across the kitchen and down the hall.

"Lorraine Dufrane?" a male voice said. Reggie got up and peeked down the hall. Her aunt's tall frame filled the doorway, but in front of her was a man Reggie recognized at once: Stu Berr. Reggie's stomach felt tight and twisted. She turned her head so that she could hear better.

"I'm Detective Berr with the Brighton Falls Police Department."

"Yes, of course. I remember you, Stuart."

"Is there somewhere we can talk?"

Lorraine stepped outside, closing the door.

"Oh my God, was that Charlie's dad?" Tara's breath was hot in Reggie's good ear.

Reggie couldn't answer. She stood frozen in silence.

"We've gotta find out what they're saying," Tara said, standing on tiptoes to look out the window at the top of the front door. Lorraine and Detective Berr were standing in the yard. "Come on, let's go out the back and sneak around the house. We can hide in the bushes." She tugged on Reggie's arm, but Reggie couldn't move, so Tara let go and ran off toward the kitchen. Reggie watched her go, then slowly, with leaden legs, walked back into the living room and took a seat on the couch beside Charlie.

"What's going on?" he asked.

"Your dad's here."

"What?"

"He's outside, talking to Lorraine. Tara went on a recon mission to see what she could find out.

She probably thinks he's gonna arrest Lorraine or something."

Was he? Or was he here to tell her they'd identified the hand?

Charlie stood up.

"Please don't," Reggie said, reaching for his arm and holding it a little too tight. "I think we should just wait here. Can we do that? Can you just wait here with me?"

Charlie nodded, looking down at Reggie's hand on his arm, probably wondering if he really had a choice.

"Reggie, there's something you should know. Something my dad told me, but he made me swear not to tell anyone, because it's like confidential police stuff."

Reggie nodded, waiting.

"Tara was caught breaking into Ann Stickney's apartment a couple days ago."

"What?" Reggie pictured the photo of the fresh-faced, smiling college student that had appeared on the front page of the *Hartford Examiner* after her body was found.

"Ann's roommate came home and found Tara in the kitchen. I guess she'd picked the lock. The roommate found her just sitting there, eating a bowl of cereal. They aren't going to press charges or anything."

"Why didn't she tell us?" Reggie asked.

Charlie shrugged. "Why would she? I mean, it's kind of a screwed-up thing to get caught doing. Nothing to go around bragging about."

Reggie opened her mouth to tell Charlie about the little doll shoe Tara carried that she'd stolen from the first victim's house, but she couldn't do it.

Instead she turned on the TV and watched a car chase that seemed to go on forever. She set the remote back down on the coffee table and noticed a safety pin there. She imagined picking it up, opening it, running the point across her skin.

In ten minutes, Tara was back. She grabbed the remote and hit the mute button, standing in front of the TV. Behind her, one of the cars had crashed and was in flames.

"It's her," she announced. Her eyes, ringed with smudgy kohl black makeup, were open wide. She looked like an excited panda bear. "The hand belongs to your mom, Reg." Tara's mouth trembled a little, and Reggie was sure she was suppressing an excited smile.

Everything started to spin and Reggie closed her eyes.

"How do they know for sure?" Charlie asked, his voice low and serious.

"Fingerprints," Tara explained. "I guess Vera was arrested once or something and they had her prints on file."

"Arrested?" Charlie said.

Reggie remembered going with Lorraine to pick her mother up from the police station. What had she been arrested for?

Reggie stood up and walked down the hall.

"Reg," Tara called after her.

"Leave her," Charlie said.

Reggie went through the front door in time to catch the taillights of Stu Berr's car moving down the driveway. The door to the garage closed with a quiet thud, signaling that Lorraine had retreated to her fly-tying workshop. Reggie followed, walking up to the door, not sure what she was going to say, but knowing she needed to find a way to make her aunt tell her everything: what Detective Berr had said, why the police had had Vera's fingerprints on file.

She's my mother, Reggie planned to say. *I have a right to know.*

She put her hand on the doorknob and was about to turn it when a sound stopped her. It began as a low moan and worked its way up to the fierce howl of an animal in pain. Reggie let go of the doorknob and stepped sideways, peeking in the small window.

Her aunt was doubled over, hands clenched into fists, screaming. When she straightened herself, she began flinging everything off her workbench: tiny hooks, feathers, thread, wire, and tools all falling to the cold cement floor. The hideously deformed stuffed trout watched from the far wall, his glass eye dull. Reggie took a step back, then turned and ran back to the house, knees wobbly, chest aching.

"The cops aren't gonna do shit," Tara was saying when Reggie walked back into the living room. Tara caught sight of her and said, "I'm sorry, Reg, but you know it's true. If we want to find your mom, we're gonna have to do it on our own."

"Right," Reggie said, trying to swallow the lump in her throat back down. "And how are we supposed to do that?" She looked back down at the safety pin, her skin feeling prickly, almost like it was begging for her to pick the pin up and open it.

"We go to the places where you know she hangs out. We look for the theater she's been rehearsing at and find some of her friends. Someone's bound to have seen her. Someone's gotta know who this guy is she was planning on marrying."

"Don't you think my dad and the other cops have already tried that?" Charlie asked.

"No doubt. But come on, who's gonna talk to cops? You're Vera's daughter. Her friends will talk to you. I'm sure they will." Tara's eyes were bright and glittering. She fingered the hourglass charm around her neck. "Your mother deserves our best shot, Reg. So do the other victims—Andrea, Candace, Ann." Tara reached into her pocket and fiddled with something. Was she still carrying around that doll shoe? Did she have something new in there as well—a little trinket picked up from Ann's apartment?

It scared Reggie a little—how *consumed* Tara had become with all of this. But deep down, she believed Tara was right—the police were not going to catch this guy. They'd had their chance and failed three times. And this time was different. This time, it was her own mother's life at stake.

"I don't know the name of the theater—it's down in New Haven somewhere. I know the director's name is Rabbit. He lives around here, I think. I know that sometimes they drive back and go to the bars on Airport Road. My mom's bag is always full of matchbooks from those places—places like Runway 36 and Reuben's."

Tara nodded. "So we start there."

Day Two

Excerpt from *Neptune's Hands: The True Story of the Unsolved Brighton Falls Slayings* by Martha S. Paquette

When Vera Dufrane's hand was indentified, the police began questioning boyfriends, past and present. The one they immediately zeroed in on was forty-six-year-old James Jacovich. Jacovich was reportedly one of Vera Dufrane's on-again, off-again boyfriends. He was a small-time drug dealer who went by the name Rabbit.

Jacovich had recently been released from prison, where he'd been serving a two-year sentence for selling cocaine to an undercover narcotics officer. He'd gotten out early for good behavior and on the condition that he would live in supervised housing and take part in a drug treatment program.

On June 21, the day after Vera's hand was discovered on the steps of the police station, Jacovich was picked up and charged with driving under the influence—the violation of the conditions of his release meant a one-way ticket back to prison. Jacovich was driving a tan Impala with a broken taillight, just like the car Vera Dufrane's daughter had witnessed her mother getting into the day of her disappearance, and similar to the one described by Candace Jacques's coworkers.

The police held Jacovich overnight, questioning him. In the end, they could find no solid evidence linking him to the Neptune crimes.

"I had an alibi," Jacovich told me when I sat down to interview him at the West Hills Correctional Facility, the July after the murders. He was a tall, thin man with nervous, watery brown eyes. "I was at a court-mandated NA meeting the night Vera got taken," he explained. "I was with my sponsor after. I was having a tough time, see, and he let me spend the night on his couch."

What about Candace Jacques, Ann Stickney, and Andrea McFerlin? Did he ever have any contact with any of them?

"The only things I know about any of those ladies are what I read in the paper. I never met any of them."

Chapter 25

October 21, 2010
Brighton Falls, Connecticut

Reggie was on her back in a cave, someplace dark and airless. Her hands and feet were bound. A bell was ringing, quietly at first, then louder, like the clattering warning of a railroad crossing—the train is coming, stay back.

She thrashed her way into a sitting position, opened her eyes. Her watch said 8:00 A.M. Reggie squinted at it, then around her childhood bedroom, up at the water stains on the ceiling.

She wondered what Tara was looking at right now.

Down the hall, Vera's bell was ringing.

Reggie was on top of the covers, still dressed, the contents of the memory box strewn out on the quilt around her: matchbooks, photographs, the wooden swan George had given Vera just before she disappeared. *Neptune's Hands* lay open on her lap. She must have drifted off around four in the morning, eyes and brain fuzzy.

The room felt hot and stuffy. She needed to get that window open. She'd bring in some tools later, see if she could loosen it.

"Coming, Mom!" Reggie shouted, grabbing the book and stashing it under her mattress, like a kid hiding porn. Her back ached and her skull was vibrating with names and little details—the men her mother dated: Rabbit, Sal the photographer, Mr. Hollywood; the bars her mother frequented, places Reggie hadn't thought of in years, places whose very names conjured up the smell of stale beer and cigarette smoke: Reuben's, Runway 36, Silver Wings—she had matchbooks and paper coasters from each of these places. She thought of the bar her mother had taken her to the day she lost her ear, the place with the spinning stools where they'd met the Boxer.

Did you know I was the Aphrodite Cold Cream girl?

Want to see a trick? Buy me a drink and I'll show you.

She could see it so clearly, her mother's perfect hand holding the egg the bartender had given her, her nails a gory red against the white of the shell.

Reggie blinked, running her fingers over the latex folds of her prosthetic ear. She stopped at her bedroom door, which was slightly ajar. Hadn't she fallen asleep with the door locked last night? She was sure she had. An unnerving feeling wormed its way through her as she stood with her hand on the knob.

The bell jangled harder, faster.

"Coming!" she called.

She pushed open the door and practically ran into Lorraine. "Shit!" Reggie yelped. "You scared me."

"Sorry," Lorraine mumbled, looking startled herself. She was in her old flannel nightgown, gray hair down and tangled-looking. "I was just going for your mother."

"I got it," Reggie said. "You go try to sleep in a little."

Reggie walked down the carpeted hall and into the bedroom, where her mother flailed a brass bell through the air with her left hand.

"Good morning," Reggie said, smiling down, rubbing sleep from her eyes.

"He's here," her mother wailed, voice shaking, eyes panicked as a mouse in a trap.

"Where?" Reggie asked, instantly awake, skin prickling from the rush of adrenaline.

"Under the bed."

Reggie drew in a breath, got down on her hands and knees, and peered under the bed.

"There's nothing, Mom," Reggie said, feeling her body relax.

Vera laughed, a terrible wheezing sound. "That's just what Old Scratch wants you to think." She shifted around in the bed, looking impossibly small under the covers.

Reggie turned and did a quick sweep of the room. The closet door was closed. She opened it slowly, standing off to the side. Nothing. Only a few old dresses on hangers and the smell of mothballs.

"Let's get a pillow behind you," Reggie said, going back over to the bed. "You don't look very comfortable. Hand me the bell."

Reggie took the brass bell, and something else fell out of her mother's hand. A tiny scrap of paper fluttered down onto the covers.

"What's this?" she asked, picking it up from the damp tangle of sheets. It was a small square of newsprint, neatly folded. Reggie opened it up to discover the article from yesterday's *Examiner*: HAS NEPTUNE RETURNED TO BRIGHTON FALLS? The edges neatly cut.

"Where did you get this?" Reggie asked. "Did Lorraine give it to you?"

Reggie looked back down at the article and saw that at the very bottom of the page, someone had printed a message in blue ink, using neat block letters:

REGINA WILL BE NEXT

She took in a gasping breath, as if stung.

Vera shook her head. “He did.”

“Mom, for God’s sake, who is ‘he’? Who are you talking about?”

“There was a crooked man and he walked a crooked mile,” Vera whispered.

Reggie’s whole body was vibrating with panic like a tuning fork. She heard footsteps creeping in the hallway, moving toward them. She looked for a weapon and picked up the lamp on her mother’s bedside table.

“Thought I’d see if I could lend a hand,” Lorraine said as she came into the room in her fluffy terry cloth robe. “Trouble with the light?”

“I’ll be right back,” Reggie said, setting the lamp down, hurrying past her aunt, down the halls and downstairs to the kitchen, still clutching the newspaper clipping. The table was cleaned off and she went for the recycling bin next to the garbage can.

“Are you okay?” Lorraine asked. She’d followed Reggie down to the kitchen and now stood, looking perplexed as Reggie pawed through junk mail, juice bottles, and tuna cans.

"Yesterday's paper," Reggie said. "Where is it?"

"I don't know. It was on the table. The last time I saw it was when you were reading it."

Reggie looked through the kitchen trash, but the bag was empty.

"You took the trash out?"

"There was fish in there. I didn't want it stinking up the kitchen."

Reggie went out through the front door, down the steps, nearly tripping over this morning's edition of the *Hartford Examiner*, which was wrapped in a blue plastic bag, tossed onto the bottom step. Reggie hurried across the driveway, where she found the tall, green wheeled can beside the garage. She opened the lid, and there, on top of the white bags, was yesterday's paper, the lead story neatly cut out of it.

So either someone came into the house, cut out the article, and gave it to Vera, or it was Lorraine. Or maybe her mother had sneaked downstairs and clipped out the article herself, writing the warning at the bottom like some kind of sibyl.

None of those possibilities gave Reggie a warm, glowing feeling.

Shit.

Her mind circled back again to Lorraine, and she told herself she was an idiot for even considering it. Still, the doors had been locked, and Reggie knew she hadn't given her mother the newspaper. But why would Lorraine do it? To threaten Vera? To keep her quiet? That would only make sense if . . . if Lorraine was Neptune.

"Impossible," Reggie said out loud as she tossed the newspaper with the cut-out front page back into the trash can. She looked down at the article in her hand with its ominous message penned in blue ink:

REGINA WILL BE NEXT

She was about to head back inside and make some coffee when she heard a car coming up the driveway. It was a dark sedan, and as it pulled up right behind Reggie's truck, she recognized the driver. Detective Levi.

"Morning," Reggie said as he got out of his car. She tried to keep her face bright and cheerful, and not let any of the morning's anxiety show through. She stuffed the cut-out article with its neatly written warning into the front pocket of her jeans.

"I was hoping I'd catch you," he said. "When I spoke to your aunt yesterday she told me you were on your way back."

Reggie nodded. "What can I do for you?"

He pulled a small notebook out of his jacket pocket and flipped through it. "I understand you and Tara Dickenson were close?"

"For a while when we were kids."

"Not so much now?"

"Last Saturday was the first time I'd seen her in twenty-five years."

"So you don't know anything about her current friends, family, a boyfriend?"

Reggie shook her head, looked back toward the house to see Lorraine watching them through the kitchen window. "The only family I ever met was her mom. She talked about aunts and cousins, but I don't know any of them."

"Her mother passed away two years ago. And I can't seem to find any other family."

"Did you check places she'd worked—the hospital, the hospice agency? Someone there might know something." Christ, it was ridiculous, Reggie feeling like she needed to do his job for him.

Evidently he didn't approve either. He gave her an annoyed look. "Of course. Those individuals have already been interviewed."

"I'm sorry I can't help you," Reggie said. She touched the piece of newspaper in her pocket and thought briefly of showing Detective Levi. But what good would it do? He'd probably put them under constant surveillance, have a cop following Reggie wherever she went, and what were her chances of finding Tara then?

"If you don't mind, I need to get back inside. My mom just got up and I've got to go get her cleaned up and fed."

"Just one more thing for now, Ms. Dufrane. I understand you and Tara were close back when your mother was taken?"

Reggie nodded, felt a lump in throat. If he asked what had happened to their friendship, she'd just give him the standard line—*people change, grow apart, we went to different schools.*

Detective Levi cleared his throat. "Can you tell me about Tara's reaction to the Neptune killings?"

"Her *reaction*?"

"See, I was going through old notes and I discovered that Tara was caught breaking into one of the victims' apartments—Ann Stickney. Thc officers who questioned her seemed to feel she was a little—obsessed—with the Neptune case."

Reggie stiffened. "We were all a little obsessed, Detective. It was a small town, a lot smaller then, and it was the biggest thing that had ever happened to any of us."

Detective Levi nodded and closed his notebook. "Did you know that Tara spent some time in a psychiatric hospital? Just after high school."

"No, I—like I said, we lost touch."

"Apparently her mother found her trying to cut her own right hand off." He studied her face, watching her reaction.

Reggie coughed to cover up the gasp that had slipped out. The ornate bird tattoo over Tara's wrist. She'd had it done to cover the scars.

"I'm sorry, but I've got to get inside," Reggie said, head spinning.

"I'll be in touch soon," Detective Levi said. He got in his car and started to back carefully down the driveway.

She was heading back toward the house when she heard a strange shuffling noise somewhere behind her. Reggie turned, her body humming, jaw locked, her one ear listening as hard as it could.

The tree. It had come from up in the tree.

A squirrel jumping from branch to branch, maybe?

No.

She heard it again. The sound of something sliding across old creaky floorboards.

Something was inside the tree house. The old tree house was about ten feet up, and the rope ladder was swinging slightly, even though there was no breeze.

Reggie listened to what sounded like footsteps.

She turned back down the driveway, watching as Detective Levi's car pulled out of sight. Shit.

Holding her breath, she walked slowly to the back of her truck, opened it up, and grabbed the biggest screwdriver she had from her toolbox.

Slowly she walked the twenty paces to the bottom of the tree house, her eyes on the framed window, where she saw no sign of movement. Her legs were rubbery and hollow-feeling, like the legs of a doll. She gripped the plastic handle of the screwdriver with its eight-inch blade tightly in her sweaty palm. Her heart pounded and her mouth went dry, the back of her throat having a strange chemical taste that she tried to swallow down. The rope ladder with its wooden slats rotted through in places was swinging gently. Above her came a dragging noise.

"Hello?" she called.

No answer.

She tucked the screwdriver into her belt like a pirate's cutlass and started to climb. She tested each step tentatively with her feet, making sure she held tight to the ropes in case the wood didn't hold. But the rope itself was frayed in places, and she wasn't sure that was too sturdy either.

Stupid, stupid, stupid, she told herself. *What if you fall and break your ankle now?*

Or what if Neptune's up there, waiting, knife in hand?

What good would a screwdriver be then?

An absurd thought came to her—maybe it was Tara. She'd escaped the serial killer and come to their old hideout to be safe. Tara, who'd supposedly tried to cut her own right hand off. *Don't think about that now.* Reggie gripped the rope tighter.

Reggie got to the top and eased the trapdoor open carefully, just a crack, worried that she'd come face-to-face with a rabid raccoon. But that's not what she saw.

There, about three feet in front of her, was a pair of men's boots. They were moving in her direction.

Chapter 26

June 21, 1985
Brighton Falls, Connecticut

"Come on, hop in. It's a heap of shit, but it goes." Sid's Mustang had a few patches of rust, but was a kickass car nonetheless. Reggie stood with her back to Monique's Wish, grateful that Lorraine was still locked away in her room on the other side of the house. She'd taken to her bed since getting the news about Vera yesterday. Reggie gave the house one last nervous backward glance, knowing her aunt would never approve of her getting into a high school boy's Mustang.

They hadn't pulled out of Reggie's driveway before Sid grabbed a joint from the ashtray. He tried, without success, to make the car lighter work, popping it in, waiting, then pulling it out, staring at its dead, cold surface and mumbling, "Fuck." Finally, he leaned across Tara and got a Bic lighter from the glove compartment, which was crammed full of napkins, ketchup packets, and loose change. Sid lit up, took a hit, and blew the smoke out the window toward Monique's Wish.

"Fuck!" he yelped again, for what Reggie realized could have been any number of reasons. Sid took another hit, then passed the joint to Tara, who took a long puff before handing it to Charlie. Tara had done her hair in punked-out spikes. Charlie said she looked like a berserk porcupine.

"No thanks. I'm fine."

"Come on, Chuckles, it'll do you good. Trust me. And all the great guitar players are total potheads, you know that, right?"

Charlie shook his head. "I said I was fine."

"You're not gonna narc on me to your pop, are you, cuz?" Sid asked.

"Of course not."

Having Sid drive them in their search for clues about Reggie's mother had been Tara's idea.

"So I hate to be the bearer of bad news and all, but remember Reggie's ankle?" Charlie had said the night before, when Reggie finally consented to go see what they could find. "How are we supposed to get to bars out on Airport Road?"

"Not to worry, Chucky, I've got it all figured out," Tara had told him. "What we need is a chauffeur. A man with a set of wheels."

Charlie had looked blankly at her for a second, then as if the name has passed through the air above them, he stepped back. "Oh no! No freaking way!"

"You have a better idea?" Tara had asked. "Come on, Charlie. Cousin Sid is perfect. He's got a killer car, a criminal nature, and I'm willing to bet he's got a sense of adventure. Plus, I hear he's got a fake ID. He hangs out at those places. I can't think of a better tour guide."

"No," Charlie had said.

"If you don't ask him, I will," Tara had said.

Charlie blew out an exasperated breath.

"Come on, Charlie," Tara had said, cuddling up against him. "We need you. You've got crime-fighting genes."

"Sometimes you really suck," he'd told her.

"But that's why you love me so much," she'd said, kissing his cheek. He flushed.

Tara held the joint out to Reggie. "Try some. It'll be good for you. It'll slow down all the craziness in your head."

Reggie reached for the joint and took a tentative little puff while they cruised through town. She'd never smoked pot before, never even tried a cigarette. Now here she was in the warm cocoon of Sid's car, doing this totally criminal thing, and it gave her a rush; a sense of slipping out of her own skin and becoming something else entirely. It was a little like the way she'd felt with the razor blade in her hand. She coughed and sputtered as the smoke prickled her lungs.

Tara rolled her eyes. "You're a total neophyte," she said, and Reggie wanted to tell her not to bother showing off in front of Sid, 'cause he wasn't exactly the type to be impressed by a big vocabulary.

"Tell me, Tara, does smoking dope bring you better in tune with the spirit world?" Charlie asked mockingly.

"Maybe it does, Chuckles, maybe it does," she said, blowing smoke in his direction.

"What's all this about?" Sid asked.

"Tara here talks to dead people. Sometimes they talk through her."

"No shit?" Sid said, looking truly impressed as he turned to Tara. "How do you do that?"

"I don't know," Tara said, closing her eyes to think about it. "I guess it's kind of like having a special antenna—"

"So now you're an insect?" Charlie said.

"No, dumb ass," Tara snapped. "I meant like a radio antenna. A super strong one that can pick up on far-off signals."

"Can you do it now?" Sid asked.

She shook her head. "It doesn't work like that. It's up to the spirits, not me."

Charlie laughed. "Riiiight," he said.

Sid started singing, "I got a black magic woman, she's got me so blind I can't see . . ."

Before long, they were on Airport Road, driving past the barns used for curing tobacco, their red paint faded, and miles of white gauze netting supported on poles and wires, laid out like medieval tents to shade the sticky leafed plants. Reggie was remembering the flat tire, the sprained ankle. When the giant headshot of the candy cane waitress came up, she looked the other way and held her breath the way kids on school buses reminded each other to do when they were passing cemeteries. As if dead souls were floating around like puffs of smoke just waiting to be inhaled.

"The best cigar wrappers in the world come from right here," Sid said. "But you never want to work in those fields, fuck no. I did it for a summer. Me and my buddy Josh. You get paid shit. It's a hundred and ten degrees under the shade cloth, and the tobacco juice is so sticky it rips all the hair out of your arms. Nature's Nair, man. Seriously."

Sid rubbed at his arms.

"And fistfights every day, no shit. Some tough assholes there. Prisoners on daylong furloughs, Puerto Ricans bused in from the north end of Hartford, day laborers down on their luck. Some of those fuckers carried guns to work."

"No way," Tara said, eyes wide.

Sid nodded. "Totally," he said.

Charlie made a disgusted chuffing sound and turned away from them, looking out the window.

Soon the road widened to four lanes and the farms gave way to low cinder block shopping plazas, cheap motels, and bars.

"So, what? We're on some kind of lost-and-found missing-person mission or something?" Sid asked.

"We're trying to find out what we can about Reggie's mom," Tara said. "Maybe track down some of her friends."

Sid nodded, then glanced in the rearview mirror at Reggie in the backseat. "Tough fucking break, huh? Are they sure it's your mom's hand?"

"Of course they're sure," Charlie said. "My dad came to her house and said so himself."

"Well if old Yogi says it's true, then it's true."

"Yogi?" Tara asked.

"That's what the other cops call him. And a bunch of other guys, too. Didn't Charlie tell you?"

Tara shook her head.

"Get it," Sid said. "Yogi Berr? You know—" Sid made a goofy face and said in his best cartoon-bear voice, "I'm smarter than the av-uh-ridge bear."

Tara laughed and Charlie gave the back of her head an icy look.

"Are your dad and Yogi pretty close?" Tara asked.

"Fuck no!" Sid said. "They fight about pretty much everything. They've been competitive as hell since they were kids—fighting over girls, who was the better football player, whose schlong was bigger—typical brother stuff. They can hardly stand each other, isn't that right, Charlie?"

Charlie gave a noncommittal grunt.

"Provisions!" Sid announced, turning fast into the parking lot of Cumberland Farms, making the tires squeal. Sid and Tara went into the store. Reggie and Charlie waited in the Mustang, listening as a jet flew in overhead, watching as its shadow passed over the car, crossed the four lanes of traffic.

"What an asshole," Charlie said. "And I can't believe you guys are actually smoking pot with him. What are you thinking?"

"Tara said it would help," Reggie said.

"And did it?"

Reggie shrugged. "I'm not sure." The pot hadn't slowed down her thoughts exactly but made them seem strung together. One flowed into the next, and on and on they went like a string of beads. Maybe thoughts were always connected like that, but you had to be high to see it. She wondered if it was like that for everyone, and if, when people got together, the strings of bead intertwined, the colors, shapes, and textures blending—if this is what conversation was. She wanted to say all this to Charlie but wasn't sure how to begin.

"My mom has this theory," she said, "that there's this big web connecting everyone on earth. That we're all strung together with serial killers and the president and the guy behind us in the checkout line at the grocery store."

"Sounds like she's the one who's been smoking weed," Charlie said.

"So you don't believe in connections?"

"I believe we're connected to the people we know. You and I might have some kind of secret string between us, but me and the president? I don't buy it."

"Do you think that if there is a web like that, or a secret string or whatever, that you could send thoughts or feelings to another person without saying anything?"

"Jesus, Reggie, you're so wasted! Next thing you know, you'll be the one channeling dead chicks."

She reached out and took his hand. "Close your eyes," she said. "I'm sending you a message." She concentrated with all her might, trying to explain all of her feelings for him in three simple unspoken words: *I love you.* It felt a little corny, but still very brave. After a minute, he broke away.

"Well?" she asked, buzzing and hopeful. "Did you get anything?"

"Yeah, I did," he said, his face serious. Reggie held her breath. He looked deeply into her eyes. "I got that you are stoned out of your *gourd.* It's a miracle. Now I believe." He turned away and started fidgeting with the door lock. "God, what is taking them so long?" he asked, sounding much too pissed off. "All we need is for some cop to pull up and take one whiff of the fumes coming out of this car. We'd be screwed."

Sid and Tara returned with four Dr Peppers and a box of powdered sugar donuts. Sid opened the box and grabbed one. He turned the donut in his hand, pulled it up to his eye, and stared through the hole.

"Have you heard about the hole in the ozone? Now that's some fucked-up shit. Know what caused it? Fucking hairspray. Aerosol deodorant. Chlorofluorocarbons. We're all gonna get cancer, shrivel up and die because we want to look and smell pretty." He took a bite of the donut. "The end of life as we know it."

He finished the donut in three quick bites, then grabbed a second. The powdered sugar drifted down like snow, covering his faded black T-shirt in white speckles. "So, Reggie, tell me about your mother," Sid said. "Like, when was the last time you saw her? Did she leave any clues or anything behind?"

And Reggie, feeling comforted by her string-of-beads theory, relaxed by how nonchalant Sid had been about the end of the world, surprised herself by telling the whole story, the highlights at least. Sid listened attentively, scarfing down donuts. He'd finished three-quarters of the box by the time Reggie was through. Tara was just licking the powdered sugar off hers. Charlie didn't take one.

"Well, no offense to Uncle Yogi, but I've gotta agree with black magic woman here—you can pretty much give up on the idea of the cops doing anything. They've got their heads so far up their asses Neptune will kill every chick in town before they catch him. Fucking retards."

Charlie sprang forward, "Hey," he said, but Tara shot him a warning look, and he sank back in his seat, crossing his arms.

Reggie reached for a donut, realized it was the first food she'd had that day.

"The cops don't have enough brain cells to handle anything beyond the mundane. Trust me on that one. No, Reggie"—Sid slapped the steering wheel—"if you want to find out what happened to your mom, you're gonna have to do it on your own. You guys were right to call me. I'm the exact right person to help."

Reggie swallowed a chunk of donut. It was powdery and dry and didn't want to go down.

"How do you figure that?" Charlie asked, fiddling with the door handle now, like he was considering taking off and walking back home.

"I might not know anything about New Haven or theaters or actors. But I know the places on Airport Road. I've got connections, cuz. I know people who hang out at those bars."

"You mean drug dealers?" Charlie said.

"Business associates," Sid corrected casually. "Now come on, we'll start with Runway 36. The bouncer there is a friend of mine. And I promised I'd drop a little something off for him tonight anyway."

Tara looked back at Charlie with an I-told-you-so smile. Charlie closed his eyes and put his head back on the red leather seat.

Reggie remembered the last time she'd been in a bar and what it had led to. She self-consciously reached out and touched the new ear, ran her fingers over its rubbery folds.

Sid slammed the car into reverse and backed up fast, missing a cement pillar by only a couple of inches, and then laughing when he finally saw it.

"Would you look at that? You all stick with me. I'm lucky as shit," he said.

Chapter 27

October 21, 2010
Brighton Falls, Connecticut

Reggie nearly lost her grip on the ladder as she scrabbled for her screwdriver. Above her, the door swung open all the way and a figure crouched down, smiling a Cheshire cat grin.

"Need a boost?" he asked, voice smooth as he reached for her.

"Charlie?" she stammered, holding her hand out to his, letting him help her up into the tree house.

"God, Reggie, I can't believe it's you. You look great. Really great."

"You scared the shit out of me!" She scrambled the rest of the way up, tucking the screwdriver back into her belt. She dusted off her knees and took a step back, letting herself take him in from a distance. He wore jeans and a brown leather bomber jacket. He was taller, much heavier around the middle than he'd been back then. His face, once thin and angular, was big and doughy, jowly as a mastiff. His hair was thinner and there were wrinkles around his puffy eyes. He looked a lot like his father, only without the big bushy mustache. Her first thought was, *God, do I look this old and crappy to him?*

"I'm sorry," Charlie said, eyeing the enormous screwdriver. "I heard about Tara on the news this morning. And they said your mother was back. Then I looked online and saw this picture of you and your mother in front of the house a few days ago. I had to come and see for myself. And to find out if you'd heard anything new about Tara."

There it was again: that old spark of jealousy Reggie had always felt when Charlie spoke Tara's name. Stupid, feeling it now. Especially now that she looked at him and felt no pangs of love or romance. She didn't even find him mildly attractive. It was strange to think that this was the boy she'd pined after for years, the very object of her unrequited love. The whole thing seemed . . . disappointing really.

This was the boy she'd grown up with and married over and over again in her fantasy life; that alternate universe where Neptune never took Vera and everything turned out the way it was meant to before some psychotic fuck messed it all up.

"So you came looking for me in the *tree house*?"

"No! Of course not. I came to your house and was heading for the front door when I saw the tree house. I couldn't resist coming up to take a peek."

She nodded. She was surprised she'd resisted until now. The tree house, like Monique's Wish, was showing signs of age and neglect. The plank floor felt springy under her feet; the roof had been leaking. The empty holes where the windows should have gone had let years of rain and snow inside, quietly rotting the wood. There in the corner was the stack of games they'd left behind: Clue, Monopoly, Life, and the Ouija board. The boxes were faded and tattered, chewed through by mice and nesting squirrels. There was a Coke bottle full of Tara's old cigarette butts. It was like stepping into a time capsule.

"Why didn't you answer when I called up?" Reggie asked.

"I guess I panicked. I realized I'd look like a crazy person, so I thought if I held still, maybe you'd just go away and I could come down in a bit and knock on the door like a regular visitor."

Reggie nodded. It seemed plausible. Strange but plausible.

"It's true, then?" he asked. "Your mother's back? She's in the house now?"

Reggie nodded.

"Unbelievable," he said. His breath had a little wheeze to it, like he'd developed asthma. Reggie guessed he was just out of shape and not used to so much excitement.

Charlie had never been big on excitement.

"Tell me about it."

Charlie kicked at a loose floorboard. "I can't believe this place is still standing. Takes you back, being up here, doesn't it?"

It certainly did. She could almost see the shadows of their younger selves behind them, oblivious ghosts watching the time slip through Tara's hourglass. *You have one minute to live . . .*

She'd been thirteen the last time she sat up here with Charlie. It felt like someone else's life—a girl she read a book about once. A girl smitten over a boy she'd never have a chance with. They'd stopped speaking soon after Reggie's mother was taken, after everything that happened that final night. Even if they'd wanted to speak, they'd been forbidden to.

Lorraine agreed to send Reggie to the Brooker School for Girls that fall, using most of the family's savings to keep her there four years as a day student.

But it was a whole three towns away, and most of the kids there were from far enough away that they knew almost nothing about Neptune or Reggie's mother. It was nothing like the torture going to Brighton Falls High might have been.

Somehow, coming up to the tree house by herself never felt right, so it sat abandoned.

She walked over to the sleeping bags, chewed through by mice and squirrels, and gave them a kick to make sure no rodent families were currently residing there. Her foot hit something hard. She leaned down, cautiously pulled back the tattered fabric and stuffing to reveal Charlie's beat-up acoustic guitar. "It's still here!" she exclaimed. "You never came back for it?"

Charlie shook his head. "It was a piece of shit compared to the ones I had at home. I guess I kind of forgot about it." He leaned down, pulled the guitar out of the tangled nest of fluff. He ran his hand over the body and up the neck, eyes wide. "I'll be damned" was all he said.

"You still play?" Reggie asked.

"Nah. Not for a long, long time." He held the guitar against his thick belly and gave it a strum; then his fingers moved into position and he played a few out-of-tune chords. He shook his head as if he still couldn't believe it and laid the instrument down, his eyes still fixed on it, misty and strange, reminding Reggie a little of the way he used to look at Tara.

"So," Reggie said, "tell me about yourself. What are you up to these days?"

"I'm in real estate, actually. I kind of fell into it by accident. I studied marine biology in college and did some research work in Maine for a while, but I got homesick and came back to Brighton Falls. I sold cars at my uncle Bo's dealership, but working for him kind of sucked. I got my Realtor's license and discovered I had a real knack for selling houses. I run my own agency now." He fumbled in his jacket for a business card.

Berr Real Estate, Charles Berr, Broker
CRB, BRI

"Any family?" Reggie asked.

Charlie seemed to squirm a little. "Divorced."

"Sorry," Reggie said.

"Don't be," he told her. "We were all wrong for each other."

"Kids?" Reggie asked.

"I've got a son, Jeremy. He's six. I see him every other weekend." He walked to the opposite corner, leaned down, and picked up an old, rusty hammer.

"We had such big plans for this place," he said, studying the hammer.

Reggie only nodded.

He set the hammer back down. "So, I hear you're some kind of cutting-edge architect," he said.

She nodded.

"That's great, Reggie. And what about you? Married? Any family?"

Now it was her turn to squirm. But she stopped herself and instead stood up as straight and tall as she could. "No," she said. "I guess you could say I'm married to my work. I've been seeing someone a while, though." She smiled as she said it, though her stomach was in knots. Len had called again last night and left a message that said only, "It's fine if you don't want to talk to me right now, but please call just to let me know you're okay. I'm really worried."

Charlie seemed to study her a moment, as if he was waiting for her to say something more. When she didn't, he cleared his throat. "So . . . do you think it's really him?"

"Who?" For a second, she thought he was asking if she thought Len could really be Mr. Right.

"Neptune. Do you think it's him or some sick copycat? I mean, shit, it's been twenty-five years. That's a long time for a killer to lay low."

"I don't know, but either way, he's got Tara, right?"

"That's another thing, isn't it?" Charlie said. "Why Tara? Why take her?"

Reggie shrugged. "Maybe she knew something. Lorraine said my mom was really agitated the night before last and that Tara was up all night with her. I've been thinking that maybe my mom gave her some clue that she decided to follow up on, and she got too close."

Charlie nodded. "Good theory. Makes sense. Especially given her background. Remember how crazy the whole Neptune thing made her? How obsessed she was? Like it was her mission to catch him and no one else stood a chance?" He was breathing too fast, taking little fish-out-of-water gulps of air.

Reggie nodded. "Is your dad still a cop?"

"No. He retired four years ago. Spends most of his time working on this old boat he bought. He's got it docked down in New London. Between you and me, I think he spends more time in the bar down there than on the boat." He smiled. "Not that he doesn't deserve it. That's what retirement should be, right? Shooting the shit with other old guys, making up fish stories."

Reggie smiled.

"You know what Tara would say if she were here, don't you?" Charlie asked. "I bet she'd say what she did all those years ago—the cops aren't going to catch this guy. If we want to find her, we have to do it ourselves."

"I know," Reggie said, her hand touching her shirt just over her collarbone, feeling through the fabric for Tara's necklace. "I've been thinking the exact same thing."

Chapter 28

June 21, 1985
Brighton Falls, Connecticut

When Reggie walked into Runway 36, she knew it was the place her mother had taken her the day she lost her ear. She recognized the red vinyl barstools, now cracked and patched with duct tape, the sad little booths on the left side of the restaurant, the pool table shimmed with a phone book. She bet if she was able to lift the table and look at the date on the phone book it would be at least eight years old.

Want to see a trick? Buy me a drink and I'll show you.

Reggie's chest felt tight. The scar tissue over her missing ear tingled.

She glanced at the glossy wood bar top, could almost see her mother's right hand, still perfect, sprinkling salt and setting the egg on its end.

Reggie blinked the past away and looked around.

It was Friday night and the place was packed with people blowing their week's pay. The place stank of greasy food, beer, cigarette smoke, and unwashed bodies. The floor was sticky under her feet. She felt a tug of fear and apprehension as she stepped into the loud, smoky space, thinking back to how the events that transpired here eight years ago led to her losing her ear.

Glen Campbell was singing "Rhinestone Cowboy" on the jukebox. A group of leather-clad, bearded bikers were playing pool on the shimmed table, and the one waiting to take his shot looked their way, sneering. He wore a black leather skullcap and riding chaps over his jeans.

A big guy in a tight Members Only jacket was standing by the door. He had a broad, sloped forehead that reminded Reggie of pictures she'd seen of a Neanderthal.

"No underage," he barked as they came in.

"It's cool, Terry, they're with me," Sid said, stepping up to shake the big guy's hand. He whispered something to Terry, then reached into his pocket and pulled out a pack of Marlboros. Terry took the cigarettes and stuffed them into his jacket pocket, nodding thanks.

"We good, then?" Sid asked.

Terry gave a noncommittal grunt and let them pass.

Reggie, Tara, and Charlie followed Sid as he approached the bar, where a thin, grizzled man was polishing glasses behind the counter. A hunched-over june bug of a man was sipping a drink at the end of the bar. The man to their left wore a blue airport security uniform. Reggie guessed him to be in his early forties. His skin had the look of someone who'd spent most of his life outdoors in all kinds of weather. Alligator hide. Reggie glanced to her right, where a man dressed like he'd spent all day in the tobacco fields was whispering in Spanish into a woman's neck, his breath tickling, making her laugh. Reggie saw she was missing a front tooth, poking her tongue out of the gap as she giggled.

Reggie leaned forward, her hands resting on one of the red stools, maybe even the one she'd sat on as a little girl, the man with the crooked nose promising to give her a dollar if she could finish her burger. Reggie imagined running into him now. Wondered if her mother had kept in touch. Jesus, maybe the Boxer was Neptune.

Did anyone ever tell you you're a dead ringer for Marlon Brando?

Reggie scanned the crowd, studied all the rough male faces. The biker with the skullcap glowered at her.

Any of these men could be Neptune, Reggie thought, her eyes turning back to the skinny bartender. *Any of them.*

"If you want to order some food, you can go ahead and sit down." The man hardly looked up from his glasses to spit out his greeting.

"Nah, no food tonight," Sid said to the bartender. "We're kinda looking for someone."

Reggie was sure that once they learned who she was they'd pat her on the back and tell her whatever she needed to know.

"Who isn't?" asked the june bug with a snicker.

"Isn't it past your bedtime, kids?" said the skinny man, sighing. "Your mamas are probably wondering where you're at." He eyed Terry at the door, but Terry was talking to one of the pool players and didn't see.

Charlie started to inch toward the front door.

"Tell 'em who you are," Sid said, shoving Reggie forward, toward the bar.

Reggie put her hands on the scarred bar top, feeling the scratches, initials of lovers long gone, drinkers who probably died of cirrhosis.

"I'm Vera Dufrane's daughter. You know her?"

"*Everyone* knows Vera," said the june bug, laughing in an ugly way.

The skinny bartender looked up, stopped polishing for a minute. His eyes were dull and watering, his nose dripping. Reggie smiled, knowing her mother's name was the ticket. Now she was getting somewhere.

"Didn't know Vera had a kid," admitted the bartender.

"Neither did I," agreed the june bug.

For a moment no one spoke. Reggie's cheeks grew hot and she felt the heat radiating out to her one real ear, making it red.

The jukebox blared "A Horse with No Name."

Runway 36 was a little behind in the music department. No Madonna or Wham! on the soundtrack.

"She's been doing a play in New Haven," Reggie said. "We were hoping we could find some of her theater friends and talk to them."

The bartender squinted at her. "A play?"

Reggie nodded. "In New Haven."

The bartender stared blankly at her.

"Reggie here said her mom was planning to get married," Sid said. "Any idea who the lucky guy might be?"

"Married?" said the june bug. "Vera?" He laughed a rusty little laugh. "Right."

"The cops were in here earlier asking about her," the bartender said. "She in some kind of trouble or something?"

"Maybe," said Tara.

"Probably just lying low," the june bug said. "Vera does that sometimes."

Behind them, one of the bikers playing pool, yelled, "Scratch!"

Reggie spun around, looking for her mother's version of Old Scratch—horns, hooves, and pitchfork. Then Reggie realized it was just the game, a bad shot. The biker in the skullcap was pounding his opponent on the shoulder, saying, "Fifty bucks! Cough it up."

Reggie turned back to the bar.

"Did you try Vera's place?" the guy in the security uniform asked. DUANE said his name tag.

"We just came from the house," Sid said.

The security guard smiled a *You kids sure can be stupid* smile and shook his head like he wasn't at all surprised.

"Not her house. Her *place.* She's always kept a room over at Alistair's. About two miles down the road. Airport Efficiencies, it's called."

Chapter 29

October 21, 2010
Brighton Falls, Connecticut

Charlie and Reggie sat across from each other at the kitchen table, steam from coffee cups rising between them. The morning edition of the *Hartford Examiner* was open on the table, Tara's face peering up at them. In the lower left corner, was an old photo of Vera. Reggie skimmed the article.

"Shit," she said. "They know everything. It says that Tara was working here, taking care of my mom."

Charlie nodded, reaching for his coffee. "I'm surprised it took them this long."

Reggie folded up the paper in disgust.

Charlie had carried his guitar out of the tree house, and it was now sitting in one of the kitchen chairs, a silent and watchful old friend joining them for coffee.

Reggie had made herself a triple espresso, and an Americano for Charlie.

"This is great," he said, taking a sip. "Sure beats my usual Dunkin' Donuts."

"Be careful," Reggie warned with a sly smile. "Once you've tasted real coffee, there's no going back."

Charlie took another sip and looked around the kitchen. "I can't believe your aunt's still here. This is a big house to live in and take of. It's a lot for one person."

"Well, as you can see, she hasn't exactly been keeping up with things."

"Think I should give her a card? Would she ever consider selling, moving into someplace more manageable? There are some new condos across from Millers' Farm—they're actually pretty nice."

Reggie shook her head. "She'll never leave here. She and this house, they're . . ."—Reggie searched for the right word—"bound."

She couldn't imagine her aunt anywhere else.

The Nautilus house Reggie was designing would be perfect for a single person on the move. Lorraine could cross the country, going from one trout stream to the next. But she'd never leave. It was as if she were a part of the house, a woman formed from stone and cement, just as cold and unyielding as the foot-thick walls that formed their fortress.

As if on cue, Lorraine wandered into the kitchen, carrying a dirty bowl to the sink.

"You remember Charlie Berr?" Reggie said.

Lorraine eyed him suspiciously. "Yes. Of course. Nice to see you again, Charles."

"You too, Miss Dufrane." He gave her his warmest smile, but Lorraine's face remained unchanged.

"How's your father?" Lorraine asked.

"Fine, thanks. Busier than ever now that he's retired. He went and bought a boat. Does a lot of fishing."

Lorraine gave a stiff nod. "And your uncle Bo, how's he?"

Charlie looked down at the floor. "Not so good. He's got cancer."

"Cancer?" Lorraine said, frowning hard.

"Yes, ma'am. Pancreatic."

"I'm so sorry." Her face softened. "How's Frances holding up?"

"As well as can be expected."

Lorraine nodded. "You give them my best, will you, Charles?" She ran water into the bowl in the sink and reached for a sponge and dish soap.

So much for cold and unyielding. Lorraine had softened in her old age. Maybe it was seeing her peers get old and sick. Or maybe, Reggie thought, Lorraine was only sympathetic to people who were dying.

"Lorraine," Reggie said, "I found yesterday's paper out in the trash can. Are you sure you didn't put it there?"

Lorraine shook her head. "I told you, the last time I saw the paper was yesterday when you were looking at it. It was right here on the table." She finished washing the bowl and put it in the dish drainer. Then she turned to face Reggie. "Maybe you put it out in the trash and just don't remember." Lorraine seemed flustered.

"Maybe," Reggie said, thinking *No way in hell.*

"I got your mother some oatmeal, but she went back to sleep before she had much," Lorraine said.

Reggie nodded. "We can try again later. If you need me for anything, we'll be upstairs."

Lorraine gave her a disapproving look that made Reggie feel like she was a teenager again, trying to sneak a boy up to her bedroom. Lorraine went back to looking at Charlie with suspicion. Then her eye caught on the newspaper and she unfolded it, saw the photos and headline, and immediately closed it.

"Is this yours?" Lorraine said, holding up the large screwdriver Reggie had left sitting on the table beside the paper.

Not wanting to admit to grabbing it as a weapon earlier, Reggie reached for it and said, "Yeah. The window in my room is stuck. I needed something to loosen it up a bit."

Lorraine nodded.

"Come on upstairs, *Charles,*" Reggie drawled in her best impression of Lorraine. It was stupid and petty, making fun of her aunt, especially after she'd just watched Lorraine being so kind. *Grow the hell up,* she told herself.

Charlie grabbed his guitar and followed, giving a respectful nod to Lorraine. When they were climbing the stairs, he said, "I don't think she's too happy that I'm here." His voice was a low hiss, air coming out of a punctured balloon.

"Lorraine's never too happy about much of anything," Reggie said. *Except when she learns someone's dying. Then she's all sweetness and sympathy.*

They stopped at Vera's doorway and looked in. She was sound asleep, head at an awkward angle, oatmeal covering her chin.

"Wow." Charlie gasped, his breath rattling in his chest. "I can't believe it's her."

"It's crazy, isn't it?" Reggie said. "Like she's come back from the dead."

Reggie gazed in at her mother's pale, skeletal face. She looked like a visitor from the land of the dead but was clearly just passing through—she'd be returning soon.

"So where'd she turn up?" Charlie asked.

"A hospital in Worcester, Mass. Before that, she'd been staying in a homeless shelter there on and off for the past two years. I'm going to call the social worker at the hospital later and see if I can find out any more. There's a woman at the shelter my mom keeps talking about—Sister Dolores. I'll see if I can track her down."

"Excellent," Charlie said. "Maybe she can tell you something helpful." It was silly, really, but Reggie appreciated the reassurance. It was good to have another semi-sane person on board.

"Come on," Reggie said. "I'm in my old room."

Charlie whistled when he walked in. "It's like stepping into a time machine." He gaped wide-eyed at the walls and bulletin board. "Nothing's changed."

"Wait," Reggie said. "This is the best part." She pulled open the closet door, revealing her old 1980s clothes, still on hangers. "Lorraine didn't get rid of a thing. I doubt she ever even came in here after I left."

"God, is that sweatshirt with shoulder pads? You could probably make some good money on eBay with this stuff," Charlie said.

"You're funny. Give me a hand with this, will you?" Reggie said, shoving the screwdriver between the sash and windowsill and prying. She could practically hear George's voice in her head: *There's a right tool for every job.* Shut up, George.

Charlie pushed up on the window while Reggie pried it from below, and at last it gave and opened for them.

"Air!" Reggie said, delighted, taking a deep whiff of autumn.

Leaving the window open a crack, Reggie plunked herself down on the bed and started pouring over the contents of the memory box she'd left on top of the rumpled quilt. "I saved all this stuff after my mom disappeared. Nothing all that useful, really. Matchbooks she'd brought me from restaurants and bars, little notes she left, a copy of Vera as the Aphrodite Cold Cream girl . . ."

"Nice bird," Charlie said, picking up the small carved wooden swan.

"Uncle George made it for my mom. He gave it to her just before she disappeared."

"What's this?" Charlie said, picking up the cutout picture of Ganesh, the elephant-headed god.

"Nothing," Reggie said. "It's silly, really. I cut it out when I was a kid. It reminded me of my father."

"Your father?"

"Or who I imagined my father might be. My mom called him Tusks. It was kind of a family joke, but it was all I had to go on."

Reggie reached into the cigar box and pulled out the ring she'd tucked there last night, and showed it to Charlie. "A wedding ring, I think. My mother had it in her coat pocket when I picked her up in Worcester. Check out the inscription."

Charlie held the ring up so that he could read it. "Wait. Isn't that—"

"The day Vera's hand showed up on the steps of the police station."

Charlie blew out a breath. "But what does it mean?" he asked.

He may have looked like his dad, but he sure didn't have old Yogi's powers of deduction.

"Probably what we've always suspected—that if we can find the guy my mom was going to marry, we've got our killer."

"So did you find any new leads about who Mr. Right might be?"

"Not a new lead, exactly," Reggie admitted. "More like taking a new look at an old one."

Charlie nodded. "Tell me."

Reggie reached under her mattress and pulled out Tara's copy of *Neptune's Hands.*

"Look, Tara underlined a few passages with a purple pen. I found a purple pen on her bedside table in the room she was staying in, which makes me think she just did it. Anyway . . . one of the things she underlined was a passage about one of the suspects, this guy named James Jacovich. The name didn't ring a bell with me, but listen to this." She looked down at the passage and read aloud, " 'Jacovich was reportedly one of Vera Dufrane's on-again, off-again boyfriends. He was a small-time coke dealer who went by the name Rabbit.' "

"Okay," Charlie said, raising his eyebrows in a questioning way.

"My mom talked about him a lot. She told me he was a director, that he had all these connections. She'd been involved with him for years. She said he was a genius, but half crazy with a bad temper."

"Did you ever meet him?"

Reggie shook her head, then looked back down at the book. "It says here that they picked him up and arrested him for DUI two days after her hand was found. You know why the cops stopped him to begin with?" Reggie asked, hearing the excitement in her voice.

"Why?"

"For a busted taillight. He had a tan Impala with a bashed-in left taillight, just like the car I saw my mom get into at the bowling alley!"

"Wait, he's involved with her, has a temper, and has a car that matches the one Vera got into the night before her hand showed up. Why'd they let him go?"

Reggie shook her head. "It turned out he had a great alibi—the night my mom went missing, he was at his court-appointed NA meeting, then ended up spending the night on his sponsor's couch. The sponsor was a reliable member of the community, according to the cops, so Jacovich was off the hook. And it also says the police couldn't find any evidence or connect him with the other murder victims either."

"But God, Reggie, there's the broken taillight!"

"There's that. But then last night, I remembered something. You know Candace Jacques, the waitress?"

Charlie nodded. "Neptune's second victim."

"Well, remember how I said my mom took me to meet her once? You know what one of the first things she said was? She asked my mom if she'd heard from Rabbit lately."

"So?"

"So, the way Candace said it like Rabbit was this mutual friend. So he's connected to not just one, but at least two of Neptune's victims!"

"You think he's still around?" Charlie asked.

"One way to find out," Reggie said. "I used my phone to do a search online and didn't come up with anything. But I thought it couldn't hurt to visit some of the places out on Airport Road. I was thinking of heading out there later on, seeing what I can find out."

Charlie nodded. "A lot of them are closed down now, but Runway 36 is still going strong. I've got some appointments, but I can be here by six to pick you up."

"Are you sure?"

"Hell yes."

"Six o'clock, then," Reggie said. She knew they were both remembering what searching the bars twenty-five years ago had led to.

She could see it so clearly: Sid crumpled on the pavement, Tara reaching down for him, her hand coming away bloody.

Reggie's cell phone rang and she jumped. Jesus. Maybe she hadn't needed all that caffeine. Reggie looked at the display on her phone: Len.

"You need to get that?" Charlie asked, standing. "I can show myself out."

"No," Reggie said, turning the ringer off her phone and slipping it back into her pocket. "I'll walk you out."

They passed Vera's room and saw she was awake.

"Hey, Mom, do you remember my old friend Charlie Berr?"

Vera peered at Reggie in the doorway. Then slowly her eyes moved to Charlie, who was a step behind her.

He moved through the door. "A real pleasure to see you again, Miss Dufrane," he said in a jovial, real-estate guy voice. Reggie saw something change in Vera's eyes, like a shade being pulled down. Then there was nothing but pure panic as Vera opened her mouth and began to scream.

Chapter 30

June 21, 1985
Brighton Falls, Connecticut

Airport Efficiencies was a single-story row of cinder block units, painted a blotchy and peeling Pepto-Bismol pink; the walls were stained from years of car exhaust, drunken urination, God only knew what else. It glowed hideously bright in the security lights around the parking lot.

"Cozy," Tara said.

"By the week or by the hour," Sid said, winking at her.

Charlie was in the backseat beside Reggie, sulking.

"Do you think your mom really has a room here?" Tara asked, turning to look at Reggie.

Reggie couldn't bring herself to answer.

"I think it's pretty fucked up if she does," Tara said, leaning forward and twisting a chunk of hair into a more pointed spike, angling it down over her left eye. It looked like a horn.

The three of them piled out of the Mustang and went into the motel's office, where they pushed a buzzer and waited for a grizzled old man to emerge from the doorway behind the desk. He eyed them suspiciously.

"Yes?" He was wearing brown polyester pants and a pea-green sweater covered in stains. His false teeth slid and clacked as he spoke. Reggie detected the faint odor of urine coming from his general direction.

"I'm looking for my mother. She's a resident here. Vera Dufrane?"

The old man was silent, gazing dully at each of them in turn. He played with his teeth, pushing them forward with his tongue, out past his lips, then sucking them back into place.

"These are my cousins," Reggie continued. "It's urgent we find her. There's been a death in the family."

Dentures reached under the counter and produced a key, which he slapped down on the Formica desk.

"You can go ahead and clean out her stuff. What you don't take goes in the Dumpster tomorrow. She's two weeks behind. Been here on and off for five years now and never missed a week's rent.

"Called last week, all apologies, said she'd be coming by to square up and clean the place out, but she never showed. A detective showed up yesterday, demanding to be let into her room. That's the last thing I need is the cops snooping around—it's bad for business." He pushed his teeth out, then sucked them in—his own punctuation mark to show he was all done talking.

Reggie took the key, attached to an orange tag with the number 8. The tag had something like petroleum jelly on it, and Reggie realized it must have come from the old man's hands. She wiped the orange tag on her jeans, thanked the man, and led the way out of the office. Stopping in the doorway, she turned back to ask one final question.

"She's getting married, you know. My mom. Did you ever meet the guy?"

The teeth were pushed forward, out past his cracked, yellow lips as the old man laughed. Reggie's face reddened, her left ear burning, and she looked down at the floor.

"There are lots of men," he wheezed, trying to catch his breath. "Hard to keep track, if you know what I mean. And we got lots of residents. I don't keep up with all the comings and goings. I can't even say for sure when Vera was here last."

"But in the last few weeks? Anyone special around since then?"

Dentures seemed to consider this.

"Nope. Last few times I saw her, she was alone. There was a light-colored car parked outside of her door a few times. That's all I can tell you."

Reggie nodded her thanks, said she'd drop the key off when they were done.

It turned out Reggie didn't need the key after all—the door had been left unlocked. She knocked first, just in case, then held her breath and pushed the door open.

Room 8 was wrecked. Not unkempt wrecked, but typhoon wrecked. There were clothes everywhere. Drawers pulled out and tossed on the floor. Broken bottles of perfume, gin, brandy, and Colt 45. The mattress was on the floor. The one chair in the room was tipped over and gutted, foam rubber padding bleeding out. Reggie's first thought was that this couldn't possibly be her mother's room. But then her eyes fell on a single stained white leather glove mixed up in the heap. And the smell of the perfume was unmistakable: Tabu.

"Jee-zuss!" exclaimed Tara. She stepped inside, walked into the center of the room, closed her eyes, and took a deep breath. "Something horrible happened here," Tara said.

"For Christ's sake," Charlie said. "Would you put your psychic antenna down?"

"Let her do her thing," Sid said. "Maybe she'll . . . I dunno, pick up on something useful."

Reggie was immediately sorry they'd come. Being in this room felt like looking at Vera naked, passing the picture around to her friends for shits and giggles.

"You think the cops did this?" Sid asked.

"No way!" Charlie said.

The smells of spilled booze and stale perfume hung in the air like invisible smog. Reggie's head spun with the sweet, sour scent. Sure she was gonna puke, she hurried to the bathroom, retched into the toilet, but nothing came up. She noticed a roach scuttle along the wall behind the toilet. She'd never even seen a roach before. It was as hideous as she'd imagined. She could practically hear its legs on the stained tile floor, scraping like tiny bones.

"You okay, Reg?" Charlie called.

"Fine," Reggie said, wiping her mouth with the back of her hand. "Never better."

She stood and looked around the bathroom with watering eyes. The mirror on the medicine cabinet was smashed, the sink full of large silver shards. Seven years' bad luck for some poor bastard. The shower curtain had been ripped off the rod and lay torn in the mildew-stained tub. Vera's makeup had been strewn across the floor: mascara, tubes of lipstick, rouge. Reggie picked up a powder compact, opened it, and smelled the sweet, talcy smell, stared at her refection in the tiny round mirror.

"Where are you?" she asked. "And what were you ever doing here?"

No answer. Only the reflection of a skinny girl with hair that was too short and a right ear that was slightly paler than the left.

She snapped the compact closed. Reggie swung open the broken-up door of the medicine cabinet and looked inside. Only a bottle of aspirin was left on the shelves. That and a safety pin. She picked up the safety pin, opened it, and touched the sharp tip to her thumb. Reggie noticed a wadded-up towel on the edge of the tub. Looking closely, she saw that it was smeared with dark reddish brown stains.

Blood.

Her mother's? Neptune's? Someone else's?

Reggie's stomach churned. She shoved the tip of the pin down into her thumb. Then she pulled it out and did it again.

"Reg?" Charlie called. "You find anything in there?"

"Nope," she said, closing the safety pin, dropping it into her pocket.

She stepped back into the other room, a combination bedroom and kitchenette. Sid was smoking a cigarette. Charlie had the door to the minifridge open and found only a couple of shriveled limes in it. There were two unwashed glasses in the sink. The other dishes were put away in the cupboard, which had been decorated with a paisley patterned contact paper. Very 1970s. None of the dishes matched. Reggie recognized a plate from home: ivory with delicate green vines decorating the edge.

"Phone's been ripped out of the wall," said Tara, holding the torn wires in her hand. Tara was all jazzed up, excited as hell about this, and Reggie kind of hated her for it.

Reggie went over to look at the phone. It was on a small bedside table next to a full ashtray. The butts in it were all Vera's—Winstons with red lipstick stains. Reggie pulled open the drawer underneath and found a phone book, a package of Trojan condoms, some matches, and a piece of paper with her mother's handwriting. She pushed the condoms to the back of the drawer before Tara could see them and took out the scrap of paper.

Second Chance was all the paper said. The words were circled.

Was Vera hoping for hers? Is that what she thought this guy was going to give her?

A nice, normal life.

Reggie stared down at the paper in her hands and thought about how cruel hope could be.

She'd made a faint thumbprint of blood on the edge of the paper.

"What the fuck happened here?" asked Sid, crushing his cigarette out in the ashtray with Vera's.

"I dunno," said Reggie, stuffing the slip of paper into her pocket beside the safety pin, "but it doesn't look good."

She decided not to tell them about the bloody towel. Christ, Tara would probably pick it up, sniff it, hold it to her heart, and go into a trance.

"But what I don't get is what she was doing here to begin with," said Tara. "I mean, she's got a home, right? And all kinds of interesting theater friends who probably have homes, too. So why come to this dump?"

"It's anybody's guess," Charlie said, kicking at the empty liquor bottles on the floor.

"Maybe she just needed a space that was all hers, you know?" Tara suggested. "Someplace she could come and think."

"Dude," Sid said, shoving his hands deep into the pockets of his jeans, "this isn't exactly a thinking kind of place, you know? I'm guessing she met guys here. Maybe made a little money off them."

"Huh?" Charlie said. "Are you saying she's like a—"

"My mother is an *actress*," Reggie practically shouted, determined not to let him say the word. If he didn't say it out loud, it wouldn't be true. And it wasn't true. Couldn't be.

They all stood in silence, no one moving or even looking at each other. Then Tara started spinning slowly around the room, hands outstretched, eyes clamped shut. She looked like a kid playing pin the tail on the donkey.

"This is where he grabbed her," announced Tara. "Right about here, I think is where it happened," she said, wiggling her fingers like anemone as she stopped in the center of the room.

Charlie snorted. "What this looks like to me is that somebody was searching for something. Just tearing the place apart to find it. Getting more pissed off by the second."

"I still think it could have been the cops," Sid said.

"No way," Charlie countered. "The cops would have treated this place like a crime scene. Been real careful. Maybe the place got torn up like this after they came. Or maybe they found it this way. No way to know. The one thing I'm sure of is that my dad and the other cops wouldn't do something like this."

"It was him," Tara said, eyes still closed, hands outstretched, as if reaching for some invisible thing. "Neptune. I know it was. I feel him in here." She gave a dramatic shudder.

"Okay, say it was Neptune who came here and trashed the place. What could he have been looking for?" asked Reggie.

Tara's eyes opened wide and glittered in the dull light. "Something that could tie her to him. Evidence. Neptune grabbed her, and came back to make sure there was nothing lying around that could connect the two of them," Tara said. "That makes total sense!"

"Assuming it was Neptune who did this," added Charlie.

"Of course it was Neptune," Tara said. She gave Charlie a scornful look. "Who else could it be?" She looked at Reggie now, like she was asking her the question.

"Anyone." Reggie sighed, remembering the old man with the dentures saying there were lots of men. "It could have been anyone."

"Dude, this is totally fucked up," Sid said, squinting around the room. "I don't know what went down here, but I'm getting some seriously bad vibes from this place."

"Totally," Tara said, giving a dramatic shiver and moving closer to Sid.

Reggie realized she had no right being in this room. Who did she think she was, trespassing like this? She was no sleuth, no superhero. This wasn't some TV show or comic book. The room and everything in it terrified her, and not simply the way it had been torn apart—it was the whole thing: the mismatched dishes, the barren refrigerator, the condoms, the roach in the bathroom. The fact that she hadn't known her mother at all. That she'd seen her as some sort of golden Wonder Woman, the Aphrodite Cold Cream girl, Homecoming Queen, Actress Extraordinaire, savior of little girls being ripped apart by dogs. But now, the curtain was being pulled back to reveal someone else entirely.

Reggie needed to go, to get away from the sweet, boozy smell. She couldn't bear to see the wrecked, squalid little room any longer. She turned and walked out without a word, leaving the key in the door, unable even to face Dentures.

"Wanna see something?" Tara asked. She was in the backseat with Reggie this time along with the cans of beer Sid had stopped for at Cliffside Liquors, where they never blinked at Sid's fake ID. Charlie was up front playing copilot while Sid smoked another joint.

"Watch it, man," Charlie warned. "You're drifting into the other lane. You're way too wasted to be driving!"

"Relax," Sid told him. "Like I said, I'm lucky as shit. And this car, she practically drives herself."

Reggie was feeling grateful that none of them had said any more about her mother or her trashed little motel room.

Tara had been chattering at Reggie since they left Airport Efficiencies—trying to cheer her up, she guessed. Reggie was taking her advice, forcing a beer down, thinking it might take the edge off. Make her skin stop crawling a little. She thought of the roach and the sound it made scuttling along the tile floor.

Sid turned up the radio. "I love this song!"

It was The Who doing "Pinball Wizard."

"Well?" asked Tara, voiced hushed and conspiratorial as she leaned toward Reggie. "Do you wanna see or what?"

"Sure," Reggie told her, taking another good slug of beer.

Tara's face was lit up, expectant. She couldn't wait to show Reggie this thing, whatever it was.

Tara rolled up the long, safety-pinned sleeve of her dress to reveal the pale inside of her forearm. Reggie squinted in the dim light of the car to see that it was covered in scars. Strange designs: neat rows of little raised white scar-tissue horseshoes, like the world's smallest pony trotted there, following the blue trail of her veins. These weren't like the delicate etched lines Tara had on her legs from the razor blade. This was something else entirely.

"Eohippus," said Reggie, remembering something she'd learned in biology about the tiny ancestor of all horses.

"I did it with a lighter," Tara whispered, the words hot against Reggie's good ear.

Reggie bit her lip as she studied the scars on the soft and vulnerable-looking underside of Tara's forearm. Her own skin started to itch in that now-familiar way—the yearning to cut, to feel the tease of the blade against her flesh just before she pushed it in. She thought of the safety pin in her pocket and wanted to open it up, see how deep a scratch she could make. She knew that it would make everything else go away, and she needed that now more than ever. She wanted it and hated herself for wanting it. It was all one big fucked-up contradiction, like thinking Tara's scars were awful, but being jealous of them at the same time.

Tara smiled. "Do you want to touch them? You can." And, without another word, she reached for Reggie's hand and guided Reggie's fingers down to her scarred arm. When the fingers made contact, Tara inhaled sharply, like the touch hurt, and Reggie jerked her hand away, only to have Tara push it back down.

"It's okay," Tara whispered as Reggie's fingertips worked their way gently over the bumps and ridges of scars. "I want you to."

Chapter 31

October 21, 2010
Brighton Falls, Connecticut

Reggie caught herself running her fingers over the scars around her prosthetic ear—a nervous habit she thought she'd broken long ago.

"I'm so sorry about what happened earlier with my mom," she said as she and Charlie walked across the parking lot toward the neon-lit front doorway of Runway 36. She'd already apologized several times, but no matter how much Charlie said it was fine and not to worry about it, she remembered the way he'd backed out of Vera's room, baffled and frightened. Vera's screaming seemed to go on forever—she clenched the bedclothes, rolled her eyes madly. She was breathless and hoarse by the time Reggie and Lorraine managed to get an Ativan under her tongue. After many minutes of hyperventilating and ragged sobs, she'd drifted off to sleep. When she woke up, she seemed to have no memory of the incident.

"It's no problem, really," Charlie said. "I'm sure it's unsettling to have a stranger pop in, after all she's been through."

"Between the illness and the meds we've got her on, she's pretty loopy."

Charlie nodded. "You have any luck reaching that social worker?"

"Yeah. She wasn't much of a help. She gave me the name and number of the shelter, though. I put in a call and was told Sister Dolores is the one in charge, but she's not working today. She's going to call me back tomorrow."

Charlie nodded.

"Shall we?" he said, eyeing the dimly lit doorway of Runway 36 with trepidation.

The door was thick steel and had several dents in it, like someone had been at it with a battering ram. There was an awning overhead with a flashing red neon airplane—Reggie was sure if she looked at it too long she'd have some kind of seizure.

The entryway of a building was supposed to draw you in, offer a welcoming transition between the outside world and the inside. The experience of entering the building influenced the way you felt once you were inside.

The only way to make the doorway to Runway 36 less welcoming would be to drape it in barbed wire.

In the parking lot off to the right, there was a small group of people smoking. One of them was a girl with a high-pitched pig-squeal of a voice who kept saying, "He never knew what hit him! I'm telling you, he NEVER knew what hit him!"

"Let's do it," Reggie said, yanking the heavy door open and stepping through first.

Not much had changed. The place was still dark and stank of beer and cigarettes, although smoking in restaurants and bars was now illegal. Reggie checked the pool table in the middle of the room and was slightly disappointed to discover that it was newer and no longer shimmed with old phone books. The red-vinyl-covered barstools had been reupholstered in black vinyl. The place was crowded, and it seemed to Reggie as if everyone had stopped what they were doing to stare at her and Charlie.

"I don't have a warm, welcoming feeling," Reggie whispered, leaning toward Charlie.

He put his arm around her. She knew it was meant to feel reassuring, but really, it just felt heavy. "I guess we don't look like regulars," he said in a low voice. He smelled like Listerine and sweet aftershave. She noticed he'd showered and shaved before picking her up, which seemed a little too I'm-thinking-of-this-as-a-date for her comfort level. She gently pulled away from him, leading the way toward the bar.

Reggie remembered following Sid across the room twenty-five years ago—his swaggering walk, the way Tara bounced along beside him; how their visit to Runway 36 had led them to the horrid little room at Airport Efficiencies.

Where would it lead them this time?

Irrational as it was, Reggie thought of turning around, walking back out before she had a chance to find out.

But then she thought of Tara. Tara, tied up in some god-awful dungeon, being shot full of morphine, her right arm ending in a mass of bandages.

But that wasn't the Tara that scared her. No, when she closed her eyes, she saw the thirteen-year-old Tara, dark eyes glimmering, pissed off and self-righteous, saying, "I guess I'm fucked if it's all up to you."

"I'm trying!" Reggie said out loud without meaning to.

"Hmm?" Charlie said from half a step behind her. The music was loud enough that he hadn't heard.

"Nothing."

Behind the bar was a sweaty fat man and a rail-thin woman with frizzy dyed red hair.

"What can I get you?" asked the woman.

"You have Beck's?" Charlie asked.

The woman frowned. "The only thing in bottles I got is Heineken."

Charlie nodded. "I'll have one of those."

"Make it two," Reggie said, knowing it wasn't wise to ask about the wine selection.

Behind the bar, up above the liquor bottles was a big-screen TV. It was tuned to a cable news channel, but the sound was off. Reggie saw a shot of downtown Brighton Falls, then Monique's Wish. Reggie felt her breath catch in her throat. It was so like stepping back in time, seeing her home on the news. Only this time it was Tara's face that filled the screen. It was a terrible picture—slightly out of focus and Tara was looking far off into the distance, squinting a little.

The frizzy-haired woman brought two beers and greasy-looking glasses.

"You know a guy who calls himself Rabbit?" Charlie asked, pushing the glass aside and taking a sip from the green bottle. Reggie could tell he was enjoying this. Hunting down a serial killer was a whole lot more exciting than selling condos and little ranch houses with remodeled kitchens and nice yards for the kids to play in.

The woman squinted at him. "You two cops?"

Charlie laughed, reaching into a pocket and pulling out a card. "Nah. I'm in real estate."

She took the card and studied it. "And what? You wanna sell Rabbit a house or something?"

"Or something," Charlie said, smiling slyly. This was so not the Charlie that Reggie knew. He was far too suave.

She took a tentative sip of her lukewarm beer. It tasted like skunk piss. Maybe she would have been better off with the house wine in the giant screw-top bottle.

The fat bartender lumbered over. "Quit yanking his chain, Evelyn," he said. He looked at Charlie. "You want to talk to Rabbit, there he is." He nodded his head and they turned to see who he was looking at. There was a skinny, grizzled-looking man at a booth by himself eating a burger. His gray hair was falling into his eyes and he had ketchup on his chin.

"Thanks," Charlie said, dropping a twenty on the bar and wandering toward the booths.

"Talk about luck," Reggie said. This had been easy. Almost *too* easy. She didn't like it when things seemed to fall into place so effortlessly—it made her suspicious.

"Yeah," Charlie agreed. "So far so good. But maybe you should do the talking. I think you've got a better chance with this guy." Reggie nodded. Charlie stayed a step behind, letting Reggie take the lead.

"James?" Reggie said, standing over the man in the booth. "James Jacovich?"

He looked up, nodding. He held what was left of the burger in his hands, which shook slightly. His fingernails were long and filthy. He hadn't wiped the ketchup off his chin. The skin on his face was thin and sagging and the whites of his eyes looked yellow. Here he was at last—the mythical Rabbit: creative genius, director of plays, the man who had connections.

"Do I know you?" he asked, voice barely scraping out through his throat, as if it hurt to talk.

"May I sit?" Reggie asked, eyeing the stained booth with trepidation.

"Free country," Rabbit said.

Reggie took a seat. Charlie remained standing by Reggie's side of the booth so he wasn't breathing down the guy's neck.

"My mother's an old friend of yours. Vera Dufrane."

Rabbit took another bite of his burger and chewed slowly and messily. Reggie could see he was missing most of his front teeth. She tried to imagine him twenty-five years ago, wondered if he'd ever been handsome.

"She's back, you know? Alive. Did you hear?"

He nodded, finished chewing, and swallowed. "I might've heard something like that."

"You wouldn't remember the last time you saw her, would you?" she asked.

He grinned. "I'm an old man. You expect me to remember something that far back?"

"See the thing is, I saw my mom the day before her hand was left on the steps of the police station. She was at the bowling alley. I saw her get into a tan car with a broken taillight. And I'm pretty sure it was your car."

He shook his head. "Wasn't me. I told the cops a million times." He went back to his burger, dismissing her.

"Rabbit," she said, voice low and soothing. "My mom used to talk about you all the time. I remember the way she'd get all giddy, singing even, when she was getting ready to meet you somewhere. I don't know much about what went on between the two of you, but there's one thing I'm sure of: she loved you."

He put down his burger and studied her a moment. Then he cleared his throat and in a soft voice said, "I wasn't anywheres near the bowling alley that day and I've got witnesses to prove it. Vera didn't want nothing to do with me. Truth is, we were on kind of rocky ground even back before I got arrested."

Reggie nodded in the most friendly way she could manage. "Why was that?"

"She had this friend. This little gal named Candy." He wiped his face with a napkin, just smearing the ketchup around. "And I guess I had me a sweet tooth one night." He gave Reggie a lecherous grin. "You wouldn't know it now, but I had a way with the ladies."

Reggie nodded, thinking he was right—she wouldn't know it, had a seriously difficult time imagining it.

"Vera was real pissed when she found out. Shit, it weren't like we were married or anything."

"But you saw my mom again once you got out of jail, right? Before she went missing?"

"Yeah. When I got outta jail we went out once or twice, but she dumped me. I was trying real hard then. You know, to get all cleaned up. To start over, I guess. But some people, they don't get second chances."

A bell rang in Reggie's brain. "Second Chance," Reggie said. "Does that mean anything to you? My mom had it written on a scrap of paper years ago."

He laughed. "It was the name of that old social work program for people just out of prison. They gave 'em a place to stay, buddied them up with some upstanding citizen. Stability, they called it. Supposed to be swayed by these great role models. Show you how good your life could be."

"And you were in this program?" Reggie asked.

"For a time. I lived in this house with four other guys. We had meetings and programs and got our piss tested to make sure we weren't using."

"And you were paired up with someone in the community? A good role model?"

"I sure was. He saved my ass until he couldn't anymore. He had a drug problem once himself, but had gotten clean. He was my NA sponsor. He had this big old house with an in-law apartment over the garage and he'd let me stay there when I was having a tough time. I was there when Vera went missing. So I didn't take her. And I had proof. An alibi."

"Sounds like he did a lot for you. What was his name?"

Rabbit looked down at the wrecked remains of his burger, like the answer was there with the crust of stale bun and congealing grease. "It was the car dealer. You know . . . the guy who used to do all the commercials with the chicken."

Reggie glanced up at Charlie, whose eyes popped open in a *holy-shit* look.

"Bo," Rabbit said. "His name was Bo Berr. A helluva good guy."

Day Three

Excerpt from *Neptune's Hands: The True Story of the Unsolved Brighton Falls Slayings* by Martha S. Paquette

On June 19, Vera Dufrane was supposed to meet her thirteen-year-old daughter, Regina Dufrane, at the Airport Lanes Bowling Alley. Regina unfortunately took a spill on her bicycle en route and was late. She arrived at the bowling alley parking lot just in time to see her mother getting into a tan sedan with a broken left taillight. The only thing Regina could make out about the driver was that he was wearing a baseball cap.

Vera did not appear to be struggling or give any signs of distress.

Dix Bergstrom, owner of Airport Lanes, and longtime friend of Vera's, reported that Vera mentioned that a friend was picking her up, and she went outside to wait for him. Bergstrom did not get a good look at the driver or the car.

Later that evening, around ten, Vera showed up alone at Runway 36. It is not known whether she drove her car, a green Vega, or got a ride. Police discovered her car the following day at the airport in the long-term lot, but found no sign that Vera had gone into the airport or taken a flight.

She had several drinks in the bar, talked to some of the people she knew, and seemed in good spirits. She left alone, just after midnight. Just before walking out the door, she was seen talking to a man with a mustache, black leather jacket, and Yankees baseball cap. When Detective Stuart Berr was asked if the man in the black leather jacket was a person of interest, he said only, "We have reason to believe that other than the killer, this man was the last person to see Vera Dufrane alive."

Chapter 32

June 22, 1985
Brighton Falls, Connecticut

Reggie slept until just after noon, drifting in and out of a dream in which she was searching for her mother and wound up back at Airport Efficiencies. The room was wrecked, but there, in the center of the bed, was a package wrapped in brown paper. With trembling fingers, Reggie opened the package. Inside was a wooden box with a neatly lettered label saying SECOND CHANCE. Cautiously she lifted the lid and opened her mouth to scream, but no sound came out. Looking up at her was a lifeless miniature version of Vera, pinned to a piece of Styrofoam amid a row of cockroaches.

Reggie sat up in bed, blinked at the clock, listened to the sound of kitchen chairs scraping against the floor, the low murmur of voices. She was supposed to have met Tara, Charlie, and Sid at the Silver Spoon for breakfast. They were going to eat, then ride out to the bowling alley to look for clues. Reggie wasn't sorry she'd slept in. She didn't really want to face the others, to have to discuss Airport Efficiencies or her mother or anything at all. She just wanted to sleep. She rolled over, closed her eyes, and saw her tiny mother impaled on a pin, cockroaches beside her.

"Fuck," Reggie yelped, opening her eyes. Her skin felt prickly. The urge to cut, strong. Maybe, maybe she'd do it with a pin.

No.

Reggie stumbled out of bed and padded down the hall and stairs in her T-shirt and sweatpants. She'd go down to the kitchen, get some juice, and pretend things were okay. That her mother was just away but would be back anytime. That Reggie was just a regular girl with no secret longing to slice herself up with razor blades and pins.

Reggie's ankle was still sore, but she could put more weight on it, her walk returning to almost normal. As she approached the kitchen, she could hear Lorraine talking. She was relieved Lorraine was up and out of bed. Reggie was starting to worry about what she might do if her aunt decided to never leave her room again.

"I just can't believe it," Lorraine was saying weakly. "I keep thinking there must be some mistake . . ."

"The fingerprints were a match, Lorraine. And the scarring." George. His voice was tired and shaky. "But I know what you mean. I keep thinking it'll be like all the other times—she'll disappear for a couple of days, then come waltzing back, all smiles, acting like she was never gone at all."

Reggie moved closer to the door, walking on tiptoes.

"It's my fault." Lorraine's voice crumbled.

"You can't blame yourself," George said, low and soothing. "There's nothing you could have done."

"If we hadn't fought . . ."

"She would have left anyway. You know how Vera was," George said. "*Is.* I mean *is.*"

Reggie got to the doorway and tucked her body behind it, peeking in. Lorraine was hunched over the table, gripping a mug of tea tightly. George was right next to her, his body pressing against hers, his arm around her.

"I suppose it was inevitable," Lorraine said, sitting up straight with effort. She ran her hand through her hair, which looked uncharacteristically unkempt. Her eyes were red, her cheeks blotchy. "Something terrible happening. I think I've known it all along, sensed it. That Vera was on a path that could only lead to destruction. Ever since we were girls, then after, when Father died, the part of her that was cracked just broke completely. I think I lost her back then. Before, maybe . . ."

"It doesn't do any good," George said, voice breaking now as he pushed his own cup away, untouched tea sloshing over the edges. "You think I haven't done the same thing? Been over it again and again in my head, fantasized about all the ways we could have saved her? If onlys do no good, Lorraine. Vera made her own choices. And maybe those choices led her to what happened. But maybe not. Maybe it was totally random."

Lorraine was crying, not delicate little ladylike sniffles, but great sobs of agony. She rested her head against George's chest and wept. George held on to her, ashen faced, his own eyes wet with tears. He leaned down and kissed the top of her head. "It just seems so unfair. So . . . surreal," he whispered into her hair.

A strange sick feeling crept over Reggie. This was not simply two good friends comforting each other—it was obvious from their body language that they were more than that. She thought of the way she'd heard George's voice the night Lorraine threw her mother out, and the whole thing was so obvious—he'd been spending the night with Lorraine. After he'd said his good nights to them, he must have doubled back, waited until Reggie had gone to bed, and sneaked back into the house, up to Lorraine's room. Or maybe, maybe they'd been in the garage, on the leather couch. Maybe that's what Vera had referred to when she said she knew what went on out there. Reggie's stomach did a disgusted flip.

She remembered the way Lorraine had looked when George gave Vera the swan earlier that night.

Had Lorraine been jealous? She wondered if this was the real reason Lorraine threw Vera out—she didn't like the way her boyfriend was looking at her sister. And just how far would Lorraine go to protect her relationship with George if she felt threatened by Vera?

She squinted in at her aunt, seeing things in a whole new light while one question rang out like an alarm bell: what other secrets were there that she didn't know?

Lorraine lifted up her head, looked at George, and said, "Last night I couldn't sleep. I was just lying in bed, imagining what he might be doing to her . . ."

"I know," George said, rubbing her back in slow circles. "I can't standing just sitting back, waiting. Knowing she's out there somewhere, tied up. That it's just a matter of time."

Reggie backed away from the kitchen and went upstairs in her sock feet, avoiding the bottom step that squeaked.

It's just a matter of time.

Her stomach churned and her mouth went dry.

George was right. The worst part was waiting. Reggie couldn't bear the thought of spending the day doing nothing but obsessing about what an idiot she'd been to be blind to Lorraine and George's relationship. Were there other things hiding in plain sight, clues that might lead her to her mother?

Reggie stood in the hallway outside her bedroom, pulled down the trapdoor that led to the attic, unfolded the wooden ladder attached to it, and climbed up.

The attic, which had once served as her mother's sewing room, was now a sort of Vera Museum. She flipped on the hanging bulb and looked around.

There were two sewing machines and three dress dummies, each wearing the last outfit she'd put on them. Headless and armless, they were three Vera-size torsos dressed in her clothes: strange oracles Reggie wished could speak.

Abandoned bolts of fabric and boxes of scraps lined one of the walls. There was a worktable with scissors, a ruler, an iron, and a pincushion. To the left of the table was a full-length trifold adjustable mirror. In front of this was a trunk full of old pictures, magazines, sewing patterns, photos from Vera's modeling portfolio, and high school yearbooks. Reggie opened the trunk and sorted through some of these relics, searching for a clue as to who her mother had been before she came along. But Vera had left few clues. There were no diaries. No old love letters. Nothing scandalous. Nothing to tell Reggie who her father might have been. Some old playbills and programs from school with her mother cast in starring roles: Wendy in *Peter Pan,* Annie Oakley in *Annie Get Your Gun.* Reggie flipped through Vera's senior yearbook and found a picture of her mother, who'd been voted *Most likely to be famous.* A girl named Lynda had written, *Shoot for the moon, Vera.* There were other photos of Vera: in the drama club, where she was in a reclining position, being held up by the other members; onstage as Lady Macbeth. Reggie closed the yearbook, holding it on her lap while she stuffed everything else back into the trunk.

Reggie gazed into the dusty mirrors, studying the images of the three faceless dummies in Vera's clothes behind her. Reggie squinted and thought she saw them move, reach for her with invisible arms, whisper in hushed tones.

She's out there. It's up to you to save her.

"What, are you thinking about sewing yourself a ball gown or something?"

Startled, Reggie looked away from the mirror and spun to see Tara nearly beside her. She'd crept up the attic stairs so silently, Reggie had no idea she was there.

"I was just looking through some of my mom's old stuff."

"How come you didn't meet us at the diner, Reg? We were gonna go out to Airport Lanes, talk to Dix, look around. Remember? We waited for you for nearly two hours. Sid had to get to work at the golf course. Charlie went off to do some lawns."

"I'm sorry. I just couldn't. I don't really see the point." Reggie bit her lip, remembering what Lorraine had said: *I suppose it was inevitable. Something terrible happening.*

Reggie put a finger out and touched the mirror, making a line in the dust, a circle that turned into a tornadolike swirl. Some things are just bigger than we are. The pull of gravity. The hand of fate.

Hand.

In her mind's eye, she saw her mother's wrecked hand in a milk carton, pointing up at her.

You. It's up to you to save me.

But Reggie couldn't. That was the thing.

She couldn't because she was stupid and selfish and didn't want to learn any more horrible secrets about her mother. She was a fucking coward.

"The point?" Tara bit her lip, studied Reggie in the dim light. "The point is that we've gotta keep trying, right? If we stop looking, it's over."

"It's over anyway," Reggie said.

"Reggie," Tara said, "just because you found shit you didn't want to see doesn't mean you can quit. So your mother had this secret little room and hung out in sleazy bars and saw lots of men. So what? She's still your mom, Reg. You can't just turn your back on her because you want to keep some fucked-up little perfect mother charade going."

Reggie looked in the mirrors. Tara was beside her and the dummies were behind them, strange phantom stalkers.

"What's this?" Tara asked, reaching for the yearbook.

"My mom's. The trunk is full of all her old stuff, but there's nothing helpful. I thought if I looked carefully, there'd be something, some little shred. Some clue."

Tara flipped through, finding a photo of Vera. "God, she was beautiful." She squinted at the yearbook, then at Reggie. "You look like her, you know. Around the eyes. And the shape of your face."

"I'm nothing like her," Reggie said.

"But the rest of it, your nose and eyebrows, they come from someplace else. Your father, probably." Tara flipped through the yearbook. "Maybe he's in here. Maybe it was some old flame from high school."

Reggie shook her head. "She got pregnant in New York."

Tara licked her lips. "So maybe it was someone she was in a play with there. Or someone she worked with. Maybe it was someone famous, Reg! Maybe that's why your mom's always been so secretive." Tara flipped through the papers, found a theater program for *The Crucible.* "Hey, isn't this that play about the Salem witches?"

"Yeah, I think so."

"And look, they did it at a theater in Hartford." Tara wrinkled her nose, counted backward on her fingers from 1985 to 1970. "October 1970," she said.

"So?"

"So . . . your mom was in this play in Hartford then, not off in New York! I'm no baby expert or anything, but I think that would have had to be around the time she got knocked up with you." Tara's face glowed in the dim light, flush with excitement.

"It doesn't matter," Reggie said, grabbing the program from Tara and dropping it back on the pile. "I'm sure whoever he is, he doesn't even know I exist. And my mom is the only person who knows who my father is, and she's gone. We can play cops and robbers all we want, running around to bars, looking for clues, but none of it makes any difference. We can't save her, Tara. No one can. It's all just a stupid, useless waste!" She leaned her head down and started to cry, hating herself for it. She was a coward and a baby, and now Tara knew it and Reggie didn't even care.

"Hey," Tara said, her voice practically a whisper as she put a hand on Reggie's back. "I know how you feel."

"Bullshit," Reggie hissed, looking up and staring at their reflections in the mirror. A thin-faced girl who looked more like a boy. She'd forgotten to put her ear on, and with the new haircut, the missing ear was obvious and made her look freakishly unbalanced. And Tara, Tara looked like some beautiful actress straight off the set of a vampire movie.

"Sometimes," Tara said, "sometimes it's all just too much, you know? All the fucked-up stuff going round and round in my brain. And people are trying to talk to me, but it's like they're underwater—they don't have a clue. I've got voices of dead ladies whispering to me, my mom screaming at me to pick up my room and telling me that maybe if I wasn't such a goddamn slob, my dad wouldn't have left us." Tara's chin started to quiver, but she sat ramrod straight, reeling herself in. When she spoke again, her voice was low and calm. "And some days I'm sure I'm gonna explode if I can't slow all the thoughts and voices down, keep them from spinning out of control."

Reggie stared at herself in the mirror, snuffling, tears and snot dripping down her face.

"But I've learned the secret," Tara said, smiling impishly. "I can stop them now. We both can."

Reggie sat down in front of the mirror, watched as Tara reached into her black bag and pulled out the silver box with the razor blade wrapped in fabric like a tiny present. She held it out to Reggie, waiting.

Reggie took the blade, pulled up the leg of her sweatpants, eager. But she stopped herself and looked at Tara.

"It'll feel so good," Tara said, leaning forward, trembling a little as she stared down at the unblemished skin on Reggie's calf. Tara looked so amazing, so pale and sparkling, like her skin was made of moonlight.

"You do it for me," Reggie said, holding out the razor blade. Tara gave a grateful little gasp, like a girl who'd just gotten what she wanted most for Christmas.

Tara gripped the blade, hovered over Reggie's skin, making the moment last. Tara's breathing got faster, more ragged. Reggie bit her lip, waiting, wanting it, but fearing it at the same time. Tara brought the blade down lightly, caressing the skin, not breaking through.

"Please," Reggie said, and Tara pushed the blade down hard, making Reggie cry out. Tara made an *mmm* sound as she pulled back the blade and let herself touch Reggie's cut, opening it up, making Reggie wince. It was deep and bled more than any of the little sissy cuts Reggie had given herself. She let the pain wash over her like a wave; felt herself melting into it.

There was no Neptune, no missing mother, no Charlie or Lorraine or horrid little room at Airport Efficiencies.

There was no one but her and Tara, whose fingers were sticky with Reggie's blood, both girls feeling invincible.

Chapter 33

October 22, 2010
Brighton Falls, Connecticut

"Shit!" Reggie yelped, the blade of the utility knife nicking the tip of her left thumb. Blood smeared on the piece of Sheetrock she'd been cutting, making a Rorschach test design that looked at first like a ladybug, then, as the blood seeped farther, like a lobster. For half a second, she was back in her old body, letting herself get some sick pleasure from the pain, getting lost inside it, thinking it made her more powerful somehow.

"Idiot," she said to herself as she moved to the kitchen sink to wash out the cut. She peered through the window over the sink and saw a news truck with a satellite dish down at the bottom of her driveway. A man was coming up with a heavy camera resting on his shoulder. A woman with immaculate hair and thick makeup followed. The press continued to come and shoot footage of the house and knock at the door, which Reggie and Lorraine never answered. The phone rang nonstop, but they always let the machine get it.

Reggie let the curtain fall closed and inspected her thumb.

She was usually much more careful than this. Hypervigilant about safety. Fortunately, the cut wasn't deep.

She still had the scar from the cut Tara had given her: a thin line on the back of her calf; the mark others noticed and sometimes asked about. (She told them she'd done it in a bicycle accident.) There were other scars, too. Fainter, paler ones across her arms and legs. Ghost scars that she could only sometimes see.

Reggie had continued to cut throughout high school. She did it in secret, the way some girls did cocaine or gave blow jobs to strangers. She did it in her room at home or locked in a stall in one of the girls' bathrooms at school. It was a compulsion. An addiction. A need to feel control, to focus her mind when it was running in crazy, nonsensical loops. Only when she left home was she able to stop—when she got to Rhode Island and began her life as a new and different girl, a girl without a past.

And now here she was, right back where she started. Her skin itched in the old, familiar way, the urge to cut strong. And the utility knife was right there. It would be so easy to pick it up, run it across her skin.

Reggie turned off the faucet and was pressing a paper towel over her thumb when her cell phone began to vibrate in the pocket of her jeans. She slid it out—Len again.

She answered it.

"Hey," she said.

"Reggie? Oh my God, I've been worried sick! Why didn't you call? Didn't you get my messages?"

"I'm sorry. Things here have been so crazy. I meant to call, but I wasn't—"

"You're back home, aren't you? Back in Brighton Falls?"

"Yes," she said. The cut on her finger continued to bleed. She reached for a fresh paper towel and put pressure on the wound with her index finger. "Len?"

"Yeah?"

"Can I tell you something? Something I've never told anyone?"

"Of course."

Reggie braced herself. She thought of backing out, inventing some other lie, but she'd come this far. If she told, the secret would be out and wouldn't have the same kind of power over her. Then maybe her skin would stop crawling and she'd stop eyeing the utility knife so longingly. "When I was a kid, I used to cut myself. On purpose."

"Okay," he said, voice calm and steady.

"I'd use a razor blade and never go very deep, just deep enough to hurt, to draw blood. I started around the time the whole Neptune mess began. When everything seemed so out of control, so hurtful and violent and scary as hell. Cutting brought this sense of order. Of calm."

Len was silent a minute. "It makes total sense. It's messed up and awful and I'm really sorry you went through it, but I get it," he said at last. "But I've got to ask, why tell me all this right now?"

"Because there's no one else I can tell it to. *That's the whole point.*" She needed Len to get this, to really understand what she was trying to say. "You're the only one I've ever wanted to tell all my fucked-up little secrets to. I was wrong to not tell you when my mother first showed up. I get that now and I'm really, truly sorry."

"It's okay," he said.

"No, it isn't. I can't stand the thought that I did something to hurt you. You're my one true friend, Len. The person I'm closest to in the world. I'm not going to pretend I know how to define our relationship, and I can't promise I'll ever be ready to move in with you. But I love you, Len. In my own fucked-up little way, I love you very much."

"I love you, too," Len said.

"I can't stand the idea of losing you," she said, biting her lip.

"I know," he said. "I can't stand the thought of being without you, either."

They were silent a minute.

"They said on the news that another hand had been found, that Neptune is back."

"He's got my old friend Tara. My aunt had hired her as a nurse to look after my mom. I think Tara found out something and went digging around and got a little too close."

"Jesus!" Len said. "I think I should come down there. I can pack a bag, be out the door in ten minutes."

"No," Reggie said quickly, looking at her blood-soaked paper towel. "I mean, thank you, but—no. You can't. It's just too much of a collision between my past life and my current life for me to handle right now. And there's nothing you can do anyway. I'm really fine."

"You don't sound fine," Len said, his voice warm and husky. She wished he were there, holding her in his arms.

"Being back here hasn't been easy," Reggie admitted.

Len made a soothing sound of agreement. "You've spent your whole life running away from that place and everything that happened there," he said.

"And now here I am. Right back in the thick of it. In some ways, I feel like I never left. Or like I've stepped back through time and gone right back to being a kid again." She started to pick at the cut on her thumb, watched it reopen and begin to bleed again.

"As painful as all this is, I know it'll be good for you," Len said. "You're facing your demons. You'll come out stronger."

Reggie sighed. "I'm facing demons all right. I'm going out to see this old son of a bitch named Bo Berr today. He was my mom's boyfriend in high school. He owned the Ford dealership here in town. He's shifty as hell, a real scumbag."

"So why are you paying him a visit?"

"You know the tan car I saw my mom get into the night she was taken? I think we've linked Bo to that car. If he knows something, we'll find out."

"We?"

"Charlie's taking me to see him. Bo is Charlie's uncle."

"Wait a sec, *the* Charlie? The infamous adolescent crush?"

Reggie sighed. Maybe she'd already told Len too much about her past.

"That was in another lifetime. *We were thirteen.* Now he's this boring, soft-around-the-middle guy with thinning hair who sells real estate. But he wants to find Tara as badly as I do."

"This is fucked up, Reggie. You're seriously tooling around town looking for a serial killer?"

"I'll be careful," Reggie said. "Look, Charlie'll be here any minute. I've gotta go. I'll call you later, okay?"

"Promise?" he asked. "Because if I don't hear from you, I'm coming down there."

"I promise," she said, hanging up before he could say any more.

Chapter 34

June 22, 1985
Brighton Falls, Connecticut

"Where's Lorraine?" Reggie had come down to the kitchen to find George doing the dishes. His clothing was rumpled, his eyes red and puffy. He looked like he hadn't slept in days.

"She went to lie down. Is your friend gone?"

Reggie nodded.

George pulled the plug in the sink, sending the soapy water in a whirlpool down the drain. "Your aunt doesn't think much of her. I'm afraid Lorraine's put off by her fashion sense. All that black. The lace and safety pins."

Reggie shrugged. "At least Tara has a fashion sense." She left off what she was thinking: not like Lorraine with her stinky old fishing vest. She didn't want to hurt George's feelings—he apparently liked the fishing vest, maybe even found it attractive. Reggie stopped that thought before it went any further. The whole idea of Lorraine and George having a secret romance made her stomach hurt.

George smiled. "You two find anything interesting up there in the attic?" He looked at her with searching eyes, and for a split second, Reggie was sure he knew about the cutting. Her leg twinged with pain and felt damp. Tara had gone deep. The cut was now covered with a gauze pad and layers of medical tape that itched and pulled at her skin.

"Not much," she said, looking away from him.

"Come have a seat," he said, pulling out a chair at the kitchen table. She sat across from him. He looked at her a long time, then lifted his glasses and rubbed his face with his damp, pruny, dishwater hands. He replaced his glasses carefully and looked out at Reggie. His eyes looked big and sad. "Reggie, your mom—"

"I know. Neptune's got her. It was her hand they found. I knew before Lorraine did—when I first heard the description of the hand. I even went to the police."

George's eyes got bigger behind his glasses. "You did? Does Lorraine know?"

Reggie shook her head. "She'd kill me. Please don't tell her."

He gave a wan smile. "Our secret, then." They were silent a minute, both shuffling their feet on the floor. Reggie looked down and saw the linoleum was strewn with crumbs.

"Reggie," George said. "If you want someone to talk to . . . about your mom, I mean . . ."

"Thanks," Reggie said, standing up like she had someplace to hurry off to. George looked relieved that she wasn't going to take him up on his offer right then and there.

"Hey, I was thinking I might head back to my place and work on Lorraine's fishing cabinet. It would be good to have something to do. Something to help me keep my mind off all this. Want to join me?" George said, eyebrows raised. Sometimes George reminded Reggie of a hopeful dog, one it was impossible to disappoint. She liked this look a whole lot better than the all-seeing X-ray vision look he'd just given her.

Reggie nodded and followed him out to his van.

"Beautiful afternoon," George said. The air smelled like fresh cut grass and grilled meat—one of their neighbors was having a cookout. The charred scent hit Reggie hard, sending waves of nausea through her. She was sure that behind it, she could detect the faint odor of her own blood as it leaked from her leg. She leaned back against George's van, steadying herself before climbing in.

George had made a lot of progress on the fishing cabinet. The sides, bottom, and top were all done but lying in a neat row on a quilt on the basement floor, waiting to be assembled.

"Want to see something cool?" George asked, eyes gleaming.

"Sure."

He reached down to the bottom of the cabinet: a small platform of sanded oak with decorative molding around the edges. He pushed on the floor of the base, and it popped open like a door.

"It's got a secret compartment," he said. "This part wasn't in the plans. I added it myself. Don't you think she'll love it?"

Reggie smiled. It was pretty cool. But still, she had a hard time imagining what Lorraine might use a compartment like that for—her extra-special top-secret best trout-luring flies? "It's great," Reggie said.

"Can I ask you a question?" Reggie said, eyes on the secret compartment.

"Shoot."

"Are you and Lorraine . . . you know, are you a couple or something?"

George closed the secret door. Without turning to look at her, he finally answered. "In a sense."

"What does that mean?"

"It means we're two adults who enjoy each other's company."

"You're not gonna get married or anything, are you?"

George made a sound that was half laughter, half snort. "Good heavens, no! I think we're both happy enough with the arrangement as it is."

"But why be so secretive?"

"What we do is nobody's business but our own."

"Does my mom know?"

"I'm not sure."

"So you never told her. Never talked about it?"

"No. Why should I? I don't need Vera's permission to have a private life."

Reggie laughed. "You know, she thought you were hanging around all the time because of her. That's what she told me. She said you'd taken her on dates, but you just weren't her type. She thought you were kind of sulky and heartbroken."

George's eyes got wide. "I've taken her out, yes. But not on dates! We went out as friends."

"I don't think she saw it that way," Reggie said.

George turned back to the platform of the cabinet, fiddling with it unnecessarily. "I guess you never know what other people are thinking, do you?"

Understatement of the year.

"I guess not," Reggie said.

"Do me a favor," George said, getting back to business. "Grab the tape measure, square, and a pencil. We'll cut the pieces for the door."

Reggie walked over to the bench with its neat rows of tools, picked up the twenty-five-foot measuring tape, the metal square, and the carpenter's pencil with its rectangular lead.

George had a six-foot piece of oak on the sawhorses. "Mark it at sixty-three and five-eighths," he instructed. Reggie measured the board, making a pencil mark first on the left side, then again when she measured from the right. Then she lined the square up perfectly and drew a line, connecting the dots. She wished everything in her life was as simple and sensible as this. If only tools and measurements would help her to find her mother. Reggie heard Tara's voice echoing in her head: *The point is that we've gotta keep trying, right? If we stop looking, it's over.*

"Good," George said. "Do you want to do the cutting?"

Reggie nodded, reaching for the clear safety glasses. "George," she said as she placed the glasses on. "Did my mom say anything to you about this new play she's in? Like the name of the theater company or anything?"

George shook his head, seemed to hesitate before speaking. "There are things you don't know. Things Lorraine and I feel it's time you learned. With your mother's—disappearance—well, a lot of stuff is apt to come to the surface. And I'd rather you heard it from me than from reading it in the paper." George straightened up and faced Reggie.

"What kind of things?"

"Your mother hasn't been in a play since before you were born, Reg."

"What?" Reggie stammered. She peered out at him through the scuffed plastic lenses of the safety glasses. She suddenly felt like she was underwater, sinking fast.

George was wrong. He had to be. Vera had been doing plays for years, that's what kept her so busy all the time.

"But she's been doing a play in New Haven. With Rabbit."

He shook his head. "There is no play in New Haven. There may not even be a Rabbit. If there is, he's no director."

Reggie's heart hammered. She wanted to cover her good ear, stamp her feet like a toddler having a tantrum, refusing to listen anymore. Instead she cleared her throat and asked in a meek voice, "But what's she been doing if she's not off rehearsing?"

George turned back to the wood, lifting onto the chop saw, lining the blade up with the line Reggie had made. "I don't know exactly. Drinking, mostly, I think. Spending time with her friends. With *boyfriends.*" He spat the last word out bitterly, sounding as prudish and judgmental as Lorraine.

"Oh," Reggie said, the word a hollow sound.

She thought of the filthy, wrecked room at Airport Efficiencies, the cockroach, and the package of condoms.

Her breath was coming hard and fast now. Tears stung her eyes behind the glasses, which were now fogging.

Everything she thought she knew about her mother was a complete lie. A lie that they'd all fed to her, year after year, thinking they were protecting her from the truth.

"Go ahead and cut it, Reg," George said, and Reggie flipped on the saw, and brought the blade down across the line, biting into the wood, making a screaming sound. Once she'd finished, Reggie turned off the saw and stepped back, taking the glasses off and rubbing her eyes.

"Your mother was wonderful onstage, Reggie. I wish you could have seen her. She had this . . . this presence. It was spellbinding, really. Lorraine and I still talk about it. About what might have happened if she'd stuck with it, if she hadn't just given the whole thing up."

You mean if she hadn't gotten pregnant, Reggie thought. *Hadn't had me.*

Reggie was feeling worse by the second. Her leg throbbed. The bandages felt damp and sticky. But somewhere behind the pain, another thought was coming to the surface. Something that had been there all afternoon, quietly festering and now refusing to be ignored.

"We found something else in the attic," Reggie said. "An old theater program from the fall of 1970. She did *The Crucible* at a little theater in Hartford."

George was over by the wood, moving another oak board to the sawhorses for measuring. He turned and stared at her blankly. "I don't think I saw that one," he said.

"But everyone always said she'd been in New York that fall, just before she moved back to Monique's Wish. That was a lie too, wasn't it?"

George sighed. "She *had* been in New York. Left just after high school graduation. But then, at the end of the following summer, she came back."

"Why?" Reggie asked.

George sighed. "I guess I can tell you. Since we're letting all the skeletons out of the closet today. Bo Berr asked her to come back. He set her up in a little apartment, promised he'd leave his wife, marry Vera instead."

George's voice had an angry edge to it, but Reggie couldn't tell who it was directed at: Vera or Bo.

"Bo? Charlie's uncle?"

"He had a real thing for Vera, always did. Even back in junior high. Hell, elementary school, probably. Anyway, it didn't last. He dumped her pretty soon after and moved back in with his wife."

"But if she was with Bo, living with him that fall, then that means . . ."

George stared at her, poker-faced.

She didn't dare say the rest out loud.

Reggie rode as fast and hard as she could to the center of town, right to Berr's Ford. She arrived sweaty and out of breath, the bandaged cut on her leg burning.

"You're a little young to be out car shopping, aren't you, Regina?" Bo eyed her skeptically as she moved across the floor room toward him. He was leaning against a brand-new F-150 pickup, the candy-apple-red paint blindingly glossy. His suit was dusty gray, the fabric worn and shiny in places. Another salesman sat at a desk in the corner; he looked up briefly from his paperwork, but got right back to it.

"I have some questions," Reggie said, stopping right in front of Bo, watching the way he smiled down at her so smugly, so dismissively. It was a smile that told her she was nothing to him. She was so close she could hear his breathing, see his nose hairs and that his shirt was stained yellow around the collar. His tie had something that looked like grape jelly on it. He licked his lips, tongue touching his overgrown mustache.

"About the fall of 1970. When my mother came back from New York."

There was a little twitch at the corners of his mouth, and the smile fell away. "Let's go to my office," he said, gesturing with one of his big, blockish hands. He'd been a football star in high school; she remembered her mother mentioning it when they watched him on TV, in one of his stupid chicken commercials. He'd planned to go to college on a football scholarship but had ruined his knee senior year.

Reggie followed him across the showroom to the big office at the end with the plate-glass window overlooking the showroom. His desk was littered with papers. There was a framed photo of Stu, his wife, and Sid. There was another shot of Bo and Stu out on a boat, holding an enormous fish with a pointed, spearlike snout—a marlin, maybe. They looked young and tan and happy. There were young women in the background, their wives, maybe, or girlfriends they'd had before they met their wives. Reggie's eye went to the Dealer of the Year plaques on the walls. Framed letters from charitable organizations thanking Bo for going above and beyond to help raise money for everything from cancer research to saving the Connecticut River from pollution.

He took a seat in the upholstered chair behind his desk. Reggie stood.

"What did she say?" he asked, his big, meaty face beginning to flush.

"Who?"

"Your mother. Whatever it was, you can be damn sure there isn't a grain of truth to it."

"She didn't say anything to me."

If only, Reggie thought. If only she'd trusted me enough to tell me the truth. Not just her, but Lorraine and George, too. They'd treated her like some kind of doll, too delicate to bear the weight of the truth.

Maybe they were right. Maybe she was.

She could feel little cracks forming already, turning rough and ragged in places, opening up in the place where Tara had run the razor blade along her skin. Sweat dripped into the cut, burning like acid.

"Well, who've you been talking to then?" Bo demanded.

"It doesn't matter. What matters is what I heard."

"And what's that?"

"That my mother came back from New York to be with you in the fall of 1970. That you got her an apartment, promised you'd leave your wife, then dumped her. Is it true?"

His face went from pink to red. "I'd like you to leave, Regina. You have no business coming here, talking to me like this."

"Is it true?"

He ran a hand over his mustache as if he was dusting crumbs out.

"Are you my father?" she asked abruptly. She couldn't believe she'd said it out loud, but there it was, no going back now. She leaned forward, resting her hands on the edge of his desk, searching his face for some sign of herself.

Bo was now the shade of a beet and moist with perspiration. "Your father . . . ," he stammered.

"I don't want anything from you. I just want—"

What *did* she want? An apology? Some kind of explanation that would help her to understand why all the adults in her life had layered the lies, spreading them sweet and thick over the years, like a sickening kind of cake that was supposed to make her feel happy and loved, but was secretly laced with poison.

"Your father could be anyone!" Bo said, the words hitting Reggie square in the chest like an arrow.

"But if my mother was living with you—"

"Your mother's a whore, Regina." He spit the words out with tremendous anger. "Haven't you figured that out by now?"

Reggie stared at him, heart pounding up into her throat. She let go of the desk, staggering backward. The pain in her leg pulsated and blossomed with each heartbeat. She glanced down and saw the blood soaking through her sweatpants, marking her for what she truly was: a bastard girl who cut herself with a whore for a mother.

"She'd let anyone who'd buy her a glass of gin slip it to her."

Now it was Reggie's face that began to color. She felt light-headed and weak-kneed. She wished she could just disappear entirely, be gone in a puff of smoke like a girl in a magic show.

"You want the truth, young lady? Here's the truth: she lived with me when she first came back, but it didn't last. Not when I learned what she was up to. That she was going out at night with other men. It's like a sickness she's got. This want, this *need,* to be loved, to be admired, to have men fight over her like goddamn dogs." His eyes blazed. "That's what got her killed."

Reggie took a step back, swaying a little. "She's not dead," Reggie said. "Not yet."

He squinted at her like she was small and far away, something he had to really focus on. "I pity you, Regina. I really do. Being born from that woman. Having her blood running in your veins. I don't know who your father is, but it's not me. She told me so herself."

"Did she say who it was?"

Bo gave a deep belly laugh, shaking his head. "I doubt she ever even knew. Could be anyone. One of those actors, a truck driver passing through. I wouldn't be at all surprised to hear that Vera put out for the goddamned devil himself."

Chapter 35

October 22, 2010
Brighton Falls, Connecticut

"How is she?" Bo asked, lower lip trembling slightly. "Your mother?"

Reggie studied the old man before her. He was shrunken, wrinkled, covered in liver spots. It was hard to imagine this was the same hulking, red-faced Bo Berr Reggie had confronted at the dealership twenty-five years ago.

Charlie had told her that his uncle Bo had recently been diagnosed with pancreatic cancer and wasn't expected to last more than six months. Even if this man had been the killer back in 1985, Reggie couldn't believe he'd have the strength and stamina to start up again now.

It seemed a strange coincidence to Reggie that both her mother and Bo were dying of cancer. Life had taken them each in such separate directions; now here they were, weak and sick, looking so much alike it gave Reggie goose bumps.

"Funny you should ask," Reggie said. "Because the last time I remember you and I having a conversation about my mother, you didn't seem all that concerned about her well-being."

Time did not heal all wounds. Sometimes they just festered.

Bo nodded, looked away. His nose began to run, and he wiped at it with a dirty tissue.

"I'm dying, you know? Did my nephew tell you?"

Reggie gritted her teeth. She refused to pity him.

"I told her, Uncle Bo," Charlie said. He was seated beside Reggie on the leather couch in Bo's home office. Charlie was wearing jeans and a Rolling Stones T-shirt that looked brand-new, like he'd just picked it up at the music store in the mall when he stopped for guitar strings. It was a little tight, accentuating his paunchy belly. On the way over to Bo's, he'd told Reggie that he'd restrung the old guitar, stayed up late into the night playing. He'd showed her raw-looking blistered fingers.

Bo's wife, Frances, had let them in, told them Bo was expecting them. Charlie had arranged the meeting by phone, telling Bo that they had some questions.

The Berrs' house was a sprawling one-story design with a curved glass block wall and a stucco exterior. Reggie remembered thinking how big and fancy it had seemed when they were kids. Now the stucco was crumbly, the glass blocks were chipped and grimy. There was a swimming pool in the back that Reggie could see from the office window—the cement was cracked, and it was half full of dark green, slimy-looking water. To the left of the swimming pool was the garage with the little apartment on the top floor where Rabbit had once stayed.

Bo cleared his throat noisily and hacked something thick into the tissue. Reggie felt her stomach flip-flop.

"What is it you want?" he asked quietly. His desk took up a third of the room and had a large, tinted glass top. It was covered in dirty tissues, cold cups of tea, and a couple of tourist brochures about Mexico.

Reggie launched right into it. "We talked with Rabbit. We know he was staying here when my mother was taken—that you were his NA sponsor and you worked with him through Second Chance. And I know damn well I saw my mother get into a tan car with a broken taillight at the bowling alley that night. Was it you?"

She fought the temptation to lean forward and shake the old man, slap his pale, sickly face over and over like a 1940s movie gangster—*Spill it, you dirty rat*—somehow force the truth out of him. Somewhere Tara was waiting in the dark, knowing that soon Neptune would come for her.

Bo sighed. "My wife, Frances, deserves a medal, you know. Putting up with me all these years. Taking care of me. Of Sidney."

Reggie cringed when she heard Sid's name. Was there a day that had gone by that she hadn't thought of him?

Twenty-five years of guilt mixed with the acid in her stomach, churning, making her twist on the couch, trying to get comfortable. She turned to Charlie. He was stone-faced. How had he done it all these years—lived with what they'd done? Sid was his cousin. And they lived in the same town. Charlie hadn't run the way she had. He'd found a way to live with what they did—to face it at every family gathering.

She remembered the dream she'd had long ago of finding a bug-size Vera pinned to a box with a collection of roaches. She felt like one of those insects now, trapped and on display.

"But you know what they say," Bo went on. "You never get over your first love? Maybe that's true."

Reggie felt her face flush as she looked down at the ground, not wanting to catch Charlie's eye. While she no longer felt anything for the man sitting beside her, a part of her still pined for that boy who smelled of fresh-cut grass and gasoline.

Reggie remembered the little Barbie shoe Tara carried around, the one she'd taken from Andrea McFerlin's house. She thought of Andrea McFerlin's two little girls, now grown women, and wondered if they'd learned to love properly, to feel safe in the world again.

"I was crazy for Vera," Bo said. "Just crazy. But whatever I did, whatever I gave her"—his eyes turned steely, and Reggie saw a glimpse of the man he used to be—"it was never enough. Vera went off to New York and I married Frances. We made our choices."

"But you asked her to come back," Reggie said. "You said you'd leave your wife. It wasn't over between you."

Bo looked down at the top of his desk. "It should have been."

Had Reggie ever loved anyone that much? There was Charlie, but that was puppy love. The truth was, Len was right: she'd never had the courage to love anyone down to the bones.

"Was it you?" Charlie asked his uncle. "Were you Neptune?"

Bo's face contorted into a look of disgust. He coughed and hacked for a minute, pulled another tissue from the box. "No. I'm no killer. I've been a junkie, I've been unfaithful to my wife, hell, I've even cheated on my taxes, but I've never lifted a finger to hurt a lady."

"Did you take Rabbit's car that night?" Reggie asked, leaning forward, holding her breath.

Bo gave a slow nod and looked down. "Vera called me from the bowling alley. Said she'd been stood up and needed a ride. I told her to call a goddamn cab, but she said all she had was eighteen cents. In the end, I went. I didn't want to take a chance of anyone recognizing me with her, so I left my car at home and took Rabbit's. He never even knew."

"So what happened?" Charlie asked. "What did she say? Where did you go?"

"We drove around. Vera was edgy, smoking a lot. We went to a drive-through, got some burgers and coffees. I asked her about the guy who'd stood her up, and all she said was that they were pretty serious, that he'd asked her to marry him. She said he was a real gentleman, someone important, with money. She wanted to know if I could picture her married."

"And what did you say?" Reggie asked.

Bo snorted derisively.

"I told her the truth. She didn't like that much."

Reggie remembered the night her mother had curled up beside her in bed. *A nice, normal life. You'd like that, wouldn't you, love?*

"What happened next?" Reggie asked.

"I dropped her off at Runway 36. I wanted to go in with her, buy her a drink, but she sent me off on my way. That was the last time I saw her."

"And the police never knew? Never figured out that it was you in that car?" Charlie asked.

Bo smiled, revealing yellowish teeth. "You know your dad, Charlie. He was a good cop. Maybe great. But he was loyal to his family. He knew it was me who took Vera from the bowling alley to Runway 36 that night. Hell, it didn't take him long. He came to ask me about it the very next morning. But he kept it quiet. He knew I wasn't the killer. Just like he knew you would never hurt anyone on purpose—right, Charlie?"

Charlie looked down at the floor.

There it was. All these years, Reggie had wondered if Bo knew what really happened to Sid that night. Reggie's mind whirred. Did Stu keep Bo from pressing charges against all of them by hiding the fact that Bo was the driver of the infamous tan car?

"People make mistakes," Bo said. "Your father understood that. He also understood that some mistakes could ruin lives. And when he could, he did his best to make sure that didn't happen."

They left Bo in his office, saying they could find their own way out. Bo coughed some more, waving them out of the room as Frances came in with a pill bottle and fresh glass of water. They paused in the hall, looking at photos of Bo and Stu, Sidney and Charlie, all of them looking impossibly young and happy, like the life that awaited them was just one big wonderful adventure.

"Do you believe him?" Charlie asked, running a hand through his thinning hair.

"Yeah," Reggie said. "I do."

"Me, too," he said.

"So we're still no closer to finding our mystery man," Reggie said.

"If there even is one," Charlie said. "I mean, maybe it really was random. Maybe Neptune wasn't the guy she was going to marry, but some stranger who happened to see her that night at the bar."

"Maybe," Reggie admitted, feeling like the whole thing was hopeless. If it was truly random, then there was no chance of finding a clue that would lead them to Tara in time.

But that was the kicker wasn't it: Tara. Why had the killer taken Tara? Why come out of hiding twenty-five years later and take another woman? The only logical explanation Reggie could come up with is that somehow or other, Tara got too close.

And then there was the wedding ring Vera had held on to—*Until death do us part June 20, 1985.* This was the biggest clue they had connecting the man she was going to marry with Neptune.

They continued down the hall, passing by the front room where Sid's wheelchair was parked in front of the TV. There was a game show on, the contestants spinning a large roulette wheel.

Reggie froze, holding her breath as she studied Sid's slumped shoulders, the way his hair, still curly and unkempt, fell over the back of his neck.

"I want to go say hello," Reggie said.

"It won't do any good. He won't know you. He doesn't remember."

So this was how Charlie managed to live with the guilt, to go to family gatherings and face Sid over the Thanksgiving turkey—he told himself over and over that Sid didn't remember. As if that made it all disappear somehow.

Reggie went into the room anyway while Charlie hovered in the doorway, hands dug into the pockets of his leather jacket.

"Hi, Sid," Reggie said, squatting down. He opened his eyes and stared at her vaguely. He was hunched over in the chair, held in by a fabric belt around his waist. A catheter tube came out of his sweatpants and into a clear plastic bag fastened to the side of the chair. The bag was nearly full with dark urine.

"Remember me? Reggie Dufrane?"

He blinked twice. A little string of drool dripped down onto his plain white T-shirt.

She reached out, put her hand on his, and gave it a squeeze. His hand was hot and sticky.

"I know you don't remember, Sid, but I'm sorry. What happened, it was an accident, but—"

"Why're you here?" he asked. Speaking seemed to be an effort, she could see the muscles of his face and neck tense and twitch as he pushed the words out. His voice was slow and creaky, like a box lid being opened, but she could understand him.

"I was just visiting your father."

He smiled. "Bo-Bo."

"Yes," Reggie said. "Bo. He and my mom, Vera, they used to go steady back in high school. Back before he met your mom. In another life."

He smiled again, dropping his head down, then bringing it back up as he concentrated on getting more words out. "Pretty girl," he said, spittle covering his lower lip.

"Your mom? I'm sure she was. I'm sure she was beautiful."

He shook his head. "Not her," he said slowly, frowning. "The girl Yogi stole."

Lorraine was in the kitchen making herself a cup of tea when Reggie walked in.

"Would you like one?" Lorraine asked, holding up her mug.

"Sure," Reggie said. She watched her aunt get down a second cup, drop a bag of Lipton into it, and fill it with water from the kettle.

"You got a call from a Sister Dolores. She said she was going home for the day but that she'd call back tomorrow."

Reggie nodded. Why hadn't the nun called her on her cell phone? She'd left both numbers.

"Detective Levi stopped by, too."

"What did he want?"

Lorraine shrugged. "The usual, I guess. He tried to talk to your mother for a few minutes, but you know how that goes."

"What'd he ask her?"

"Mostly about Tara. Then if she could tell him anything at all about Neptune."

"I'm sure she was quite forthcoming."

"Actually, she sang him a song: 'Oh do you know the Muffin Man.' "

Reggie laughed.

Lorraine filled a little cow creamer with skim milk and carried it to the table.

"Was that Charlie Berr who dropped you off?" Lorraine asked.

"Yes," Reggie said, bristling as she picked up her tea and took a sip, burning the roof of the mouth.

"You're seeing a lot of him."

"We're old friends," Reggie said. "That's all." Charlie and his Rolling Stones shirt, the fresh aftershave he had on when he met her. Was he hoping for this to develop into something more?

Lorraine nodded, stirring milk into her own tea. "So is there a man in your life, then?"

"No," Reggie answered too quickly. "I mean yes. Maybe." She pulled the bag of tea out of her cup, played with the label attached to the string by a tiny staple.

Lorraine smiled at her. "It's not good to be alone, Regina."

Reggie nodded, her fingers working at the little staple, opening it, then, realizing what she was doing, setting it down.

"I don't know what I'd do without George. He's my lifeline. Especially now."

Reggie took another sip of tea. What an odd couple they made, Lorraine and George. But somehow they were perfect together. Both of them sort of lost and awkward, two misfits. George with his ducks, Lorraine with her fish. It was kind of endearing to Reggie, the idea that their relationship had lasted so many years. They'd never married, never even lived together. They'd invented their own definition of romance: they cooked dinner together a few times a week, George gave Lorraine rides to doctors' appointments and shopping, Lorraine did all his mending.

Was this how she and Len would be in years to come? Each in their own separate space, coming together when they needed each other?

Maybe she and her aunt weren't so different after all.

Lorraine set her cup down and turned to Reggie. "I'm glad you're here. I couldn't do all this on my own. George helps all he can, but he's so busy with work. You being here makes such a big difference. George, George is my family, but you and your mother, you're more than that. You're blood." She reached out and put her hand on Reggie's, giving it a tentative squeeze.

Reggie nodded and squeezed back. "Thanks." They felt like the first kind words she'd heard from Lorraine in a long, long time. But Reggie was to blame for that, wasn't she? She'd shut Lorraine out, been needlessly cruel in the way that only teenage girls can be.

Reggie felt suddenly guilty for her fleeting thoughts just days ago that Lorraine might have something to do with Neptune, that she might have been the one who'd given Vera the newspaper article.

"I'm sorry that I ran away like that last week, when Mom first came home."

Lorraine nodded. "It was a lot to take in all at once, I imagine."

"And I'm sorry for blaming you when Mom disappeared. It wasn't your fault. I was just so devastated, so furious, I guess I needed someone to direct all that at. It wasn't right, leaving home and never coming back. I just couldn't face things. I didn't know how. It was cowardly, and I'm sorry."

Lorraine bowed her head down, as if studying her shoes. "I understand," she said.

They were silent a minute. Outside, a siren wailed in the distance.

"I went to see Bo Berr today," Reggie confessed, grateful to be changing the subject. "I thought maybe he was Neptune."

"Why on earth would you think that?"

"Because of something George told me once. About Mom coming back and living with Bo after being in

New York. Then I did some digging and found out Bo was the one who picked her up from the bowling alley that night. He came and got her in a borrowed car."

Lorraine pursed her lips. "Your mother and Bo, that's ancient history. Heavens, I felt so bad for him back when they were still in high school. She treated him terribly. Both of them. Stringing them along, playing them off each other like puppets."

"Who?"

"Bo and his younger brother, Stuart."

"Wait . . . Mom dated Stu? Charlie's dad?"

Lorraine shrugged. "I can't say for sure what was happening when. But in the end, I think she broke both their hearts when she ran off to New York."

Reggie found her mother's senior yearbook right where Tara had set it down years before—on top of the trunk in the attic.

Reggie could hear Tara's voice: *She was beautiful. You look like her.*

Reggie held the yearbook and glanced into the three mirrors, Vera's dress dummies behind her like old, familiar ghosts. She did look like her mother. She saw it now. In the eyes, the cheekbones. She was a darker version of Vera—the proverbial black sheep.

Reggie opened the yearbook and went through it page by page, reading the notes and autographs. And there, near the end, a photo she'd missed before. Vera and a dark-haired, serious-faced boy with their arms around each other. Her head was on his shoulder and she looked peaceful, content. Next to it, in neat cursive he'd written:

> *They do not love that do not show their love.*
> *The course of true love never did run smooth.*
> *Love is a familiar. Love is a devil.*
> *There is no evil angel but Love.*
> —Shakespeare
>
> *Always and forever,*
> *Stu*

Suddenly, like the tumblers of a lock turning, everything clicked into place.

Stu Berr.

Stu Berr, who'd led the investigation. Who'd let his brother off the hook. Stu, a man in a position of power.

Reggie remembered her mother's horrified reaction at seeing Charlie's face. And didn't Charlie look just like his father?

Oh God. It all made sense.

Reggie pulled out her phone and dialed information, asking for Bo Berr's number. She got it and punched it in.

Frances answered. "Hello?"

"Mrs. Berr, it's Reggie Dufrane. I was hoping I could speak to your husband."

"He's resting. I'm afraid your visit wore him out. And he's just had his pain medicine."

"Please, it'll only be a minute. I wouldn't ask if it wasn't important."

Frances put the phone down and Reggie heard muffled voices. Then Bo got on the line with a groggy "Hello?"

"Mr. Berr. It's Reggie Dufrane. There's something you said earlier that I've been wondering about."

"Is that right?" His words were ever so slightly slurred.

"You said that the morning after you dropped my mother off, your brother came to see you to question you. Are you sure it was that morning?"

A few wet coughs and throat clearings.

"Yeah, it was early morning. Right after they'd found the hand, I think. He knew right away that I'd been the one who dropped her off at the bar. He was the one who told me the hand was Vera's."

There was only one way Reggie could think of that Stu had known it had been Bo who'd dropped her off.

A chill ran through Reggie. The hand that was wrapped around her cell phone began to tremble.

"Thanks, Mr. Berr. Take care of yourself."

She hung up and dug the tiny staple from the teabag, the one she didn't even realize she'd brought upstairs, deep into the skin of her thumb.

Day Four

Excerpt from *Neptune's Hands: The True Story of the Unsolved Brighton Falls Slayings* by Martha S. Paquette

It's almost a cliché: after a murderer is brought to justice, his neighbors and coworkers come forward in complete disbelief, saying what a nice guy he was. He went to work every day. Kept his lawn mowed. Seemed friendly enough. He blended in, camouflaging himself effortlessly, passing for normal.

It's my strong belief that that's just what they'd say about Neptune.

He's everyman and no man. Someone you'd pass on the street and not give a second thought to. He probably owns a house and lives alone. He's an intelligent man. He's methodical. Patient. He's probably good-looking, charming even—there was no sign that any of these women struggled when he abducted them. They must have gone willingly, trusting their killer right up until the end.

Chapter 36

October 23, 2010
Brighton Falls, Connecticut

Reggie pulled up in front of Stu Berr's house and saw a pickup in the driveway. She'd thought of calling first but decided a surprise visit might yield more results.

She only hoped he didn't have any surprises waiting for her: a rag soaked in ether and a surgeon's saw.

Stop it, she told herself.

Her phone was ringing. Len again. She answered, thinking that hearing his voice might soothe her, stop her hands from shaking and help give her the strength and courage she needed to go knock on Stu's door.

"You didn't call," Len said.

"I'm sorry," Reggie told him. "I got a little swept up in things here. I think I know who Neptune is."

"Jesus. Who?"

"Charlie's dad. Stu Berr." She looked across the street at the neat little ranch house, saw movement inside. "He was the lead detective on the Neptune case and now it turns out he and my mom went out back in high school. I think he never got over her. I think—"

"Have you gone to the police, Reg?"

"Not yet. I don't have any proof. And he was a cop himself, so that makes things a little complicated."

"Listen," Len said. "I'm on my way."

"What? No. I can—"

"No arguments. I'll be there in three hours or so, depending on traffic. I don't want you to do anything until I get there, okay? Just stay at home with the doors locked. We'll figure out the next move once I arrive. Deal?"

"Okay," Reggie said, thinking she should be angry, but really, she felt relief.

"Don't do anything stupid, Reg," he said.

"I won't," she promised. "See you soon."

She hung up the phone, counted to ten, opened the door of her truck, and crossed the driveway. The place had been kept up well. The driveway had been resurfaced recently, and there was a fresh coat of paint on the house. The shrubs were neatly trimmed and the leaves raked. Stu Berr had not been idle in his retirement. To the right of the front door was the wooden plaque with the house number—21. She remembered the key that used to be hidden in the little carved-out niche behind it. She rang the bell and heard a dog barking behind the door. Reggie considered turning around and running.

But then the door open slowly and Stu Berr stared out at her. Reggie was startled by how much he looked like a slightly older version of Charlie. In fact, he could have passed for Charlie's older brother rather than his father. Gone were the jowls and the rolls of fat above his waist. He wore a T-shirt and running shorts, showing sculpted muscles. His hair was short and gray. The mustache was gone.

With his right hand, he held a large German shepherd by his thick leather collar. The dog continued to bark and growl, pulling on Stu's arm as his muzzle pressed against the flimsy screen.

"Help you?" he said.

"Mr. Berr. I'm Regina Dufrane. Vera's daughter?"

He stared at her a minute through the screen door. "Oh my goodness, yes," he said. "I heard she was back at home. Come in, please." He unlatched the door, then stepped aside, waving her in. He continued to hold the dog.

Reggie hesitated.

"Don't worry. He won't hurt you."

Reggie reluctantly opened the screen door and stepped inside, keeping her back to the wall, not taking her eyes off the enemy. Her body went rigid and cold. The dog continued to roar at her, teeth bared. Reggie felt a strange tingle at the scar tissue under her prosthetic ear.

She still hated dogs. They were the one fear she couldn't seem to conquer.

"Duke!" Stu said in a firm voice. "Go lie down."

The dog stopped barking, put his ears back in defeat, and sulked off to a corner of the living room. He walked in circles over his plaid flannel dog bed, then settled down, curling himself into a surprisingly small ball.

"Smart dog," Reggie said, letting out a breath she didn't even realize she'd been holding. Her entire body was chilled with cold sweat.

"He was a police dog, but he was getting a little gray in the muzzle, so they let him retire with me."

"Nice," Reggie said.

"We're good company for each other," Stu said. "Can I offer you some coffee? I just made a pot."

"Sure," Reggie said. She followed him into the kitchen and watched while he poured her a cup of coffee.

"Cream and sugar?"

"No thanks. I take it black."

"Let's go into the living room. It's more comfortable there."

She took the coffee from him and followed him into the living room, choosing the seat that was farthest away from Duke. The dog raised his ears, kept his eyes trained on her.

"Does the dog bother you?" Stu asked. "I can crate him."

"No. I'm fine, thanks. I'm not sure he likes me much, though."

Stu smiled. "Dogs smell fear."

Reggie swallowed a sip of bitter weak coffee and set her cup down on the table. "Charlie says you've got a boat you're fixing up?"

"Yeah. Down at the shore. She's a mess, but I'll get her into shape. I'm actually heading down there today to do some painting."

Reggie nodded, picked up her coffee, and took another sip. Stu stared at her with his best ex-cop look. It was the same way he'd looked at her years ago when she went to the station to explain that she believed the scarred hand that showed up was Vera's. His eyes were steely and alert, taking every detail in, but his face showed no emotion.

"So what can I do for you, Regina? I'm guessing you didn't come out to see me to ask about my boat," he said.

Reggie set the cup down, pushed it away. "No. No, I didn't."

"It's about your mother, then?"

Reggie nodded.

He looked at her, waiting. Then said, "Has she remembered anything? Anything at all?"

Reggie shook her head. "Not that we can tell."

Stu took a sip of his coffee.

"I found something when I was going through my mother's things. Her old high school yearbook. There was a picture in it of the two of you. And you'd written down a poem."

Stu's jaw clenched slightly. He nodded, but said nothing.

"But she was also involved with your brother Bo, right?"

He sighed. "Ancient history," he said.

Reggie smiled. "But history repeats itself, right? Like my mother coming back and moving in with Bo?"

"Vera and I were over before she left for New York. Nothing between us was ever rekindled."

"So you weren't involved with her in any way before she went missing?"

"Not that it's any of your business, but, no."

"But you were there in the bar that night, weren't you? At Runway 36? You either saw Vera get out of Bo's car or she told you he'd given her a ride."

Stu gave her a long hard look; then his serious face broke into a smile. His teeth were so perfect and white that Reggie wondered if they might be dentures. "I'm afraid you missed your calling, Regina. You may be a world-class architect, but you would have made one hell of a detective."

Had he been keeping tabs on her over the years? She thought of the mysterious phone calls she'd been getting since leaving home—had it been Stu Berr on the other end, breathing into her good ear?

Reggie looked at the dog, who was still lying down, but his eyes and ears showed that he was at full attention, much like his owner. Reggie was close to the door and had no doubt she could get to it quicker than Stu, who was several feet away with a coffee table between them. But she doubted she could outrun the dog. She touched the cell phone in her pocket, wondering if she could dial 911 without looking at the numbers.

"I was there that night. I was the man in the Yankees cap that people saw talking with Vera."

"Why didn't you ever say so?"

"Because my visit with her was part of an ongoing investigation into the Neptune killings."

Reggie gave him a questioning look. She didn't want him to know the full extent of her suspicions. "Why Vera? Did you know she was going to be taken next?"

He shook his head. "No. I was there to talk to her because she was a suspect."

"Suspect? In what kind of case?"

He cleared his throat and gave her a long serious look. "I was fairly certain your mother was the Neptune killer."

Reggie sank back in her chair. "You can't be serious."

"Detective work is all about finding threads. Connections. In the case of Neptune, all these threads led me back to your mother. She was the one thing all the victims had in common."

Reggie remembered all her mother's talk of threads and connections, how everyone was linked, whether they realized it or not.

"But she only knew Candy! Not the other two."

"True. Which is where the real detective work comes in. Candace Jacques had been dating James Jacovich. In fact, Jacovich dumped Vera for Candace. Andrea McFerlin had been dating a man named Sal Rossi. Does that name ring a bell?"

"My mother dated a guy named Sal. She said he was a photographer."

Stu shook his head. "Sal Rossi was the manager for Airport Cab company. He didn't date your mother long. When he broke up with her, he took up with Andrea McFerlin. They met through a dating service."

"And what about the young woman—the film student?" Reggie asked.

"Here's where things get interesting. Ann Stickney was making a documentary about the tobacco sheds and the men who worked there. One of the men was Wayne Abbott."

"Never heard of him."

"You mother dated him for some time. He was a younger man. Dark hair, very handsome. He drove a VW bus and went around telling people he'd had small parts in movies. Total bullshit, by the way."

"Mr. Hollywood," Reggie said under her breath.

"Young Wayne thought Ann was a better prospect than your mother, so he ditched poor Vera, thinking that maybe Ann's film would make his fictional movie star identity a reality. It didn't work out that way."

Reggie's head spun. "So all three women . . ."

"Had taken men away from Vera."

"But this doesn't make sense!" Reggie said. "Because the killer came for Vera next!"

Stu smiled. "Clever, isn't it? What better way to cover your tracks than to be the final victim, the one whose body is never found?"

Reggie sat forward, perched at the edge of her chair. "What? You're saying she cut off her own hand? That's insane!"

Stu shrugged. "My theory wasn't very popular with the rest of the police force, either, and of course there wasn't enough evidence to pursue it. But it made sense to me."

"And what about now? Is my mother supposed to have taken Tara and cut off her hand, too? Just hopped out of her deathbed for one last go-around with the saw?"

"Unlikely," Stu admitted. "I'm guessing it was a copycat. Or maybe Vera had an accomplice? Someone who was in on her secrets. Or maybe it's just some random sicko drawn out of the woodwork by the news that Neptune's last victim is alive. I don't know. Your guess is as good as mine. I'm afraid I'm more of a boat-builder than a detective these days." There was a little twitch at the corner of his mouth.

Reggie's head began to pound as all the new information flooded in, swirling around in her brain like a logarithmic spiral. And there, at the center, was the one thing she felt certain of, held to like clinging to a rock in a storm: Stu Berr was wrong.

An hour later, Reggie sat in her truck down the street from Stu's house, waiting for him to leave, hoping he hadn't been telling a story about going down to do some painting on his boat today. The bag from her quick trip to the Super Stop & Shop was on the seat beside her. She wasn't sure if Stu still kept a key behind the street number plaque, or what she would do if he didn't (break a window in the back maybe?), but she had to get into that house. She wasn't sure just what she hoped to find—Tara bound and gagged in the basement? Not likely. No, if Stu was Neptune and did have Tara, he'd have her more carefully hidden, not in a quiet residential neighborhood.

In spite of her best intentions, Stu's theory worked its way into her brain like a parasitic worm. Once there, it got its hooks in and held tight. She was sure—no, positive—that he was wrong. Vera was not a killer.

But what if . . .

She pushed the thought away, went back to watching the house. The curtains were closed now.

She eyed her cell phone, thrown on the passenger seat, then picked it up and dialed the number for Monique's Wish. Reggie spoke to the answering machine until Lorraine picked up.

“I’m here,” Lorraine answered, sounding a little flustered.

“Listen,” Reggie said. “Do you remember—was Mom gone when each of the women Neptune killed first disappeared?”

She could hear her aunt breathing, but she didn’t answer. At last Lorraine said, “Regina, what’s this about?”

“Nothing, probably.” Reggie bit her lip, feeling like an idiot.

Across the street, Stu Berr emerged, duffel bag in hand. Reggie sank down in her seat. “I gotta go,” she said to Lorraine.

Stu got into his truck and pulled away. Reggie waited a good ten minutes, just to make sure he hadn’t forgotten something and decided to double back. Then she slung her messenger bag over her shoulder, grabbed the plastic grocery bag, and headed for the front door. She turned the plaque on the siding, and there, just where she remembered its being all those years ago, was the key.

Bingo.

She replaced the numbers and unlocked the door. Then, before opening it, she reached into her grocery bag and unwrapped one of the two T-bone steaks she’d bought. Gingerly, she pushed the door open.

"Here, Duke," she called, voice wavering. "Here, boy!" Cold sweat beaded between her shoulder blades. Her scar tissue tingled. As she heard his toenails clicking against the floor, she imagined the three-headed beast, guardian of the underworld, coming for her.

Duke (with only one head—thank God) came trotting over, gave her a warning growl. She held the door open for him and tossed the steak into the driveway.

He hesitated a moment, glancing from her to the meat.

"Good boy, go ahead. It's for you."

He licked his lips nervously.

"Go on," she said, gesturing to the driveway.

At last his desire for meat overpowered his guard-dog self and he trotted into the driveway, pouncing on the steak. Reggie slipped into the house, locking the door behind her. She left the second steak by the front door to use for her escape.

Stu had tidied the kitchen, washed out the coffeepot and cups. The place smelled like bleach. Too clean.

She went back into the living room, saw the neat bookshelves with old encyclopedias, sportsman's guides to hunting and fishing, boatbuilding books, some marine biology textbooks that must have been Charlie's. Her eye caught on the old photo of Stu with his buddies in Vietnam, all in uniform, raising tin cups in a toast, an ambulance behind them. "Holy shit," she mumbled, another piece of the puzzle coming together. She'd forgotten he'd been a medic in the army—that's where he'd had the medical training, where he learned about tourniquets and pressure dressings. And didn't they sometimes have to do amputations right on the battlefield to save soldiers? Reggie was sure she'd read that in a book about the Civil War, so maybe it was true for Vietnam, too.

Reggie hurried down the hall to Stu's bedroom. It contained a double bed—carefully made with a dark spread on top, a bureau, a wooden chest, and a walk-in closet. The wooden chest contained extra sheets and blankets. In the bureau she found the usual—socks and boxer shorts in the top drawer, T-shirts in the second, a few pairs of jeans in the bottom. While rummaging around in the drawer with the jeans, she felt something cold and metallic. Even before lifting it from its hiding place, she knew what it was: a gun. Some kind of automatic pistol. Reggie didn't know enough about guns to identify it beyond that. She tucked it back right where she'd found it, between two pairs of pants.

No big deal, she told herself. Lots of people keep handguns in the house, especially ex-cops. Still, it made her shiver. But this was no proof. Neptune wasn't a shooter. What she needed to find was surgical tools, bandages, a fine-toothed saw for cutting bone.

She reminded herself she had to hurry. Who knew how long it would be before Duke dropped his steak bone and started barking to alert the entire neighborhood that there was an intruder in his house. She checked the closet and found neatly pressed shirts and pants hanging. She felt along the top shelf and found only a few mothballs.

Charlie's old bedroom was across the hall from his father's. It was empty now, except for a twin bed, neatly made, and an empty chest of drawers. There was nothing in the closet, no homey artwork on the walls. It felt abandoned.

She walked across the hall to Stu's office, the heels of her boots clicking on the hardwood floor. Back when Charlie was living at home, Stu had kept his office locked. Now, Reggie was happy to discover, he didn't bother. The old hasp was still bolted to the outside of the door, but there was no heavy padlock in place.

What she saw when she stepped into the room sucked the breath from her chest, as if she'd stepped into some kind of vacuum chamber.

The room was cluttered and chaotic, the walls, desk, and floor covered with notes, photos, police reports, and newspaper clippings on the Neptune case.

"Son of a bitch," she murmured.

It was like going back in time.

Pinned to the wall were police photographs of each hand inside each milk carton, and of the three victims as they were found: Ann Stickney on the town green, Candace Jacques at the base of the *Knowledge* statue in front of the library, Andrea McFerlin sprawled in the fountain at King Philip Park. Each woman was naked, left in a strange, contorted-looking pose, each with a big white paw of bandages covering the place where her right hand had been.

Reggie felt stomach acid burning its way up into her throat. She swallowed hard, trying to keep it down. It was one thing to read about the bodies, to hear it talked about in the news, and to imagine what they might have looked like. But actually seeing them—noticing little details like the C-section scar on Andrea McFerlin's stretch-mark-covered abdomen; Candace's Jacques torn earlobe from Neptune's ripping at her earring during their struggle; the waxy, dappled light that made Ann Stickney's body seem almost blue-ish—brought the killings to life in a whole new, sickening way. These were real women, not just names on the news. She'd known that before, yes, but never truly understood it till now.

And there, in the last photo on the right, was her mother's right hand inside the milk carton, the scar tissue looking like plastic, like maybe the hand had been made of modeling clay—something from a Hollywood special effects department. But it was Vera's hand, no doubt. And even now, the finger was stuck pointing in Reggie's direction.

Reggie's legs turned to jelly and she grabbed the edge of Stu's desk, lowering herself into his padded office chair. She took a few calming breaths, then flipped on Stu's computer, but it was password protected. She tried NEPTUNE, DUKE, YOGI, and CHARLIE and then was officially out of ideas, so she turned if back off. There was an avalanche of papers and file folders covering the top of the desk and spilling over onto the floor. A lot of them had names of the victims and suspects written across the tab: ANN STICKNEY, ANDREA MCFERLIN, CANDACE JACQUES, JAMES JACOVICH, SAL ROSSI, WAYNE ABBOTT. And there, on the top of the pile was a file marked VERA DUFRANE. There was a note paper clipped to it. Reggie picked up the file and read the note:

10/18/10

Detective Berr,

I doubt if you remember me—my name is Tara Dickenson, we met years ago. I'm an old friend of Charlie's. I work as a nurse and was recently hired to care for Vera Dufrane. Vera said something last night, something that I was hoping you might help me make sense of. My cell is 860-318-1522. Please call as soon as you get this. I'd like to meet today, if possible.

—Tara

"So this is how you got her," Reggie said. He'd just called the number, arranged a meeting, and grabbed her. This was the evidence Reggie had been searching for. She'd go straight to the police. But she had to be careful, didn't she? They were all friends of Stu's. Maybe she should go to the state police? Or call the FBI even.

She checked her watch. Less than two hours until Len arrived. He could go with her. She could do this with his help.

Reggie flipped open her mother's file. Inside was a mug shot and arrest report dated December 3, 1976. The charges were driving under the influence and assaulting a police officer. According to the report, when she was pulled over, she lashed out at the officer with her car keys, catching him in the cheek. He needed three stitches. She had to do six months of community service. There was a second arrest report and mug shot, this one dated April 25, 1981. According to the report, Vera was brought in after agreeing to have sex with an undercover officer for $100. Reggie looked down at her mother's disheveled wardrobe, the smudged mascara around her eyes making her look like an exhausted raccoon. Why would she do it? What could she have needed a hundred bucks for that badly?

Reggie's head felt as if it were in a vise, being tightened at the temples.

Flipping through Vera's file, Reggie found notes Stu Berr had taken after an interview with Vera on June 15, 1985:

> Ms. Dufrane admits to knowing the most recent victim, Candace Jacques. When asked the nature of their relationship, Ms. Dufrane stated that Ms. Jacques "was someone I know from the bars. We go way back." Ms. Dufrane denies having any animosity toward Ms. Jacques, in spite of the fact that James "Rabbit" Jacovich left her to be with Ms. Jacques. "She can have him," Ms. Dufrane stated.

Stu asked her where she'd been when Candace disappeared and she couldn't recall. She denied knowing

Andrea McFerlin, but admitted to having a relationship with Sal Rossi, whom Andrea was involved with at the time of her death.

Reggie's eyes jumped ahead a few paragraphs to where she saw her own name:

> Ms. Dufrane has one child, Regina Dufrane, age 13. Regina lives in the family home, Monique's Wish, with Vera's older sister, Lorraine Dufrane, as her primary caregiver. When questioned about the identity of Regina's father, Ms. Dufrane laughed and muttered something unintelligible, then recited lines from a child's nursery rhyme:
>
> *"Georgie, Porgie, pudding and pie,*
> *Kissed the girls and made them cry,*
> *When the boys came out to play,*
> *Georgie Porgie ran away."*
>
> Of note, Ms. Dufrane was clearly under the influence of alcohol during this interview and I believe this may have colored some of her answers.

Chapter 37

June 23, 1985
Brighton Falls, Connecticut

"The killer comes here," Tara said as soon as they walked through the door of Reuben's.

Reggie followed Sid, Charlie, and Tara in a daze. She hadn't wanted to come, wanted to be back in her room, hiding under her grandmother's quilt, but Tara had talked her into it.

"This is the last night, Reg," she'd said into the phone, voice tinged with desperation. "Our last chance to find your mother. If we don't save her—" Tara didn't let herself finish, just left the words hanging, letting Reggie do her own gruesome fill-in-the-blanks. "So, here's the plan," Tara continued. "You're gonna get your ass out of bed and get dressed. We'll pick you up in half an hour, take a ride over to Reuben's." Reggie hadn't said anything about her talk with George or her visit with Bo Berr, but the events of the day before were eating away at her, pulsating, like the pain in the leg Tara had cut.

"How do you know Neptune comes here?" Charlie asked.

"*They* told me—Andrea, Candy, and Ann. They say we're on the right track. Their voices are coming in loud and strong. They're here with us now." She licked her lips. Tara looked paler than usual, like a girl made of paper.

"Give me a break," Charlie said.

"Chill out, cuz," Sid said, putting a hand on Charlie's shoulder. "Let our black magic woman do her thing."

Charlie shrugged Sid's hand off and looked back at the door, like he was considering bolting. His eyes were furious. Then he looked back at Tara and seemed to calm down, deciding to stay put for the time being.

Reuben's was about half the size of Runway 36, and as Sid explained, the big draw wasn't the atmosphere but the food. Reuben's didn't have a pool table, jukebox, or neon beer signs. The walls were covered in cheap faux wood paneling with photos, newspaper clippings, and postcards tacked to it. There was a bar with worn stools and a dozen wooden tables with mismatched chairs. In the corner, by the hallway that led to the bathrooms, was a Ms. Pac-Man machine. Lively accordion music drifted from the kitchen along with wonderful, spicy smells. A chalkboard behind the bar listed drink specials and a simple menu: gumbo, jambalaya, red beans and rice, and a Cajun burger. Underneath, in small letters, someone had added: FORTUNES TOLD, $5. ASK AT BAR.

"How's your leg?" Tara whispered.

Reggie shrugged.

"I did the inside of my arm just before Sid picked me up." Tara breathed. "I'll show you later." Reggie let go of Tara's hand.

Sid nodded at the bartender, a tall man with light brown skin and pale eyes, and headed for a corner table. When they got to the table, Tara sat next to him. She was wearing a black long-sleeved leotard and tights with jeans that were more hole than fabric. Charlie had on his *Sticky Fingers* shirt with a Levi's jacket on top of it.

Reggie surveyed the room. The dinner crowd hadn't arrived yet. There was a couple eating at a table near the door, speaking in hushed tones between bites. Two people were seated at opposite ends of the bar: an old woman in a fuchsia coat with a poodle on her lap and a chunky bald man who was dressed in a black vinyl suit, complete with a long vinyl trench coat. Reggie could see that the guy was perspiring horribly, red in the face. The top of his head glistened. He was drumming his fingers on the bar. On each of his fingers was at least one ring.

"Get a load of Vinyl Man over there," Charlie whispered.

Tara rolled her eyes. "It takes all kinds," she said, pulling a pack of cigarettes from her ratty purse. Sid lit her cigarette for her. He'd cleaned himself up, shaved, moussed his hair into place, put on black jeans and a black blazer over a Zig-Zag Rolling Papers T-shirt.

The man from behind the bar came over to their table.

"What can I do for you folks tonight?" Reggie couldn't place his accent. It was lilting. Musical. His skin was smooth and mocha colored, his eyes a startling pale blue that reminded Reggie of aquamarine. The bartender had a leather string tied around his neck, with what appeared to be a chicken foot tied at the end. Reggie couldn't take her eyes off the foot, the reptilian toes dry and curled.

"A Bud and a Cajun burger—rare," Sid said.

"And for the lady?" he asked, nodding in Tara's direction

Tara smiled. Licked her lips. "I'll have a Long Island iced tea, please."

The bartender laughed. "You expect me to believe you're twenty-one?"

"I look young for my age," Tara said.

The man stared at her, then looked at the rest of them. "How about a pitcher of soda?"

"Coke, please," Charlie said. "And I'd like a Cajun burger, too."

"I'll take the gumbo," Tara said, sinking back into her chair and playing with a chunk of hair.

"Good choice, miss." The man smiled. "It's the house specialty."

"And for you, miss?" he asked, looking at Reggie.

"I'm not really—" Reggie started to say.

"She'll take the gumbo," Tara interrupted.

The bartender turned and headed back behind the bar and through the swinging doors into the kitchen.

Reggie went back to scanning the bar like she was waiting for the old woman or Vinyl Man to do something unusual that she didn't want to miss. Exchange some secret look, a few words, a kiss maybe. You never knew what might happen.

"So what do you think?" Charlie asked, his voice breathy and light. "Is that guy Reuben? Should we ask him about Vera?"

Vera. New York Vera. Aphrodite Cold Cream, gonna-be-a-star Vera.

Vera the whore.

"I'm pretty sure that's Reuben," Sid said. "I guess his mom does most of the cooking. She grew up in Louisiana. Out on the bayou or whatever. They say she practices voodoo—you know, dolls and dead chickens and shit like that. Did you catch the foot around Reuben's neck? Pretty fucked up, huh?"

"Like I said before, it takes all kinds," Tara said. "Want a cigarette, Reggie?"

Reggie shook her head.

Sid reached for the pack and lit one. "You smoke like a movie star," Sid said to Tara.

"Thank you, darling," Tara said, blowing smoke into Sid's face. She reached for her lighter and started flicking it over and over, making sparks.

"What'd you do yesterday, Reg?" Charlie asked.

I let Tara slice my leg open with a razor. Then I went and saw your uncle and asked him if he was my father. I found out my mother was a whore.

"Nothing," Reggie said, sinking lower into her seat, wishing she were anywhere but here.

What if Bo had lied? Said all that stuff just to cover up the truth—that he really was Reggie's dad? The thought made her sick. She looked up at Charlie, whom she'd been in love with since first grade. Was it really possible that he could be her cousin?

Reggie's head began to pound.

"You okay?" Tara asked, rubbing Reggie's shin with the toe of her boot under the table.

"Fine," Reggie said, swallowing hard.

The bartender returned with their drinks, and when Sid asked, he confirmed that yes, he was Reuben, proprietor of the place since 1976.

"Pleased to make your acquaintance, Reuben," Tara held out her hand demurely. The tall man took it, gave it a slight squeeze.

"I wonder if you can help us. See, my friend Reggie here is Vera Dufrane's daughter. We heard Vera spends a lot of time here."

"Can't say I know her," Reuben said. The guy was poker-faced.

"Really?" Tara asked.

"Can't say as I recall anyone with that name," Rueben said.

"She's about five five, platinum blond hair, wears a lot of makeup," Charlie said, trying to sound like his dad. "She's an actress. And a model."

Did you know I was the Aphrodite Cold Cream girl?

Want to see a trick? Buy me a drink and I'll show you.

Reuben shook his head. "Not ringing any bells. Your food'll be out in no time," Reuben said before heading back to the bar. He refilled Vinyl Man's glass and said something that made the large man turn on his stool and look toward their table. His eyes were too small for his broad, flat face. His wet skin shimmered under the lights above the bar.

Reggie, feeling self-conscious, turned to Charlie, whispered, "I don't like it in here. I want to go home."

Charlie nodded. "I know. I don't like it either. But let's just stay and eat, huh?" He moved closer to her, put his arm around her. It made her feel all glowing and warm, but then she realized he was just doing it because Tara had snuggled up next to Sid.

"This is all so fucked up," Reggie said, meaning all of it: her mother being gone, everything she'd found out today, the way Charlie had cozied up beside her in a sad attempt to make Tara jealous, the fact that she'd let Tara slice her with a razor blade yesterday.

"Welcome to the world, Baby-O," Tara said, playing with her hourglass necklace.

"I don't know why we even came here," Charlie said. "It's obviously a big waste of time. This Reuben guy doesn't even know Vera."

"Oh God, he's *obviously* lying," Tara said.

"Did the dead ladies tell you that, too?" Charlie snapped.

"No," Tara said. "I could just tell."

"I agree with Tara," Sid said.

"Of course you do," Charlie said bitterly.

"I'm gonna go to the bathroom," Reggie said, standing. Her knees felt strange and rubbery. The cut on her leg stung horribly.

"Want me to go with you?" Tara asked.

Christ, what was she? Six? Did Reggie really seem that pathetic to her friends?

"No thanks. I'm fine."

"You sure?" Tara asked, opening her purse just a little with her right hand, giving Reggie a peek at the little silver box with the razor blade inside.

Tara was taking things to a new level, inviting her to indulge in their secret pastime in a public place, showing the wrapped-up razor blade right in front of the boys, who were oblivious. Reggie's skin itched as she looked down at the blade. She felt the secret between them beating, throbbing like a toothache. It gave her a thrill but made her feel slightly ruined, like a bright, shiny apple with a rotten spot no one could see.

"No thanks," Reggie said again as she turned away from Tara's disappointed face.

On her way past the bar, Reggie peered back into the kitchen through the windows on the swinging doors. She saw Reuben standing at a counter, laying out a whole plucked chicken. Reuben caught Reggie watching, gave a long, slow smile, then raised a huge cleaver and brought it down, expertly slicing the bird in half along the breastbone, with one quick stroke.

Chapter 38

October 23, 2010
Brighton Falls, Connecticut

"Where's George?" Reggie asked Lorraine. She'd found her aunt in the upstairs bathroom, rinsing out Vera's bedpan. Reggie stood in the doorway, her messenger bag strapped across her chest, Stu Berr's file on Vera and Tara's note to him inside.

On the drive home, everything made sense: the way George was always there for her, giving her gifts, buying her school supplies. Her mother had always said she and George had been involved once. Maybe Lorraine didn't know.

"I think he's working from his office at home today. He said something about driving down to the warehouse in Brattleboro, but I'm not sure if that's later today or tomorrow."

"Lorraine, can you give me a minute alone with Mom?"

Her aunt eyed her skeptically. "Of course. I've just given her an Ativan. She might be dozy."

Reggie found her mother cocooned in sheets and blankets, her face pale as a moth. Reggie thought of what Stu had said earlier and tried to imagine Vera a killer. She nearly laughed out loud.

"Hey you," Reggie said, carefully sitting at the edge of the bed, reaching out to touch her mother's shoulder.

"Hay is for horses," Vera said.

Reggie smiled. "Mares eat oats and does eat oats—"

"And little lambs eat ivy," Vera finished.

"Mom?"

Vera looked up at her, eyes half open.

"What can you tell me about Stu Berr?"

Vera smiled and started to sing, "If you go out in the woods today, you're in for a big surprise. If you go out in the woods today, you better go in disguise. For every bear that ever there was, will gather there for certain because, today's the day the teddy bears have their piiiic-nic."

Reggie leaned down and whispered in her mother's ear. "Is Stu Berr Neptune?"

Vera laughed.

"Can you tell me, Mom?"

Vera closed her eyes, started to drift off.

"I have one more rhyme," Reggie said as she stroked her mother's cheek, which felt dry and papery. "Georgie porgie, pudding and pie," she said.

Vera's eyes opened, but she did not speak.

"Kissed the girls," said Reggie.

"And made them cry," her mother said.

"I remember, Mom. Everything you used to say about George. How he loved you, but couldn't have you. I remember how you used to talk about George and his ducks, you'd tease him all the time, said it wasn't natural, a grown man spending all his time making those damn wooden ducks."

Vera smiled. Her lips were dry and chapped.

"Then you asked him once, you said, 'How come you've never made one of those ducks for me, George?' So a few days later, he gave you a box and you opened it and pulled out this tiny, beautiful carved wooden swan. 'This isn't like any duck I've ever seen,' you told him. And he said, 'Yes it is. It's the ugly duckling. All her life she thinks she doesn't fit in; then she grows up and sees that she's really a beautiful swan.' "

Reggie had tears in her eyes as she told this story, remembering the way George had looked at her mother, the way she held the swan so delicately, like it was made of glass. The little wooden swan Reggie had tucked into her memory box all those year ago, after her mother was pronounced dead by the rest of the world.

"George is my father, isn't he?"

Vera looked down into her sheets like the answer might be there.

"Please, Mom," Reggie pleaded.

"I'm cold," Vera said.

"I'll get you another blanket," Reggie said, going to the closet.

"If it's cold here, it's hot in Argentina," Vera said.

"Well," said Reggie, layering another blanket on top of her mother, "I don't think we'll be going there any time soon."

"Oh it's not far," Vera said, closing her eyes. "Eva Perón lives there. And they grow the most wonderful pears."

"Lovely," Reggie said, tucking in the edges of the blanket, watching her mother drift away.

Reggie sneaked out of the room and across the hall to her bedroom. She took the memory box down from the closet and pulled out the wooden swan, George's gift to Vera. She ran her fingers over the delicate cross-hatching of feathers, the smooth curve of its long neck. The swan was carved from a softwood—pine, she guessed. Reggie tucked the swan carefully into her messenger bag. She only hoped the papers she had inside would be enough to save Tara. It was the final day and time was running out. She checked her watch for the thousandth time. One hour until Len was due to arrive. Should she wait and go to the station with him? She took out her cell and dialed his number, but it went right to voice mail.

"It's me," she said. "Just wondering about your ETA. Call me when you get to town and I'll give you proper directions."

He could be anywhere. And every second counted. The sooner she got her information to the police, the greater the chance of finding Tara alive. And if they didn't believe her, refused to even listen, then she'd call Charlie and find out where Stu kept his boat. She and Len would head down to the shore, find Stu, and tail him until he led them to Tara. It wasn't the greatest plan, but it was better than nothing.

She tucked the phone into her bag as a chill washed over her, a cool breeze blowing through the window she'd left cracked open. She closed it. Her screwdriver was still sitting on the windowsill. She dropped it into her messenger bag. She'd put it back in the toolbox when she got down to her truck.

"Everything okay?" Lorraine asked when Reggie walked downstairs and into the kitchen.

"Fine. Mom's sleeping."

"I think I'll fix us all some lunch," Lorraine said.

"None for me, thanks," Reggie said. "I need to run out and do a couple of things."

"Surely you have time for a bite to eat."

Reggie shook her head. "Maybe when I get back."

Reggie's cell phone rang. She recognized the Massachusetts area code and answered.

"Hello?"

"Miss Dufrane. This is Sister Dolores of Our House in Worcester. I hear you've been trying to reach me." Her voice was low and quiet, with a slight rasp to it.

"Yes," Reggie said. "Thanks so much for getting back to me."

"How is your mother?" Sister Dolores asked.

"She's doing all right. As all right as can be expected. She's talked about you quite a bit since coming home. She seems to think very highly of you. I wanted to thank you. For being there for her when we couldn't."

"Mmm," Sister Dolores said understandingly. "I've been praying for her. You tell her that, will you?"

"I will. Sister, I was wondering if there was anything more you could tell me about my mother."

"Such as?"

"How she came to be with you. If she ever said anything about her background."

Sister Dolores was silent for a few seconds. "Miss Dufrane," she said at last. "I run a one-hundred-bed facility. I've been doing this for over twenty years now. I've learned not to pry into people's business. The people we serve, they haven't had the happiest lives. If they want me to know what brought them to Our House, they'll tell me in good time."

"My mother was there on and off for two years, right? And she obviously thought the world of you. She must have said something."

"Oh, sure, she said lots of things. She told us her name was Ivana. That she'd been an actress."

"She never said anything about how she lost her hand? About Neptune?"

"Nothing. Just like I told the detective who showed up here—she never said much about where she'd come from. It was like she'd dropped out of the sky."

"A detective from Brighton Falls?" Reggie asked. "A young man? Edward Levi?"

"No, no. This was an older man. Very pleasant. I'm afraid I couldn't help him at all, but he didn't seem to mind, even after driving all that way. Detective Berr, that was his name. I imagine you must know him?"

"Yes," Reggie managed to say through a tight throat.

"Awfully nice fellow. I wish I could have told him more."

Chapter 39

June 23, 1985
Brighton Falls, Connecticut

Charlie was waiting for Reggie in the hallway outside the women's room door, studying the postcards and snapshots on the walls.

Hello from Reno. Get Your Kicks on Route 66. Greetings from the Roadkill Cafe.

Reggie nearly ran into him.

"What's up?" she asked.

"I was hoping you'd talk to Tara. Tell her to slow it down with Sid."

Reggie looked behind Charlie, out to the back table where Sid and Tara were making out. Tara was practically sitting in his lap and kissing him. Sid was licking at her mouth like an overly friendly dog. It turned Reggie's stomach, but she couldn't stop watching.

"Why should I?"

Sid was groping at Tara's breast now, and Tara pushed his hand away, said something that made him laugh. Then they went back to kissing.

Charlie looked furious and desperate. "Because. He's no good for her and you know it."

"Maybe that's what she wants," Reggie said. "Someone who thinks he's as badass as she wants to be."

"But Tara's not really like that," Charlie whined. "I think she's really pretty normal. All the fucked-up girl, psychic stuff . . . it's just acting."

Reggie was so sick of it all. The things people knew (or thought they knew) about other people. Maybe everyone had a secret life, not just Vera. She suddenly hated all of it. She wanted people to be as see-through as fish tanks, no more murkiness, no misdirection. No lies and bullshit. No secret rooms or lies about being the star of some goddamn play that didn't even exist.

Most of all, right now, she was sick of the fact that somehow the whole world seemed to be revolving around Tara and her moods and predictions—never mind the fact that her own mother was being held prisoner by a psycho murderer.

"Tara cuts herself, you know," Reggie said, her voice laced with a venom she hadn't expected.

"Huh?"

"And burns herself with a lighter. Her arms and legs are a mess of scars. She's way more fucked up than you think."

And I am too, she thought.

He stared at her blankly, and she continued. "Trust me, Charlie, she's not into you. And there's not a damn thing you can do to change it."

His eyes blazed. "You don't know that," he said. He started to walk away, but Reggie caught him by the arm.

"Charlie"—her voice was soft and pleading as she gently gripped his arm—"I'm sorry."

Charlie looked at Reggie and opened his mouth to say something, then seemed to think better of it. He shook her off with a disgusted sigh and hurried back to the table.

Fuck. Now she'd done it. Maybe it was something she'd inherited from her mother—this unique ability to be able to completely screw over the people you care most about.

Reggie picked at her gumbo, half listening to the ridiculous conversation Sid and Tara were having. All she wanted in the world was to get out of there, go home, put a pillow over her head, and stay there for days. She wouldn't get up tomorrow because she knew what would happen when she did: she'd turn on the news and hear that her mother's body had been found. Cops, reporters, and people from town would gather around Vera's naked body, shaking their heads, clicking their tongues.

Too bad, too bad. Such a shame. Such a pretty woman.

Did you know she was the Aphrodite Cold Cream girl?

Reggie's solution, pathetic as it was, was to stay locked in her room, buried in her covers, doing her own version of the little kid's trick of "If I can't see you, then you can't see me."

"I didn't say all sausage, just some sausage," Sid said. "There's different kinds, you know."

Charlie threw his cousin a furious glance.

Tara laughed. "I'm thinking little breakfast link, here."

"Not hardly," Sid said. "We're talking King of the Kielbasa."

Tara snorted. "Eew! I hate kielbasa!"

Sid leaned in and whispered something and Tara snorted again. "Just leave off the sauerkraut," she guffawed.

Jesus. Didn't these people get it? Her mother was in some torture chamber with a serial killer, probably eating her last meal of lobster at this very minute. Reggie stirred her gumbo, found a shrimp, and dropped the spoon, disgusted.

She heard her mother's voice: *It's all about connections. There's a big web linking all of us together—you and me and the president and the guy who build the goddamn atom bomb. Don't you feel it?*

"Hello? Anybody home there?" Charlie asked, obviously irritated.

"Mmm?" Reggie murmured.

"I asked if you were ready to get out of here," Charlie said.

"Definitely," Reggie said, pushing her bowl of gumbo away.

"I don't think she wants to leave yet," Tara said, clamping a hand down on Reggie's arm. "Do you, Reggie?"

Charlie glared at her. "Why is it you always have to be the expert on everything?" he asked. "Now you're the freaking expert on Reggie?"

"I never said I was an expert," Tara shot back. "I just thought—"

"Maybe it's time you start keeping all your goddamned thoughts to yourself. 'Cause I, for one, am really sick and tired of hearing them all the time."

"Relax, dude," Sid said.

"Don't fucking tell me to relax!" Charlie snarled. He was shouting now, and several of the other diners had turned to look their way. "You're so relaxed you can't see the road in front of you half the time. And you're so clueless you think you've got yourself a nice piece of ass there, but you have no idea how totally screwed up she is."

"That's enough," Sid said, standing.

"Why don't you show us your arms, Tara?" Charlie said, standing now, hovering over her. Charlie was breathing hard, almost wheezing.

Tara stared up at him in disbelief. Then she turned and looked at Reggie, dark eyes smoldering, their message clear: *you betrayed me.*

Reggie held her breath, waited for Tara to turn the tables and tell them all the truth about Reggie: *while we're at it, why don't we look at Reggie's legs, too?* But she stayed silent, glaring. This was worse than Reggie's having her secret revealed. It was like having her heart doused in ice water.

Charlie reached for Tara's sleeve, and she flinched. Sid grabbed Charlie's wrist, holding it tight. He knocked a glass from the table and it shattered on the floor.

"Problem here, kids?" Reuben asked. He'd moved in swiftly and was now right behind Sid.

"Nah," Sid said, dropping Charlie's arm and sitting back down. "No problem at all, right, cuz?"

Charlie sat, too, pulling his hand away from Tara's arm. He was breathing like a steam train.

"Glad to hear it." Reuben nodded. "Why don't you all just finish up your dinners and go on home, then?" He studied them a minute, then turned and walked back to the bar.

"Let's get out of here," Sid said, standing and throwing money to cover the bill down on the table.

No one else moved. Tara was glaring at Reggie. Charlie was glaring at Tara. And Reggie was looking at the shards of glass and melting ice cubes on the floor.

"Come on," Sid said. "Before they kick our asses out." Reggie stood and Tara and Charlie followed.

The lights in the parking lot were out. They stood a second, letting their eyes adjust, then moved toward Sid's car.

"Well, I don't think I'll be showing my face in there any time soon," said Sid.

"It's your fault," Tara snapped at Charlie. "If you hadn't made such a damn scene in there—"

"Oh sure," Charlie said. "Blame me. You've been slicing and dicing yourself, breaking into dead ladies' apartments, and now you're turning into this complete slut. You're not psychic, Tara. You're psycho!"

Sid lunged forward, grabbed Charlie's T-shirt, and put his face right in front of Charlie's. "That's enough, Charlie."

Charlie pushed at Sid's chest with both hands, sending the older boy toppling backward onto the asphalt.

"Jesus!" Sid yelped, starting to get himself back up off the ground. Charlie lunged at him, and they both went down, rolling around. Sid struggled to get Charlie off him and to duck the hits and kicks.

Tara raced forward, grabbing the back of Charlie's shirt. "Get off him!" she yelled. Charlie swung back, and Tara lost her balance, falling onto the parking lot. "Asshole!" she yelped. Reggie went to help her up, and Tara jerked away from Reggie. "What the fuck did you do?" she asked. "What did you say to him?"

"I'm sorry," Reggie said.

Tara shook her head violently. "You've ruined everything!" she hissed.

Sid and Charlie were up again, holding on to each other. Charlie was smaller than Sid, but his movements seemed more careful, more directed than Sid's, who moved like a slow, gangly scarecrow.

Charlie grabbed Sid's throat, and Sid was trying to pry Charlie's fingers off.

Tara jumped up and clawed at Charlie's arms. "Let him go!" She was standing sideways, up against Sid, her left leg behind him.

Reggie stood paralyzed, knowing she should do something, but unsure what it should be. Sid was making horrible choking sounds. Reggie approached Charlie, saw that his arms were bleeding from the scratches Tara was giving him. "Please, Charlie," Reggie said. "This isn't who you are."

Charlie looked at his own hands wrapped around Sid's neck in disbelief, like they weren't his at all, then let go. Sid gasped for breath, hands clutching at his crushed throat.

Reggie leaned toward Charlie, touched his bleeding arm. "It's all my fault," she said. "I shouldn't have said those things about Tara. I was just mad . . . jealous, and I . . ." She stumbled over words and knew that if she didn't say it now, she never would.

I love you.

She screamed the words inside her head, but when she opened her mouth, the only thing that came out was a pathetic "I'm sorry."

"Get away from me!" Charlie yelled, shaking her off. "All of you! Everyone just leave me alone."

They all stood frozen, wide-eyed.

"Get the fuck out of here," Charlie hissed, lunging forward one more time, pushing Sid with both hands. Sid's feet caught on Tara's leg, and he flipped backward, legs flying up, head hitting the pavement with a sickening crack.

For a second, no one moved. Time stopped, and Reggie felt herself slip away and view the scene as if she were looking down at a photograph. There was Charlie, arms in front of him like Frankenstein's monster; Tara stood sideways, the left leg Sid had fallen over planted firmly against the pavement; and Reggie's eyes were on Charlie as she wished she could take it all back.

"Sid?" Tara called. "Oh Jesus, Sid?" She went down on all fours to check on him.

Charlie nervously shifted his weight from one foot to the other. "He's okay," Charlie said.

Tara looked up. "No! He's not fucking okay. His head's hurt. There's a lot of blood."

"He'll get up in a second," Charlie said. "He's just stunned."

Reggie got down and studied Sid's crumpled body in the dim light. His eyes were open and a dark pool of blood surrounded his head. Reggie put her hand in front of Sid's nose and mouth. "Guys, I don't think he's breathing at all. I think he's hurt bad." Her voice rose in pitch.

She had done this. Her love for Charlie, her jealousy. If she hadn't said those things to him, he and Sid wouldn't have fought. Sid wouldn't be lying here on the asphalt.

The rotten spot deep inside her was spreading.

"He's dead!" moaned Tara, looking up at Charlie. "He's fucking dead and you killed him!"

"Shut the fuck up!" Charlie yelled. He was rocking. "I thought—oh, shit! It was an accident!" He came over, kicked at Sid's body. "Get up!" he yelled.

"We've gotta get help," Reggie said, standing, backing up slowly, moving toward the front door of Reuben's.

"No," Tara said, jumping up and grabbing Reggie. She clamped her hand tightly around Reggie's arm, pulled her back. "It's too late for that. What we've gotta do is get out of here. Now."

A car turned into the parking lot, its headlights illuminating the whole gruesome scene: Reggie looked down at Sid's face, pale and stonelike, and saw the lake of blood spreading out behind his head like a halo. The car sat for a few seconds, idling, and with the bright lights in her face, Reggie couldn't see who was inside.

"Run!" Tara squealed, pulling on Reggie, dragging her away. And Reggie and Charlie ran, following Tara. Reggie turned to look over her shoulder and saw the car back up, turn around, and leave the parking lot, tires squealing.

It was a light-colored sedan with only the driver inside.

Chapter 40

October 23, 2010
Brighton Falls, Connecticut

"Reggie," George said when he greeted her at the door. "Everything okay?"

"Can I come in?" she asked.

"Of course." He stood aside and she stepped in.

"Come on back to my office," he said, leading the way down the hall.

George sat down behind the heavy wooden desk and Reggie took the upholstered chair across the desk from him. After the chaos of Stu Berr's office, George's seemed almost like a monastery. The wood floors were clean and polished, the books in neat rows on the small set of shelves built into the wall. A green banker's lamp illuminated the desktop, which was empty except for a few invoices George had been going over. The sense of order comforted Reggie, made her believe in a world where things just might turn out okay.

"Your mom all right?" he asked, taking off his glasses and setting them down on the neat desktop. Even his glasses were spare and clean with neat wire rims.

"She's fine. You know, considering."

He nodded understandingly. "I'm sorry I haven't been over much to help out. I've been swamped with work. We lost one of our big suppliers, and we've run into some snags with the construction on the new Brattleboro warehouse."

"It's okay. We're holding our own, I guess. Look, George, I need a favor."

"Shoot," he said.

"I was hoping you'd go to the police station with me."

"The police station?"

"I think I know who Neptune is. I've got evidence, but I'm afraid they won't believe me. Especially that young cop Levi. I'm going to need all the help I can get. My friend Len is on his way down from Vermont, but I don't want to wait."

George's eyes were huge. "You know who Neptune is?"

Reggie nodded. "What do you know about Stu Berr?"

"The detective?"

"He and my mom were involved in high school," she said.

"Yes," George said. "I remember. She also dated his brother Bo. Things got a little messy, as I recall."

"I think Stu Berr might be Neptune," Reggie said.

"What?" He pushed forward in his chair, leaning forward, as close to Reggie as he could be with the desk between them.

Reggie reached down into her messenger bag and pulled out the file on Vera, the note from Tara, and showed them to George, filling him in.

"He was the one in the Yankees cap who talked to her in that bar that night. He said he was questioning her, that he thought she might be Neptune."

"Vera?" George chortled. "That's crazy!"

Reggie nodded. "I know. I think he was trying to distract me, to throw me off his trail."

George shook his head. "It's absurd."

"What if Stu was the one who promised to marry her? What if he was luring these women away in whatever twisted way he could manage?"

George pushed back, rubbed his face with his hands. "My God," he said. "Just imagine it. He'd be in the perfect position to commit those crimes and get away with it. He was the detective working the case! No one understood how the hands got left on the steps of the police station without anyone noticing. But everyone was used to seeing Stu Berr come and go."

Reggie nodded. "I need to go to the police, show them the note from Tara. I'm worried though—the cops there all know Stu. They'll stand up for him, maybe even refuse to look at evidence."

"I'll go with you," George said. "It may take some convincing, but this is the last day, Reg. If he's following the same pattern, he'll kill her tonight, dump her body in the morning."

Reggie shut her eyes tight, trying to blink away the image of Tara, naked, wrist wrapped in gauze on some early-morning-dew-covered field. "I know. Thanks for offering to go with me. Whatever happens, it'll be easier with you there."

"It's no problem at all." He stood.

"Wait," Reggie said. "Before we go, there's one more thing I need to ask."

"Okay," he said, sitting back in his chair. He looked suddenly worried.

Just ask, Reggie told herself. Best to get it over with. To know for sure one way or the other.

"You and my mother were involved once, weren't you? Before you got together with Lorraine."

"Reggie." He sighed. "We've been over all of this, haven't we? And I told you—"

"You told me what you thought I should hear. My whole childhood and adolescence, you worked so hard to protect me from the truth—you and Lorraine created this whole mythical reality about who my mother was and where she went when she wasn't home. Now I think there are other things you were hiding from me, too."

"Such as?"

"Are you my father, George?"

His face turned to the side, like the words had slapped him. Recovering, he took in a breath and faced her, but only stared.

"Please, George. No more secrets."

He nodded wearily. "She never wanted you to know," he said. "Your mother said I could be as involved in your life as I liked in the role of family friend, but that I mustn't ever tell you the truth. She thought it was better, I guess, for you to imagine all the people your father might have been than to have all the complications of it being me."

Reggie bit her lip, remembered the way Vera used to talk about George: calling him a dud, teasing him about his ducks.

"Does Lorraine know?"

"No . . . Well, maybe. I think she suspects, but she's never asked. She knew about my history with your mother, such as it was." He looked down at his shoes.

It amazed Reggie—the tangled nest of secrets they'd all been living inside.

Reggie wondered what to say next. She felt a little like she'd been dropped into a bad daytime television movie: daughter realizing the man who'd been a father figure to her was her actual father after all—she could practically hear the cheesy music building to some sort of climax. And here was the part where she was supposed to say something touching, something meaningful; something that would end with the two of them in a tearful embrace.

Her mind went blank, everything spinning too fast to grab hold of any one thought or idea long enough to say it out loud.

George gave her a weak smile and stood up. "We'd better be on our way. Just let me go grab my coat and turn some lights off. Be right back."

Back to the practical world.

Reggie sank back into her chair. It would be over soon. They just had to make the police check out Stu, go down to his boat. Maybe that's where he was keeping her.

Reggie tucked the file on Vera and note from Tara back into her bag. There, at the bottom, was George's swan.

George. Her father, George. It would take some getting used to, yet on some deep level, she knew it to be true. She felt it, a part of him inside her—the logical, practical part. She understood the genetic origin of her love for order, for plans and blueprints, for seeing the beauty and possibility in a single piece of wood.

She ran her fingers over the carved wooden swan, pulled it out of the bag.

It's the ugly duckling. All her life she compares herself to others, thinks she doesn't fit in; then she grows up and realizes she's really a beautiful swan.

It wasn't just her mother's story, but Reggie's as well, wasn't it?

Reggie turned the bird over in her hand, noticing the fine cross-hatching of feathers. She pictured George bent over his workbench, chisel in hand, paying careful attention to each detail.

But there, in the center of its chest, right over its nonexistent solid-wood heart, was something that didn't belong.

Not feathers, not a name or initials an artist might leave.

No. There, buried in the pattern of its breast, was a hidden message. A warning. A confession.

A tiny, carved trident.

"Oh shit." Reggie gulped, the jolt of adrenaline hitting her like a hundred shots of espresso, all her senses on overdrive.

Reggie ran her trembling fingers over the trident, thoughts exploding in her head, one message loud and clear above all others: *Run! Get of there, now!*

"Ready?"

Reggie jumped. George was standing right behind her in the doorway, a smile on his face. His gaze fell on the swan in her hand and his smile seemed to change, just a bit.

"Sure!" Reggie said, overly chipper. Damn it, she had to get herself under control. "Remember this?" she asked, turning the swan and holding it out, not wanting to draw suspicion. "I think you gave it to Mom once. I just found it in a closet at Monique's Wish. It's quite lovely." She kept her voice as steady as she could and dropped the swan back into her bag.

George nodded, eyes on the bag. "We'll take the van," he said calmly.

"I can drive," Reggie offered, trying to keep the tremble out of her voice.

George pulled the keys out of his pocket and opened the front door.

"Oh no," he said. "I insist."

Part Three

Excerpt from *Neptune's Hands: The True Story of the Unsolved Brighton Falls Slayings* by Martha S. Paquette

"I think, in so many ways, that before the murders we were living in an age of innocence," says Reverend Higgins of the Brighton Falls First Congregational Church. "We thought nothing bad could happen here. Neptune took something from us, beyond the lives of those poor women. He took away our sense of safety and showed us the true face of evil. It's hard to imagine going back to the way things were before. I don't think Brighton Falls, or any of its residents, will ever be the same."

Chapter 41

October 23, 2010
Brighton Falls, Connecticut

George whistled as he drove, both hands clasped safely on the steering wheel of his van. Reggie studied his hands; they were small, dainty almost, with neatly trimmed nails. They looked smooth, nearly hairless, and Reggie was sure they'd be soft to the touch. She'd always pictured Neptune's hands as being larger, rougher. These were the hands of an artist, a surgeon, and the fact that they looked so harmless disturbed her.

She was still spinning from the shock of it—George, the man who helped her with her algebra, taught her to ride a bike; meek little George with his Uncle Mouse face—he was Neptune. It just didn't seem possible.

Reggie made herself say the words over in her mind, trying to get them to sink in:

George is my father.

George is Neptune.

Neptune is my father.

She thought back to her astrology chart, the tiny blue trident in the twelfth house, a piece of Neptune tucked away inside her, giving her bad dreams and artistic visions. Now she understood it was so much more than that: half her DNA—the building blocks that made Reggie the person she was—had come from him.

She studied his profile, searching for some familiar piece of herself. Did she have his forehead, his chin?

In addition to her love of plans and order, did she have some small piece of what it took to be a killer buried deep down in her cells?

Reggie rode in the passenger seat, bag on the floor, tucked between her calves. Her stomach cramped and she took in a deep breath, going over her plan. When they got to the police station, she'd go through the motions with George, tell the cops about Stu Berr. Then she'd find an opportunity to get one of them alone, to show them the swan and say that George was really Neptune. She'd be safe with the entire Brighton Falls Police Department there with her. And they'd have their guy, just like that. They'd hold him, question him until he confessed, told them where Tara was. It would work. It had to.

She just had to make sure that if he had any suspicions whatsoever after seeing her with the swan, they were laid to rest. She licked her lips, wished that some of her mother's acting skills had been passed down to her.

"I still can't believe it was Stu Berr all along," Reggie said. "And to think he actually tried to convince me that my mother was Neptune."

She glanced at George. He had an expression on his face she had never seen, a small smile with mirthless, determined eyes. And she knew he knew.

He'd seen her notice the trident. There was no doubt. And now, she was in deep, deep trouble.

"Your mother," George said reflectively, "is an extraordinary woman."

"Mmm-hmm." Reggie nodded. Her palms were sweating, her heart was beating all the way up into her throat.

She looked around in a panic. He'd turned the other way. They weren't going downtown at all. He was taking her the long way around, the back way to Airport Road.

"Shouldn't you have turned left?" She tried to sound calm and matter-of-fact. *Silly George, you missed the turn.*

"I have a little errand I need to run first." He gave her a wolfish grin, all teeth. "You don't mind, do you?"

Reggie swallowed hard. "Actually, I was kind of hoping we could get there soon. I think the sooner they see the note from Tara, the sooner they'll be on Stu's trail. The better the chances at rescuing Tara."

"This won't take long," George promised.

"My friend, Len," she said, grasping at straws, "he'll be arriving in town any minute. He'll wonder where I am."

"Mmm," George said, eyes on the road ahead, completely uninterested.

They drove in silence for a few minutes. Reggie contemplated opening the door and jumping, but all the lights were green and George was driving at a steady clip. The last thing she wanted to do was land wrong and crack open her skull or get pulverized under the wheels of an oncoming truck. She needed air and pushed the button to lower the window, but nothing happened. He'd locked them. Had he locked the doors, too? Shit.

"Are you too warm, Reggie?"

"A little."

"I'll turn on some cool air."

They were passing the old tobacco barns. Not many actually grew tobacco these days. One had been turned into a Christmas tree farm. Another sold chrysanthemums. But most were just abandoned, the empty barns leaning, the tattered shade cloth flapping on posts, like the handkerchiefs of ghosts.

George cranked up the AC and the fear sweat on Reggie's body was now giving her chills. She bent forward a little, picturing the cell phone in her bag, wondering how she could get to it without him noticing. She leaned farther forward, scratching an imaginary itch on her leg.

"Everything all right, Reggie?" he asked, staring at her.

"Fine," she said, sitting upright.

She kept her eyes fixed straight ahead, out the windshield, but watched George in her peripheral vision. He wasn't a large man—about as tall as Reggie, as a matter of fact. His shoulders slumped and a little belly hung over his pants. She doubted he could overtake her using strength alone, and Reggie had seen no weapons in the van. Surely she stood a good fighting chance.

"I was saying," George said as he pulled into the passing lane to go around an airport shuttle van, "your mother is an extraordinary woman. Think of it—everything she's been through, all the lives she's changed."

Reggie bent down to scratch her leg again, hand brushing the top of her bag. George glared at her and she sat back up.

"And do you know the most amazing part—the part that had always confounded me?" George's voice was getting louder, faster. She watched a little vein on his forehead bulge and pulse.

Reggie shook her head. "No," she admitted. "What?"

"That she's never had any idea of the power she wields over other people. This unique ability to crush and destroy."

"I'm not sure what you mean."

There was that hungry-animal grin again. "Oh, I think you do."

They'd turned onto Airport Road and were going by the Silver Spoon Diner, once-upon-a-time employer of the late Candace Jacques. Reggie stared at the art deco building, saw the reflection of George's white van on the side of the polished silver diner.

"Look at what she did to you," George said.

Reggie winced. "She did the best she could."

"A dog would have been a better mother to you than Vera," he said. The vein on the side of his head stood out more. Sweat formed on his brow. He was spitting out the words now. "Abandoning you to go off drinking with her boyfriends. Always up for a fuck if it meant a few free drinks, a dinner out now and then."

"I don't think—"

"And then," George interrupted, "they'd always leave her in the end. They'd see her for what she was and know they could do better."

They passed Reuben's, which had a big FOR SALE sign in front. The windows were boarded up and the parking lot was empty. Reggie remembered Sid lying on the pavement in a puddle of blood, heard Tara's voice, *Run!* They came up to a yellow light, and Reggie fiddled with the lock as surreptitiously as she could, her heart leaping when she heard a tiny click. George gunned it through the yellow light. They passed the airport and headed out into the no-man's-land of warehouses, abandoned factories, and pay-by-the-hour motels. Airport Efficiencies was on the left, still painted Pepto-Bismol pink.

"Choices," George said. "That's what life comes down to, isn't it? The choices we make. We're each in charge of our own destinies, Reggie, whether we realize it or not."

"I agree," said Reggie, looking frantically around as the buildings got farther and farther apart. They crossed railroad tracks. Empty lots full of knee-high scrub brush and dead grass.

"You may think that Vera was the victim here, but the truth is, she got to where she is by the choices she made along the way. One bad choice after another. When it would have been so easy to stop, to choose another way. A decent life. That's what I offered her. And she turned me down, again and again. Mocked me."

He grimaced. Licked his lips. The van slowed as they approached a bend in the road. Reggie yanked the door handle, praying it would open. The door swung out and she jumped, hitting the pavement, rolling like a sack of potatoes, her elbows and hips skidding on the asphalt. She heard the screech of brakes, and not looking back, heaved her body up and started to run. If she could just get into the overgrown brush, she'd have a chance. She was a fast runner, used to long distances. George was a good twenty years older. If she could just get enough distance between them at the start, she'd be okay.

She was facedown on the ground before she even realized he was close. She lay stunned for a second, felt George's weight shift on top of her. She bucked up, trying to throw him off, but he held steady. She'd underestimated his strength. He flipped her over onto her back. She kicked up at his groin but didn't make contact.

"It didn't have to be this way," he said, lifting her up by the shoulders, then slamming her down against the ground. The sky behind him darkened, the whole world dimming, turning into one narrow tunnel, and all she could see was his face there at the end of it, grinning down at her like a sinister moon. Then he too was gone.

Chapter 42

June 24, 1985
Brighton Falls, Connecticut

Reggie cranked the pedals of her Peugeot as she rode through town. The sun was just coming up, making the sky in the east, over toward the airport, glow Martian red. Reggie felt like she must be on some other planet. There were hardly any cars on the roads, just the occasional delivery truck bringing fresh bread, milk, and gasoline into town. A few commuters were off to an early start, heading into offices in Hartford before the traffic got too bad. There were lights on in some houses, and Reggie could see movement through the uncurtained windows: a woman making breakfast, a man in boxer shorts turning on the television. Lawn sprinklers were running, keeping the grass a perfect sea of green. The streetlights were still on, and when she got downtown, it was a little like being in one of those zombie movies where you're one of the last survivors. The stores were all empty, windows dark like closed eyes. There was this sense that the town was holding its breath, waiting.

She looked at the sunrise again, the pinks and reds spilling out across the horizon, and remembered Sid's blood on the pavement last night. She squeezed her eyes shut tight a second, pushing it all away.

She circled the downtown streets, checking every grassy area, every storefront. She passed a police cruiser, knowing the cops were doing the same. She pedaled harder, faster. She didn't want some uniformed cop, a total stranger with a gun and radio strapped to his belt, to be the one who found Vera. Reggie needed to be the first; she'd take her jacket off to cover her mother's naked body before the hordes of onlookers came—snapping pictures, scraping under Vera's nails, combing through her hair looking for shreds of evidence. Mostly, what Reggie would do—what she needed to do—was to say she was sorry. She'd failed her mother. If she'd been more clever, had paid more attention and been a better daughter, then maybe she might have found her in time.

Now, not only would she be the daughter of a murder victim, but also a murderer herself. An accomplice, at least. If she hadn't screwed things up so badly last night, let her own selfish feelings take control, then maybe things would have turned out differently.

Unable to find any sign of her mother's body downtown, Reggie crossed Main Street and headed out toward Airport Road. As she rode, images of last night popped into her head: Sid falling like that, hitting the pavement with a crack, Tara telling them all to run. Her stomach churned as she remembered the three of them running, not speaking, then all turning their separate ways as Tara shouted, "Remember, it never happened."

Remember.

It had been an accident, yes, but running away had been wrong. Reggie knew that. She'd known it at the time but had been too stunned, too frightened, to stand up to Tara. Now they were probably all wanted for murder.

Reggie cycled past the tobacco barns, where men were just starting to show up for work. One of them whistled as she rode by, not a sexy lady kind of whistle, but more like something you'd do to call a dog. Reggie kept her eyes on the road ahead, didn't look back.

She passed the billboard that still had Candace Jacques's huge face on it. HAVE YOU SEEN ME? God, why hadn't someone taken that down?

And soon it would be her mother's turn. Reggie imagined Vera's picture in the paper tomorrow: NEPTUNE'S FOURTH VICTIM, VERA DUFRANE. And what would they say about her? Surely it wouldn't take reporters long to dig up the truth. They'd find out about the squalid little room at Airport Efficiencies. The failed acting career. The list of men. The bars. Would Reggie even be mentioned? Reggie concentrated, visualizing tomorrow's headline, trying to scan the imaginary article to find out where Vera's body had been found. Stupid. Like it could really be that easy to see into the future. If Tara had been here, she might have pretended she could. But pretending was a whole different thing. And Reggie was no Tara.

The two-lane road turned to four lanes and Reggie passed by the Silver Spoon Diner, which had a dozen cars in the lot and more pulling in. The traffic was heavier out here, taxis and airport shuttles, delivery vans, travelers hurrying to catch their flight. The air smelled like diesel fumes and fried food. A plane came up overhead, taking off to some far-off destination: San Francisco, Puerto Rico, Rome.

She tried to imagine the people on the plane above her, what the view was like from up there. Could they see her, a lone girl, bicycling along the expanse of asphalt, past the corrugated metal storage units, the Pepto-Bismol pink motel, a bar called Runway 36? Reggie studied every parking lot, every side road and alley. No sign of her mother's body. She rode on, ankle aching, sweat dampening her T-shirt, making her cold in the early morning air.

When she got to Reuben's, she half expected it to be blocked off with crime scene tape and crawling with cops trying to reconstruct what had happened to Sid. But the lot was empty, his body, gone. She wanted to pull in, look at the place in the parking lot where his crumpled body had lain still. Was there a bloodstain there, marking the place?

She didn't dare turn in. The police could be watching, wondering if the killer would return to the scene of the crime. Everyone in Reuben's had seen her, Charlie and Tara with Sid. It was only a matter of time until the police found them. And then what? Would they all be arrested, taken off to juvenile detention, to actual prison even? Reggie didn't care. It didn't matter really. They deserved it. Part of her even wished for it—to be locked away from the rest of the world.

Reggie pedaled on, past the airport, out to where the buildings thinned out, the four lanes turned back to two. She passed a driveway that led down a dirt road to one of George's warehouses. A Monahan Produce truck was pulling out, off to make an early morning delivery. Suddenly afraid that George would catch her out here, Reggie turned her bike around. Maybe she'd try the airport, circle through the parking lots and garages.

A mechanical chirp sounded behind her, and she turned, looked back over her shoulder. It was a police car, lights flashing. She was being pulled over. She stopped her bike and turned to see Stu Berr hop out of the car.

"I've been looking for you, Regina," he said.

Chapter 43

October 23, 2010
Brighton Falls, Connecticut

"We're both dead, Dufrane," Tara said, face swollen, lips sticky with blood. Her head was drooping forward, like it was too heavy to hold up. Her eyes were barely open.

"Are you okay?" Reggie asked. Stupid question. Reggie had just woken up moments ago, Neptune standing over her, his breath chugging like a train, his voice scolding:

It didn't have to be like this.

He'd taken off her blindfold and left, but Reggie had the sense that he wouldn't be gone long. She had to act quickly.

The cement under her back was cool and gritty, scraping her where her shirt had pulled up and bare skin made contact with the ground. Her arms were pulled above her head, elbows by her ears, her wrists around a pipe and bound with duct tape. The pipe, old electrical conduit, was firmly attached to a ridged metal wall. She could feel the wall when she reached back with her fingers. She lifted her head up and saw that he'd used half a roll or so on her ankles, too.

The tray of tools he'd left out for her amputation seemed to glitter and sparkle in the dim light, the only bright shiny things in the room. They were laid out on the floor about five feet to her right, taunting.

"I'm fucking great," Tara said, spitting blood. Tara was sitting upright against another iron pipe on the other side of the building, about twenty feet across from Reggie. Her torso had been wrapped round and round with silver duct tape, holding her against the pipe. Her arms were free, but there was nothing within reach. The end of her right arm was a mass of white bandages.

"Does it hurt?" Reggie asked, looked at the place where Tara's right hand had been.

"You could say that," Tara said, grimacing. "The son of a bitch hasn't given me morphine since last night."

Reggie's eyes went back to the saw and scalpel, the pile of bandages.

Don't look at them, she told herself. *Don't panic. Just think.*

Reggie's head exploded with a great dark blooming flower of pain as she tried to look around the abandoned warehouse. Her skinned elbows and right hip throbbed. Her cheek felt torn and crusty.

She looked down at her own chest and saw that the hourglass necklace was lying on the outside of her shirt, the glass cracked, the pink sand spilling out.

You have one minute to figure a way out of this. If you don't, you both die.

"Where are we?" Reggie asked, trying to still her racing heart.

"Hell," Tara answered dully.

Reggie craned her aching neck. Saw the curved metal walls arching over them, like they were inside a giant tin can cut in half lengthwise. The building was about twenty feet across, forty feet long. There were no windows, only a large wooden sliding door at the end, and a huge ventilation fan above it.

"It's a Quonset hut," Reggie said, feeling a strange sort of relief. This was not some magical madman's cave: it was a building. A building Reggie happened to know a great deal about. She'd studied at the Rhode

Island School of Design, the same state where the Quonset hut was developed. And she'd gotten to know the building intimately when she did the retrofit for the couple in Bennington.

"They're named for Quonset Point in Rhode Island," Reggie said, slipping into the voice she used for university lectures. "They were originally developed by the navy at the start of World War II. They needed a shelter that was inexpensive, lightweight, portable, and could be put up quickly using only hand tools." Reggie looked around at the corrugated metal walls, the steel arches supporting them. The metal was tarnished, rusted in places. This building had been here for a long time.

"As impressed as I am by your wealth of knowledge," Tara said, "it doesn't do us a damn bit of good."

But Tara was wrong. It did Reggie a world of good. To be able to break things down, to categorize and name them, to focus on the structural elements—it took things, for the moment at least, out of the realm of nightmares and into the real, tangible world.

Reggie remembered the *Boston Globe* article highlighting her work on the Bennington Quonset hut. There was a picture of the owners at the kitchen table, light streaming through the south-facing windows, the cabinets painted a cheery lemon-drop color with cobalt-blue accents. "Dufrane is a magician," they'd told the reporter. "She makes the impossible possible."

The hut Reggie found herself in now was far from bright and cheery. A few dim lightbulbs glowed overhead from ancient fixtures. The sliding door was framed with a crack of sunlight, and wind blew the fan on top, casting spinning shadows across the stained and cracked concrete floor. There was an old wooden table near Tara. In back, behind that, some broken-down machinery—old truck axles, the front of a forklift, a rusted-out pulley system.

Scattered here and there were piles of shipping pallets and old wooden crates. They were fruit and vegetable crates, Reggie realized. PRODUCT OF ARGENTINA, the one nearest her said. There was a colorful label showing a dark-haired woman with seductive eyes holding a big, juicy pear. She looked at another, showing a bunch of smiley-faced purple grapes who appeared to be singing. The lyrics hung in the air above them, surrounded by music notes: THE WEATHER IN ARGENTINA IS ALWAYS LOVELY.

A chill ran through Reggie.

He'd taken her mother to this same place. Probably the other women, too.

She pictured them, the faces she'd seen only hours ago on Stu Berr's wall: Andrea McFarlin, Candace Jacques, Ann Stickney. They'd all spend their last days on earth here, in this filthy, cold place that stank of rotting fruit and oil, of things forgotten and spoiled. They'd laid on their backs here under the arched cathedral-like ceiling, tied up and trapped in this twisted Church of Neptune.

She lifted her head to look at Tara. "Were you awake when he brought you here? Do you remember anything about the outside of the building?"

"No. But we must be in the middle of fucking nowhere. I screamed and screamed at first. But no one ever came."

Reggie listened, heard airplanes overhead, coming and going from somewhere behind her. She looked at her watch. 2:15. The sun was right behind the spinning fan. She guessed they were a couple miles west of the airport. George had some old warehouses out at the end of Airport Road. They must be in one of those.

"How long was I out?" Reggie asked.

"Not long. Ten, fifteen minutes. I heard the car outside. Then, a couple minutes later, he carried you in. How long have I been here anyway?" Tara asked. "I've lost track."

Reggie thought of lying, but couldn't. "It's day four," she said.

Tara let her head drop all the way down and closed her eyes. "It won't be long now," Tara said, voice remarkably cool and matter-of-fact.

"How did you know it was George?" Reggie asked.

"I didn't know for sure," Tara said. "Vera got all worked up one night. It was right after he'd visited her. She kept going on and on about how she wouldn't go back, how he couldn't make her. We were up half the night and I didn't understand a lot of what she said, but I'd heard enough to make me think that George was Neptune, and that before she turned up at the homeless shelter, he'd been holding her somewhere. I went to Charlie's dad, but he wasn't home."

"Why go to him? He's retired."

"I figured no one knew the ins and outs of the Neptune case more than Stu Berr. I thought he'd know what to do. But . . . George caught up with me." She was quiet for a moment. "I guess Lorraine had told him how upset Vera had been, how I'd been up with her all night. I dunno, somehow he figured out that *I'd* figured it out—maybe with his fucking serial killer psychic powers. He caught up with me, and he jumped me, and practically fucking choked me to death—I thought I was dead then, but I woke up here. He's told me things.

He's crazy, Reggie. Scary, batshit crazy. Between what he and Vera told me—he kept your mother in a little rented room of some kind for years up in Worcester, not far from one of his warehouses there. Pretended she was his wife. Told her that if she ever left, he'd come after you."

"Oh Jesus," Reggie whispered.

"Yeah. He brought her food, cigarettes, booze. She wasn't locked up or anything—but she was too scared to leave. He'd bring her a cell phone, dial your number, and let her hear your voice when you answered. That was how she knew he was keeping to his word, that you were okay for now. And it was also a threat, showing her that he knew just how to find you."

"It was her," Reggie said, remembering all the phone calls over the years, the strange breathing on the other end, the sense she'd had that the person on the other end was on the verge of speaking.

"But how did she finally escape?" Reggie asked.

Tara laughed raggedly.

"He let her go. I guess it got to be too much—keeping her there in secret all those years. And of course she wasn't a beauty queen anymore, she was sick and crazy, more work than ever. Lorraine was needing him more and more, starting to ask questions about all his trips. He dropped her off at the homeless shelter himself, swore that if she breathed a word about him or who she really was, he'd come after you."

The thought of the lengths her mother had gone to in trying to protect her astounded Reggie; the idea that love could run so deep. Vera had sacrificed her own life, her own sanity, to save her.

Reggie heard her cell phone ringing. She turned and saw her leather messenger bag tossed on the floor on the other side of the building, near the sliding door. Totally out of reach.

Reggie tested the strength of the duct tape that bound her wrists together on the other side of the iron pipe. There was no way she could break it. What she needed was something sharp. Her eyes went to the tools laid out on the metal tray about five feet from her: scalpels, a saw, metal trowel, propane torch, clamps, and bandages. It was a bold move on his part, leaving them out in the open. He'd done it to scare her, give her a prelude of what was to come. But he'd made a critical error in judgment. If there was one thing Reggie was good at, it was geometry, spatial relations, visualizing the radius of a circle. She saw patterns other people didn't, invisible lines, planes of trajectory. She knew the tray of tools was not out of reach.

The phone stopped ringing.

Reggie began to shuffle in a clockwise motion, feet pushing her along, butt lifting, bound arms pivoting around the pipe. Her whole body hummed with pain. She tried to lift her head to watch her progress but couldn't manage it. She pushed onward, slowly, carefully.

She thought of spirals and curves, the orbit of planets. The way Len told her she had Neptune in the twelfth house; that it was what made her a great architect, but also had the potential to bring her to the brink of madness.

She thought of the way her mother always used to say that everyone was connected by invisible string; that we were all bound to one another in ways we could never even begin to imagine.

She felt those strings now, binding her to her mother, to Tara, to the other women Neptune had killed; women who had looked up at this same ceiling in their final moments on earth.

It was slow going, writhing and bucking along like a bug stuck on a pin, but finally she made contact. Her right foot hit the tray full of tools with a satisfying metallic clank.

"What are you up to, Dufrane?" Tara had lifted her head again and looked at her with one eye open, the other mostly closed with swelling.

"Making the impossible possible."

"Huh?"

"If I can just move these, get the saw, knife, or scalpel to where I can reach it with my hands, then I can cut myself free."

Tara made a hissing sort of laugh. "Ironic."

"What is?" Reggie said, resting a second.

"The idea of being saved by a blade."

Carefully Reggie used her foot to edge the tray and everything on it clattering toward her across the cement floor. She writhed and contorted, pulling the tray closer to her body. When it was close enough, she rolled over onto her right side, her injured hip screaming in pain as it grated against the rough concrete floor. She pulled her knees toward her chest to keep the items corralled as she spun like the crooked hand of a clock. Ticktock. Ticktock. She'd done almost half a turn, was at the eleven o'clock position, about as far as she could go without hitting the wall.

There, just to her right, was another fruit crate—El Diablo Oranges, São Paulo, Brazil. A red devil was smiling out at her, pointing his pitchfork in her direction.

Old Scratch.

She knew she'd only have one shot. She studied the trajectory, picturing the invisible line between the saw and scalpel on the tray and her bound hands. At last she took in a breath, and with the force of her whole body, she kicked up with her knees, knocking the tools off the tray. She hit the scalpel perfectly, sent it skidding across the cement and heard it hit the metal wall. She couldn't turn and see it, and only prayed it hadn't bounced out of reach. The saw had come closer, too—she could just see it by twisting her head viciously, but it looked out of reach. She shoved herself back toward the wall and began feeling behind the pole. Her fingertips just grazed the edge of the saw but couldn't move it closer.

"Shit!" she said and she tried to stretch them, imagining her body made of elastic. But it was no good. She gave up and began to search for the scalpel, fingers doing a frantic spider-crawl along the reachable edge of the wall behind her. Where the hell was it?

Her fingertips danced over the floor, searching. At last she felt it: a slender cylinder of cold metal wedged between the floor and the wall. She worked her fingers to the end, only to discover it was the wrong end when she grabbed for it and felt the sting of the blade.

Just like that, she was thirteen again, sitting in the attic with Tara, who was holding a razor, wet with her own blood. She remembered the guilty pleasure at feeling such relief when Tara drew the sharp edge across her own skin: this exalted moment where there was nothing else in the world but her and her pain: no mother held by a serial killer, no secret longing for Charlie, nothing. Just the pain and the way it drew her deep inside herself, to a place of perfect calm.

Reggie allowed herself to run her fingers over the edge of the scalpel once more, feeling the kiss of the blade, emptying her mind of everything else, which was such sweet relief.

"How's it going there?" Tara asked.

"I'll have us out in no time," Reggie promised.

She took a deep breath and reached for the handle of the scalpel, fingertips sticky with blood. She fumbled with the scalpel until she managed to get it at the right angle to cut the tape. It was a tedious process, even with a sharp blade, the awkward, upside-down stabbing and sawing motion. At last she made it through and her hands were free.

Her phone was ringing again.

She sat up, scuttled across the floor to her bag, and answered.

"Reggie," Len said. "I'm here with your aunt. Where the hell are you? We were about to call the cops."

"Listen carefully. You need to call 911. Tell them Tara and I are being held in an old Quonset hut a couple miles west of the airport. It's owned by Monahan Produce. George Monahan is Neptune."

"Oh my God, Reggie," Len said.

"Hurry," Tara said, giving Reggie a desperate glance. "I think I hear a car."

Reggie froze, listening. There it was, the faint buzz of a motor, getting closer.

"I've gotta go," she said.

"I love you, Reggie," he said.

"I love you, too. And I'm sorry, Len. I'm sorry for always being so scared, for pushing you away."

"Not the time for a tender moment, Reg," Tara interrupted. "He's almost here!"

"Reggie, I—" Len said.

"Call the police. Tell them to hurry." She hung up.

She heard the crunch of tires on gravel.

"Do you have a knife or something in there?" Tara asked.

Reggie rummaged through her bag, pushing aside the wooden swan, her sketchbook full of Nautilus drawings. She grabbed a fountain pen, thinking it might be better than nothing, then saw that there, at the bottom of the bag, was the large screwdriver.

"Hurry," Tara gasped. "He's here."

Reggie slid the screwdriver across the floor to Tara. "It's all I've got," she said.

Tara reached awkwardly for it with her left hand and tucked it inside her black motorcycle boot.

Outside, a car door opened and closed. Footsteps approached.

Reggie scooted back and grabbed the tools and bandages, threw them onto the tray and pushed it back to where she thought it had been.

There was a metallic thumping sound as he worked to unlock and unlatch the door.

Reggie grabbed the scalpel, slipped it into her sleeve, then lay back down, hands over her head, around the pipe, the sliced duct tape pushed back together.

The door opened and light spilled in, Neptune's shadow long and enormous in the center of it.

"Miss me, ladies?" he asked, voice booming like a clap of thunder.

Chapter 44

June 24, 1985
Brighton Falls, Connecticut

"I stopped by your house and your aunt said you were out on your bike."

Reggie stood with her hands on the handlebars, the bike placed protectively between her and Stu Berr. He wore a blue polyester sports coat that was too tight in the shoulders and didn't button. She could see a gun in a holster strapped to his left side.

"Have they found her?" Reggie asked. "My mom?"

Stu shook his head. "Not yet."

Reggie nodded, looked down at the pedals and chain of her bike, the toothed chainwheels and front derailleur.

"Is that what you're doing out here?" Stu asked. "Looking for her?"

Reggie gave a timid shrug. "I wanted to find her first. I thought," she said, looking up at last from the gears of her bike to meet his eyes, "that she'd want it that way."

Stu nodded and looked at her for what felt like a long, long time.

If he hadn't come to tell her about her mother, then he'd come to arrest her for killing Sid. She waited, wondering if he'd handcuff her or if she'd be allowed to get into the car on her own. She tried to imagine Lorraine's face when she heard the news: *your niece and her friends killed a boy last night.* She felt almost sorry for Lorraine, having to live all alone in that big, stone house now, only ghosts for company.

"Reggie," he said at last, "I know what happened last night. In the parking lot at Reuben's."

"Oh," Reggie said, the word a hollow sound.

"Early this morning, Charlie broke down and told me the whole story."

Stu ran his fingers over his mustache and studied her a minute, like he was contemplating what to do next.

"Are you going to arrest me now?" Reggie asked.

Stu blew out a long, slow breath. "No, I'm not."

"We shouldn't have left him like that," Reggie said, tears coming. "Just lying there dead. What happened was an accident, but we shouldn't have run away. I'm so sorry. It's all my fault. I'm the reason everyone was fighting. If I hadn't told Charlie—"

Stu interrupted her. "He's not dead, Regina."

She looked up, wiped at her eyes, heart fluttering with hope. "You mean he's okay?"

Stu gave her a grave look. His face had aged so much lately. Dark baggy circles hung under his eyes. "No," he said. "His head was badly injured. There's nothing the doctors can do."

"So he's going to die?"

"I don't think so. But there's a good chance he won't be able to walk again. Or speak. He'll never be the same, Reggie. Do you understand?"

Her chest went from feeling light and fluttery to having the sensation of a wrecking ball smashing into it. "It's worse than being dead," she mumbled.

Stu didn't answer. They looked at each other a minute, neither of them speaking. Reggie imagined Sid in a hospital bed, hooked up to an IV and oxygen, head wrapped up in a huge white bandage like a swami—a pot-smoking mystic on a transcendental journey he'd never wake up from.

And it was all her fault.

"Here's the thing," Stu said, his voice low as he leaned closer to her, his breath coming faster now. He smelled like stale sweat, coffee, and cigarettes. Reggie was sure he hadn't slept last night and was probably still in yesterday's clothes. "No criminal charges are going to be pressed. The police investigation will say he was alone in the parking lot when he tripped and fell."

"But that's not what happened!" This wasn't supposed to be what cops did. They were the good guys. They were supposed to uncover truth, not tell lies.

Stu nodded. "Isn't it bad enough to have one life ruined?" Stu asked.

"But we were all there!" Reggie objected. "If we hadn't left him, if we'd gotten him help right away . . ."

He held up his hands in a stop gesture. "What's done is done," he said, voice firm and full of authority. "Now here's what I need from you. Are you listening, Reggie, because this is important?"

She gave a weak nod.

"I want you kids to stay away from Sid. And from each other, too."

"But Charlie—"

"No buts. My son is going to have a normal life. He's going to high school in the fall. He'll work his ass off to get good grades, maybe play a little ball, get into a good college. I'm not going to let his life be ruined by this." Stu bit down on his words, grinding them up and spitting them out.

"It's best if you all take a little break from each other right now," he continued. "And with all that's happened with your mother, I think you need to spend some time at home. Your aunt needs you."

"Does she know about what happened with Sid? Did you tell her?"

Stu shook his head. "Like I said, there's nothing to tell. Sidney tripped and fell. He was alone in the parking lot. He'd had a couple of drinks and smoked a little pot. He hit a rough spot in the pavement, lost his balance, and fell backward. Accidents happen. Do you understand?"

Reggie nodded, but the truth was, she didn't understand at all.

Was it really possible to reinvent the past this way? Reggie thought of the years of lies she'd listened to about her mother, how eager she must have been to believe them when the truth seemed so obvious now. Shouldn't she have been suspicious when her mother never invited her to any of her plays, never let Reggie meet any of her eccentric theater friends? Maybe what it came down to was that people believe what they want to believe.

"And you're not going to contact Charlie or Tara for a while, right? No visits, no phone calls."

"Right," she stammered.

"Good girl," he said. "Can I give you a lift home?"

"That's okay, I'll ride back."

She got on her bike and pushed off.

"Reggie," he called, and she hit the brakes and looked back at him. "Neptune's other victims, their bodies were found very early in the morning."

"Yeah, I know."

"I'm just saying, maybe it's a good sign that your mother's body hasn't turned up yet. Maybe this time it will be different."

Reggie hated him just then. It seemed the cruelest thing a person could do—to invent hope where there was none.

"Maybe," Reggie said, and started to pedal back home.

Chapter 45

October 23, 2010
Brighton Falls, Connecticut

Reggie turned her head and watched as Neptune carried two grocery bags over to a small wooden table near Tara. Whistling, he pulled a white cloth out of one of the bags and used it to cover the table. He set a place for one with a plate, knife, fork, spoon, and crystal wineglass. He moved slowly, methodically—smoothing the napkin, checking the distance between plate and glass, polishing the fork till it shined. As a finishing touch, he added two silver candlesticks with red candles, lighting them with a box of matches drawn from his pocket. He ignored Tara and Reggie completely.

When everything was perfectly laid out on the table, he opened the bag, pulled out a large plastic container, and opened it. As the smell wafted out, Reggie's stomach somersaulted and she tried to breathe through her mouth. She stared, fixated—like someone who sees a terrible accident but can't look away—as he gently pulled off the lid of the container to reveal a boiled lobster dinner, which he moved carefully onto the plate; lobster red and steaming, little white potatoes on the side.

"Almost time, my love," he said to Tara. She had her chin on her chest and eyes closed. Then he glanced toward Reggie and seemed to study her a moment.

She hadn't had time to arrange the tools neatly or cover her wrists properly. Had he noticed?

No. He simply smiled, went back to the lobster. He cracked it open, slicing the carapace down the center, exposing the meat. Then he drizzled it with melted butter from a smaller container. When he was finished, he licked his fingers, packed up the containers, and stepped back to admire his handiwork.

"Perfect," he said, looking to Tara. "Don't you agree, darling?"

She didn't lift her head. He walked over, crouched down, and lifted it for her, peeled open her eyelids, making her look.

"Lobsters are incredible creatures," he told her. "They're able to regenerate appendages lost in battle."

Tara kept her eyes blank and doll-like, but somewhere in there, Reggie was sure she saw a little spark of terror.

"They molt regularly, growing a new shell and eating the old one." She seemed to twitch a little here. "They molt five or six times in the first season, and as adults once or twice a year."

"The lobster," he said, taking out his pocketknife, "is an expert at transformation."

Tara looked right at Reggie and rolled her eyes.

He worked carefully, cutting the tape that bound her to the pipe. "Stand," he commanded.

"I'm afraid I'm not much of a lobster fan," she said.

"Move, bitch!" he said, grabbing hold of her arms and jerking her to her feet, where she staggered and swayed. He puppet-walked her over to the table, propping her up in the chair. He took out a roll of silver duct tape and used it to bind her ankles to the chair's front legs.

"Tonight you dine like a lady," he said. "Tonight you will be redeemed."

"Thanks, but seriously, lobster's not really my thing," she told him. Her voice only trembled slightly.

He slapped her face hard, the skin against skin sound echoing through the warehouse. Her nose started to bleed.

"Eat," he told her, leaning down to hiss in her ear, "start eating, or I'll gut your little friend Regina *right now.*"

She picked up the fork, dug out a piece of white lobster meat, brought it to her mouth, and began to chew. Butter dripped down her chin. She chewed a long time. When she finally swallowed, she seemed to gag a bit.

"Good girl," Neptune said. He was just Neptune now, not the George that Reggie had known her whole life, the George who was her father. "Now you enjoy your dinner while I tend to our new guest."

He walked over to Reggie slowly, smiling, savoring every second of this. His hands were deep in his pockets, his eyes on Reggie's face. Was he looking for a trace of himself there? Did he feel an ounce of regret at being about to cut the hand off his own daughter?

"Can I ask you something?" Reggie said.

He nodded. He was beside her now, still looking down at her. She knew at any minute, he'd turn his attention to the tray of tools and notice the missing scalpel. She could feel it tucked into her sleeve, cool against her wrist. She just needed to get him close enough, catch him off guard.

"Did she say she'd marry you? Were you the one she told everyone about?"

He turned away, his face twisted with disgust. "No. I'd asked her, yes. The first time was just after she told me she was pregnant. I took her out to dinner, her favorite place, Harry's Steak House down by the shore. We ordered lobster, and I had the waiter bring a bottle of champagne." His eyes had a wistful, faraway look. "I got down on one knee, offered her a ring. And do you know what she did?" He stared down at Reggie, fury replacing wistfulness. "She laughed. She actually laughed."

Reggie shook her head. She remembered laughing at Len's drunken idea that the two of them should move in together. Like mother, like daughter.

"I'm so sorry," she said, suddenly understanding the scene before her.

Neptune turned away from her, watching Tara force down bites of lobster meat obediently. Tears streamed down Tara's face, but she made no crying sounds.

"But I didn't give up. I asked her for years, over and over again. Even when I was with Lorraine, I told Vera that the offer always stood. I could give her a good life. A nice home. Be a real father to you. Take care of you both. But she always said no."

"But then she said yes to someone else?" Reggie guessed. She tried to sound a little disgusted, like she was on his side, she understood the pain and torment her mother must have put him through.

He turned back to face her, looking more like a broken-hearted lover than a malicious killer. "I never found out who it was," he said. "But she was very excited. She was actually going to go through with it. Try and have the magical, normal life that had always eluded her. I tried to tell her. No one could love her like I did. I begged her to change her mind. To choose me instead."

"It wasn't fair," Reggie said. "Her choosing him over you. You'd been there for her all those years. You'd given her so much."

The corners of his mouth twitched, then stayed downturned. "Life isn't fair, Reggie. I learned that a lot time ago. You did too, didn't you?"

Reggie understood, twisted as the whole thing was. George had loved Vera his whole life, done his best to win her over, suffered rejection year after year. Watched as this woman he loved threw her life away, drank and went out with one loser after another. And when she was in trouble, George was always there for her. Then, when she finally decided to marry and settle down, she chose someone else. It seemed so cruel. Something inside of him snapped then, when he heard the news. And he had to punish someone. But he couldn't bring himself to hurt her—not yet.

"The other women—Candace, Andrea, Ann—they were all seeing men who'd dumped Mom."

"Whores," he said. "Unworthy whores. They deserved what they got." The little vein on the side of his head bulged again.

He got down on his knees, stroked Reggie's hair. "I wanted to save you from all of this. If she had only said yes, changed her mind, everything would have turned out differently."

He was so close she could smell his breath—it was sour and tinged with menthol.

"But why not just kill them? Why cut off their hands first?"

"It didn't seem fair, did it? Your mother's beautiful hand being ruined like that, ugly with scars, while these other women, these tramps, had perfect hands. So I took them for Vera." He was reaching for the saw now, his fingertips giving the handle a loving caress.

"Did you know," he asked, "that the human hand has twenty-seven bones: fourteen phalanges, five metacarpals, eight carpals? Such perfect engineering."

He looked down at Reggie's right hand. She held her breath, waiting. He took her hand, twisting it so that he could look down at her palm.

"The hand is a map. The Gypsies, Greeks, Chinese, Egyptians, Hebrews—they all knew it. They honored hands. Used them to diagnose and heal.

"The left hand is the hand you're born with. The right hand is the hand you make. Remove the right hand and you erase the record of how badly these women lived, send them on to the next world with only their birth hand, their pure hand."

His eyes glistened behind the wire-rimmed glasses.

"I helped them to transform," George told her, voice firm but soothing. "To transcend."

Reggie's head swum as a wave of nausea overtook her. If she could just keep him talking, get him closer, she might have a chance.

"Why keep them alive after?"

He dropped her hand and hung his head. "Regardless of what you might think, I'm not a killer, Reggie. I don't enjoy it." He glared down at her, as if daring her to contradict him. "It doesn't come easily for me. I waited, with all of them, to give Vera a chance to save them. If she came around, said yes to marrying me, I'd let them go."

"But she didn't," Reggie said.

"I was nothing but a joke to her," he said, eyes blazing. "The deaths of those women, they were her fault."

"I see," Reggie said, locking eyes with him as she reached for the scalpel in her left sleeve, touching it with the fingertips of her right hand. "It was her fault. All of it. But still, once you had her, you didn't kill her. You kept her alive year after year. You threatened to come after me if she left you."

"We all have our destinies, Reggie. Your mother's was to be with me."

"But you let her go."

His body tensed. "A mistake. Clearly. I thought her mind was too far gone. All that drinking. Honestly, I'm surprised she even remembered who she was. And I thought the threat of coming after you was enough to keep her quiet about anything she did remember."

"Did you mean it? That you would have come after me? Hunted me down and killed me?"

He smiled, shrugged his shoulders like a shy little boy. "Like I said, I'm no killer."

"But you're going to kill me now." Her fingers wrapped around the handle of the scalpel.

Closer. She needed him to come closer.

He made a tsk-tsk sound. "Your fault, I'm afraid. If you hadn't found that damn swan, seen the little clue I'd left for Vera, the little warning that was supposed to make her realize she had the power to stop the killings . . ."

Reggie lowered her voice to almost a whisper, closed her eyes. "There's one thing I don't understand."

"What's that?" he asked.

Reggie gave an incoherent mumble and George leaned forward so that his face was inches from hers.

She lunged up, swinging her arm in a perfect arc, slicing into his neck with the scalpel, feeling the impact, the pressure, then release as she pushed the blade as far in as it would go.

Chapter 46

June 24, 1985
Brighton Falls, Connecticut

"I'm not supposed to talk to you," Reggie said into the phone.

"I know," Tara said. "Yogi told me the deal, too. Just one more time, though, okay? Meet me in the tree house in half an hour."

"I don't know. I —"

"I'll see you then, Reg," Tara said. Then she hung up before Reggie could respond.

Reggie rolled out of bed and walked downstairs. Her legs felt like they were made of lead. She ran her hand along the wall of stone, cold and damp against her fingertips.

Lorraine and George were in the kitchen, drinking tea, waiting for news. But there hadn't been any word. And now it was after five.

Vera's body still had not been found.

George had brought over a pot of turkey soup that was simmering on the stove, making the kitchen steamy and giving it a Thanksgiving dinner kind of smell that made Reggie's mouth water. She hated herself for it. How could she be thinking of food when her mother was dead and Sid was lying in a hospital, brain damaged? How was she supposed to eat turkey soup when it was all her fault?

Reggie snuck out the front door and crossed the yard to the tree house. She climbed the swinging ladder, then sat back in a corner and waited. She peeked out at Monique's Wish, saw her bedroom window. She could make out the outline of the bulletin board with her drawings, her bed with its Drunkard's Path quilt, the edge of her closet. She squinted her eyes and thought she saw a shadow move across the room, a ghost version of herself. The Reggie she used to be. She wished so strongly then that she could go back in time, warn that girl what was to come: the killings, losing her mother, Sid's accident. *The world is not the way you think it is,* she would tell herself.

"Hey," Tara said, pushing open the trapdoor and scrambling up. She crawled over to Reggie and sat so that their sides were touching. “Want a cigarette?” Tara asked as she pulled out her pack.

“No.”

“How ’bout this?” Tara said, holding up the little silver box that held the razor blade.

Reggie shook her head, brought her knees up to her chest, and hugged them close. Part of her longed for it: to punish herself in some way, to feel something beyond the dark weight of guilt.

“Did you call Charlie, too?” she asked.

Tara picked at a hole in her jeans. “He didn’t pick up. I’ve been calling all day. I’m sure he’s home, but he’s not answering the phone.”

“If Stu finds out . . .”

Tara nodded. “He won’t. And I won’t try to talk to Charlie anymore. Maybe it’s for the best anyway.” She shook a cigarette out of the pack.

“So was there a reason you wanted me to meet you?” Reggie asked. If Tara was here to make her feel like shit, to remind her that all this was her fault, she might as well get it over with. Reggie braced herself as best she could and waited.

Tara lit her cigarette. “I just wanted to say I was sorry.”

“What for? I’m the one who fucked up and told Charlie about the cutting. I don’t even know why I did it. I guess I—”

Tara shook her head. "I don't even care about that! Well, I do, but it doesn't matter. Not compared to what I did to Sid."

"We were all there, Tara. And what happened to Sid, it was an accident."

"But I'm the one who said we should run. If we hadn't . . ."

"And I'm the one who blurted out your biggest secret just because I was jealous. I'm the one who got Charlie so pissed off. If I'd kept my mouth shut, they wouldn't have even started fighting. Sid wouldn't have—"

"Do you know why I said to run?" Tara interrupted. "Because when I stood there, looking down at Sid, sure he was dead, all I thought was that I had to protect you. That you and Charlie couldn't be caught there like that. And I knew you guys were too good to leave on your own. I made you."

Reggie shook her head. "You weren't dragging us along in chains, Tara. We chose to follow you."

Tara exhaled more smoke, watched it drift up to the unfinished ceiling.

"It was always my choice, Tara. The cutting, going to the bars, leaving Sid like that. You didn't make me do any of it."

They were silent for a minute, listening to crickets, to a helicopter overhead droning like a giant insect.

Tara dropped her cigarette into an empty Coke bottle. "Still no word about your mom?"

"Nothing. Which is almost worse in a way. I just keep thinking her body's out there somewhere, naked, undiscovered."

Tara nodded.

"Then I keep thinking, what if she's not dead?" Reggie said. "Which just seems so totally deluded. Having this little tease of hope . . . it's just stupid. I almost wish they'd just find her body. Get it over with, you know?"

"You know that old saying," Tara said. "Be careful what you wish for."

"I know, but—"

"You know what I went to sleep wishing last night?" Tara asked. "That Sid wasn't dead. I played a little game with myself, imagined going back to the parking lot, and there he was, sitting up, waiting with this stupid *I-sure-fooled-you* grin. Then this morning, old Yogi comes around telling me it's true, Sid's not dead. Then he tells me that he's all fucked up, brain damaged, and you know what my first stupid thought was? That I'd made it happen by wishing he was alive."

"But you didn't," Reggie said. "I mean, wishes don't have that kind of power."

"How do you know?" Tara asked, staring at Reggie with intense, desperate eyes.

"*Because.* They don't. We can't change things by wishing. Only by doing. It's our actions, Tara, not our thoughts."

Tara smiled a cynical smile and pulled out her hourglass from inside her shirt. "The world we know is going to end in one minute. Tell me one true thing before we die. Then I'll tell you one."

"I'm not in the mood for a game."

"It's the last time, Reggie. The last time ever. So make it a good one."

Reggie watched the pink sand fall through the hourglass.

"Part of me has always hated you," Reggie said, looking down at the floorboards.

"Why?" Tara asked without a trace of surprise or anger in her voice.

"Because Charlie loves you. Because when I see him looking at you I know I'll never see him look at me that way. Because me, I'm just me. But you . . . you're like the sun and everything is revolving around you, wishing it could get just a little bit closer."

Tara wrapped her fingers around the hourglass and yanked hard, breaking the chain. She held the broken necklace out to Reggie, who stared at it, unsure what to do. Finally, Tara grabbed Reggie's hand, pried her fingers open, and placed the hourglass in her palm.

"And part of me has always loved you," Tara said. "It's kind of fucked up and ironic, isn't it? Charlie loving me, you loving him. You hate me for being me, and me, all I've ever wanted was to be more like you. The normal girl who draws these totally amazing pictures and has this glamorous movie star mother and lives in this cool castle of a house." Tara stood up and crossed the floor to the trapdoor. "It's kind of a shame, isn't it?" she asked. "That none of us ever got what we wanted."

"Can I ask you something?" Reggie said.

Tara shrugged. "You've got the hourglass now. You get to make the rules."

"Was it real? When Andrea McFerlin got inside you? When they told you stuff? Did you really hear the voices of dead women?"

Tara picked at a tear in the sleeve of her shirt. She seemed so . . . so broken, to Reggie right then. A cut-up girl held together with safety pins and staples.

"I thought I did," Tara said. "But now I'm thinking maybe it was just me. Maybe they're all just me."

She lifted the trapdoor and slid through it. Just like that, she was gone, leaving Reggie with the little hourglass, which she kept turning in her hand, watching time run out over and over.

Chapter 47

October 23, 2010
Brighton Falls, Connecticut

"Bitch," he gurgled, placing a hand over the gash on the side of his neck. Blood pumped out between the fingers he'd wrapped over the wound. With his right hand, he reached for the tools on the tray, grabbing what looked like a hacksaw—the tool Reggie knew he'd intended to use to cut off her hand. He lunged forward with it, sinking the teeth into Reggie's neck. She screamed, twisted away, which made the blade bite harder into her skin. Using both hands, she grabbed the metal frame of the saw and pushed up, away from her neck, relieving the pressure, getting it off before it went too deep. He took his left hand off his neck, the blood coming out in spurts now, and tried to regain control of the saw, but his hands were slippery, and she jerked it away. Reggie threw the saw, hearing it clatter against the cement floor, but unable to see where it landed.

He came at her again, with bare hands this time, wrapping them around her neck, his fingers warm and sticky. She was amazed by their strength. She felt as if he'd completely crushed her windpipe. The blood on his hands mixed with the blood seeping from her own neck, half of their DNA matching. Father and daughter.

And she felt him inside her then; not the calm, rational man she'd known all her life, the one she went to with all her troubles, but the dark man, the killer, Neptune. She was Neptune's daughter, and she knew, at that moment, that she, too, carried the power to kill.

Clawing at his wrists and arms, she tried to loosen his grip, but it only got tighter. She bucked her hips, swung her knees, trying to connect, knock him off of her or at least distract him. The blood from his neck dripped down onto her chest, soaking her silk blouse.

"You're just like your mother," he said, spitting the words out.

Reggie wanted to answer, to give some kind of witty response, famous last words, but without air and with a crushed throat, speaking was impossible. For the first time in years, she wanted to be just like her mother. She wanted to be the kind of person who loved someone so fiercely, she would do anything to protect her.

She thought of her mother, trapped in that little apartment all those years, playing the good and happy wife, chain-smoking, downing glass after glass of gin, having nothing but memories and the television to keep her company most of the time.

She felt light-headed, and things began to turn gray and fuzzy, as they had once upon a time when Tara had choked her. The strength seeped from her limbs.

She could see it so clearly now, Tara's face above her own. *I'm Neptune. Why do I do what I do?*

Then she felt herself floating up, leaving her body. She looked back down and saw herself on the floor, eyes frantic, mouth in a grimace of pain and fear as he strangled her with his delicate hands. Only it wasn't just herself she saw, but all the women he'd killed, the faces changed, clicking through like images on a child's viewfinder: Candy the waitress, Ann Stickney, Andrea McFerlin—all of them with that same wild-eyed look of terror.

And she understood it then. This was why he did what he did. It was the look on their faces in these last moments, the power he must have felt just then, their lives fading in his hands. At last, for a few brief minutes, he got Vera back for all the times she'd rejected him, laughed in his face.

As the grayness faded toward black, as the scene below her became more abstract, less personal, and the relief of just giving up began to take over—Reggie suddenly snapped back into her own body, and it was Tara's face she saw rising above her. Not the Tara of her childhood, but the grown-up version, battered and bruised, chin covered in blood. She was standing behind Neptune, and she had something in her left hand, something narrow with a metallic tip. She raised it above her head, then slammed it down into Neptune's back, let out a strangled grunt of effort. The screwdriver.

Reggie could hear George's voice in her head—not the Neptune George, but the George who'd taught her to read a plan and to fix her bicycle: *There's a right tool for every job.*

He released his grip on Reggie, and air rushed into her aching throat. He twisted, tried to rise, but staggered back down, weak from all the blood he'd lost. Reggie sucked in oxygen raggedly, her wits and strength coming back with each breath. Neptune was down on his knees, one hand on his leaking neck, the other reaching uselessly around to his back as he groped for the screwdriver lodged between his shoulder blades like the key of a broken wind-up toy. Tara stepped back out of his way, watching him with narrowed eyes and bared teeth, as if she would go for his throat with nothing but her fangs if necessary. Reggie struggled to a sitting position, looked him in the eyes. It wasn't terror she saw there, but stunned disbelief. Then his body crumpled forward.

It was over.

Afterward

November 1, 2010
Brighton Falls, Connecticut

"Don't you have to get back to work?" Tara asked. They were in Vera's room at Monique's Wish, the dappled late afternoon sunlight hitting the floorboards, making them glow.

Len was beside Reggie, holding her hand. He seemed hesitant to leave her for even a minute since meeting her at the hospital last week. In the old days, this would have driven Reggie mad, but now she found it comforting. She gave his hand a squeeze.

Vera had just drifted off to sleep after a confused card game that was half crazy eights and half rummy, with a touch of five-card stud thrown in. Tara kept saying it was like living inside the beginning of a bad joke—*this couple sits down to a card game with two one-handed women . . .* Vera and Tara had to lay their cards out, trusting no one would peek.

"I can work from here just fine," Reggie said, gathering up the cards. "And while I'm here, I can get some repairs under way."

Len had settled right in at Monique's Wish, too. He'd completely charmed Lorraine and put himself to work cleaning, cooking, and running household errands. He seemed in awe of the house, said it was like living inside a giant sculpture.

"Oh," Len said. "I almost forgot. The guy at the home center gave me some names of roofers who do slate. But I still think it would be kind of fun to do it ourselves." He gave her a wry smile.

"I think I've had enough adventure for a while," Reggie said, cringing a little at the idea of their crawling around on the steep-pitched roof. "Let's leave the high stuff to the experts."

Her hand went to her throat, as it had done a thousand times a day since her escape from the warehouse, feeling the bruises and cuts, which ached and itched as they healed.

In her dreams and nightmares, she was back on that cold cement floor, feeling Neptune's hands around her neck. She woke shivering, crying out, and Len would turn on the light and hold her, say, "It's okay. I'm here. You're safe." And she'd look around, see the solid stone walls of her grandfather's castle, feel the soft weight of the Drunkard's Path quilt covering them, and know he was right. She was safe. She was home.

"Parts of the house are in such ragged shape," Tara said, "wouldn't it be better to tear it all down?"

Tara wore jeans and a sweatshirt, white bandages covering the place where her right hand had been. She was already starting to talk about a prosthetic hand and had an appointment to be measured and fitted. She didn't want just one new hand, though. She said she wanted a hand for every occasion: a hand with sequins and glitter for nights on the town; a hand covered in tattoos; a hand with a poem written across it.

"Tear it down? No way!" Reggie protested. "Not with all the work that went into building it. This place was a labor of love. My grandfather must have wanted to quit a thousand times over, but he didn't because he'd promised his wife a castle."

Tara smiled in her familiar, teasing way. "Romantic."

"The idea is," Reggie said. "But building it must have been hard as hell. Hauling all these rocks. Laying the walls up by hand."

"It's an amazing accomplishment," Tara agreed. "And quite a legacy to leave behind."

"It's a work of art," Len said.

"You know, I've been thinking," Reggie said. "My whole professional focus has been on sustainable design, and really, what's more sustainable than people staying right where they are? Just fixing up the houses they already have—making them more green, more energy friendly. I was thinking I might do some new projects along those lines, starting right here, with Monique's Wish. I was up late last night sketching some ideas—a new roof with a rain catchment system and solar water heaters. Replace the windows, add a few more on the south side. Maybe radiant floor heat. I was thinking I could renovate the attic, make it a workspace for while I'm here. Add some dormers and skylights, maybe."

"Ambitious," said Tara.

"That's me," Reggie said, smiling.

"What about the project you've been working on," Tara asked, ". . . the little snail house?"

"The Nautilus is on the back burner for now," Reggie said. She was less sure now about her idea that people were better off as nomads, wandering from place to place with their homes on their backs. Maybe Len had been right all along: home was a solid place where you put down roots; where the walls held memories and your family gathered around you.

"I want to put all my energy into Monique's Wish. I'm even thinking about teaching some renovation workshops here in the suburbs."

"I think it's great that you're going to stick around. It'll make a big difference with your mother. And even if she doesn't say so, it'll mean a lot to Lorraine."

Reggie nodded. Lorraine had said little about George. Reggie hadn't pushed her—her aunt had never been one to process her feelings out loud. Reggie had also decided not to tell Lorraine about George's being her father or about a lot of the details of George's psychosis she'd uncovered. There was only so much a person could take. The most important thing was that they were all safe. It was over at last. They had the rest of their lives to try to make sense of it, to put the missing pieces into place. But right now, there were more pressing things. Like card games and chocolate pudding with Vera.

The doctors didn't know how long Vera had—weeks, months at the most. But whatever time they had left, Reggie was determined to make the most of it.

Reggie stood up and walked to the dresser to put the cards away. There, on top, next to the box of medicines, was a framed picture of the old Aphrodite Cold Cream ad. Her mother, young and radiant, strangely immortal, smiled out at them, her perfect right hand holding the jar of cream. *Treat Yourself Like a Goddess.*

Reggie turned back to see that the real Vera had opened her eyes and was giving Reggie a slightly puzzled look.

"It's you," Vera said, surprised, as though Reggie hadn't been there playing cards all afternoon.

"Yeah, Mom. It's me." Reggie walked over and sat down on the edge of the bed, smiling down at her mother.

"You're here," Vera said.

Reggie took her left hand, gave it a squeeze. "Where else would I be?"

Acknowledgments

Huge thanks go out to the usual suspects: my agent, Dan Lazar who tells it like it is and always finds a way to make me a better writer; my editor, Jeanette Perez, who can take something rough and help me polish it until it shines; and to everyone at William Morrow—all your energy and input has been invaluable.

I'd also like to thank all the wonderfully wild misfit kids with whom I spent the mid-1980s—Lynn, Betsy, Debbie, Becky, Charlie, Billy, and all the rest—cruising the backstreets of suburban Connecticut in my Camaro with warm beers, blasting Stevie Nicks, chain-smoking menthol cigarettes, looking for trouble and sometimes finding it. May all our secrets stay safe.

This book is, at its heart, about family, about home. So I would be remiss not to give heartfelt thanks to my own family and everyone in it. Yeah, we're not exactly the Brady Bunch or the Waltons, but we've got *way* better stories. I love you all.